RUTHLESS
GIRL

BOOKS BY EMMA TALLON

RUTHLESS GIRL

EMMA TALLON

bookouture

Published by Bookouture in 2020

An imprint of Storyfire Ltd.
Carmelite House
50 Victoria Embankment
London EC4Y 0DZ

www.bookouture.com

ISBN: 978-1-83888-142-9
eBook ISBN: 978-1-83888-141-2

This book is a work of fiction. Names, characters, businesses,
organizations, places and events other than those clearly in the
public domain, are either the product of the author's imagination
or are used fictitiously. Any resemblance to actual persons, living or
dead, events or locales is entirely coincidental.

For my beautiful children, Christian and Charlotte. That I have been gifted with you makes me so thankful each and every day. This book, like everything else I do, is for you.

I love you always.

PROLOGUE

Her heart rate increased with excitement and her breath caught in her throat. She was so close now. He was just inside that door, totally unaware of what was about to happen. With steady fingers she reached into her pocket and pulled out the gun.

She took the last few steps to the door and smiled. It was slightly ajar, which was perfect. There would be no need to alert him to her presence by rattling the handle. She exhaled slowly, savouring the moment, revelling in the feeling of power, then gently pushed it open.

It swung silently open and she pulled the silencer out of another one of her pockets. With deft, experienced hands, she screwed it onto the end of the gun and lifted it ready to shoot. She licked her bottom lip, her eyes wide and alert like that of a predator. The bookcase came into view, then the filing cabinets and finally the end of the desk, bathed in the weak, warm glow of light from a desk lamp. Finally, as the door swung wider, he came into view.

Her eyes narrowed as she stared at him across the room. She had been so quiet and he was clearly so engrossed in whatever he was doing that he hadn't yet turned around. He sat hunched over the desk, peering over a load of papers with his back to her and the door.

For a moment she considered getting his attention. It would be the icing on the cake to see his face as she ended his life. Seeing the helplessness play out as he realised he was cornered would warm her for years to come. But sense won out and instead she just lifted her arm, aiming the gun at the back of his head. Her breathing slowed and years of training took over. This was nothing but a hunt. And today he was her prey.

He froze, and as he began to turn, alerted too late to the presence behind him, she pulled the trigger.

The muted clap of the gun going off bounced through the room and faded away as the bullet found its mark. As he slumped forward a heavy silence fell across the room. It was all over. He was dead.

The great Freddie Tyler was gone.

CHAPTER ONE

Anna Davis took one stiletto-heeled step back and rested her hands on her slender hips as she cast her eye critically over the back wall of the premises for their latest venture. She nodded slowly. The guys she'd hired had done a good job of resurfacing it. It looked perfect, not even a hint of the bullet holes which had pockmarked it just a few days before.

'What do you think?' asked the man next to her, as he wiped the last of the plaster off his hands onto his work trousers.

'You've done a great job,' she replied, with a look of appreciation.

'It was certainly a mess before we started,' he said with a small laugh.

Glancing sidewise at the beautiful and slightly intimidating woman who'd hired him, he wondered again at her calm and collected attitude towards the state the place had been in. It had given him the shivers when he'd first walked in. There had been patches of blood on the floor, glass and broken furniture strewn around and bullets lodged in the walls almost everywhere you looked. No one quite knew exactly what had happened, but there were rumours going around and they all seemed to loosely match up.

'Rumour has it there was a bunch of Russians in here before you took the place,' he continued. Anna nodded distractedly as she checked the wall for any imperfections. 'Some say they had a disagreement between themselves, but I don't think that's what really happened here.'

'No?' she asked, turning to face him. 'And what *do* you think happened then, Mr Butler?'

Lowering his voice, Steve Butler leaned in a little closer. 'Well,' he said conspiratorially, 'my cousin was having drinks a few doors down from here that night, and they were just out having a fag when they heard the shots. Well, they thought they might have been something else at the time. You hear all sorts round here, don't ya? But sure enough, they *was* shots,' he confirmed, his expression serious. 'My cousin said he saw a load of men in balaclavas coming out after and getting in a van. Swears blind he recognised one of them and it was a guy who works for none other than the Tyler brothers, the bigwigs who own this area.' He lowered his voice to a whisper, his eyes gleaming with the juiciness of his gossip. 'He reckons they was there to get the Russians out of Soho. It was a turf war,' he summarised with a smug nod.

Anna's expression grew cold and her dark blue eyes flashed dangerously, causing Steve to blink in confusion.

'If that were the case, Mr Butler,' she said, her measured tone deadly, 'I would be a little more careful about who you voice that opinion to. I don't imagine the Tylers would take too kindly to those who added that sort of thing to the rumour mill.'

'Yeah, but…' Steve floundered a little as he started to catch on to Anna's swiftly cooling demeanour. He had found her a little intimidating to begin with, a woman with such natural power about her, but now something in her hard stare was causing his heartbeat to quicken. He laughed slightly, trying to lighten the mood. 'I mean, it's not like it could be that really, when you think about it. I mean, it's not like the Tylers have taken over here. Whatever happened paved the way for you ladies to step in with your restaurant.'

There was a long silence as Anna stared at him, her cold gaze level. He shifted his weight awkwardly and was trying to think of something to say to fill the silence when she suddenly smiled, the action not quite reaching her eyes.

'Pop me over the invoice when you're ready and I'll have it paid this Friday.' Anna turned back towards the wall. 'And good job. It's as though it never happened.' Without another word she walked back through the bar area towards the office.

Watching her go, Steve shivered involuntarily. He had no idea what just happened, but he sure as hell wouldn't be mentioning the Tylers again. Whatever her connection was to them – and he was starting to think there was one – Anna Davis was a formidable woman in her own right. He stared at the clean, blank wall he had just finished. Russian or not, he wouldn't want to be the man who stood in her way. Not for all the money in the world.

CHAPTER TWO

Freddie ended the call with a grim expression and slipped the phone back into his inner jacket pocket. Smartly dressed in their infamous tailored Savile Row suits as always, he and his brother Paul stood out like sore thumbs in the tired, rundown neighbourhood they'd just pulled up in. Flicking his cigarette butt out of the window, Paul killed the engine.

'This definitely it?' he asked in his deep, craggy voice.

'That's the one,' Freddie answered, staring up at the dingy high-rise block of flats across the road. 'First storey, number five. Some sort of safe house Aleksei set up for his men. There's at least three of them in there, keeping their heads down, Billy confirmed. Could be more, but that's all he's seen.'

It had been nearly a month since they had raided Aleksei's strip club in order to gain the ground back that the Russian had so disrespectfully stolen from them whilst they'd been away. But for some strange reason, Aleksei had not been there that night as expected, and even more bizarrely he hadn't been seen or heard from since. The Tylers had been ready for him, had hunted high and low, ready to finish what they'd started, but their searches had been in vain. For once they were well and truly stumped. Aleksei – the Russian mobster who'd attempted to overtake part of Soho – had disappeared off the face of the Earth and his men had scattered. Most had gone home, some had stayed and gone underground, none seemed to have much of a plan as to what to do next. Freddie had never seen anything like it. Their men had been tracking as many of them as they could over the last few weeks and had watched to see if Aleksei made contact, but he hadn't, so now it was time for them to go in themselves and find out what these men knew.

Leaving the car, the pair walked up to the building and in through the badly fitting double doors to the stairwell beyond. Paul wrinkled his nose at the stench of piss and the suspicious stains worn into the cracked plastic flooring. They both pulled leather gloves from their pockets and put them on as they mounted the stairs in silence. The only sound around them as they made their way up was the buzz of a TV behind the door of one of the flats and the roar of a plane taking off above them. This part of Stanwell was a dreary place, an estate right next to Heathrow airport where the dreg ends of society seemed to gather in force, making it about as appealing to visit as a nuclear test site.

Reaching the front door of number five Paul glanced at Freddie, his eyebrow raised in question. 'Want to do the honours?' he asked.

'It would be my pleasure,' Freddie answered. Pulling his foot back he booted the flimsy wooden door in with one hard kick.

As the wood splintered the brothers pushed through into the hallway beyond and swiftly gathered their bearings. The open door in front of them led into an open-plan lounge and kitchen where three startled men quickly jumped to their feet from where they had been chilling in the mismatched furniture around the room. Two were still in their underwear, hair tousled from sleep, and the other had been about to light a cigarette which promptly dropped out of his mouth onto the dirty carpet below. He went to reach around to the back of his belt but the brothers were way ahead of him, pointing the loaded guns from their inner pockets.

'I wouldn't if I were you,' Paul warned, marching forward and placing the cold end of the barrel against his temple. The man immediately raised his hands up high. The other two followed suit, unarmed as they were. Paul reached into the first man's waistband and threw the gun back towards Freddie.

'Right then,' Freddie bellowed, waving his gun between the other two as if deciding who to focus it on. 'Where the fuck is Aleksei?'

CHAPTER THREE

Seamus leaned over the ropes at the edge of the ring and watched the lads who were currently sparring. 'Footwork, Tim,' he called out. 'You're supposed to be as light as a bird, not jumping around like a bloody drunken bear.' Tim corrected his footwork and immediately the sparring match became a lot more even. 'Good lad. Fists up, Al, unless you fancy sporting a flat nose on your date tonight.' Al raised his arms.

Nodding in approval at a particularly skilful shot, Seamus felt a pang of longing to get into the ring surge through his chest. His need to be up there doing what he did best was beyond physical. But it was the one thing he couldn't do right now, not with his hand being bust. The reminder of this current weakness brought the constant dull ache he felt in the slowly healing bones to the forefront of his mind and he gently flexed his hand. A few weeks before, two of Aleksei's men had pushed a stack of heavy crates down on top of him in a bid to hospitalise him and antagonise the Tylers. It had partially worked. Seamus had jumped back at the last moment and it had only bust his hand, saving him the trip to hospital as he'd been swiftly patched up behind closed doors – however it had still greatly antagonised the Tylers.

It was no longer strapped up, for which he was grateful. His bosses had lied to the boxing league board about why he'd had to pull out of all his arranged matches so suddenly, claiming a death in the family back in Ireland. He'd had no choice but to keep a low profile for the first few weeks whilst it had been wrapped up in tight bandages. If anyone from the boxing world had seen, news would have spread like wildfire. He'd have been forced through a medical assessment and kept out of the game until he was deemed officially fit. His opponents would have found out and used his weakness against him and it would have damaged the position he had worked so hard for. By keeping it quiet, Seamus could work on getting back to the point when *he* felt ready to get back in the ring and not be denied.

There was still a long way to go. The bandages had only just come off and so he had returned to training his boys in the ring in the gym, but it would be a few months before he would be able to get back up there himself. He could tell his boys were curious as to why he wasn't training or entering matches himself. There had been whispered conversations and curious glances, but none of them had had the balls to ask him outright. He doubted they ever would. They all knew who he was. Seamus was a prize-winning boxer, top of his game and one of the legendary Tyler firm. The youths that came to the gym to learn how to let off steam without violence knew better than to show any disrespect to one of the Tylers' men and were not stupid enough to get on the wrong side of someone who could put them on their arses with one strategic blow. So, Seamus was shown the respect he deserved and suffered no struggle in avoiding the questions everyone was dying to ask.

Suppressing a sigh, Seamus stretched his hand out and pulled it in, careful to do his physio exercises under the small towel he held in his other hand so that no one could see. Feeling, rather than hearing the presence of someone walk up to stand beside him, Seamus glanced sideways. It was Sammy, another of Freddie's men, one of the more senior-ranking individuals in the inner circle – the man who'd taken Seamus under his wing when he'd first joined the firm several years before. Pulling himself off the ropes, he greeted his friend with a smile.

'Come, let's talk in me office,' he suggested, the melodic lilt of his Irish accent still as clear as ever. 'We can catch up properly.'

Sammy nodded and followed him through, his broad shoulders swinging from side to side in his beige suit. The men in the gym nodded their respect as they passed and Sammy returned the gesture. He often worked out there himself, priding himself on keeping his muscular physique on top form.

Closing the door behind them as they entered the office, Seamus pulled out a chair and waited for Sammy to sit down before he took his own seat. 'You been on the sun bed?' he asked, with a small frown.

'Nope,' Sammy replied cheerily.

'You always look as though you've just spent a week on the beach,' Seamus said with a chuckle and an envious look. 'I don't know how you do it. I could spend a month in the Maldives and not tan like you do.'

Sammy's naturally light blond hair, pale blue eyes and tanned complexion always drew a lot of interest, though no one knew where this unusual combination had come from. Certainly not his parents, who had both been an average mousy brown and pale. Freddie often joked that he'd been swapped at birth by a Swedish body-building couple.

'How's the hand today?' Sammy asked. 'Still in pain?'

'Yeah, it's not the best,' Seamus replied with a grimace. 'But I'm getting by. Tim out there is shaping up, ya know,' he said, changing the subject. 'I'm t'inking we should start putting him in for proper training soon.'

'Yeah?' Sammy raised an eyebrow in interest. 'You think he'd be a contender?'

'He definitely would,' Seamus confirmed. 'He came through the youth offender system and took to the programme well. He's had it tough, just needed a bit of direction. He's been edging for an in with Freddie, but obviously I shut him down for now. He'd be sound to play the game though, if we got him up to match level. It would take some time,' he shrugged, 'but it's worth getting the ball in motion, if you're up for it.'

Sammy nodded slowly. They had been talking about expanding their reach in the boxing world. Seamus had been winning and throwing matches strategically for them for the last few years and it had been a solid earner. They couldn't spread themselves too far for fear of being noticed, but if they found the right sort of people, they could have three or four boxers in the leagues and make an absolute killing.

'Keep working with him and I'll sit in on some matches. Then when he's ready for the lower trials we'll set up a meet with Freddie,' he replied.

'Perfect. So, what have we got on today? I could do with getting out of here. The ring is calling to me soul and it hurts,' he admitted with a groan.

'We've got protection collections to do, but I'm also a man down on the coke run. The guy who picks up from Alfie's men and drops to the top of the dealer tree has been arrested for a domestic.'

'What?' Seamus exclaimed with a look of disgust.

'Yeah,' Sammy said in a grim tone. 'Beat up his missus, I heard. He's going to have to go. Can't have a liability like that walking round with that much product. But until we reshuffle, the drop needs to be picked up. Could you run it today?'

''Course,' Seamus replied, 'no problem. Just give me the details. Can't have all that lovely cocaine not reaching our customers now.'

'Great.' Sammy pulled out a sheet of paper and handed it to Seamus. 'Burn that when you're done.'

'Will do.' Seamus reached into his pocket and pulled out a bottle of pills. Unscrewing the lid, he popped two of them in his mouth.

'What are they, painkillers?'

'Christ the lord, no!' Seamus replied in disgust. 'I wouldn't touch the things. Don't you know how addictive they are?' He shook his head. 'No, these are iron and magnesium. Helps speed up the healing. Anyway...' he pushed the bottle back into his pocket and zipped up his dark green aviation jacket, 'I'd best be off then. The coke won't deliver itself. I'll catch up with you on the collections after, yeah?'

'Sure,' Sammy replied, opening the filing cabinet by the desk. 'I should be in Soho, just give me a bell when you're on your way. What did you say that boy's name was again?'

'Tim Eaves,' Seamus called back as he opened the office door. He couldn't wait to get away from his beloved gym today. 'Second drawer down.'

As the office door shut behind him, Sammy checked his watch. He had some time before he needed to meet Freddie at the club. He reached into the drawer and ran his fingers down the files until he found the one he was looking for. 'Bingo,' he muttered. Settling back into Seamus's chair behind the small desk, he opened it up and began reading through the boy's history and list of offences. He chuckled at a couple of them and got comfortable as the file continued.

Seamus had been their prize fighter for a long time and they had made a lot of money from his games. But with him out of action for the foreseeable future, now more than ever, Sammy wanted to get the ball rolling on the next step in their plan. Because when all was said and done, time was money and money was power – and in their game, power was everything.

CHAPTER FOUR

Later that night, having gathered everyone together in the office at Club CoCo, Freddie opened one of the desk drawers and pulled out a battered old map of London and the surrounding areas. Unfolding it, he flattened it out as best he could over the desk. Black and red marks were dotted all the map. They would mean nothing to the untrained eye, but to those in the know each mark indicated either a Tyler-owned building, a road which held no cameras, or marked the boundary edge for the area in which they could do business.

'I've had an offer on a bulk load of weed from a contact over in the East End, but only if we can take the lot and store it ourselves until it's been distributed,' he said, leaning over the map.

Anna peered at the map from her seat on the other side of the desk out of interest. She knew that the details of this particular job wouldn't have much to do with her, but looked to see if she could come up with a viable location suggestion anyway. Most of their barns and warehouses outside London to the east were already being used for various other enterprises, she knew.

Sammy waited for Freddie to continue, but Paul frowned. 'What contact?' he asked.

'Lily Drew,' Freddie answered.

'What's Lily doing with a bulk load of weed? And why are we taking it? We have our own set-up already,' Paul questioned.

'Those boys of hers, the twins,' Freddie replied, 'they got their hands on a job lot from the Jamaicans in the South. Only the Jamaicans don't know it was them and Lily don't want them finding out.'

'No…' Sammy exclaimed under his breath in surprise. He threw his head back and laughed. 'They didn't? Those little fuckers. I bet she's steaming.'

'She certainly is,' Freddie replied. 'She can't distribute it round there, they've not dealt in weed before so it would be too obvious where it came from if they suddenly had some. She needs to get rid of it somewhere it can be filtered off quietly. I wouldn't usually entertain it but she's practically giving it away, so it would be silly not to. We can just add it in to our orders, no one will be any the wiser.'

'I don't know, Fred, I don't like the idea of having to store it,' Paul said with a worried grimace.

They had only been out of prison for a couple of months and were still being watched loosely by the police. It wasn't that Paul had lost his nerve – storing illegal substances like this was what had tripped them up last time. He'd been caught moving a large bag of cocaine and it had ended up being enough to send them both down for nearly three years. It had been the one and only time they had stored any of the drugs they distributed. Usually they had an efficient, constantly moving chain in position, moving the goods straight from supplier to the top of the dealer tree. That way, the risk was minimal.

Freddie nodded. 'I know, I don't exactly relish the thought either. But if we plan carefully and make sure we don't personally go near it, I don't think it poses us any real risk. It won't sit there for long and we can get it pushed out in a week. Plus, it's Lily,' he added. 'We ain't exactly going to say no when she's up against a wall, are we?'

'Mhm,' Paul grunted grudgingly in agreement.

'Who's Lily?' Anna asked, crossing her arms with a frown, a small needle of jealousy prickling her at the way Freddie had spoken her name to Paul. She'd never heard any of them talk of a Lily before.

'Lily was one of our neighbours on the estate we moved to after Dad died,' Freddie explained, hiding the small smile of amusement at Anna's reaction. After all they had been through over the years, it warmed his heart to see how protective she felt of their relationship. 'Her mum was friends with ours. When we were little, she used to come watch us sometimes so Mum could work extra hours. She was a few years older than us.'

'Oh, OK,' Anna replied, her stance relaxing. 'Well, if she's one of your own of course you have to help her out,' she agreed, understanding where Freddie was coming from.

'Exactly.'

'What form is it in?' she asked.

'Bagged. They have a few trees too, but I've told her to destroy those. We haven't got the equipment or time to dry them out.'

There was a knock on the door before it immediately opened. Tanya walked in with a broad smile. 'Hey, how's it going?' She closed it behind her before walking forward to take the seat next to Anna.

Anna twisted her lips to one side as her eyes swept over the map. There was nowhere obvious under the radar that wasn't already being used, but, 'What about the storage in the roof at The Sinners' Lounge?' she said, suddenly. 'It's been empty since we moved in and it's out of the way of the general public.' Anna saw Paul's face drop even further. 'I know it's central but think about it. There are people coming and going all the time. No one would notice your transporters coming in and out and they wouldn't have to travel so far to get it. If this Lily can get it in there unnoticed it's the perfect solution.'

'If *who* can get *what* into The Sinners' Lounge?' Tanya asked, glancing from Anna to Freddie.

'Weed,' they replied in unison.

'Oh, right. OK. Sure. Because that makes complete sense,' she replied sarcastically.

'Freddie needs to store a few bags of weed—' Anna began to explain.

'More than a few,' he interrupted.

'Freddie needs to store *more than a few* bags of weed for a week or so and we're looking at options,' Anna finished.

Tanya frowned. 'One-off?' She shot the question at Freddie.

'Total one-off. It won't be repeated. We still have our usual process in place,' he replied.

Tanya exchanged a look with Anna. 'It's fine with me,' she said eventually. 'But you'll have to talk to Josephine about it, she'll need to know what's happening.'

Anna looked away and pursed her lips, her expression hardening at the sound of Josephine's name. 'No problem,' she replied. 'I'll sort it.'

'OK, that's settled then,' Freddie said, folding away the map. 'I'll make the arrangements.'

The beep of an incoming message sounded and everyone looked down to their phones.

'Mine,' Tanya announced.

'Shit, is that the time?' Freddie said, more to himself than anyone else. 'Wait here,' he added, looking at Paul and Sammy as he marched towards the door. 'I'll be back in a second, just need to grab Gavin before he locks up.'

Tanya scanned her text and scowled. 'Oh, for fuck's sake.'

'What's wrong?' Anna asked.

'My date for tomorrow night has cancelled.' She sighed dramatically and sank deeper into the chair, crossing her long, shapely legs in front of her. 'I'm destined to be man-less forever, me.'

'No, you aren't,' Anna replied, rolling her eyes.

'I am. Honestly, my charm has worn off. It don't work anymore. I'm practically days away from being a spinster.'

'Oh, for God's sake,' Sammy said from behind her with a laugh. 'Your charm is as intact as ever, Tanya Smith.'

Tanya twisted round to stare at him. 'And what authority do you have on the matter, eh? My charm never worked on you, did it, you big blond giant?'

'Well, you never actually tried throwing your charm my way, did you, you little red firework?' he replied, an amused glint in his eye.

Tanya opened her mouth to respond, but for once found she had no response to give. She closed it again, folded her arms and looked him up and down. Sammy was right, she never had tried her luck in his direction, despite the fact he was one of the most attractive men she knew. She knew why, of course. Sammy had never been an option for her in the past, not really. When she'd first met everyone many years before, she'd only had eyes for Freddie. They'd dated for a while when they were young and naïve. And when, years later, they all became friends and eventually she'd been accepted into the Tyler crime family, she'd just written him off as being too close for comfort. Tanya lived by the rule that one should never shit on one's doorstep. And Sammy was as close to her front door as someone could possibly get.

She couldn't even think about it. What if they started something up and then it went south? What if it all just went horribly wrong and then suddenly there was nothing but tension where there had been friendship before?

Then again – a small internal voice whispered – *what if it didn't?*

Anna began discussing plans for the restaurant with Paul and the moment of flirtation between Tanya and Sammy passed. Sliding her gaze sideways, Tanya discreetly looked Sammy up and down once more. His piercing blue eyes and full lips were accentuated by a tanned, chiselled face. She didn't usually like blonds, but Sammy pulled it off so ruggedly she decided she'd make an exception. His beige summer suit was expertly tailored, showing off his broad, defined physique to the max; she bit her lip as she wondered what his chest was like under his crisp white shirt. Was it smooth or did he have chest hair?

Catching her staring, Sammy's lips curled up into a smile of amusement and Tanya immediately pulled her attention away. She pursed her lips and joined in Anna and Paul's conversation. She might have been thinking about it, but no way did Sammy need to know that. Not yet, at least. If she did decide to do anything about him then it would be on her terms. And she'd make damn sure he didn't know what hit him.

Downstairs, Freddie finished up his business with Gavin, the club's general manager. '... so if you see him in here again call Ricky through to deal with it quietly. Just make sure you close off the cameras in the alley out back beforehand. OK?'

'Got it, no probs,' Gavin answered.

The rogue pill-seller Paul had suspected had been found and warned off with a small slap in the back alley for his troubles. It would leave a bruise perhaps but nothing had been broken. He was only a young kid, so Freddie wanted to give him a chance to fuck off quietly. But as far as chances went, he never gave more than one. If the kid turned up in the club trying to peddle his wares again he'd suffer the beating of his life.

'Great, catch you tomorrow.' Freddie walked back to the stairs that led up to his office just as the music stopped and the lights came on. It was closing time – time for all the stragglers and the die-hard stop-outs to vacate the premises.

Unbeknown to Freddie, a pair of eyes that had been staring at him from the corner of the room narrowed. 'There's a time and place for us, Freddie Tyler,' the voice that came with the watching eyes whispered. 'And it's coming very, very soon.'

CHAPTER FIVE

The sound of laughter travelled up the narrow staircase from the floor below, alerting Josephine to the arrival of the girls. She checked her watch and raised her eyebrows in surprise. It was later than she'd realised. She'd been lost in her thoughts and memories for most of the evening again. That happened a lot these days.

The whorehouse – or out-of-hours club, as Anna referred to it – which Josephine ran for her and Tanya, was a place that opened up for horny customers once their main club around the corner closed for the night. The main club – Club Anya – served drinks, food and fun to the public and put on an array of impressive entertainment night after night. Burlesque dancers sashayed around rope climbers, fire breathers pranced below ring gymnasts, and pole dancers slid up and down from floor to ceiling, all wearing only the bare minimum. After finding one of the girls offering extra services in the back alley one night, Anna and Tanya decided to open somewhere more discreet that catered for the men who wanted more than just a show. Now, once the girls were done for the night there, they relocated here – The Sinners' Lounge – to make some real money.

Dragging herself off the sofa where she had been sitting for the last few hours, Josephine turned on the light. It had grown dark without her even realising. She rubbed her eyes, tired despite all the extra sleep she had been giving in to lately. Walking through to the bedroom, she sat down at her dressing table and looked herself over. She didn't look too bad, having already piled her curls up on top of her head and got dressed ready for the evening earlier on. She just needed to touch up a bit. Running her hand down her face she continued to her neck and lingered on the Adam's apple that stuck out there, an ever-present reminder of her roots. Up until a few weeks ago getting rid of it had been one of her biggest priorities, the next surgery on the list that she'd been saving for in her quest to become all woman. But now it all just seemed so incredibly unimportant.

Sniffing, she dropped her hands and refocused on the task of preparing for the evening ahead. She had to look her best. If she didn't, the girls would start wondering why. Talk would begin and suspicion could form – and this was something that couldn't be allowed to happen. Anna and Tanya had been very explicit on that point.

Josephine reached for the tube of concealer and squeezed some onto her finger, then rubbed it into the dark circles under her eyes. Checking it was all smoothed in, she nodded and opened the box containing her collection of lipsticks. She rummaged through, looking for a shade of pink that would match the fuchsia stripes that ran through her black dress. Finding one, a brief smile of triumph played across her lips. She leaned in and began to apply a thick layer to her lips, before slowing to a stop as the memory hit her.

This particular lipstick was one she had bought over a year ago to go with a flamboyant little number she'd worn on a night out spying on the enemy for Anna. It had been the night she had first met Aleksei. He had asked the barman to send fuchsia cocktails over to her table, to match the lipstick. Later he had sent over his number too. Josephine had known it was a bad idea – she was, after all, part of the opposing team, not that he knew that at this point – but something in Aleksei interested her and curiosity had won out. They had met, hit it off and secretly embarked on what had been the most beautiful and heartbreaking relationship of her entire life.

Aleksei had seen her like no one ever had before. He had loved her for who she was, and she had loved him. It had been hell, keeping him a secret, knowing that her love was a complete betrayal to the people she worked for – people who were her friends, the family she'd never known before. She couldn't have walked away from the love she shared with Aleksei any more than she could have stopped drawing oxygen into her lungs. But of course, as she had known it would eventually, it had all come to a head a few weeks before.

Aleksei hadn't earned the right to be working on the Tylers' patch – he had bullied his way into his corner of Soho, completely ignoring the rules of underworld society. The Tyler brothers had been inside, and Anna had managed the situation as well as she could, but the day the brothers got out everyone knew that Aleksei was on borrowed time. Aleksei knew this too. It was why he had tried to kill Freddie and tried to rope Josephine into helping him do it.

Josephine had finally been pushed to make a decision. It had not been an easy one, she loved Aleksei with all her heart, but she also loved Anna and the rest of her friends and she owed them her loyalty. The night she had been ordered to lure Freddie into Aleksei's trap, she had instead tried to scupper Aleksei's plans. It had backfired and he'd turned on her, even tried to kill her for her betrayal, but unbeknown to Josephine, Anna had been following her and had saved her life, killing Aleksei in the process.

It had been a shocking chain of events, and she'd been forced to come clean to Anna and Tanya about everything. They'd covered up Aleksei's death and had sworn never to speak a word to anyone about what had happened that night – not even Freddie. There was too much at stake, too many complicated threads to untangle.

There was a knock at the door and she jumped, the lipstick she had still been holding to her lips shooting across her cheek and leaving a bright trail. She tutted and quickly grabbed some tissues and tried to wipe it off before walking over to the door and opening it.

Tanya stood the other side, a wide smile of greeting on her face. 'Alright? How's it going?' She waltzed in leaving a cloud of Chanel Coco Mademoiselle in her wake.

Josephine wafted the air with her hand as she closed the door behind her. 'OK, thanks,' she replied.

'You've got a bit of, um…' Tanya pointed a long, polished finger towards Josephine's face and made a circular movement. 'Lippy.'

'I'm aware of that,' Josephine replied drily. 'Thank you.' She continued rubbing her face with the tissue and walked into the small kitchenette to put the kettle on. 'Cuppa?' she asked.

'Go on then, quick one,' Tanya replied, checking her watch. She still had what felt like a million things to do this evening, but was pointedly aware of how fragile her friend was at the moment, so didn't want to just run out after getting what she came for. 'Do you have the accounts ready?' she asked.

'On the coffee table,' Josephine called over her shoulder.

Tanya picked them up and sat down on the couch, making herself comfortable as she flicked through them. Like many of the businesses under the Tyler empire there was only one set of accounts for The Sinners' Lounge, which were coded and kept carefully hidden from anyone outside of the inner circle. The accounts were handwritten by Josephine and passed over once a month either to Anna or Tanya who would then launder the profits through Club Anya. It was a fairly straightforward process with card payments, as they just used one of Club Anya's card machines and put the payments through as food or drink, but they also took a vast amount of cash. Once the girls and the overheads were paid from this, the rest had to be carefully trickled back into the more legitimate company so as not to raise suspicion.

'Jesus, Rose has been a busy bee,' Tanya remarked, raising her eyebrows with a smirk.

'Born for this life, that one. Loves it more than a fat kid loves chocolate,' Josephine replied, placing two cups of tea on the coffee table and taking a seat in the armchair opposite Tanya. 'How are plans for the new place coming along?'

'It's getting there. The walls have been replastered and painted now, so no trace of the carnage.' Tanya's gaze briefly flicked up towards her friend. 'You know you can come down and see it anytime you like,' she said carefully.

Josephine flinched. 'I can't,' she said in barely more than a whisper. 'There's just... It would be too much of a reminder of everything.'

Tanya nodded sagely, choosing not to reply. The premises for their new restaurant was Aleksei's old club, taken back into the fold now that he was gone. It was a difficult position that they all found themselves in at the moment. As far as the world knew, Aleksei was just missing. She, Anna and Josephine were hiding the truth and it was still a very tense time. Barely a few weeks had passed and although no one had found his body underneath the rubble of the building that had collapsed on top of his corpse, that wasn't to say they were completely out of the woods yet. And on top of this, Josephine was also grieving. Whatever else Aleksei had been, he was the man she'd loved. But although Tanya sympathised with her, she couldn't support her in the way one usually would a friend who had just lost their lover. It was a tricky situation.

'How is Anna?' Josephine asked, tentatively.

Tanya sighed and put the accounts down before running her hand through her long red hair. 'She's OK,' she replied. 'Busy with all the new stuff going on.'

Josephine nodded and bit her lip. 'Is she ever going to be normal with me again, do you think?' It was a question she had wanted to ask for a long time but had been skirting around, afraid of the answer.

There was a short silence, before Tanya leaned over and squeezed her friend's arm. 'Give her time,' she answered gently. 'She still loves you, Josephine, you're still family. But Anna is a very black-and-white person. You hooking up with Aleksei, hiding everything from us…' Tanya trailed off and bit her lip, not wanting to say anything that would upset Josephine further. Whilst she understood Anna's feelings on the matter, she also felt Josephine had been through enough. She didn't want to add to it.

'I know,' Josephine mumbled.

'Just give it some time,' Tanya repeated. 'Anna might be a bit of an ice queen at times, but all ice melts eventually.'

'The polar caps haven't,' Josephine replied glumly.

Tanya smiled and grabbed the accounts as she stood up. 'I'll catch you later. Chin up.'

As she walked out, her smile dropped. For all her hopes and her jolly words, deep down Tanya wasn't sure that Anna was ever going to be able to forgive Josephine. Anna's bar was set high and made from reinforced steel. Right now, she was still warring with this bar and her heartfelt wish to forgive their friend. But there would come a point when Anna would realise that she couldn't change how she felt. And what that would mean for Josephine and her future here, Tanya didn't dare think about.

CHAPTER SIX

Balancing one of the hot coffees she held on top of the other, Sarah Riley lifted the latch on the old wrought-iron gate and walked into the sprawling graveyard. With a groan and a clang it closed behind her and she set off towards the far corner where she knew Freddie would be waiting for her. She looked up at the bright blue morning sky and then around at the neatly kept graves that sat in rows in the short, thick grass. As far as graveyards went this one was pretty beautiful, situated as it was on a rolling hill overlooking the lush countryside just outside the city. And this was, of course, why Freddie had chosen it. He wanted nothing but the best for the people he cared about, even after death.

As she turned a corner by the small chapel in the middle of the grounds that was rarely used, Sarah caught sight of Freddie sitting on the bench he'd had installed behind his sister's grave, staring out at the view. He appeared lost in thought and didn't turn to acknowledge her until she was just a few feet away.

'Here.' Sarah passed one of the steaming coffees to Freddie. 'I figured you might need some caffeine. This is a bit early for you, isn't it?' Most of Freddie's business was conducted at night-time, Sarah knew, so mornings were usually pretty quiet as far as he was concerned.

'Thanks.' Freddie took the offered takeaway cup and waited as Sarah sat down next to him. He continued to watch as the shadows from the few sparse clouds above made their steady journey across the rolling hills beneath. 'What's the latest?' he asked, taking a sip of his coffee.

Sarah Riley was a DCI for Thames Valley Police. She worked directly under Ben Hargreaves, the secretary of state for justice. She also worked for Freddie and despite day-to-day appearances, it was with him that her true loyalties now lay. When Ben had formed a task force to bring the Tylers down, it had been Sarah who had worked hard to sabotage their plans from the inside. She'd done a good job for the most part – they had nearly been home and dry when one of the officers had stumbled across something that even she couldn't cover up or warn them about in time.

Sarah placed her coffee down on the bench beside her, pushed her fists into the pockets of her short leather jacket, and crossed one leg over the other. 'Nothing much has changed. He has Daniels keeping tabs on you still, but I've made sure to increase his workload, so he doesn't have a lot of time to spare on a project that isn't a priority. Still, he has flags on most of your accounts.'

Freddie shrugged. 'That's not a problem. I'm not stupid enough to put anything through there that ain't legitimate. How itchy is he getting, with us on the outside still?'

'Pretty itchy,' Sarah admitted, pushing her short dark hair back behind her ear. 'But he doesn't seem to be making plans to move on you again. He can't justify it really, not after what he spent getting that arrest on you before. He had to answer to the board for that, you know. Spending such a big portion of the budget on the team to bring you down, to only bag you on a mere drugs charge.' Sarah raised her eyebrows and gave a small smirk. 'He pissed off a lot of people. He can't justify putting any of the budget on you again unless you give them a seriously big reason.'

Freddie nodded. 'What have you heard about that Jamaican weed heist, south of the river?' he asked, changing the subject.

'That wasn't you, was it?' she asked with a guffaw of amusement, turning to look at him.

'Nah, 'course not,' he replied. 'Do you know what they've got on it so far, though?'

'Not a lot. It was in the middle of a housing estate so no cameras. All they have to go on is the witness accounts, but the description was pretty generic. Young white males, nondescript clothing. I'm not running the team on that one, but the DI in charge is one of mine. Why?' she asked.

'Try and bury it, if you can. Or at least take it off their priority list. It's nothing to do with me, but it would be doing a friend a favour,' Freddie answered.

'I'll see what I can do. I've just had a murder come in last night, I'll see if I can put that on their plate perhaps.' This reminded her how much she had to do today. Pushing up her sleeve, Sarah glanced at her watch. 'Is there anything else?'

'Yeah.' Freddie leaned forward onto his knees and cast his gaze down to the white granite gravestone in front of him. It belonged to Thea, his little sister who had been murdered three years before. 'Hargreaves.' His feelings of disgust for the man soured his tone. Hargreaves had been the one who'd insisted the SWAT team burst in and take the Tyler brothers from Thea's funeral, not even having the decency to wait until it was over. 'I want you to build a file on him for me. Collect details of his comings and goings. Patterns, habits, any unusual activity.'

Sarah raised her eyebrows in surprise but kept her thoughts to herself. 'OK. How deep?'

'As deep as you can without making ripples,' Freddie replied. 'I know you say he's not planning anything but we're better safe than sorry. I like to keep a few steps ahead.'

'Gotcha. I'll start today.' Sarah stood up and straightened her jacket. 'I'd best be off. Catch you later.'

Walking back the way she came in, Sarah pondered how she was going to set about following her boss without being noticed. There were a variety of options at her disposal, but most of them could be easily traced back to her if she wasn't careful enough. She almost immediately dismissed the idea of using the equipment available to her through the force for this reason and made the decision to contact Bill Hanlon, one of Freddie's men who had a certain skill with security and technology. He could get practically anything she needed on the black market and it was usually better than what the police had to hand anyway.

As she passed through the gate once more, she almost turned to walk up the hill, but something about the car that was passing made her pause. She frowned and stared at it. The large black Range Rover seemed out of place cruising down the deserted country road of the little village at this time of the morning. But more than that, there was something about it that she was sure she'd seen before. Aside from the blacked-out windows that were not, in fairness, uncommon, the black wheel rims were personalised with a bright red trim. That *was* uncommon. Range Rover didn't make rims like that, the car had been purposely detailed. And Sarah had seen it before. Outside Freddie's club.

As her attention swiftly moved up to the windows, the car sped up with a screech and raced away around the corner.

CHAPTER SEVEN

Anna took a deep breath, braced herself and walked into the main room of The Sinners' Lounge. It was empty, being so early in the day, other than the cleaner running the hoover round the bar area and Bill, who was seated at one of the tables near a window, waiting for her to arrive.

'Hey.' She greeted him with a smile. 'Thanks for meeting me here so early.'

'No worries,' he replied. 'Show me where you're thinking then we'll work out some options.'

'Great. There's an empty space in the loft which is almost a room but not quite – the ceiling is too low. No one has need to go up there, so I figured that would be a good place to keep it.' Anna was referring to the bulk load of cannabis she had been discussing with Freddie the night before.

After leaving the club she had called Bill and asked him to meet her at The Sinners' Lounge to discuss the privacy and security of the product. It might only be one load of drugs right now, but should they need to use the space going forward, it would be handy to have everything set up to the highest standard.

Footsteps entering the room sounded behind her and, knowing who it was likely to be, Anna locked her jaw with a grim expression. She swiftly hid this behind a polite smile, so that Bill didn't pick up on the tension between the two of them. The footsteps faltered and then resumed moving closer at a slower pace. Anna forced herself to turn around.

'Anna, how are you?' Josephine asked with a hopeful smile.

Anna smiled tightly in return. 'Well, thank you. And you?'

'All good.' Josephine looked down at the coffee in her hand before walking over to Bill and setting it down in front of him. 'Would you like one?' she asked, gesturing towards the steaming cup.

'No, I'm not staying,' Anna replied curtly. 'Too much to do,' she added in a softer tone, seeing Bill's gaze sharpen and his brow furrow. 'I'll catch you later though, OK?' She shot Josephine the brightest smile she could and saw hope light up in the other woman's eyes. This caused a strange mix of emotions to start swirling in her stomach and she looked away. Sadness at the awkward distance between them and a wistfulness at the thought of the good times they used to have danced with feelings of anger and betrayal. This was why she had been avoiding Josephine. She couldn't find it in her heart to forgive her for everything, not yet at least.

'OK, well, let me know if you change your mind,' Josephine replied.

'This way, Bill,' Anna said, walking swiftly past Josephine towards the stairwell beyond. She didn't trust herself to respond. The strain between them was evident.

Bill took a big swig from the coffee cup in front of him and wiped the foam off his lip as he stood up. 'Thanks, Josephine,' he said with a friendly grin.

'What's happening, exactly?' Josephine asked, tentatively, her gaze darting towards Anna's retreating back.

Anna paused and rolled her eyes, cursing internally. She couldn't just leave Josephine out of the loop, this was her home and workplace. Placing her hands on her hips she turned back around.

'Sorry, Josephine, I'm not thinking straight today. I'll pop down in a few minutes and explain, I just need Bill to come and see the roof first.'

'OK, great.' Josephine held the smile as Bill joined Anna. As they disappeared from view, she stopped faking it and let the misery spread back over her face. Anna couldn't even bear to be in the same room as her. The same Anna who had been one of her closest friends just a few weeks before. Were things ever going to get back to normal?

Anna opened the door to the last room at the top of the building. It was filled with odds and ends of furniture and a few half-used cans of paint. At the back of the room was a small door, about half the height of a normal door, that led into a wide space between the storeroom and the eaves. Anna opened this and stepped aside to let Bill see.

Bill hunched over and peered into the space. It was bigger than it looked from the outside, spanning a good few metres each way, but with the ceiling sloping sharply down making it impossible for anyone to stand upright in there. He nodded slowly.

'Yeah, this should do. We'll need to block up that window.' He pointed to the small Velux window that was currently the only source of light. 'I'll change your security system to one that operates the cameras individually, like in CoCo.'

Anna nodded. 'Got it.' That made sense. Their current system meant that all the cameras were operated by one switch. This new system would allow her to turn off the back door and hallway as the product was moved in and out, whilst keeping the others up and running as usual.

'Then it's up to you how tight you want the security.' Standing back upright, Bill turned to face Anna. 'Either we can just put a decent lock on the door to the main room and then a heavy bookcase in front of this door. That should be enough of a deterrent for anyone trying their luck. Or we can go a step further, have motion sensors with linked nanny-cams on the inside. I'd set it to cover the door rather than the product, so worst case scenario it don't show nothing incriminating, of course.'

'Let's do both,' Anna replied, her tone resolute. 'We never know when we may need it again.'

'OK. I can have it all set up by tomorrow night.' Bill pulled out his phone to check a message. 'I've got to shoot. Tell Lily no earlier than nine if she comes tomorrow, just to be on the safe side.'

'Will do. Thanks, Bill.'

They made their way back down the stairs and Anna waved Bill off before re-entering the main lounge with a heavy sigh.

'Right,' she said in a curt tone as she reached Josephine. She was seated at a table under the window, looking over the stock take for the bar. 'Bill will be in and out of the loft over the next day or so, fitting some security. I'll then be arranging for some products to be kept up there, for Freddie.'

'What kind of products are we talking?' Josephine asked.

'That doesn't matter,' Anna replied, dismissively. 'But this is to be kept quiet, I don't want the girls or anyone else knowing. I'll have you updated on who to expect and when.'

She made a mental note to pass future correspondence on the matter through Tanya, after she had overseen the initial delivery. She could have arranged for Tanya to be here for that too, but as much as she wanted distance from Josephine, she was also curious about this Lily person, for whom Freddie seemed to have such a soft spot.

Josephine bit her lip as Anna stood stiffly, staring at the door. She was about to leave, this much was evident; she always ran off as soon as she could these days. Anna pushed the sleeve of her red chiffon blouse back off her wrist to look at her watch, and then released it, absent-mindedly smoothing her black pencil skirt with her hands.

'Well, I'd better—'

'Anna,' Josephine interrupted her. 'Listen, um, I need to talk to you about something.'

'Tanya will be around later on, I need to head off,' Anna responded.

'It's not about the Lounge, it's about the diamonds.' She sat up taller and a small sparkle momentarily returned to her eye. 'One of my guys has hit a real jackpot. Almost twice the amount of diamonds we've been able to get our hands on before and they're untraceable, no marks. Must have been conflict diamonds by the sounds of them, which means no heat, no details on any system and nothing to have lasered off. We can charge a premium for them.'

Anna turned her gaze towards Josephine for the first time since entering the room. 'You know we don't have Roman set up to do the run any more.'

'Yes, but I thought you were trying to find someone else?'

'I was. But I'm not now.' Anna's eyes turned cold. 'Aside from the fact that I'm already up to my ears running everything else, I have no desire to continue this arrangement with you. Not for now, at least.'

Josephine's jaw opened and shut like a fish as she tried to find an appropriate response. It hadn't occurred to her that Anna would put a stop to something so lucrative for the both of them.

Anna stepped towards her, her heels tapping sharply on the floorboards as she decided suddenly to address the issue. 'You keep asking Tanya when things are going to get back to normal again, but you just don't get it, do you?' she snapped. 'You betrayed us, Josephine. I took you in, gave you a home, a job, friendship,' her voice lowered to a hiss, 'and yet you lied to my face.'

Josephine felt the tears begin to prickle the back of her eyes and she blinked rapidly. 'I never meant to—'

'What you did or did not mean to do is of no consequence,' Anna interrupted her with a dismissive wave. 'This world we inhabit…' She swept her arm out and turned in a circle. 'This isn't normal life. It comes with rules – hard rules, that have to be followed if you want to keep *breathing*.' She glared at Josephine.

'And you waltzed around, playing your little game as though this was a fucking school yard.' She snorted, humourlessly. 'Pairing off with the enemy. I sent you in there with full knowledge of who Aleksei was and what boundaries he had crossed. And instead of doing your job, you *fucked him.*'

Josephine flinched and swallowed the hard lump in her throat. It had been so much more than that, and Anna knew it. She wanted to defend herself, defend her broken heart, but the warning light in her head told her that it wasn't wise. She'd never heard Anna speak like this; so full of raw, vengeful anger.

'You ran around with the man who had rolled in and started undermining our business on *our* turf. The man who tried point-blank to kill both Freddie and Paul and who, when he didn't succeed, then put even bigger plans in place to take them out. Even when you *knew* he was trying to take us out you still snuck around like some loved-up teenager and lied to our faces – your *family's* faces.'

'But I didn't, Anna,' Josephine said with a shaking voice. 'When I found out what he was going to do—'

'You *still* didn't come to me. You didn't tell us that Freddie and Paul's lives were in real, genuine danger. And if I hadn't followed you there that night and stopped him from choking you to death,' she spat, 'he might have actually succeeded in taking us all out.'

Anna paused and took a deep breath, trying to calm the rage within that was so strong she could feel it shaking her body.

Josephine felt a hot tear escape and quickly wiped it away with her hand. 'I couldn't come to you, Anna. Not after all of that,' she said miserably. 'But you know I went in there to stop him. You *know* when it came down to it my loyalties were with you.'

Anna stared at Josephine for a few moments with cold eyes. 'And that,' she said quietly, 'is the only reason you're still here.'

The hardness in her words sent a shiver through Josephine. The memory of Aleksei's grip around her neck loosening, his body slumping off hers as the bullet ended his life, ran through her head. She'd looked up to find herself staring into the barrel of Anna's gun, waiting for her to pull the trigger a second time. It had only been Tanya calling Anna's phone, warning them to get out of the building, that had saved her from the same fate.

'Do you really hate me this much, Anna?' Josephine whispered, not bothering to wipe away the tears that now rolled unchecked down her face.

There was a long silence before Anna answered. 'I don't hate you, Josephine. I hate what you did. I hate that you lied. And I hate that you fucked up so damn badly.' She paused then continued, her wrath unabated. 'I hate that in order to protect you from what you did, I've had to lie to Freddie – to everyone. I hate that you put both me and Tanya in that position. If any of this came out, we'd be considered untrustworthy too. Do you even get what that means? We could lose everything, just for covering for you. That's the reality of this situation now.' She shook her head. 'But most of all, Josephine… What I hate the most is that I don't know how, or if, or when I am ever going to be able to look at you without feeling all this hatred again.'

The calm honesty in Anna's words as the flare of anger seemed to subside into exhaustion was the undoing of Josephine. She squeezed her eyes shut as the tears ran faster, and bowed her head in shame.

Anna's heart hurt as she looked at the broken woman in front of her. She wanted to comfort her and punish her, all at the same time. In the end she did neither, quietly turning and walking back out of The Sinners' Lounge and away from Josephine entirely.

CHAPTER EIGHT

Mollie huffed as she reached the apartment block where Freddie and Anna now lived with her beloved grandson Ethan. She could never understand what they saw in flat living, in owning an apartment surrounded by other apartments in the city. There was no lovely garden to grow flowers in and no front yard to make nice and be proud of. She just couldn't understand it. It wasn't like they didn't have the money.

Smiling at Ethan as he trotted along beside her, she squeezed his hand lovingly. He was the apple of her eye these days. He reminded her so much of her little Freddie at this age. Though Freddie had had to grow up far too quickly not long after, when his father had died. They'd had nothing to their name and no money coming in. It had been a terrifying time for Mollie, with four children to feed and house. If Freddie hadn't gone out after school helping out at the markets and on building sites, Mollie wasn't sure how they would have survived. Ethan would never know that sort of struggle and she thanked the Lord for it almost every time she saw him.

'Come on then, let's get you dropped off. Do you know what Anna's making you for dinner?' she asked as she entered the code to get into the building.

'Dunno,' Ethan answered with a shrug. 'Maybe shepherd's pie with the orange potato on top,' he continued hopefully.

'Sweet potato,' Mollie corrected. She had to hand it to Anna, she couldn't fault her cooking – however hard she tried. 'Still,' she said conspiratorially, 'whatever you get, you know you've got Nan's banana bread for afters, don't you?' She patted the little bag she'd packed for him to take home.

'Aw, yeah!' Ethan replied in glee. 'That's my favourite.'

Mollie smiled smugly as they travelled up in the lift. She'd come to care for Anna greatly over the years and she could give her the praise she deserved on the cooking – so long as she was always her boys' favourite baker.

Letting herself into the flat with the spare key she had for times such as these when she was dropping Ethan off, she called out to see who was home. Nobody answered.

'Hmm,' she muttered with a small frown.

Walking into the kitchen she found the note Anna had left that morning.

Hi Mollie, I should be back but in case I'm not Tanya is in downstairs and will watch Ethan till I get back. Call you later – Anna X

Pursing her lips and raising her eyebrows, Mollie turned back to Ethan. 'Right, kiddo, get your coat back on, you're going down to your Auntie Tanya's.'

'OK. She's not cooking my dinner though, is she?' Ethan asked warily. As opposed to Anna, Tanya was well known for being a terrible cook, though to Ethan's dismay this never stopped her trying.

'I don't know,' Mollie said, pulling a face. 'Hopefully not. Come on.'

They walked down the short flight of stairs to the floor below and Mollie knocked twice before trying the handle to Tanya's front door. It opened immediately and she walked in, Ethan half a step behind her.

'Tanya, it's only me— Oh my goodness grief!' Mollie shrieked as they turned the corner into the lounge. 'Ethan!' Grabbing the boy close to her she quickly held her hands over his eyes, as her own bulged in shock.

'Mollie!' Tanya cried accusingly, quickly trying to cover herself up and standing up from where she had been draped across the sofa in her sluttiest underwear taking naughty photos of herself. 'Gordon Bennett, don't you bloody knock?' she asked, her cheeks flushing crimson with embarrassment.

Ethan giggled loudly, having seen the situation through a crack in Mollie's fingers.

'What on earth are you doing, Tanya Smith?' Mollie asked, outraged, pulling herself up to full height.

'Taking naughty photos for her date,' Ethan responded cheekily.

'Ethan Tyler! Talk like that again and I'll wash your mouth out with soap,' Mollie warned, rounding on him. 'As I should do to you, young lady,' she added, turning back to Tanya. 'Or your dirty mind, one of the two. Taking photos of yourself in your underwear.' She tutted. 'Is that what you think nice young women do?' she admonished.

Tanya let out a long, frustrated breath through her nose and pulled a tight smile as she tied her green silk dressing gown around her tightly. 'I'm not sure, Mollie,' she replied, 'I haven't asked any of them.'

Mollie gave her a withering look. 'Well, it certainly wasn't what young women did in my day. And you didn't see many of them get to your age unmarried, let me tell you.'

'That's probably because they didn't have camera phones and internet back then, ain't it, Mollie?' Tanya replied brightly. 'Or electricity, or running water, you ancient bat...' she muttered scathingly as she walked through to the kitchen.

'What was that?' Mollie asked sharply.

'Just saying it's a shame I didn't have a mum like you to teach me how to act all proper and that,' she lied with a broad smile.

Ethan hid his smirk behind his hand. He'd heard what she'd said.

Mollie nodded self-righteously. 'That ain't your fault, love,' she said, with a sympathetic look. 'You just go and get yourself dressed and I'll put the kettle on.'

'Oh, you're staying for a cuppa?' Tanya asked, raising her eyebrows.

'Might as well,' she replied, shrugging off her jacket.

'Well,' Tanya murmured to Ethan as she passed with a roll of her eyes, 'we'd better both behave for now then, hadn't we?'

CHAPTER NINE

Freddie walked out through the front door of the club into the bright sunshine and busy street beyond. Lifting his face up to the sky he allowed the warmth to rest on his skin for a moment before turning and walking swiftly down the road. Bypassing an arguing couple and a mother with a pushchair, he dived down a smaller side street and slowed his pace a little as he pondered on his recent conversation with Sarah.

She had called this morning and told him about the car outside the graveyard, after spending the previous day trying to find out who owned it. All her searches had come to a dead end. The plates were fake and she couldn't find a match for the detailing. It could have been a coincidence, of course, but it wasn't likely. What were the chances of the same person being outside his club and at the graveyard he had buried his sister in so many miles away? No, whoever it was, they were following him. But why? It wasn't the police. That much he could work out himself. The police didn't roll round in jacked-up Range Rovers with blacked-out windows and fake plates for a start.

At the end of the alley Freddie paused for a few moments and checked his watch. Not really looking at the time, he focused as the man in his peripheral vision also paused and half turned, ready to walk back, since there was nowhere to hide in the narrow alleyway. Freddie's jaw locked in a grim line as his suspicions were confirmed. He carried on in the direction he had been going and disappeared around the corner, backing into the small crevice he knew to be in the wall just beyond.

A few seconds later, the man following him appeared and looked around, trying to figure out where Freddie had gone. Stepping forward, Freddie pushed his pocket knife into the man's back, hiding it from view with the open sides of his jacket. Immediately the man froze, groaning as he realised he'd been caught.

'Hello, treacle,' Freddie hissed into the man's ear. 'I suggest you tell me who the fuck you are and why you're following me, before I decide to carve myself a nice bit of pork.'

'I ain't no rozzer,' the man replied, indignantly. 'I got more pride than to work as a bloody pig, thank you.'

'Oh, I'm aware of that,' Freddie replied, walking the man towards the back of a collection of industrial bins, out of the public eye. 'I wouldn't be holding a knife to your back if I thought you were filth. I was referring to the fact you look like a squealer. Are you a squealer, when a little pressure gets applied, Mr Whoever-the-fuck-you-are?' Freddie pushed the knife harder against his back and the man let out a small sound of discomfort. 'I reckon we might have to find out, if you don't start talking soon.'

To Freddie's surprise the man began to chuckle. 'Christ, you're more like your old man than I thought you'd be.'

'You what?' Freddie asked, his brow furrowing as he pulled the knife away. He roughly turned the other man around, searching his face for any familiarity. 'Who are you? And what do you know of my dad?'

The other man dusted himself off and straightened his T-shirt. 'I'm Jim. Jim Martin. I was friends with your dad. Well, before, you know…'

'I've never seen you before, or heard talk of anyone called Jim,' Freddie replied. 'And that still don't answer my question as to why you've been following me.'

'I'm sorry for that,' Jim said, holding his hands out. 'I didn't mean to shit you up, I just wasn't sure when best to approach you. I know who you are, I know I can't just walk up to you and expect an audience. I was just trying to find the best opportunity. And as for not knowing me, you wouldn't. I went down when you were just a kid still. Took the rap for a murder I helped clear up, back in my days working for Big Dom. Could have got out for good behaviour a few years back, but, well,' he chuckled, 'I wasn't that good.'

Freddie studied the man in front of him. Slightly shorter than he was, Jim was still fairly tall but beginning to stoop with age. He had a well-rounded belly, but still seemed strong and agile despite this. Several of the tattoos on his arms looked like inside jobs, which backed up his story. Glancing down the alleyway they'd walked along, Freddie squinted as he pondered what to do.

'So, you say you wanted an audience with me?' he asked.

'Yes,' Jim replied.

Freddie chewed the inside of his cheek before responding. It had been a long time since he had heard anyone talk about his dad and that had piqued his curiosity. 'OK, then. There's a café up here. We can talk there. Come on.'

Slipping the blade he was holding back into his jacket pocket, Freddie strode off towards the small café. Jim followed and the pair walked in silence until they were inside and sitting at a table in the window.

The woman behind the counter bustled over with her order pad, flipping to a fresh page as she reached the table. 'Hello, Freddie,' she said with a grin. 'What will it be today?'

'I'll have a tea please, Sheila,' he replied, 'and a…' He rose one eyebrow at Jim in question.

'Oh, I'll have the same, cheers,' Jim said.

'Two teas then,' Sheila confirmed. 'Coming right up.'

Waiting until she'd left, Freddie stared at Jim, his expression hard and unreadable. Jim held his gaze, seemingly unfazed by this.

'So, go on,' Freddie prompted.

'Right, yeah.' Jim repositioned himself, lacing his fingers together on the table in front of them. 'I've er, well, I've recently got out and to be honest life out here has changed a lot. It's been twenty-five years since I last roamed these streets.' He half smiled. 'And as for my bosses, the men who used to rule round here, one of them is dead and the other can't remember his own name anymore.'

Freddie felt his muscles tighten at the reference to his mentor, Vince Castor. Back in the day, Big Dom and Vince had ruled the central belt together. They had built the foundations of the empire that the Tylers had taken over and paved the way of life that they all now lived and breathed. Vince had groomed Freddie as his successor from an early age after seeing his potential and, unlike Big Dom, still lived, but was no longer the force to be reckoned with that he once had been. A few years ago he had moved into a retirement home after the untimely death of his young wife, then a couple of years later, whilst Freddie had been in prison, he had developed dementia, a cruel strain which had ripped like wildfire through his brain. Some days he remembered things, but most of the time he no longer had any idea what was going on. It had broken Freddie's heart to see how much he had declined in the time he had been inside.

'When I went away, Big Dom saw me right for my troubles. He paid off some debt I had and put some money aside for me, for when I came out. And I've got that,' he added, 'but what was a decent sum twenty-five years ago don't really go far today.' He shifted uncomfortably. 'So, I need a job.'

'You want to work for me?' Freddie asked.

'Pretty much,' Jim replied.

There was a long silence as Freddie studied Jim across the table. Jim looked to be easily in his late fifties and whilst – if his back story was the truth – he might have been handy back in the day, everything worked differently now. It would be like teaching a rookie everything from the very start again, which was not easy with the young ones, let alone an old dog like Jim.

'I know I might not be your most exciting prospect,' Jim continued, picking up, rightly, on Freddie's initial reservations, 'but I'm not looking to jump into the sort of position I was in before. I'll take anything you've got, even if it's just as a runaround. I just want to be on someone's payroll again, somewhere with a chance my skills might come in useful. And I do still have skills,' he pushed. 'Plus, after doing a twenty-five year stretch for Big Dom, you wouldn't be able to question my loyalty.'

Freddie nodded. This was true. *If* Jim's story checked out. The question was, though, how exactly was he going to verify those details? It wasn't like they kept some sort of historical HR record on all the criminals who had worked for the firm through the ages. And aside from Vince, who was no longer a viable source of information, everyone from that golden age of villainy was either dead or had retired abroad and was off the radar.

Sheila bustled over with the teas and set them down on the table. 'Here we are. Sugar's in the pot.'

As she walked away Freddie rubbed his face and thought through his options. He could just decline, tell the old man 'no' and send him on his way. He might have worked for Big Dom and Vince, but Freddie didn't owe him anything. Then again, wasn't loyalty the backbone of their firm? Did it matter that it had been twenty-five years and the old faces were gone? Freddie was only in the position he was in now because of Vince and Big Dom. And so, it would seem, was Jim.

Making a decision, Freddie straightened up. 'Look, I might have a job going behind the bar at the club. Come by around eight and I'll talk you through what shifts are going spare.'

Jim blinked and his face dropped. 'That wasn't really the kind of job I was hoping to get. I can pick up bar work anywhere – I'm talking about working for the firm. I might be long in the tooth but I've still got all the same skills I did back in the day,' he argued.

Freddie looked at his watch and took a deep gulp of the hot tea in front of him, before standing up and straightening his jacket. 'I'm sure you do, but I don't know you from Adam, mate,' he said. Pulling a ten-pound note out of his pocket he gave it to Sheila. 'I've got to shoot, keep the change.'

'Oh, thanks, love,' Sheila replied with a warm smile. The Tylers were always so good to her when they came in. Her favourite customers.

Jim stood up too, his face a picture of dismay as he realised his time with Freddie was up. 'Just give me a chance. I ain't fussy about what I do, so long as I'm back in the game. You must need someone, a runner, anything. I ain't cut out for the legal lifestyle.'

'Eight o'clock, if you decide you do want those shifts,' Freddie repeated, walking out of the small café. The door clanged shut behind him.

As Freddie made his way back to the club he pulled out his phone. He hadn't really needed to go out, but after Sarah's warnings that he was being followed he had started to notice Jim's presence more clearly. He'd been coming to the club quite often, always alone, always watching. Freddie had made a slow, preoccupied exit today in the hope the man would take the bait and follow. His gamble had paid off. This was the man who'd been following him, watching him, all this time. It still seemed a bit fishy, though, the way he had gone about things. Why not just introduce himself in the first place?

Placing a call, Freddie waited for it to connect, glancing behind to make sure Jim hadn't followed him out. He hadn't, this time.

'Hey, Bill. I need you to look into someone for me. A Jim Martin. Reckons he just got out from a murder stretch and used to work for Big Dom. Find out what you can and get back to me ASAP, yeah? Good man.'

Freddie put the phone away and took a deep breath before exhaling slowly. Jim said he'd known his dad. More than anything, he'd wanted to ask the man to tell him everything he remembered, to share stories and give the father Freddie missed so badly life again, just for a few minutes. That was why he'd offered him the bar shifts instead of telling him to sling his hook. It had been many years since Richard Tyler had passed, Freddie had only been ten years old, but not a day went by when he wasn't reminded of his absence in some way. They had been close, the pair of them. Freddie had been Richard's little shadow, looking up to him, wanting to be just like him. It had been a cruel twist of fate that had taken him from them so early on.

Shaking off the pang of grief that still shot through him whenever he thought of his dad, Freddie walked into Club CoCo. There was a time and place to dwell on old memories, and it was neither here nor now. What he wanted to know now was whether or not Jim's story about working for Big Dom and taking the rap for one of the murders was true. Part of him was inclined to believe it was – it was unlikely someone would be stupid enough to make up something like that to someone as dangerous as Freddie Tyler. The man would have to have some kind of death wish.

But still, there was something that didn't sit quite right about Jim. And Freddie couldn't put his finger on what it was. Suddenly, he hoped that Jim did show up for the bar shifts he'd offered. Because if nothing else, at least having him in the bar meant he could keep a closer eye on the puzzling newcomer. Was he friend or was he foe? Only time would tell.

CHAPTER TEN

The sound of drilling on the floor above finally stopped and two pairs of feet pattered down the stairs. Patting her hair and checking herself over one last time in the mirror, Josephine walked out of her small flat and locked it behind her. Bill and Tanya reached the bottom of the stairwell leading up to the attic and smiled at her in greeting.

'Alright, Josephine?' Bill said.

'Where you off to?' Tanya asked.

'Oh, just the shops. Need to get some food in,' she answered.

'OK.' Tanya glanced at her watch. 'Will you be about tonight?'

'Yes, what's happening?'

'Anna's just asked that you stay down with the girls and keep them out of the way of the back stairwell. Anything they hear, they need to unhear. That OK?' Tanya replied.

Josephine nodded with a humourless smirk. Of course Anna wanted her out of the way. 'Sure,' she said, plastering a fake smile on her face for Bill's benefit.

'Great, OK, well…' Tanya looked at Bill and the pair moved on down the hallway. 'I'll catch you later.'

'What's going on with her and Anna?' Bill asked Tanya under his breath as they walked out of hearing range.

'Oh, don't ask.' Tanya rolled her eyes. 'It's all to do with women's problems,' she whispered conspiratorially.

'Oh, OK.' Bill clamped his mouth shut and Tanya hid a grin. It was amazing what those two little words could do.

Josephine watched as they disappeared and sighed heavily, hugging her arms around her chest for a few moments. She lived in a busy brothel with people all around her, but she felt more alone than ever right now. Most of them had no idea of the trauma she had been through or the grief coursing through her veins, and those who did were doing their utmost to bury all evidence of it. She understood why, but it meant that she had to process everything that had happened and mourn the loss of the only man she had ever loved entirely on her own.

Sniffing back the tears that threatened, she pulled herself upright and forced herself to walk down the stairs and out of the building. She found the best way to contain her emotions was to carry on as though everything was normal. It wasn't easy, but it was necessary. And right now, that meant going food shopping. She would walk into the supermarket and place the tomatoes and the cheese and the bread in her basket. She'd check the expiry date on the milk cartons and tut at the price of oranges as if the few pence that had been added since last time actually meant anything.

She closed her eyelids for a second, allowing them to be warmed by the sun. The horn of an impatient taxi driver forced her attention back to the pavement. The streets were filled with the usual buzz of Central London life and seemed to pulse with an unseen energy. It brought a small smile to Josephine's lips. Whatever else was happening in her life, the sights and sounds of the city on a sunny day were always a welcome distraction.

As she walked, Josephine reached into the oversized pocket of her thin summer jacket and checked she still had her shopping bag, folded away neatly there for just this occasion. Distracted by this as she turned down the side road that led towards the supermarket, she didn't notice the big black Range Rover following at a crawl, a few metres behind. The pathway thinned and she stepped into the road to allow a young couple to pass and didn't register the sound of the engine roar as it sped up behind.

''Ere, watch out,' a voice yelled.

Someone grabbed her by the elbow and jerked her out of the road, swinging her round so roughly that she nearly hit the wall of a nearby shop. Almost losing her footing, Josephine reached out to the wall with her other hand and steadied herself.

'What the hell?' she asked, as the Range Rover screeched off angrily down the road and around the corner, disappearing out of view.

'You OK?' the same voice as before asked, and Josephine turned to the man who had pulled her out of harm's way.

'Yeah, thanks for that,' she said, straightening her dress and jacket. 'What a bloody maniac.'

'What you done to piss them off, then?' the man asked.

'What do you mean?' Josephine frowned.

'Well, they were crawling along till they saw you step off the pavement. Looked like they were aiming for ya,' the man replied earnestly, scratching his head. 'It was only 'cause I was looking that I caught you in time.'

'Oh.' Josephine blinked. 'I'm sure it's probably just coincidence. I've never even seen that car before.'

The man pulled a face, not convinced. 'If you say so, love.' He carried on walking and Josephine's frown deepened.

The man was being paranoid. Probably a conspiracy theorist looking for something to gossip about. Because she didn't have anyone who would want to run her over, not any more at least. Did she?

CHAPTER ELEVEN

'Seems his story checks out,' Bill said, as he sat down at the desk opposite Freddie. 'From what I could find so far, anyway.' He reached into his pocket and pulled out his cigarettes, offering one to his boss and lighting up. Taking a deep drag, he blew out a long plume of smoke. Freddie did the same and settled back in his big leather chair, biting his lip thoughtfully. 'Obviously there's no paper trail connecting him to the firm,' Bill continued, 'but he did just get out after a stretch for Tom Long's murder. Tom Long was one of the rebels who tried to overthrow Vince and Big Dom back in the day. They got rid of him just at the right time, but the body was found. An investigation was launched and there was a lot of talk of gang wars. Big Dom was even taken in and questioned – his mug was all over the papers at the time. But then the following stories say that Jim just walked into the station one day and handed himself in for it. The case was closed and the firm was out of the limelight.'

'So he did take the rap for them, like he said,' Freddie mused. He took another drag of his cigarette and exhaled the smoke slowly.

'Seems so,' Bill answered. He eyed his boss's expression critically. 'You still ain't sure about him though, are ya?'

'No, I'm not.' He flicked his ash into the crystal ashtray on the desk. 'All this following business is a bit off. He's been in here for weeks, had plenty of opportunity to approach me.'

'Could just be wary. He's been away a long time. Prison does things to ya. You know that as well as anyone.'

'True,' Freddie conceded. He took no offence at this statement. Bill had done time himself, a few years back. He flicked his ash once more and took another drag. 'He wants a job with the firm. I've offered him bar work. Can't just take on a complete stranger, we have no idea if he's friend or foe.'

'I can't see any benefit for him to be a foe after already taking a lifer for the firm,' Bill said.

'Me neither, if I'm honest. But there's something off about him.' He frowned. 'I'm only entertaining him at all because he helped out Big Dom, but that don't mean he gets an instant in.'

There was a short silence. Freddie wasn't sure what it was that bugged him so much, but there was something not quite right. Why had Jim acted so shady? And if he had known his dad *and* been part of the firm, why had they never heard his name before now? Surely someone who had taken one for the team at that level should have been celebrated, gone down in underworld history as a hero?

'Well, if he turns up he can have a few shifts. But chances are he won't bother. He ain't after straight work.'

'Can't say I blame him,' Bill replied.

'By the way, we're a man down on the dealer tree,' Freddie informed him.

'Yeah, I heard.' Bill stubbed out his cigarette.

There was a knock at the door, before it immediately opened and Sammy walked in. 'Alright?' he said with a grin.

'Yeah, good. I've got an odd one for you,' Freddie said, 'but it might just work out to our advantage—'

There was another knock at the door, a light rapping, and Freddie frowned. He wasn't expecting anyone else for at least another hour. Surely Jim hadn't turned up early?

Tanya's head peeped around the door and her body swiftly followed as she walked in. 'Oh hey, I was hoping I'd find you here,' she said to Freddie. Nodding at Bill and Sammy she strode confidently across the room as fast as her restrictive leather wrap dress would allow her. With no more chairs readily available, she leaned against the desk and crossed her shapely legs, resting one hand on her hip and turning her head towards Freddie.

'I hear you're a man down on the dealer tree,' she said, cutting straight to the point.

'Everyone has, apparently,' Freddie replied, bemused.

'Anna mentioned it this morning and I had an idea. Alice, one of our girls, is up the duff and starting to show. We're moving her over to waiting staff until she has the baby, but obviously it's cut back her income a bit. She's looking for something extra on the side. If you want, you can use her until you've sorted out something long term. She's trustworthy,' Tanya pressed. 'One of our best. And she'd really appreciate the money.'

Tanya took a deep breath in and let it out slowly, causing her generous bosom to rise and fall above the low cut of her dress. She arched her back slightly and pulled her thick red hair over one shoulder. Sammy, sitting directly in front of her, raised his eyebrows and held her stare with an amused glint in his eye, when she finally looked his way. It was subtle, but not that subtle and Freddie hid a grin.

'And you couldn't tell me this over the phone?' he asked, tongue in cheek.

'What, and miss the opportunity to come and say hello to such good friends in person? That wouldn't be any fun now, would it?' she replied, giving him a cheeky wink and a grin. 'Oh, and I almost forgot.' She stood up and straightened her dress, running her hands over her hips. 'Anna and I were talking; we should have a get-together tomorrow night at Club Anya. We have the VIP space free, so thought we might as well make use of it.'

'How convenient,' Freddie replied.

Tanya ignored the not-so-hidden jibe and just smiled broadly. 'It is,' she replied. 'So get your guys together, let's let our hair down and have a good old knees-up, shall we?' She raised one perfectly arched eyebrow and looked around at the three men. 'I've already texted Amy, Bill. She's looking forward to it.'

'I'm sure she is,' Bill replied. Amy was Bill's wife and a good friend of both Anna and Tanya.

'Great, well, see you then. Bring your drinking boots, I'm in the mood for some fun.' Winking at Sammy, Tanya waltzed back out of the room and as the door closed behind her the room fell into silence once more.

The three men looked around at each other.

'Well, that weren't for my benefit,' Bill said with a deep chuckle.

'Nor mine,' Freddie continued, a smile creeping up slowly on his face as he turned to Sammy.

Sammy shook his head with a grin. 'I believe that display was for me.' He stated what they were all thinking. Staring at the closed door, he felt the first tug of intrigue pull at him. He'd always admired Tanya for her feisty demeanour and her strong, upbeat ways – and she was, of course, a very attractive woman. But she had never shown him any interest and, never short of female attention, Sammy was not interested in being the one to chase.

Reading his friend's mind, Freddie nodded his head. This was going to be an interesting show to watch, that was for sure. There was a definite spark and sparks like that tended to lead to a full-on fire. And if that happened, perhaps this was the relationship which would finally work out for each of them. They were all cursed, those in the know. There were so many secrets to keep and dark deeds to be hidden, when you belonged to a firm such as theirs. It put heavy restrictions on relationships with people in the normal world. But these two would never have any reason to hide any part of themselves from the other.

Clearing his throat, Freddie decided not to comment further. 'Right, so where were we?' Only time would tell what was to unfold between those two.

CHAPTER TWELVE

Jim exhaled heavily and drew himself up to full height before knocking on Freddie's office door. Freddie had shut him down almost immediately earlier and he hadn't been ready for it. He should have expected it, looking back on the conversation. He knew, better than most, how secretive and private the firms of London could be. It was just good sense. It was survival. They couldn't afford to take a chance on someone they didn't already completely trust. So he needed to show Freddie he could be trusted.

'Come in,' came the muffled response.

He opened the door and walked into the office. Freddie was seated at the desk looking over a heavily marked map, but he folded it and filed it away as soon as he saw Jim.

'I wasn't sure you'd come,' Freddie said, as Jim took a seat opposite him. 'But I'm glad you did, I'm a man short on the rota.'

Jim shook his head as he took his seat. 'I'm not taking the bar shifts. With all due respect – and thanks for the offer – I'm not that desperate for money. I didn't come to you because I needed just any job, I came to you because I want to get back into what I know, what I'm good at.'

Freddie laced his fingers together on the desk. 'And what exactly *are* you good at?' he asked.

'Grifting,' Jim answered. 'I'm a grifter by trade. And I'm good. I'd have the glasses off a blind man without him feeling a thing,' he boasted. 'I could snatch the knickers off a nun and she'd just be sat there wondering which door the draught was coming from.'

Freddie shook his head, dismissively. 'I don't need a grifter.'

'I'm not just a grifter, I'm a jack of all trades when it comes to the life,' he continued, trying to sell himself as best he could. 'I'm skilled at breaking and entering and I'm good at negotiating the trade of stolen goods.'

'Your skills all revolve around thievery.' Freddie shrugged. 'Which all sounds good, but I still have no need for anyone in your area.'

'I'm also loyal to a fault,' Jim pressed. 'I went down for twenty-five years – *twenty-five years of my life*, for Big Dom.' He held Freddie's stare intently. 'That ain't small change in this world, and I think you know that.'

Freddie sat back in his chair as he pondered the unexpected predicament in front of him. Jim was right: someone who would take a life stretch for their boss was indeed something rare in this life and the ultimate show of loyalty. Bill's research had backed up his story too.

Taking Freddie's silence as a promising sign, Jim pressed forward. 'I was loyal to my firm then and I'd be just as loyal to it now. And let's face it, it might be under new management but it's still the same firm, is it not? You still run the same rackets through Soho, you still run the parlour girls, the cocaine is still distributed to the same places, I *know* this business already. I just want a chance to come back in now that the hard time I took for Big Dom is done.'

Freddie picked up his cigarettes and lit one, taking a deep drag before flicking the excess ash into his crystal ashtray. Jim was not so subtly pressing on the responsibility button, reminding him that although Big Dom was out of the picture, it was this firm he had done time for. Part of him wanted to be annoyed, but a bigger part of him knew that these comments were fair game. Jim had every right to press the issue.

Jim looked down at the cigarette packet on the desk and suddenly grinned. 'Your grandad used to smoke those, you know,' he said.

'Eh?' Freddie frowned at the unexpected change in conversation.

'Yeah, your dad's dad. They were his brand. Your dad hated the things, couldn't bear to be around anyone who smoked 'em. He always used to duck out and sit on his tod when anyone else lit up.' He chuckled. 'Even down the pub.'

Freddie smiled. He could actually remember Richard's aversion to smoking quite clearly. His dad had been a boxer, focused on keeping his body on top form for his fights. He had warned his children of the dangers of smoking from an early age. For the first time in his life, Freddie suddenly felt a pang of guilt at his lit cigarette and he leaned forward and stubbed it out. 'I remember that,' he said with a wry smile.

He studied Jim for a moment. The man was certainly past his prime, the firm Freddie now ran having taken the best years of his life. And it was true, the fact that Jim was trying to get across without saying it outright. The firm owed him. Freddie knew that if Big Dom was around today he would insist that any man who had taken a murder stretch for him was given a job when he got back out. It was only right.

Freddie nodded. 'Alright, listen. I'll put you on some of the collection rounds with my men. Pick up the routes, get to know the people and we'll go from there. You can start tomorrow, I'll put you on payroll from tonight.'

'Thank you,' Jim said with a grateful smile. It wasn't much, collecting money for protection services, but it was an in, and that was all Jim needed.

'I expect hard graft, mind,' Freddie warned. 'My men are on call day and night, seven days a week. When I need them, I expect them to be there. Nothing comes before the needs of the firm if you work for me. You get a bird, a hobby, a desperate need to go on a jaunt, that's fine – but nothing you can't drop at a moment's notice if I need you. You think you're up to the task?'

''Course,' Jim answered. 'Wouldn't expect any different.'

'Good,' Freddie responded.

Jim smiled, happy that he'd been able to change Freddie's mind.

It was true that he'd done time for one of Big Dom's murders. So the firm did owe him. But he had lied about his loyalties. He held no loyalty for this firm. And that was something Freddie was just going to have to find out the hard way.

CHAPTER THIRTEEN

Waking in the weak morning light, Freddie rubbed his bleary
eyes and turned towards the mass of dark hair peeping out from
under the covers next to him. He smiled and moved closer, pulling
the covers back and wrapping his muscular arm around Anna's
sleeping form. She stirred and turned her head a little, and Freddie
nuzzled into her neck, breathing in her warmth. He closed his eyes
and savoured the moment, as he did every single morning now.

Prison had changed him. A little for the worse, and some for
the better. Three years had been a long time, and they had been the
most dismal years of his life. Not because he was locked away, that
he could cope with. It was something you came to terms with, if
you chose to take the sort of risks that they did. No, they had been
the worst years of his life because they had taken Anna from him.

He had never expected her to wait. A lot of men would have,
but not Freddie. He loved her too much to lock her down in such
a way. The time and distance between them had been too great,
and their relationship had had no way of continuing to flourish.
She'd done her duty, though. Anna had kept the firm going strong
and had raised his son as her own. If he had come out the same
man he had gone in, perhaps they would have reunited a lot more
quickly. But Freddie's radar had been off, he'd been all over the
place. He'd seen enemies where there were none and his paranoia
had known no bounds. He'd turned on Anna, accused her of
professional betrayal. It had almost broken them, but somehow,
once he'd come to his senses and fought to turn things around,

she had managed to forgive him. He had never been more grateful for her inner strength than in that moment. The flame that had burned brightly in both their hearts for so many years was still there, despite everything they'd gone through, and they had started their relationship again, just a couple of months before.

Now, when he woke up each morning and he found he was no longer alone in his bed in a cold cell, but was in fact at home with the love of his life, Freddie felt a renewed sense of gratitude and he savoured every moment with her.

Anna turned over and pressed her body to Freddie's, snuggling deeper into his chest. Feeling his own body respond to hers instantly, Freddie lifted her chin with his fingers and sought out her mouth. It curled into a sleepy grin as she kissed him and she wrapped her arms around him, pulling him on top of her.

Freddie gave a small groan of pleasure as she wrapped her legs around him, but this was swiftly cut off as the bedroom door suddenly opened with a bang. Freddie fell back to the side, his groan of pleasure turning to one of frustration as they both pulled the covers up to hide their nakedness from their son.

'Anna, I'm hungry, can we have breakfast now?' Ethan asked, completely oblivious to what he had just interrupted.

'Mhm,' she murmured through a forced smile. 'Of course, I'll be through in just a minute.'

'Ahh,' Freddie laughed through his frustration and rubbed his hands through his hair. 'OK.' Swivelling to the side, he pulled on a pair of boxers and stood up. 'Come on, mate, I'll make you some toast.'

'Oh.' Ethan looked disappointed.

'What?' Freddie asked, as they walked through to the kitchen.

'Well, Anna usually makes proper breakfast on Saturdays. Sausages and eggs and bacon and everything.'

'Well, Anna has a prior engagement this morning,' Freddie replied, 'so how about I make you this toast to keep you going for now, then I'll take you both out to the café in a bit and you can choose whatever you want?'

'What's a prior engagement?' Ethan asked, slipping onto one of the breakfast bar stools and watching as Freddie put the bread in the toaster.

'I'll tell you when you're older. Juice?' Freddie replied, opening the fridge.

'Yes please.' Ethan picked up the TV remote and found his favourite programme.

'What's this then?' Freddie asked, as he waited for the toast to pop up.

'Oh, this is *Trollhunters*,' Ethan said, eagerly. 'It's really good.'

'Oh. Don't you watch that dog show anymore? *PAW Patrol*?' Freddie asked. He hadn't seen it on the TV at all since he'd been home.

'Nah, that's for babies, not big boys like me,' Ethan scoffed.

Freddie felt a pang of sadness at these words. Ethan was growing up so fast and he had missed pretty much all of it so far. He thought back to their first ever conversation. *PAW Patrol* had been the thing they had bonded over, when Freddie had first discovered Ethan's existence a few years before. They'd barely got to know each other properly and Ethan had only just come to live with Freddie when he'd been sent down.

The toast popped up and Freddie buttered it and placed it in front of Ethan, who was now completely engrossed in his programme.

'Thanks, Dad,' he muttered, without looking round.

Freddie stroked his head and rested his hand on Ethan's shoulder for a moment. 'We'll go do something fun today, yeah? Before you go over to Nan's tonight. Your choice, have a think about it.'

'OK.'

Leaving the young television zombie to his toast, Freddie walked back through to the bedroom where Anna was waiting for him still curled up in the bed. He closed the door firmly behind him and the intensity in his eyes deepened as they locked with hers.

'Now,' he said in a low, deep voice, 'where were we?'

As he reached the bed and crawled upwards towards Anna, the silence in the room was once again shattered by the shrill ring of his phone. 'Oh, for the love of God!' Freddie exclaimed, throwing his head back in despair.

Anna laughed and pushed him away. 'Go on, answer it and get rid of them. The quicker you do that, the quicker we can get back to this,' she purred, running one shiny, manicured nail down Freddie's bare chest.

He gave her a smouldering look. 'Don't you move, Anna Davis,' he replied, grudgingly pulling back and reaching for his phone. He looked briefly at the screen then answered. 'What is it, Riley?' he asked, curtly.

'I'm sorry to call you so early, but it's important. That car that was following you...'

'Belongs to Jim Martin, I'm aware,' Freddie cut her off irritably. 'I caught the fucker following me yesterday. It's all sorted out.'

'No, that's just it,' Sarah replied. 'The car isn't his. The plates were fake but the detailing was very distinctive. I did some digging and – I can't be a hundred per cent – but if I'm correct, that car belongs to Aleksei. He had a black Range Rover of that spec and had it detailed just like that. It would be a major coincidence if it's not him.'

'Aleksei?' Freddie sat up, all thoughts of anything else forgotten.

Anna sat up too, her attention sharpening at the sound of Aleksei's name. She pulled the sheet up around her as she sat back against the pillows and strained her ears, trying to make out everything Sarah was saying on the other end of the phone.

'He has several cars, all of them black, all detailed with different types of unique red trim. Perhaps it's some sort of throwback to "mother Russia" or something, I'm not sure. But it's him, that much I am sure about,' Sarah pressed.

'No, you're right. It makes sense that it's him.' Freddie squeezed the bridge of his nose. 'I knew he hadn't just disappeared off the face of the Earth. That would have been far too easy.' Freddie stood up and leaned onto the windowsill. He sighed and looked down over the busy streets of London. 'I was hoping we'd find out where he's been hiding before he came back at us – start off with the upper hand. But it's too late now. If he's following us, he already has a plan and is already a step ahead.' He bit his lip. 'I've got to go. See if there's anything else you can find out.'

'Will do.'

Freddie lowered the phone as Sarah ended the call and stood staring out of the window for a few more moments. Eventually he turned and shrugged a handy T-shirt on. 'I've got to go out,' he said to Anna. 'I need to get the men together. Can you see if my mum will have Ethan a bit earlier and then come join me so we can go over all this before tonight?'

'Of course,' Anna replied. 'Go.' She held an encouraging smile on her face as she watched Freddie walk out to get washed and dressed, but as soon as he was out of sight her face dropped into an expression of deep worry.

The Aleksei problem hadn't been closed off; Freddie still had men out searching possible hideouts and tapping up potential sources of information. But due to the lack of news it had begun to sink lower and lower on the priority list. Whilst they were not yet out of the woods, the stress around the situation had lessened as the weeks had gone on, with Freddie's attentions moving elsewhere. Now, though, this was throwing Freddie and the firm back onto high alert and that was worrying.

And as for the car which was following them, who on earth was behind those tinted windows? she wondered. It wasn't Aleksei, that was for certain. Aleksei was dead, Anna had pulled the trigger herself. His body was buried beneath tonnes of rubble, and so, they'd assumed, were the two men who were with him that night.

The shot Anna had fired had been heard by the two men in the car on the road outside the building site. As she had raised the gun from Aleksei to Josephine, Tanya had called her and warned her to get out of there as quickly as possible, as these men were running towards the building to check on their boss. The women had got out safely, bolting back over the side fence where Anna had originally entered. And as they had stood on the other side wondering how on earth they were going to cover it all up, Josephine had produced the detonator she had stolen from Aleksei. They'd set it off, blowing the building and running away into the night as the huge structure collapsed on top of Aleksei and his men, destroying all evidence of what had happened that night forever.

But what if his men had come back out before the explosion? Or what if one of them had run around the perimeter instead of going inside? It had been so dark, and they had been so set on getting away, that they hadn't stopped to double-check.

If that was the case, if one of them was still alive, that could be a big problem indeed. Because whilst they couldn't have known of Anna and Tanya's involvement, they *had* known Josephine. They had watched her go inside to visit Aleksei not long before all of this had played out. And if they had survived and were watching from a distance, they would know that Josephine was fully alive and well.

Pulling off the covers, Anna picked up her own phone and wrote out a text.

Urgent meeting. My place. One hour.

Walking to her wardrobe, Anna hurriedly pulled out some clothes. It had to be them. Who else could it be? And knowing this, how was she going to deal with it and still keep up the façade in front of Freddie and the others? Was the wall of deceit they had all constructed with such careful lies about to crumble for good?

CHAPTER FOURTEEN

Josephine looked nervous as they reached Anna's floor so Tanya nudged her with her arm. 'Chill out, babe. We're going to Anna's, not hell.'

'I'm Jewish, we don't believe in hell,' Josephine responded.

'Oh. Well, what do you believe in, then?' Tanya asked.

'Well…' Josephine tilted her head to one side. 'I guess the closest thing we have to that is Gehinnom. But that's not exactly a bad thing. It's more like a sort of spiritual washing machine. Your soul gets cleansed of all the bad.'

Tanya stared at her. 'Well, I can't use that in this scenario, can I?' she said. 'Just…' she waved her hand. 'This is not the worst place in the world to be, is what I was getting at. Come on, put on your big-girl pants and suck it up.'

Josephine prepared herself. She did not feel confident walking into Anna's home at all, but she could at least try and look like she did, for Tanya's sake if no one else's. Tanya rapped lightly on the door, then opened it without waiting for an invite. 'Anna?' she called out.

'Here,' came the immediate response.

Anna walked into the hallway from the lounge. She glanced back towards Ethan, who was sitting on the sofa with his hand-held games console. His tongue stuck out of the side of his mouth where he was concentrating so hard.

'Ethan?' Anna called. He glanced up. 'Can you pop into your room with that for a bit? I just need a catch-up with Tanya and Josephine.'

'Sure,' he replied.

'Thanks, darling.' Anna ruffled his floppy light brown hair as he walked past.

As he disappeared from view, Anna beckoned the two women through to the kitchen and they each took a seat at the breakfast bar, opposite Anna who leaned over it from the other side.

'What's going on?' Tanya asked, keeping her voice low so it wouldn't travel into Ethan's hearing. 'Everything OK?'

'No, not really,' Anna replied heavily. 'There has been a car following Freddie and he had Riley look into it. She rang him this morning with news. It's Aleksei's.'

Josephine gasped and then clamped both her hands over her mouth as her eyes widened in shock. 'It can't be,' she whispered through her fingers. 'He's dead.'

'Obviously,' Anna replied, giving her a withering look. 'But it's still his. Which means whoever is driving it, is following Freddie. They may be following more of us, at the moment we don't know. But that much is certain.'

'Shit,' Tanya muttered under her breath.

'Yeah.' Anna exhaled slowly. 'The one thing I keep coming back to in my head, is that we can't be certain that both of Aleksei's men were inside the building when we blew it.'

'They definitely went in, I saw them when I was watching out for you through that knothole in the wood,' Tanya replied.

'Yes, but what if one, or both of them, came back out after you stopped watching?' Anna replied. 'The second you saw us you got ready to help us over, then we were talking for a good couple of minutes before we pressed the detonator. They could have seen us, already started running our way. Or one could have come out to do a perimeter sweep.'

'It is possible,' Tanya admitted. She sat back and ran her hand down her face.

Josephine looked down at the breakfast bar, her skin greying as the weight of what this could mean hit her. 'And if they did,' she said slowly, 'they knew I was there that night. By now they would know I'm alive and not under the rubble with Aleksei. Which means they would know I had everything to do with it.'

'Bingo,' Anna replied. 'Which, if looked at closely, could unravel everything. Your betrayal of this firm...' Josephine's cheeks flushed red and she re-hung her head, '... and mine and Tanya's involvement in both keeping that betrayal a secret, and in everything else that happened that night. If all – or *any* – of that comes out, we're all completely fucked. You know as well as I do that loyalty means absolutely everything in this game. And if Freddie finds out we've been hiding things from him...' She trailed off, not wanting to voice any of the potential horrible outcomes.

Tanya blew out a long breath and crossed her arms as she thought it over. 'OK. We're only assuming we're dealing with one of those men at the moment, right?' she said eventually. 'It might not be them. What are the other options?'

'It could just be someone else who worked for Aleksei, out for revenge for the club shooting,' Anna admitted. 'But it seems unlikely. If they have no boss – no idea what even happened to their boss – why would they continue on the vendetta? He didn't have the biggest following after fleeing Russia and none of his men were leader material, not really.'

'What about his family?' Tanya asked, glancing at Josephine. She wouldn't enjoy the question, but they needed to know.

Josephine shook her head. 'No one that would come back at the firm like this. The only family he had were his wife and sons. The boys are kids, not even as old as Ethan. And the wife, Sophia, she was just there out of duty. She raised the kids and put up with him so long as he brought home the bacon. That was it.' She looked down at her hands and blinked rapidly as the threat of tears began to prickle. Reminders of Aleksei were always hard, but especially ones like this.

Anna straightened up and paced the kitchen, pushing her dark hair back off her face. 'We need to find out who is in that car somehow. And before Freddie,' she added, exchanging looks with Tanya. 'And somehow, we have to do this entirely under the radar.'

'How the fuck are we going to do that?' Tanya asked, her expression drawn.

'For once I have no idea whatsoever,' Anna replied. 'But we're going to have to come up with something good. And fast.'

CHAPTER FIFTEEN

Seamus pulled the car to the side of the road and leaned over to open the passenger door for Jim, who was waiting on the corner as had been arranged by Freddie the night before. Freddie had asked Seamus to take him along on the errands today and acquaint him with some of the lighter tasks. Seamus knew of course that by 'lighter tasks' Freddie meant jobs that didn't give away too much information to this newcomer. He was being tested, watched to see if he could really be trusted.

'How're you doing on this fine afternoon then, Jim?' Seamus greeted him brightly, his melodic Irish accent cheery in the quiet car.

'Yeah, good thanks, mate,' Jim replied gruffly. He looked around at the inside of the Audi Seamus was driving and raised his eyebrows appreciatively. 'Nice motor you've got 'ere. It yours?'

'Yes, she's me pride and joy,' Seamus said proudly.

Jim eyed the luxury interior and the high-spec tech and nodded. 'He must be paying you a fair wedge, to afford one like this, eh?' He glanced sideways towards Seamus.

'I do well enough,' Seamus answered shortly. He didn't make a habit of discussing his finances with people he knew, let alone strangers.

Jim took the hint and changed the subject. 'So, what are we doing today then?'

'We are collecting payments from clients in Soho,' Seamus answered.

'What sort of clients?' Jim asked. 'Protection?'

'That's the one.' Seamus glanced sideways at him. 'You'll probably remember how it all works from your days with the old faces.'

'Yeah, yeah, 'course,' Jim replied. 'It's just been a long time since I've been out in the real world. It's all a bit of a distant memory these days, the ins and outs of it all. Plus, a lot has changed. We didn't even have mobiles back in my day,' he said with a chuckle. 'Or these bloody cameras everywhere,' he continued, pointing at the CCTV head on top of a traffic light which was angled down towards them. 'I mean, what's that about? Seems they record everything down to your fucking bowel movements nowadays. I don't know how anyone gets away with anything.'

'With great planning and skill,' Seamus responded. He turned the next corner as the light went green.

'So, what's it like working for Freddie?' Jim asked.

'Well, it's both of the brothers I work for really,' Seamus replied. 'As will you. And it's wise to remember that,' he advised. 'Paul may be the quieter of the two, but the brothers work as partners. And it's good. They're fair bosses. If you're willing to work hard, get your hands dirty and prove your loyalty, they reward you well.'

'That's good.' Jim looked out of the window, then back to Seamus. 'So the brothers work together. The family, they close? They see much of their mum and that?'

'Mollie?' Seamus remembered what Freddie had said about Jim being friends with his father, years before. He must know Mollie too. 'Yeah, they see her all the time. They look after their own.'

'She keeping well, is she?'

'So far as I know.'

'They still in the same area, are they, the rest of the family?' Jim probed. The last time he'd seen Mollie, she was still living in the dusty rows of the East End. Seamus gave Jim a sharp look and Jim held his hands up. 'I'm just thinking about dropping in sometime to say hi. We're old friends, it would be nice to catch up.'

Seamus exhaled through his nose. This game of twenty questions was annoying him already. He wished Freddie had asked someone else to take Jim out today. 'Freddie and Paul moved their mother to Wanstead about ten years or so ago. Hermitage Close.'

'That's nice of 'em,' Jim replied. 'Looking after their old mum like that, eh?' He gave Seamus a crooked grin and rubbed his hand over the salt-and-pepper stubble of his chin and meaty cheeks thoughtfully. 'Very nice.'

They continued the rest of the journey in silence, much to Seamus's relief. Jim's blue eyes, already slightly hooded with age, crinkled further. Seamus had given him some food for thought. It had been a long time indeed since he had last seen Mollie. On this side of the hard twenty-five years he had endured, out of all the people related to his murder charge, she was the last one standing.

Hermitage Close. He committed it to memory. He would be paying a visit to Mollie, when he got the chance. Because they had a lot to talk about.

Staring into the depths of the crystal glass as he swirled the amber liquid it held, Freddie racked his brains for somewhere they hadn't already thought of. They had checked all of Aleksei's businesses, contacts and previous known whereabouts a hundred times. He wasn't in any of them and every single one of his men they'd found seemed to genuinely have no idea where their boss had gone. But he was somewhere. He had to be.

Bill shook his head and sighed heavily. 'There's nothing, Fred. I can't think of a single fucking thing. Which, to me, says he's grabbed his stash bag and is holing up in a hotel somewhere we wouldn't think to look.'

'Meaning we have more chance of finding dirt on Mother Teresa,' Freddie replied, his tone flat.

They all had stash bags. It was only sensible in their line of work. In a hidden location, known only to themselves, each of them had a bag filled with clean money, a fake passport, some form of weaponry and a spare set of clothes. That way, should it ever come to it, they could go on the run at a moment's notice with no chance of the police – or enemies – being able to trace them.

'It's the only explanation. But if he's still local maybe Sarah can pick up the car on CCTV, see where it goes back to,' Bill offered. 'And if she can't, perhaps me and Zach can hack the city cameras and have a look ourselves. If we know a day and time it's been around we could give it a go.'

'Maybe,' Freddie responded. 'She's looking into that at the moment. Give her until tomorrow and then we'll revisit it.'

The door opened and Anna walked in, closing the door behind her quietly. 'Well, you're certainly a sight for sore eyes,' Freddie said with a tired smile. 'And dressed to kill. What's the occasion?' He looked her up and down appreciatively. She was wearing her deep red fitted dress with matching lipstick; his favourite dress on her. The red seemed to accentuate her long dark hair and deep blue eyes.

'We're all going out tonight, remember?' Anna replied, walking over and touching his shoulder affectionately. 'Club Anya. All of us.'

'Oh, shit.' Freddie sat upright and placed his glass on the table. 'I've been so wrapped up in this Aleksei business I completely forgot. What time is it?' He looked at his watch.

'It's OK, no one is meeting for another hour. Ethan's settled at your mum's.' Anna frowned in concern at the lines of stress etching into Freddie's face. 'Look, we can just cancel if you'd rather.' Half of her hoped he would agree so that she could focus on launching her own investigation into who was behind the wheel of the blacked-out Range Rover. Underneath her calm exterior the dark mystery was eating away at her.

'No, let's go. We could all use some fun,' Freddie replied, pushing his chair back. 'Come on.' Putting his hand in the small of Anna's back, he guided her out of the office. Bill followed after them, grabbing his jacket from the back of the chair.

Feeling the warmth of Freddie's hand through the thin material of her dress, Anna couldn't help the brief smile that flickered onto her lips. But as the tinted car windows flashed through her mind once more, the smile faded. Were her days of peace and love with Freddie numbered once again?

CHAPTER SIXTEEN

The club was heaving, the atmosphere was alive and the drinks were flowing in the VIP area of Club Anya where the group had gathered, when Tanya finally made her appearance. Anna laughed at the joke Freddie had just shared with them all and looked up in time to see her friend crossing the busy floor. She immediately stood up and walked to meet her at the rope which separated them from the rest of the room.

'Hey, where have you been?' she asked, signalling to one of the bar staff to bring Tanya a champagne glass.

'Well, I wanted to look me best, didn't I?' Tanya replied with a broad smile.

'You always look fabulous,' Anna commented, before looking her up and down. Tanya was wearing the emerald green dress she usually only broke out when she was trying to seduce someone who had caught her eye. They jokingly called it her 'hunting dress'. Anna raised an eyebrow. 'My, my,' she said with a grin, 'we're breaking out the big guns this evening, I see. And who's the lucky man?'

They walked back towards the table, where the rest of the firm and their close friends sat enjoying the evening. 'Who says this is for a man?' Tanya replied. 'Maybe I just fancied wearing it.'

'Really…' Anna replied, her tone full of amused sarcasm. She opened her mouth to pursue the conversation but was cut off by their good friend, Bill's wife Amy.

'Well, if you ain't a sight for sore eyes, Tanya Smith,' Amy greeted her warmly. 'It's been a bloody age since I've seen you last and that just won't do.'

Amy Hanlon was as small and slight as Bill was big and burly. Physically they made an odd match but in every other way they were the perfect couple. She was Bill's source of strength and motivation and although not part of the firm herself, was very involved through her support of him. Anna and Tanya had become very close to her over the years.

'I know, everything has been so nuts lately,' Tanya replied, leaning in for a hug. 'The new restaurant is pretty much ready now though, so we won't be such absent friends for too much longer. You're coming to the opening, aren't you?'

'Wouldn't miss it for the world,' Amy replied. 'Tuesday, ain't it?'

'Yes, assuming everything goes to plan,' Anna replied.

'It bloody needs to,' Tanya said with a laugh. 'Now that we've sent out all those fliers with the date on.'

As they took a seat around the main table, Tanya's glass arrived and Freddie immediately picked up one of the chilled bottles of champagne and leaned over to fill it. 'Alright, Tan?' he asked. 'You look lovely tonight. Don't she, Sammy?' he called, looking over to Sammy with a glint in his eye.

Sammy grinned. 'You certainly do, Tanya.'

'Oh, really?' Tanya responded casually. 'Well, thanks, both of you. I haven't stopped today, barely had a chance to look in the mirror.' She smiled and sipped from her champagne, relaxing back into the rounded booth and crossing her long, slim legs as she locked gazes with Sammy.

Anna watched with amused wonder, shutting her mouth as she realised it had gaped open. Freddie winked at her, before turning back to his conversation with Seamus and Bill. 'Well, well, well…' she muttered to herself under the music. So this was who had piqued Tanya's interest then. That was certainly a turn-up for the books.

Turning to open up a conversation with Amy, Anna watched Sammy and Tanya's silent exchange more subtly. Was this a good thing? It would be if it worked out. They could just be themselves with no need to hide any part of their less-than-legal lives. But if it didn't work out – if things turned ugly – then this could be very bad indeed. They would still have to work together and be in close contact. It was certainly a risk. Though, of course, she reasoned as her eyes wandered towards Freddie, nothing worth having ever came without risk.

The small clutch bag Anna had with her began to vibrate and she pulled her phone out, apologising to Amy for the interruption. The call was coming from The Sinners' Lounge. Grinding her teeth briefly, Anna took the call and moved away from the table, holding her hand over her other ear so that she could hear.

'Hello?'

'Anna, it's Josephine,' came the hesitant reply down the line. 'Listen, I'm sorry to call you, but we have a big problem here and apparently only you can deal with it.'

'What sort of problem?' Anna asked.

'A blue one.'

Anna closed her eyes and cursed silently. Blue was the code word to indicate that the issue was with law enforcement. She had thought all their bases had been covered on that front. All the local plods were either on payroll, or they were kept in check by people further up the chain who were.

'I'll be five minutes, don't say anything.'

Ending the call, Anna quickly walked over to Tanya. 'Listen, we've got a code blue at the lounge, I've got to go. Just wait here, I'll be back soon.' She didn't bother asking whether Tanya wanted to join her. If this was about to turn pear-shaped it would be better for only one of them to deal with the fall-out.

With a grim expression she turned and strode out of the club.

CHAPTER SEVENTEEN

Anna marched into the bar area of The Sinners' Lounge and looked around. There were only two clients in there with girls as it was still very early in the evening. Leaning against the bar, looking on at one of these couples with amused curiosity, was the man Josephine must have been talking about. Anna immediately knew it was him. Despite the fact he was wearing plain clothes and had made an obvious attempt to hide what he was, anyone in their game would have been able to tell a mile off. Practical, nondescript clothes made from good-quality materials and designed for long-lasting wear were matched with painfully sensible shoes, and deep frown lines that had been earned through a lifetime of taking on trouble adorned his face, despite the fact he looked to only be in his mid-thirties.

Josephine hovered nervously behind the bar a few feet from this man. As his back was turned to her, she started furiously pointing at him and pulling wide eyes at Anna. Anna nodded and lifted one hand to tell her to stop.

She plastered on a smile and walked over to their unwelcome guest. 'Josephine,' she turned to address her as the man turned towards her, 'could you get a drink for myself and for Mr...?' She raised an eyebrow at him in question.

'Matthews. DI Matthews,' he responded, pointedly.

'For myself and Mr Matthews here,' she continued. 'We'll take it by the window. What would you like to drink, Mr Matthews?'

'I'll just have a water.'

'Water and a bottle of champagne, two glasses.'

Anna led the way over to the vacant table by the window and offered DI Matthews a seat, before taking her own. As she settled, she crossed her legs and shot him her warmest smile. 'So what is it that I can do for you, Mr Matthews?'

DI Matthews settled back in his chair and looked Anna up and down, his gaze resting a little longer than appropriate on her bare legs. She noted this with narrowed eyes, but was swift to replace this with a placid smile as his gaze eventually returned to her face.

'We'll get to that,' he said, a strange smile creeping up his face. 'Let's start with talking about what you do here, shall we?'

'In what respect, exactly?' Anna answered.

'Well, you run a whorehouse for starters,' he replied bluntly.

'Oh, I'm afraid you're rather mistaken,' Anna said with a small laugh. 'This is an odd place, I grant you that, but it is no whorehouse. This is actually a late-night massage parlour and, as you can see, a relaxing bar where clients are welcome to have a few drinks and socialise with the therapists.'

'Socialise?' DI Matthews looked pointedly at one of the clients at another table, who had pulled his companion's boobs out of her top and was now loudly sucking on one of them.

Anna cursed silently. She couldn't exactly ask them to stop though. To alert one of their clients to the threat of the police would be professional suicide. She forced a smile. 'Well, I guess you can't control the driving force of true love when it strikes, even if it's not at the most ideal time.'

'That's what you're going with?' he replied with a raised eyebrow.

Anna exhaled slowly and there was a short silence as Josephine arrived with the drinks. She poured out two glasses of champagne and placed them on the table. As she moved away, Anna picked hers up and took a long sip. Placing the glass back on the table, she twisted the stem with the tips of her fingers before speaking again.

'You're not from around this area. You don't usually work this patch at all, in fact, and you're too high up to be on the beat. Which leads me to wonder why you've developed such an interest in my business.' Anna twisted her mouth to the side as her sharp brain moved through all the possible scenarios that could have led him here. 'How much is a DI's salary these days, anyway?'

DI Matthews smiled, the action not quite reaching his eyes. 'That's what you think you can do with everyone, isn't it? Buy them off. Put them on payroll. Use them.' His face twisted into an ugly sneer as he uttered the last few words. 'You're right, I'm not from around here. I'm from Surrey. You don't remember me, do you?'

Anna frowned and studied his face. Stress lines and short dark stubble surrounded a naturally downturned mouth and his cheeks were slightly too gaunt for the rest of his skull. Blue brooding eyes stared back at her from under dark brows that matched his hair, though this had a few smatterings of grey here and there. There was nothing about him that rang any bells at all.

When she didn't immediately answer, DI Matthews continued. 'I came up one night for a mate's stag do. Not really my kind of thing, your club round the corner, but it's clearly popular. I saw you that night, asked one of the bar staff about you. You'd caught my eye, you see.' He shifted in his seat and picked up his drink, taking a sip himself and then turning up one side of his mouth in a strange cocky half smile. 'You're a very attractive woman. I did my research and found out you were the owner of that place and looking after some other clubs for some ex who went to prison.'

Some ex, Anna repeated in her head. This Surrey-based plod clearly knew nothing about the Tylers if he was talking about Freddie as flippantly as that.

'I thought to myself, *nice one, this bird's got some gumption. You know?*' he continued. 'So I came back the next night and I asked you if you wanted a drink with me. Don't you remember?'

Anna resisted the urge to roll her eyes. If they had a pound for every time a drunken customer asked either her or Tanya out, they'd have been able to buy half of Soho by now. Club Anya with its burlesque dancers and scantily clad performers made the men horny. They were all Romeos by the end of the night, trying to get their leg over anywhere they could.

'I'm afraid I don't recall that,' she answered simply.

'Nice,' he snapped, narrowing his eyes. 'So you'll date a scumbag criminal, but when a decent man comes along for once, you can't even be bothered to remember his face?'

Anna's jaw tightened at the sharp change in attitude. *What was this guy's problem? Surely his pride couldn't have been that wounded?*

'I think we'll leave this conversation here now, Mr Matthews,' Anna replied coldly. She made to stand up but paused as he continued.

'Oh, I don't think we will actually. I couldn't really understand your logic there, you see. So I had a little dig around and found out you also had this place. I found out that all the guys on the force around here turn a bit of a blind eye to it, too. And they have to give it a blind eye, don't they? Because it is really just a full-on whorehouse. Now, you might be able to smooth over the surface with your "massage parlour" crap, but if someone actually had this place investigated…' He smiled. 'Someone like me…' He paused again for effect. 'Well.' He shrugged. 'I wouldn't imagine your cover story would hold up for very long. One only has to scratch a touch beneath the surface.'

Anna narrowed her eyes. 'What do you want, Matthews?'

'Well.' He pretended to consider it. 'I feel like we started off on the wrong foot. I'd like a chance to change that for the better.' He sat up and leaned forward, placing his hand on Anna's knee.

Her jaw tightened, but other than that her poker face stayed intact. Resisting the urge to slap his hand away, Anna stayed totally still, waiting to hear what he was about to suggest so that she had the whole picture to work with.

'Perhaps I could be persuaded *not* to bring this illicit business to my superiors' attention, if you and I were on more, shall we say, *friendly* terms.' His brooding gaze bored into hers. 'I think we can both find much happier ground, in this case, wouldn't you say?'

Anna reached forward and calmly lifted his hand off her leg, swivelling to one side so that she was out of easy reach. 'If it's sex you want, Mr Matthews, then it's sex you'll get.' He blinked at this response and hope filled his face. 'You pointed out yourself that this is whorehouse. You may take your pick out of any of my girls and visit twice a month free of charge.'

'No.' His response was swift and strong and Anna watched as the redness of suppressed anger crept up his neck. 'I don't want a filthy whore, thanks. I want *you*.'

Anna's blood turned cold and it took all of her willpower not to turn her nose up in disgust. What kind of man went about trapping a woman this way? *A psychotic control freak. The force is full of them*, her mind answered.

DI Matthews let his gaze roam freely down her dress towards her legs again. 'You're a fine specimen. You're successful and sexy as fuck.' He grinned. 'I'd give you a good time, you know. And it's a small price to pay, really, to save your business and protect your freedom, wouldn't you say?' He let the threat hang in the air between them for a moment. 'You've got until Monday to decide whether you prefer the thought of time on the inside, or whether you want to come and have some fun with me. I'm sure you'll make the right decision. And when you do…' He stood up and leaned down over her, pausing to sniff her hair. 'I can assure you we'll both be satisfied.'

Anna suddenly stood up, pushing the chair she had been sitting on back with force, then turned to stop him. 'DI Matthews.' He paused and she walked over to him. 'I don't need any further time to think on it. I will always do what needs to be done in my business's best interests,' she said, heavily. 'Come here Monday night at nine thirty. I'll be here waiting for you.'

DI Matthews let a broad smile creep over his face. It had been a bold move but he'd known it would work. Headstrong women like this always had a weakness that could turn them into meek little mice. And with Anna it was simple. She'd do anything to protect her hard-earned business and her freedom.

'Good decision,' he said, lifting his hand to her face. He ran his fingers over her cherry red lips, already getting excited at the thought of what he was going to make her do with them soon. 'Enjoy the rest of your weekend.'

Anna watched as he walked away, a bounce in his stride now that he had got what he'd come for. She blinked in anger and disgust before turning on her heel and striding back to the table to down her glass of champagne. As she slammed the glass back on the table it smashed, and she watched as the dregs of champagne slipped away through the broken shards. It was true, what she'd said. She would always do what was in her business's best interests. But when DI Matthews finally realised what that meant, he was going to be in for a very big shock indeed.

CHAPTER EIGHTEEN

The early morning sun crept in through the bedroom window, its occupants having been too preoccupied to think to close the curtains as they fell into bed the night before. The warm rays slowly made their way down the walls, across the bed and shone off the fiery gold mass of curls that lay sprawled across the pillow.

Tanya stirred as her body began to wake up and then frowned as she realised sleepily that it was far too early to be moving just yet. Opening one eye she peeked out and groaned as she realised she hadn't closed the curtains. A slight shift enabled her to see the clock. It wasn't even six o clock.

'Motherfucker,' she murmured to herself.

Moving slowly, still mostly asleep, Tanya stood up and shuffled to the window to pull the curtains across and throw the bedroom back into relative darkness again. As she turned around, she jumped, startled, and put a hand to her chest.

'Jesus Christ,' she exclaimed as she caught sight of Sammy propped up on his elbow in her bed, watching her with a lazy grin. 'Oh my God,' she said with a giggle. 'I forgot you were here for a minute.'

'Oh. Well, that doesn't say much for my skills then, does it?' he replied with a laugh.

Tanya grinned and walked back to the bed, rubbing the sleep from her eyes. She slipped back under the covers and turned to face him, aware for the first time that she was as naked as he was. The memory of the night before played out in her mind. They'd drunk and danced the night away and she had lured Sammy in to exactly the position she'd wanted him. It wasn't hard, she was an expert when it came to luring men. It was the after part that she wasn't so experienced in. And now that their initial night of passion had come to an end, she wondered how things were going to go next.

Her smile broadened as she remembered their antics in the bedroom. She had always thought Sammy's quiet, brooding ways were hiding a wild animal underneath, and he hadn't disappointed.

'Your skills speak for themselves,' she replied, reaching over and running the tips of her fingers down his bare torso. It had always been obvious that Sammy favoured the gym, but seeing him now, naked in her bed in the light of day, she marvelled at how chiselled his broad chest and abs were.

'So, Tanya Smith,' Sammy murmured, grabbing her and pulling her body up against his, 'you got what you were after. What now?'

Tanya felt her body respond and leaned into the kisses that Sammy was now raining on her mouth and neck. 'I don't know,' she answered honestly. 'What do we do now?'

Sammy had been a friend for many years, they were involved in all the same things, running in the same circles. This could be a blessing or a curse.

'Well *right now*,' Sammy said, 'I'd quite like to do that all again.' He pushed himself against her harder, making himself very clear. 'And then after that, I'd like to get some breakfast with you and see where we go from there. What do you think?'

'Well,' Tanya became slightly breathless as Sammy's hands wandered downwards. 'I think… Oh, sod *thinking*. Come here.'

A couple of hours later, Tanya pulled her dressing gown in tighter as she stood at the coffee machine, making them each a much-needed latte. Sammy sat behind her at the breakfast bar in his boxers, watching her with an amused smile.

He'd known this fiery vixen for years; watched her fight her own battles like a warrior, seen her use her loud humour to cover up any chinks in her almost impenetrable armour. He'd seen her grow from nothing into the successful independent businesswoman she was today. She was someone he liked and admired. And now that romance was on the table, he found he wasn't averse to the idea of taking things further, the way he usually was. Most women he met were too soft or too boring for his tastes. He needed someone strong and interesting. But finding that combination in someone he actually liked was a whole other ball game. Let alone finding someone who he didn't have to lie to or hide certain things from.

'Here you go,' Tanya said, bringing two steaming mugs of coffee over and placing one in front of Sammy. She leaned over the breakfast bar in front of him with her own and smiled. 'Some liquid energy. I'm sure you need some after this morning.' Her green eyes glinted cheekily.

'Thanks.' Sammy took a sip and studied her for a moment. 'So, do you fancy going for breakfast? And then maybe, if you're free later, a drink tonight? As more of a date drink, than a group outing, this time.' He laid it out openly.

'I do.' Tanya looked down at her coffee, wrapping her fingers around the warm mug. 'I do fancy that. I um, I think that we should keep this to ourselves for now though.' She looked up at him. 'I don't mean that in a bad way or anything, I'm just thinking it would be good for us to hang out and figure out what we're doing before anyone else gets involved. You know?' Tanya bit her lip. There was so much at stake here, whichever way things went now. It was best that they knew where they each stood before making waves throughout their whole circle.

Sammy nodded. 'I agree.' He understood completely. It was the sensible approach. 'And in that case,' he paused to take another sip of his coffee, 'you'd better start thinking about how you're going to sneak me out of this building without Freddie, Anna or Ethan seeing me.'

'Dear Lord,' Tanya said, her eyes widening. 'I hadn't even thought of that.'

CHAPTER NINETEEN

Walking down the road in the midday sun towards Ruby Ten, one of his less demanding clubs these days, Freddie wrote out a quick text asking Sammy to meet him there. He looked up and noted that Seamus's car was already there ahead of him. As he reached the car the doors opened and Seamus stepped out, as well as Jim. Freddie raised his eyebrows in surprise. As far as his closest men went, there were no specific working hours. Every and any day was a working day. But Jim was just a lackey at present – someone on the payroll to do all the running around that no one else had time for. He hadn't expected to find him hanging around on the weekend without being asked to come in.

'Jim,' Freddie said, as he stopped beside them on the pavement. 'What are you doing searching out jobs on a Sunday? Trying to win employee of the month?'

Jim grinned. 'Ahh, I'm old school, Freddie. Just because it's Sunday, don't mean there's nothing to be done, does it?' Freddie conceded this with a nod of the head. 'Plus,' he added, 'it ain't like I've got much else going on. You get out the clink after twenty-five years, no one even remembers ya. There weren't no family waiting for me to come home. It's just me on me tod. I'd rather be out here than sat staring at the four walls.'

Nodding again, Freddie looked away. His own time in prison had been enough to make him feel misplaced in this world when he came out and that had only been two and a half years. He'd had family and loyal friends all waiting for him and it had still been difficult. He couldn't imagine how odd life must feel for Jim right now.

'Well, there's certainly a lot to be done today, so the more the merrier,' he said. He turned his attention to Seamus. 'We need to start thinking outside the box about where Aleksei could be hiding. We've been thinking too logically.' He glanced at his watch. 'Go get settled in the office, I just need to run and grab some fags. I'll be five minutes.'

'Sure thing. This way then, Jim.' Seamus led the way down the road to the side alley that led to the back entrance of the closed club premises.

Turning back the other way, Freddie strode down the road to the corner shop a few buildings down. Greeting the familiar shopkeeper, he made his purchase and left the shop, checking his phone to see if Sammy had responded. He had. Sammy was en route. Satisfied with this, Freddie slipped the phone back in his pocket and as he looked up, stopped dead in his tracks.

The car they had all been searching for was pulling up right outside the front entrance of Ruby Ten. He raised his eyebrows in disbelief. That was ballsy, even for Aleksei. Glancing at the small window on the first floor, Freddie wondered what the chances were of Seamus looking out. Slim to none, he quickly decided, as the window was nowhere near the desk where they would likely be sitting waiting for him.

'Shit,' he cursed under his breath. He had no weapons on him or back-up. The only thing currently in his favour – if Aleksei was in there with several of his armed goons – was the fact that the street was relatively busy. It wouldn't do Aleksei any favours to be seen attacking him.

He could retreat, wait until he had back-up. But for all he knew, Aleksei could be gone by the time he managed to gather his men. Plus, it just wasn't in him to run from a fight, even if the odds weren't in his favour. It just wasn't who he was. Pushing forward, Freddie puffed out his chest and made his way to the vehicle showing much more confidence than he really felt. As he came within a few feet he paused. The back door opened and out of the tinted back cabin stepped a long, slender pair of legs, followed by the rest of an attractively dressed woman. Freddie blinked, confused, until finally her head came into view.

He had never met her before, had only seen one picture that Sarah had sent him as part of her reconnaissance pack on Aleksei. But he hadn't needed to see any more to remember someone so striking. This dark-haired, tanned beauty was Sophia Ivanov. Aleksei's wife.

Sophia positioned herself to stand square on to Freddie, a few feet down the path, her hands resting loosely on her hips as she appraised him. For a few moments there was nothing but silence as he waited for her to make the first move.

'There is no need for you to continue your search,' she finally said, a thick Russian accent colouring her deep, sultry voice. 'I know your little police dog has been trying to find me. So, here I am.' She held her arms out, before dropping them down to her sides. She moved towards him and Freddie noted the driver stepped out to stand behind her. 'I have been thinking about how best to meet you.'

'And why would you want to meet me?' Freddie asked, keeping his tone neutral until he could figure out where this was going.

'Because I have a potential business arrangement that you may be interested in.'

Freddie barked out a short laugh. 'A business arrangement? Unless it involves you handing me your husband's head on a plate, I can't really think of anything you'd be able to offer that could catch my interest.'

Sophia's dark eyes flashed with something that Freddie couldn't quite place and a cold smile played across her deep red lips. 'But how on earth could I offer you that, when Aleksei is already dead?'

CHAPTER TWENTY

Freddie stepped behind the empty bar in Ruby Ten and reached up for the vodka on the top shelf. This was where he knew his bar manager kept the good stuff – the Russian stuff. Walking back over to the table with the bottle, some ice and three glasses, he sat down and poured them each a generous measure. Sophia's bodyguard, as Freddie had already come to think of him, staunchly ignored the glass meant for him and continued to stand silently behind Sophia's chair.

Freddie lifted his glass politely. 'Cheers.'

'*Za zdorov'ye*,' Sophia replied, before shooting the large measure back in one.

'So, Mrs Ivanov,' Freddie started, his mind still whirling, trying to connect the dots. 'You say Aleksei is dead and that you have some sort of proposition. Please elaborate.'

Sophia reached forward and refilled her own glass from the bottle. 'My husband is dead. His body lies underneath the weight of an entire building.' She looked up at Freddie, her eyes strangely icy for such a dark, warm shade of brown. 'So I cannot give you his head, I am afraid.' Reaching over, she refilled Freddie's glass and put the bottle down. 'That being said,' she continued more pleasantly, 'there are some other things of his that you may be interested in.'

'And why would you want to come to me with these things?' Freddie asked. He was curious to find out what she was talking about, but at the same time he was wary. Freddie and Aleksei were known enemies. Indeed, each had tried very hard to kill the other. Why would Sophia want anything to do with him?

Sophia sat back and studied Freddie for a few moments. 'Did you know much about my husband, Mr Tyler?' she asked. 'Did you ever hear anything about our marriage, let's say?'

'I can't say I did,' Freddie answered truthfully. As he said this though, another conversation he'd had about Aleksei with Bill popped up in his mind and he suddenly had an inkling as to where Sophia was going.

'My husband had… certain tendencies, that came out a few years into our marriage. These led to us becoming a less than typical husband and wife duo.' She held her head up high and stuck her chin out, the confident action clearly forced to cover her embarrassment. 'We remained friends for our children's sake and kept up appearances. But we were not in love, as you expect people to be in a marriage.' Looking down for a moment, Sophia flicked an imaginary fleck of dust off her immaculate skirt. 'What I care most about now, is what I cared most about a month, six months, a year ago. My two sons. I need to continue to drive them onwards towards a bright future the way we always have, and it is like I have been left with the vehicle to do so, but no keys to start the engine.' She stared into Freddie's eyes intensely. 'This is where you come in. I have the car, as I say, but you are the only person I can think of who may hold the key to get it going.'

Freddie sat back and studied Sophia. Calm and collected, her logical and detached manner seemed to be genuine. There were none of the tears or the grief or even hysterics that one would expect from a widow speaking to her deceased husband's enemy. But then again, if all they had between them was a false front of a marriage held together only for the sake of their children, why would there be?

'And what kind of key do you think I have, exactly?' Freddie answered. 'So far you've talked to me in nothing but riddles. If you don't lay out what it is you're after, I have no way to answer you.'

'My husband's club is now back under your firm's control. I realise that it was your patch to begin with and I have no right to it. But that has left us in a financial corner,' Sophia replied. 'The only other things I have been left with are Aleksei's gun routes.' She sat upright and leaned forward onto the table. 'I know you don't run guns. But there is a market for it, one that Aleksei found very lucrative. And I may not have a husband or a steady income any more, but what I do have is knowledge. I know Aleksei's routes, his stock, his supplier arrangements, everything. What I do not have, now that he is dead and his firm has fallen apart, are men to carry out the work. Men who are not afraid of getting their hands dirty, of it being illegal.'

Freddie nodded. 'I see.'

'If you will run the operation alongside me and provide the men, I am willing to offer you a straight fifty-fifty partnership.'

Freddie shifted in his seat and frowned. 'Why?'

'What do you mean?'

'I mean, why are you asking me? Surely you have other contacts in this world you can go to?'

Sophia lifted her chin. 'I do not,' she replied. 'Aleksei burned our bridges when we left Russia. And although I was an advisor to my husband, I had no direct day-to-day contact with the business. Until now, of course. He made sure that should anything happen, I knew enough to be able to step up.'

'Yet still, you know that your husband and I were enemies. Even if what you're saying is true, if he really is dead, that still makes no difference on this particular point.'

'You were an enemy to my husband because he trod on your turf,' Sophia replied. 'And, of course, because he tried to kill you.' She held his stare, her expression brazen. 'I understand your feelings, but neither of these actions were taken by me. You have no quarrel with me directly.'

'And you expect me to believe that you have none with me?' Freddie questioned, raising one eyebrow disbelievingly.

'None whatsoever,' she replied, levelly. 'My husband took risks, eventually one did not pay off. That was the choice he made. I make choices too, and my choice right now is to not be left without money to raise my sons. You have a son, do you not? Surely you can understand that, parent to parent.'

Freddie exhaled heavily. He did not take kindly to his son being brought into any discussion linked to his work, but he could grudgingly understand why Sophia was bringing the point to light on this occasion.

'I'll have to think about it,' he answered. 'One thing I would like to know though… Why have you been following me around?'

'I thought that much would be obvious, Mr Tyler,' Sophia replied, standing up and picking up her purse. She opened it and pulled out a card with her number on, placing it on the table between them. 'It is always wise to know who you are getting into business with. Or if it does not work out,' she added over her shoulder as she walked away, 'one's enemy. Do let me know your decision. By tomorrow night, if you do not mind. Children are expensive and my time to get this set up is limited.'

Freddie watched Sophia walk out of the door, followed by her bodyguard, with a thoughtful frown and played with the glass still full of vodka in front of him. He looked down at the card she had left on the table then picked it up and slid it into his inner jacket pocket. Of all the ways he had predicted this situation to go, that hadn't been one of them. And the fact that Aleksei was dead was very surprising news indeed – if of course it was true. It could just be an elaborate set-up to get their guard down. Freddie wasn't ruling this possibility out.

Pulling out his phone, Freddie made a call. 'Paul, I need you to come in to Ruby Ten, ASAP. There's been a development we need to discuss. Seamus is here, Sammy's on his way. I'll ring Anna now – can you get hold of Bill? Jim's here too. I'll find something for him to do, this is for our ears only right now.'

Ending the call, Freddie bit his lip as he thought over every-thing Sophia had said. Placing his next call to Anna, he didn't notice the door to the stairs move slightly as Jim closed the small gap he'd been listening through and slipped away back to the office as silent as a mouse.

CHAPTER TWENTY-ONE

Anna stood at the top of the stairs, ushering the girls out of The Sinners' Lounge as politely as she could. They closed a few hours early every Monday, as it was the quietest day of the week, but tonight she was closing it even earlier than usual.

'You sure you want us to head off?' Erica asked, as she passed. 'We do sometimes get a few last-minute stragglers.' She'd been hoping to pick up at least one or two punters tonight, for some extra cash.

'Don't worry,' Anna replied cheerily. 'We won't lose business closing an hour early once in a while.'

'Well, OK then,' Erica answered, her tone glum as she walked towards the exit.

'Rose, can you stop and help with the stock take tonight please? Josephine has a lot on, she could do with a hand,' Tanya called out.

'Oh, no problem,' Rose answered, putting her bag and jacket back in the cloak cupboard.

The last of the girls trailed out, shouting their goodbyes, and the downstairs door closed with a bang. Tanya and Anna exchanged glances. 'Right,' Tanya said to Rose. 'Hop to it. You know what to do.'

'Sure thing.' Rose smiled and headed off to do as she'd been instructed.

'Drink?' Tanya asked with a raised eyebrow.

Anna looked at her watch for the time. 'Yes, let's. I still need to talk to you about this whole Sophia thing.' After her meeting with Freddie yesterday she had gone straight to tell Tanya about the unexpected turn of events. Just as she had finished download-ing everything Freddie had told her, though, he had arrived and joined the discussion, meaning they had not been able to talk about it freely. Anna hadn't been able to get Tanya alone again until now, to find out what she thought of everything.

Tanya nodded and walked behind the bar to pour them each a glass of wine. 'Yeah, I didn't see that coming.'

Anna sat on one of the bar stools and took the drink Tanya offered her. 'Me neither. Maybe she's a bigger player than Josephine thought,' she replied.

'What's that?' Josephine piped up as she came in from the hallway.

'Sophia,' Tanya said, after checking first for the go-ahead nod from Anna. 'She's the one who's been tailing Freddie.'

'What?' Josephine turned white, her hand flying to her neck as her eyes widened in shock.

'She wants to partner up on the gun-running,' Anna continued. 'And somehow she knows where Aleksei's body is.'

'But how could she?' Josephine whispered. 'There is no way she could have known.'

'There are ways,' Anna replied with a heavy sigh. 'She could have been in the back of that car—'

'No.' Josephine cut her off with a shake of her head. 'She was definitely not there. Aleksei kept her away from the business and even if this was an exception he would have said when I got there. She was definitely not there that night.'

'I don't think she was as in the dark as he led you to believe, Jojo,' Tanya said softly.

'She was *not* there,' Josephine insisted.

'She may not have been,' Anna cut in. 'But she knows everything there is to know about the gun routes, their suppliers, everything. And she knew everything about the club too, from what we hear. She says Aleksei left her with enough knowledge to take over, should she ever need to.'

'Oh.' Josephine seemed taken aback, but swiftly recovered. 'Well, I guess living with him she will have picked up a lot.'

'That may be so, but what I'm concerned about right now is exactly how much she knows about Aleksei's death.' Anna picked up her glass and took a deep drink of the crisp white wine Tanya had poured. 'She knows he is under that building. So what else is she aware of? Does she know we were there, that it was us?' Anna and Tanya exchanged a worried look.

Josephine walked over to the bar wearily and took a seat on one of the stools. Her heavy features looked even heavier than usual under the weight of the questions they all now had to consider. She fiddled with a dangly bright purple earring. 'There is a chance,' she said slowly, 'that Sophia might know about me.'

'What?' the others cried in unison.

'Josephine…' Tanya breathed in horror.

'You never said anything about this,' Anna snapped angrily. 'What the *hell*, Josephine?' Her dark blue eyes flashed with anger. As if they didn't have enough on their plate, this was the last thing they needed.

'I only said *might* know,' Josephine said, feeling flustered. 'She didn't know before all this. But the day it all happened, Aleksei told her he was sending her and the boys to Estonia to live with her mother. It was to clear the way for me to move in. He did it to try and manipulate me into doing what he wanted, clearing her out and leaving the position of leading lady open for me to fill.' She looked down, her face turning red in shame. 'Obviously I never considered it, but he did it thinking that would be enough to sway me. He told her he was sending her away the next day and to pack their bags. I don't know if he told her specifically why, or even if he did, who I was. But there is that possibility.'

'Jesus Christ,' Anna spat, seething. Why were they only just learning about this now? Standing up, she began an agitated pacing.

Tanya leaned forward on the bar and rubbed her forehead. 'If she knew about that or of our involvement, surely she would have already brought it up? It's been weeks, there's been nothing. Surely if she knew, she would have confronted us by now. Or at least not offered to partner up with Freddie,' she added.

'But what if that's exactly why she has?' Anna countered. 'What if it's some weird mind game she's playing, to get to us?'

There was a long silence. Eventually Tanya answered. 'It's possible, but I don't see how it would be in her favour to go down this route. If she wanted to mess with us, she could have done it much more effectively by coming to us directly.'

Josephine bit her lip, suddenly reminded of the car that nearly ran her down in the street. It had seemed odd at the time. Could that have been Sophia? She shook her head, deciding not to pursue the thought. It was sure to be nothing but her paranoia.

'I'm inclined to agree with you,' Anna said slowly. Her face remained troubled. 'But I think we need to see how this plays out and keep a sharp eye on things. Freddie asked my opinion on whether or not we should agree to the gun-running deal. She wants an answer tonight. I said I wanted to discuss it with you again quickly first.'

'Tell him to go for it,' Tanya replied. 'Carefully, of course.'

'OK. Let's do it.' Anna pulled her phone out of her purse and wrote out a quick text to Freddie. 'OK. It's going ahead then.'

Tanya nodded. 'Good. Always best to keep your enemies close.'

Anna glanced at her watch. 'And on that note, it's time. Make yourself scarce,' she said to Josephine. 'Tan, I'll see you in a minute.'

Tanya and Josephine walked out into the hall and began to climb the stairs.

'Is she going to be alright, do you think?' Josephine asked quietly.

'Anna?' Tanya laughed. 'She'll be more than alright. Hard as nails and twice as clever, that girl. That stupid twat will rue the day he ever thought he could pull some bullshit like this.'

Pacing around the bar, Anna took another few sips of her white wine as she waited for DI Matthews to press on the buzzer downstairs. Glancing at one of the long wall mirrors that were strategically placed around the room she checked herself over one more time. She'd gone with a particularly seductive black number for this evening, ready to play her part, not wanting to disappoint her pushy, unwelcome guest.

The buzzer sounded and she glanced at her watch again. He was dead on time. With a dark smile, Anna walked over and buzzed him in.

CHAPTER TWENTY-TWO

'DI Matthews,' Anna said, with a nod of greeting.

'Miss Davis,' he replied, looking her up and down apprecia-tively. 'You look ravishing in that dress. Though I suspect it looks even better on the floor.' He licked his lips in anticipation.

Ever since this stuck-up woman had turned him down that night, it had boiled like an angry sore in the pit of his stomach. The more he'd found out about her, the more it burned. Sophisticated, accomplished and clearly business-minded, she was the perfect match for an upstanding man like himself. He had worked hard to get to where he was, just as she had. If she'd given herself the chance to get to know him, she'd have realised just how much they had in common and how well-matched they were. But instead, she was too busy hanging around the kind of scum he spent his days putting behind bars. It had left a bitter taste in his mouth that this woman thought herself above him whilst she was off shagging criminals.

It was something he found he just couldn't let go of, and the reason he had pushed her into a corner like this. If she was going to go around acting like she belonged with scumbags, then he'd treat her like one. Perhaps that was what she liked, after all. And once he'd had his way with her and screwed her out of his head once and for all, he'd move on to someone more worthy of his time. But for now, this was starting to be all sorts of fun.

'Follow me,' Anna said pleasantly. 'I've had one of the rooms made up for us especially.' She beckoned him to follow as she mounted the stairs to the next level.

DI Matthews couldn't contain the wide grin that spread across his face as he followed her up. He watched her pert backside move from side to side as she went up each step and bit his lip as he thought of what he was going to do with her. He imagined himself ripping the dress off her and throwing her down on her front, spreading her legs with his. He'd lift her backside high in the air and take her from behind. He almost let a groan escape as he thought of this, but contained himself. Only a few minutes longer to wait. Her long, dark hair flowed down her back, he noticed with approval. This was what he'd hold on to as he thrust inside her again and again. Maybe he'd tug it a little bit hard. He imagined she'd like it rough, with the sort of men she usually dated. That should turn her on, he decided.

They walked in silence through the hallway at the top of the stairs, to the door at the end. As they reached it, Anna paused and turned with a smile, her hand on the doorknob.

'Here we are,' she said, her deep voice seductive. She allowed her gaze to burn his enticingly, and watched as his excitement rose threefold. She pushed the door open and his gaze shifted to the four-poster bed in the dimly lit room. 'After you.'

Not needing a second invitation, DI Matthews strode into the room and began to shrug off his T-shirt, eagerly. He barely managed to get one arm out before something dull and heavy was smashed around the back of his head and rendered him unconscious.

DI Matthews awoke with a groan as the dull thud in his head intensified. He tried to remember what had happened, but he couldn't. All he could remember was Anna opening the door and then himself stepping inside. He tried lifting his hand to his aching skull, but his hand wouldn't move. It was bound, somehow. With a nervous squint, he opened one eye and found that he was lying face up on the four-poster bed. Opening his other eye he tried to locate his hands, struggling still to move them. He looked up and found to his surprise that they were bound by ropes to the posts at the top of the bed.

What's going on? he wondered. *Is this some sort of kinky roleplay?* As he searched his surroundings more, now that his brain was beginning to un-fuzz, he realised his feet were tied in a similar manner to the bottom of the bed. As his eyes rested on them, he realised a few other things all at once. Firstly, he was completely naked. And secondly, he was not alone. Aside from Anna, two other women were there, casually watching him from the side of the room. One of them he recognised as Anna's red-headed business partner, but the other he hadn't seen before. She was a slender, attractive brunette with the rosy cheeks of youth and piercing big blue eyes who looked as though butter wouldn't melt. Her outfit told another story though, naked other than a bondage collar and a leather garter holding up a pair of fishnet stockings. As he watched, she picked up a bright red lipstick and applied a thick layer to her generous lips.

'Good evening, DI Matthews,' Anna said from her chair in the corner of the room. 'So good of you to finally join us.'

He frowned. 'Well, I wasn't expecting to be knocked out. You realise that's a serious offence, right? Knocking out a police officer. Not to mention the restraints.'

'Oh, you want to talk offences?' Anna said, her eyebrows shooting up in mock surprise. 'What sort of sentence does sexual blackmail come with, these days?'

He narrowed his eyes. 'I really wouldn't test me, Anna. You either want this, or you don't. And if you don't…' he tried to shrug, 'that's fine. But I can't promise I won't be looking into your businesses with a fine-tooth comb. It's your choice. Make it fast.'

Anna smiled coldly. 'I'd like to introduce you to Rose. Rose here is one of our finest girls. She loves to do things that most others wouldn't even dream of. Don't you, Rose?'

Rose giggled and looked coyly in his direction.

'I've told you already. I'm not interested in shagging one of your prozzies,' he spat. 'It's you, or nothing.'

'Oh dear,' Anna said, feigning dismay. 'And I so hoped we might have come to a more amicable solution.' She nodded to Rose and sat back in the chair, crossing her arms.

Rose slinked forward and climbed onto the bed, like a prowling tigress. Hiding a smirk of amusement, Tanya pulled out a camera and began taking pictures of the two on the bed.

'What are you doing?' DI Matthews demanded. 'Stop that, right now.'

'But why?' Anna asked. 'I need the photos to protect myself.'

Rose began rubbing her body over the tied-up officer, jiggling her boobs in his face and opening her legs in front of his eyes to show him the goods. Turning around and straddling him so that everything was on display to him, she started kissing his lower abdomen, leaving bright red lipstick marks everywhere her lips touched.

'You see, I will do everything I can to protect my business. Which is, of course, what you were trying to play on.' Anna stood up and began slowly pacing the room as she talked. 'But do you really think I got to where I am by letting fuck-boys like you scare me into sleeping with them for their silence?' She stopped and pulled a face of disgust and pity at him. 'If you did, then you're really not as smart as you think you are.' She shook her head.

'So what exactly do you think you're going to do with these pictures?' DI Matthews asked. 'It's pretty obvious they're staged. I'll have you in cuffs the second you have me out of ropes.'

'It's not that obvious it's staged, though, is it?' Anna replied, looking pointedly at the response DI Matthews' body was having to Rose grinding and sliding around above him. 'In fact, I'd say it looks like you're having the time of your life. And whilst you might want to try fighting me on that in court, I'm not sure you'd want to try fighting the same argument with your wife now, would you?'

'What did you just say to me?' he snarled, panic beginning to show in his eyes.

'I think you heard me perfectly well,' Anna replied, her tone hard. 'Angela Matthews, your wife of seven years – nearly your ex-wife, so I hear, after your last infidelity was uncovered.'

'Ohh, tut tut…' Tanya chimed in with a shake of the head. 'You have been a bad boy, haven't you?'

'Oh, piss off,' DI Matthews said, shooting a look of hatred towards her.

'He's not very friendly, is he?' Tanya mused, pulling a face.

'It seems not,' Anna agreed. 'It doesn't feel good, when you're pushed into a corner now, does it, DI Matthews? But going back to your sweet, forgiving wife Angela – from what I understand she only *barely* took you back the last time.' Anna stepped forward and leaned down towards his face. 'So, I'm going to make *you* a deal. You may leave here tonight and never return, and never look in any of my businesses' direction ever again. No charge.' She smiled. 'Or,' the smile dropped, 'if you try to make trouble for me in any way, shape or form, these photos will be hand-delivered to your wife, possibly even by Rose herself, along with a tearful account of how you roped her into this kinky secret world of yours only to then break her heart by letting slip you were already married.'

'Ooh, I like that,' Tanya enthused.

'Yes, quite apt, I think.'

'You bitch…' DI Matthews glared at her through narrow eyes. 'And to think I even considered you as dating material.' He snorted and sneered at her. 'Not any more.'

'I can assure you, the feeling was never mutual,' Anna replied, in a matter-of-fact tone. 'So, which side of this deal would you like to accept?'

'I'll leave,' he spat. 'Wouldn't touch you with a fucking barge-pole now. But you hear me, Anna. You go near my wife and I'll make you rue the day.' His bluster covered his seething anger at how well Anna had turned the tables. He bucked, trying to throw Rose off him, annoyed by the way his own body had betrayed him and fully embarrassed by the turn of events.

'Then we have an understanding,' Anna responded. 'Tanya, you take that camera and get the pictures printed, will you? Then pop the SD card somewhere safe, just in case we need it later.'

'Of course,' Tanya replied sweetly as they exchanged exaggeratedly pleasant smiles.

Anna turned her smile back to DI Matthews as Tanya exited the room. 'She's a dear, isn't she?' she said, her tone clearly mocking him as he struggled against his restraints. 'Oh, I wouldn't do that. You don't want to mark your wrists. What would Angela think?'

He stopped struggling and growled at her across the room. 'You'll pay for this.'

'Actually, I won't,' Anna responded, dropping the fake smile. 'Because you so much as look in my direction again, your marriage, your whole happy family routine, will be down the pan. Not only that, but I have a vast network of people at my fingertips I can get to make your life a living hell. People you no doubt despise, but who outsmart you ten to one,' she added, curling her lip as she allowed the disgust she felt for the feeble man in front of her to come to the fore. 'I am one of the most dangerous people you will ever have the stupidity to cross. I've let you off with a warning this time. That won't happen again.'

Reaching over to the table where she had placed two large, sharp knives, she passed one to Rose.

'What the hell?' DI Matthews yelped. His eyes widened in shock as she approached him with cold hatred in her eyes. 'Listen, whatever, OK?' He held his hands up as high as he could, considering his bindings. 'I tried to play the game, you won. It's over. I took the deal.' His voice cracked into full-on panic as Rose approached him from the other side and Anna gave her the nod. 'I took the deal, I took the deal,' he screeched, squeezing his eyes shut and trying – unsuccessfully – to shuffle away from them.

'Yes, we already went over that,' Anna replied, her tone bored.

Lifting the knife to the ropes that bound his wrists to the bed, she sawed through the bindings until the last thread snapped, allowing DI Matthews his hand back. Rose mirrored the action on the other side. DI Matthews immediately sat up and began trying to undo the leftover rope that was still secured around his wrists as the women cut through the ropes holding his ankles.

'You don't have time to do that here, I'm afraid. Take them off in your own time. I want you off my premises, immediately,' Anna said, running her fingers up and down the back of the large blade.

DI Matthews didn't need to be told twice. Shifting off the bed, he winced once more and touched the back of his head where they had knocked him out, before grabbing the pile of clothes that had been neatly folded on the bedside table. He pulled his underwear on and his trousers, not bothering to waste time with socks before shoving his feet into his shoes. Keeping one wary eye on the two women still holding the blades, he threw his T-shirt over his head and grabbed the rest of his things under one arm, still pulling his T-shirt down as he hurried out of the door.

'You were right, by the way,' Anna called after him, mockingly. 'Allowing you to come over did give me great pleasure, after all.'

Running down the stairs, furious and embarrassed, but knowing he could never do a thing about what just occurred, the last thing DI Matthews heard was the sound of the two women's laughter.

Shaking her head, amused, Anna turned back to Rose. 'Strip the bed and sort this room out for tomorrow, will you?' she asked. She opened her purse and threw a wedge of notes onto the side. 'And that's yours for tonight's work.'

'Easiest money I've ever made,' Rose replied with a throaty chuckle, as she began to pull the sheets off the bed. 'Probably the most fun, too.' She glanced at Anna. 'Can I ask you something?'

'Of course,' Anna replied.

'You could have just threatened him with Freddie. Surely that would have been enough without all this?' She glanced up towards Anna and back to the bedsheets a couple of times in quick succession, not sure if she had overstepped the mark by making such a forward comment. Anna was a fair boss, but she had a hard streak. She wasn't someone Rose wanted to piss off.

Anna smiled and looked down at the knife, running her finger gently over the sharp edge. 'There's no need to threaten a man with one side of the axe, when he's already got his neck up against the other.'

CHAPTER TWENTY-THREE

Freddie nuzzled into Anna's neck as she stood at the small mirror in the back office of their newly set up restaurant, trying to put on her earrings.

'Stop it,' she half-heartedly complained with a laugh. 'I'm trying to get this on.'

'Like anyone would notice something as insignificant as your earrings when they have the dazzling beauty of your face to focus on,' he murmured into her neck, completely ignoring her protests. Wrapping his arms around her waist more securely, he pulled her back into him, breathing in her perfume. 'This face, this neck…' He kissed her further down her shoulder and grinned as he felt her respond. She leaned back into him. 'This dress, which is coming off the second I get you home, Anna Davis,' he promised, in a low seductive voice.

She turned around to face him and couldn't help but smile as she looked at his handsome features and kissed him hard on the lips. 'Good,' she replied, nipping at his bottom lip with her teeth, teasingly. 'I'll hold you to that. But for now, we have a restaurant to open.'

'Yeah, plus, it's getting really uncomfortable for the rest of us in here,' came a strained voice from behind the desk. Paul rolled his eyes at them exaggeratedly as they turned around and Anna laughed.

'Sorry, Paul.' She pushed Freddie away and opened the office door. 'So, I'm going to go and cut the ribbon with Tanya, get things moving and then once the press have gone, we'll join you guys in the VIP area, OK?'

'Gotcha,' Paul replied. 'I'll save you girls some champers.'

'Good stuff.' Anna disappeared and the door shut behind her, leaving the brothers alone.

Although this restaurant was unofficially a joint venture between the four of them, only Anna and Tanya were on the lease and set up as directors. Neither Freddie's nor Paul's name was noted down anywhere. This way there was no paper trail to the Tylers, keeping the business several degrees safer, should they be looked into for anything by the police going forward. To keep up appearances, although it was an exciting night for them all, it would only be the two women walking out into the limelight of the local press and greeting customers as they entered ready to be fed and entertained for the first time.

'So, did you speak to Sophia today?' Paul asked, as Freddie took a seat in the chair opposite.

'Yeah, I met with her earlier, told her we had a deal. She ran through the general routes and the supplier details. He had a good operation running, I'll give him that,' Freddie conceded with a grudging expression of approval. 'If nothing else he wasn't a bad businessman.' He reached into his pocket and pulled out his cigarettes, offering one to Paul. Paul took one and they both lit up.

'When does she want to start? How many men does she need on the run?' Paul took a drag. 'And are you sure you're happy to risk trying this out? For all we know, she could have the plod waiting to collar us the second we have our hands on the product. Or Aleksei waiting in the wings. I'm still not sure I buy the whole death story.'

'Which is why we won't be anywhere near the product. And why we'll keep a second team scouting the pick-up and drop-off points before and after, and scouting ahead on the route for any unexpected guests,' Freddie answered. Paul nodded his approval.

'Also, I do buy the Aleksei story,' he added. Paul raised an eyebrow in question. 'It makes no sense to open up the inner workings of the gun-running to us, just as some ploy to tempt us into a trap. It's too risky and there are far easier ways. No, she's telling the truth, I'm sure of it. Aleksei would have made his play by now if he was still in the game. And his men would be united, not scared and hiding in safe houses with no clue what's going on. Aleksei is gone. I asked her where the building was and sent someone to check it out. It was half built, not scheduled to be brought down. Someone blew it up with a shit tonne of dynamite, Aleksei was apparently inside when the detonator went off. No body, no record. At the moment anyway.'

'You think Aleksei was rigging it himself?' Paul asked, surprised.

'Must have been. Idiot must have triggered it before he was clear. That's all I can think of.' He took another drag on his cigarette and returned to Paul's earlier questions. 'Now, the run itself needs four men in total. I want to get six on the second team watching their backs. She wants to start this week, depending on if she can get everything back up and running how it was. Obviously, there's been a disruption to the usual routine and she'll need to talk the suppliers round to the new arrangement. But she reckons that won't be an issue.'

'Who are they?'

'Ukrainians. They keep a solid supply chain for protection, so apparently won't intend on meeting us themselves so long as Sophia vouches for us.'

Paul nodded and bit his lip. 'And you're sure this is the right time for us to be getting into moving weapons? We've always steered clear before, and with good reason.'

It wasn't that they hadn't had the chance to run guns before now, they'd had plenty of opportunities. Other firms within London ran guns. The Jamaicans in the South had a thriving enterprise, the Jews in the West could always be counted on for stock and Ray Renshaw's firm had been known to procure the odd weapon when asked. But it was something that the Tylers had always left well alone. The risks were significantly higher than a lot of the businesses they ran, the stock was bulky and therefore harder to hide and the clientele could not always be trusted. They had watched suppliers get burned in the past, when the trail had led back to them off the back of a bank job gone wrong, or when a client had had their guns discovered out of sheer bad luck.

'If we were looking at setting this up from scratch, then no,' Freddie answered. 'It wouldn't be worth it. But this is already a well-oiled arrangement and it's more of a middle-man job, rather than a shop front. The clients have already been vetted and they buy regularly in bulk. Whatever their reasons are, I'm not about to ask, but these aren't wideboys after a handgun to wave around so they can look like Billy Big Balls. They're serious.' Taking one last drag, Freddie stubbed his cigarette out in the ashtray between them. 'It would be stupid to pass up. We stand to make a lot of money.'

'OK then,' Paul said with a nod. He stubbed his own cigarette out. 'So long as you're sure, let's see where this goes. Now…' Easing himself up from the chair he had been so comfortably seated in for so long, Paul straightened his suit and glanced at himself in the mirror. 'While they're busy cutting the ribbon and smiling for the camera, let's go get the drinks sorted. Our lot will be arriving any minute and it ain't going to be much of a party if there's no booze flowing.'

'Good idea,' Freddie replied, standing up and following him out. As they reached the bar he couldn't help but smile. The first night of any new venture was exciting and as this was his first with Anna involved it seemed even more of a special occasion than usual. The firm and all their friends would be here soon to celebrate with them and it was one step higher up the ladder of life. Right now, Freddie felt on top of the world. Life was perfect. And for tonight at least, nothing could possibly go wrong. Could it?

CHAPTER TWENTY-FOUR

Tanya chatted animatedly to Amy about the acts they had planned for the few weeks ahead, her cheeks flushed pink by the several glasses of champagne she had enjoyed so far. A server from the bar passed her and she held her glass out to be filled up again. The bar staff had been told to make sure that everyone in their VIP section was not to be left with an empty glass all night. This was a celebration.

'So then the firebreathers and the trapeze artists from tonight's show will make a second appearance in about a month, but not as main circus acts like tonight, they will be performing with this amazing singer we found down on the South Bank. Honestly, she is sensational. I've never heard such a set of pipes before in my life. I was walking past and just had to stop and book her in for this place right there and then. I'll tell you what night she's on, you should definitely come over for that. Maybe we can make it a girls' night, get us lot together here for dinner and cocktails?'

'You're on,' Amy replied enthusiastically. 'Just let me know the date.'

Tanya cast her gaze around the room and grinned, happy that everyone seemed to be enjoying themselves. The tables in the restaurant area were almost completely full, the empty ones reserved for people who were due to arrive shortly. The atmosphere was buzzing, people dazzled by the fantastic entertainment and the beautifully cooked food. They'd hired only the best chefs, who had been trained up in Michelin-star restaurants, and the servers were all silver service. With dark décor complemented by small chandeliers hanging subtly around the room, the entire room gave off a sophisticated air.

Shaking her head slightly, Tanya mentally pinched herself once more. If someone had told her a few years ago that she would be standing as joint proprietor in a place as classy and respectable as this, she'd have laughed in their face and asked for their dealer's number. She marvelled at how far she had come in life. From the penniless, clueless runaway she had been at the tender age of seventeen, convinced into working as a stripper in one of London's seedier clubs, to a successful club owner and now to this. They'd really taken a step up with this one. Of course, it was still mainly to launder money through, but that was neither here nor there as far as she was concerned.

Josephine walked over and touched her on the elbow, to gain her attention. Tanya turned and greeted her, noting that for once Josephine looked relaxed and was even smiling.

'Hello, Josephine, how are you doing? You look nice this evening.'

Josephine looked down at the garish purple number she was wearing and her face lit up. 'Do you like it?' She pulled at the feathers that adorned the pleats of the skirt and matched the ones woven into her intricate updo, and twirled around. 'I bought it especially for tonight.'

'I love it,' Tanya lied. Josephine's style was as unique as she was herself and although Tanya rarely actually liked her outfits, she greatly admired Josephine's strong sense of self, and so made sure to support and nurture it wherever she could. 'It's nice to see you looking happy, Josephine,' she said more sincerely. 'It's been too long since I've seen you properly smile.'

Josephine's smile faded to a slightly sadder one, but it still lingered on her face. 'These last couple of months I've been reliving that night over and over,' she said quietly, checking that no one else was listening. 'And I've been punishing myself for all my mistakes, every single day, on top of grieving for a man I loved. But…' she sighed, 'I realised I can't keep punishing myself forever. I have Anna for that,' she added with a grimace, glancing over to where Anna was chatting away to a small group of friends. 'So I initially decided I would just allow myself to grieve in peace. Only, when I did that, I started to feel angry. Angry because when it came down to it, he didn't really love me the way I thought he did. I was no safer with him than any other enemy, once I had to stand against him. I meant nothing. And yet here I am, *grieving* for what I thought I shared with the guy, even though it clearly wasn't real.'

'It was real on your part,' Tanya reminded her. 'Don't let that slip under the rug, just because he wasn't who he made out he was.' She touched Josephine's arm. 'Sometimes when we grieve it isn't actually grief for the other person, it's grief for what we gave away – for what we gave them of ourselves and they destroyed. And that's OK.'

Josephine swallowed the lump of emotion that had risen in her throat at Tanya's words. 'Thank you,' she said quietly. She wiped just below one eye, stopping the stray tear that was forming from falling, then sniffed and plastered the smile back onto her face. 'But I'm fine. Honestly, I am. Right now, at least. I know there will be times I won't be. But I refuse to be down all the time. It doesn't suit me. So I'm holding on to the good times, like tonight, from now on.' She looked around at the large group she was part of and felt a touch of warmth in her heart. 'This is a good day,' she confirmed with a nod.

'Well, I'm pleased to hear it,' Tanya replied.

'By the way, Sammy has not stopped staring over at you all night.' Josephine changed the subject. 'Is there something I should know about you two?' she asked with a curious expression.

'What are you on about, you daft bat?' Tanya responded with a forced laugh. 'It's *Sammy*.' She laughed again and shook her head as if the idea was ludicrous.

'If you say so,' Josephine replied, pursing her bright purple lips with a smirk. She didn't miss much when it came to people-watching, so as subtle as the man was trying to be, he still wouldn't get much past her notice.

Tanya rolled her eyes with a chuckle of apparent amusement and pulled her phone out of her purse. Careful to shield the screen from Josephine, she tapped out a quick message to Sammy.

J's noticed you staring at me, you pervert. Keep your eyes to yourself. Until later. Then you can give me more than just the eye. Wink wink. Tx

Tanya slipped her phone back into her purse and moved strategically, so that to look at her Josephine would have her back to Sammy, who was currently pulling out his own phone to read her text.

'Anyway,' Tanya continued the conversation brightly. 'Have you tried the food yet?' She was referring to the canapés that were floating around their area. They'd decided not to bother with a sit-down meal themselves. 'The chefs we hired are blinding.'

Glancing over at Sammy she saw a grin creep over his face as he shook his head. Masking the movement as a weight shift as he continued talking to Seamus, he tensed his upper arms and chest, giving her a display of what she could expect later that night. Looking down, Tanya had to bite her lip to stop herself from laughing.

'Yeah, they um… Oh my God…' Josephine trailed to a stop and Tanya looked up. Josephine's face had turned a deathly shade of white that even the heavily applied layer of make-up couldn't hide, and her eyes were as wide as saucers.

'What?' Tanya asked, looking over to where her friend was staring to try to see what was causing her such distress. 'What is it?' But Josephine didn't answer, just stood rooted to the spot.

Frowning, Tanya searched the area near the door again more closely. The maître d' was welcoming two sets of new guests and as he ushered the group of four in front towards their table, she got a clear look at the two people behind for the first time. The man was heavy-set, dressed in black and his miserable scowl looked out of place in the happy atmosphere of the room. The woman he was with stood a confident step in front of him, dressed impeccably in a new line Gucci dress Tanya had been coveting herself, her raven hair shiny under the light, her seemingly natural tan glowing and her chiselled face made up like the cover of *Vogue*. The woman was a stunner, that was for sure. So much so that Tanya couldn't help but stare too, for a moment. As she turned back to Josephine though, the look on her face suddenly made everything click into place.

Who else could turn the vivacious Josephine into a pale mute just by walking into a place? It could only be one person. It could only be Aleksei's wife, Sophia.

CHAPTER TWENTY-FIVE

Freddie's hand paused halfway to his mouth as he was about to take a sip of his whisky. After a second he lowered it, the sip forgotten. Bill joked away beside him, but he tuned out, leaving Paul to laugh heartily in his stead.

'Excuse me for a minute, will ya?' he said, walking off without waiting to see if either of them had heard him.

Leaving the VIP area he strode through the busy bar of the restaurant to the front, where Sophia was waiting to be seated.

'Mrs Ivanov, this is a surprise,' he said, greeting her with a friendly but controlled smile. 'I hadn't realised you'd booked a table.'

'Yes, well…' her smoky gaze bored into Freddie's, 'I wanted to see what had been done with my late husband's club.' She looked around and nodded in polite approval. 'It looks nice. Much nicer than it was as a strip club.'

'Thank you,' Freddie replied.

There was an awkward silence and Freddie realised with annoyance that he was going to have to invite her to join them. He couldn't be seen to rudely snub her as a new business partner, as much as he wanted to right now. Tonight was supposed to be about pleasure, but now it seemed it would have to be turned around back to business. And mouths would have to be guarded.

'We're, er, having a few drinks over here,' he said, gesturing back to the VIP area from where Anna was now curiously looking over. 'A celebration for the opening. You must join us, come and meet my brother and some of the men who will be working on the runs.'

'Oh, I couldn't possibly interrupt your party,' Sophia said half-heartedly with a smile.

'I insist.' Freddie parroted the response that was expected.

'Well, if you're sure.' Sophia walked forward confidently towards the area where the rest of the firm were still in full celebration, leaving Freddie to follow behind, bemused.

Anna stepped forward with a slight frown of confusion underneath her polite smile as she met them at the rope.

'Anna this is Sophia Ivanov, the new business partner we've been in talks with.' Freddie dived smoothly into the introduction as though her appearance was expected.

Anna took the hint and after only a millisecond's pause, smiled broadly and held her hand out to shake Sophia's. 'Great to meet you in person,' she enthused.

Glancing at Freddie she guided Sophia into the VIP area and over to where Bill and Sammy stood watching. Bill, she could tell, already knew exactly who Sophia was. This was to be expected. He had done a lot of research on her during the firm's search for Aleksei. 'Come and meet some of the men. Sophia, this is Bill and this is Sammy, they'll be working on the runs initially.'

She paused as they greeted her politely and subtly appraised Sophia. She was a very attractive woman indeed and for a moment she wondered how much of this Freddie noticed when he looked at her. She ran her hands over her hips in a self-conscious gesture, before straightening up and pushing the thought back out of her head. What was she, some insecure schoolgirl? she chided herself. What she and Freddie shared was deep and strong and beyond the kind of set-up that a pretty face could ever undermine.

'What can I get you to drink, Sophia? Champagne?' Anna asked.

'That would be lovely, thank you,' Sophia replied politely, her Russian accent richly curling around her words.

'I'll be back in just a moment.' Giving Freddie a subtle instruction to meet her at the bar, she sidestepped the server she could have gone to on the way and went to order another bottle.

Freddie joined her and leaned his back against the bar, casually watching the newcomer as she stood talking to his men. Her own man stood just behind her, silent as always.

'When did you invite Sophia?' Anna asked quietly.

'I didn't. She just turned up,' he replied grimly.

'Ah, I see.' Anna ordered another bottle of champagne and a glass and then turned to wait, facing the same way as Freddie. 'What do you think she's doing here?'

The question was placed casually, but Anna felt anything but that. Her insides had turned to ice as Freddie had introduced the woman and her eyes had searched for any small clues that she was here to taunt them. She knew that Aleksei was dead and that his body was in the rubble underneath the building. How did Sophia know that? How much else was she aware of? What was her plan here? All of these questions had been swirling around in her brain for days, like a poisonous fog that wouldn't dissipate, and now that the woman was here they seemed to be hammering at the sides of her brain, demanding answers.

'She said she was curious to see what we'd done with it,' Freddie answered. He glanced at her face and saw the hardened jaw and the twisted mouth of doubt. 'But you don't think so,' he continued. 'You think there's more to it?' He looked back over to Sophia, who was now talking to Amy, who Bill had tactfully introduced to keep her company.

'No, no,' Anna quickly lied, smiling reassuringly. 'Not at all. It's clearly curiosity, like you say. That's natural, given the circumstances. Plus,' she continued, seeing that Freddie still wasn't quite convinced, 'it's a good distraction, coming out to a new restaurant. Better than sitting at home alone now that her husband is gone, I would imagine.'

'Yeah, I guess there's that,' he replied.

The bottle and fresh glass arrived and one of the servers from their area hastened over to pick it up. 'Sorry, Miss Davis,' she said with wide eyes. 'I didn't realise we'd run out.'

'Don't worry, Letty, we hadn't. Just add it to the circulation and make sure that lady over there gets this glass,' Anna responded. As the waitress rushed off to do as she'd been bidden, Anna took a deep breath and walked back towards the group. 'We'd best make sure everyone knows to be on their guard and that she has a good night,' she said resolutely.

Freddie straightened his jacket and fell into step beside her. 'You took the words right out of my mouth.'

CHAPTER TWENTY-SIX

Sophia twirled the slim stem of her champagne glass between her fingers and took a small sip as she looked around – the polite smile she'd fixed upon entering not once slipping from her lips, despite the anger that bubbled inside. That she had been curious to see what they had made of the place wasn't a lie. She wanted to see what her husband's blood had bought this firm. And it was most certainly his blood which had bought it. Had Aleksei been alive, they would never have got their hands on this place again. Had they not killed him. They were curious to know how much she knew, of this she was certain. All of them were sneaking glances at her, their faces guarded. They knew she knew – she'd made no secret of her knowledge, letting Freddie know outright that she knew exactly where her husband's body lay, crushed and festering beneath thousands of kilos of rock and cement.

She turned in a wide circle as if admiring the place, to hide the snarl that was threatening to take over her expression. Yes, they knew that she knew. But they did not know how much, and she was enjoying having this power for the time being. Until such a time as she made her deeper intentions clear, at least. Because whilst she had been curious to see what they had done, this was not the only reason she was here tonight. There was someone here that she wanted to speak to. Alone.

Leaving the small group she had been pretending to engage with to talk amongst themselves, Sophia wandered over to the side table where some of the canapés had been set down for the group to enjoy. One man stood there stuffing his face with his back to her. As her shadow fell across the platter in front of him he turned, licking his fingers unceremoniously.

'Oops, don't mind me,' he chuckled. 'You dive in. Those little beef things are blinding.' He pointed with a freshly licked finger and Sophia had a hard time hiding her distaste for a moment. She just about managed it though and smiled at him instead.

'Oh, I'm not hungry, thank you.' She turned slightly, checking that they were still safely out of earshot of the others. Luckily, it wasn't too hard with the music and general sounds of activity in the busy establishment. 'I was wondering, what's your name?' she asked.

'Me? I'm Jim,' he said with a grin, chuffed that he was being singled out to be spoken to by the attractive young woman. Maybe she liked an older bloke, he thought to himself, oblivious to the lack of charm his balding head, pot belly and absence of manners afforded him.

'Jim.' Sophia nodded. 'I'm curious, Jim. Do you spy on all of your employer's meetings?'

Jim's smile faded and he glanced around to make sure no one had heard her. 'You what?' he responded.

'Mr Tyler may have had his back to the door you were watching us through the other day, but I did not. And you were not as covert as you thought you were.'

'I don't know what you're talking about,' Jim continued, his face clouding over angrily.

'Yes, you do,' Sophia responded. 'You don't have to worry,' she added casually. 'I'm not going to tell him. I just wondered why you felt the need to eavesdrop.' She looked him up and down critically. If what her man, Ali, had told her was correct, he was the new guy and was an odd fit for the firm. There was a chance he was exactly what she was looking for. 'Perhaps he isn't paying you enough. Perhaps you were hoping for some bit of juicy information you could sell on.'

'Eh? How dare you—' Jim started, puffing his chest out in self-defence.

'I'm just saying, if that were the case, you might not have been that far off the mark,' Sophia said, cutting him off. She paused to gauge his reaction and then continued when he fell silent. 'Yes, I thought so.' She smiled at him, turning on the full charm. 'I'm new to working with this firm and could do with someone on the inside, who could give me any information I lack, perhaps sometimes to locate specific information for me. I'd be happy to pay that person very well indeed. They could end up being on two payrolls. Infinitely better than just one, I find.' Watching Josephine disappear to the ladies out of the corner of her eye, Sophia reached into her clutch bag and pulled out a card. She handed it to him discreetly. 'Think about it and contact me if you're interested. Oh, and, like the incident of you spying behind the door, this conversation is to stay between us.' She walked off, leaving Jim staring after her.

Next Sophia approached Freddie and Anna, smiling widely as if they were old friends. 'Well, tonight has been a pleasure, thank you for inviting me.'

'You're leaving so early – can we not entice you with a few more drinks?' Anna responded. She'd barely had a chance to talk to Sophia in the couple of hours she'd been at the party and was still no closer to finding out what she needed to know.

'Thank you, but no. I need to get back. I'll speak to you both soon, I'm sure.' With a nod, Sophia turned and walked away towards the front door. Freddie and Anna watched her go, their expressions sombre, until she disappeared from view.

*

Sophia paused in the entrance hallway for a few moments before turning back inside. 'Stay here,' she ordered her man, Ali, curtly. Keeping her head down, she quickly slipped up the side of the room until she reached the toilets. Entering, she checked the cubicles and found only one occupied. As the sound of the flush came through, Sophia stepped back and waited for Josephine to appear.

The door to the cubicle opened and out she came, almost jumping back in surprise as she saw Sophia standing just a couple of feet away, staring at her with a cold, hard expression.

'Oh, er…' She looked away and stepped forward to the sink to wash her hands, her cheeks burning.

Sophia looked her up and down in disgust. The tacky purple garment she wore was ill-fitting and the sprays of feathers everywhere could have been placed by a five-year-old. No amount of make-up could hide the masculine features that made up her large face and her big droopy brown eyes reminded Sophia of a dog her father once owned. She hated her even more in person than she had from afar.

As Josephine turned on the tap, Sophia's hand shot over and slammed it shut. Josephine let out a small squeak of surprise and fear.

'Do you not think that I know who you are?' Sophia snarled. 'Why are you pretending we are strangers, *Josephine*? I know exactly who – or should I say *what* – you are, you foul, disgusting creature.' She looked her up and down cruelly. 'Acting as though you are something you could never be, whilst still taking the benefits of the parts of you that you try to hide. You're a disgrace.' Spit flew out of Sophia's perfect mouth as her rage and hatred began to make her shake.

Tears pricked behind Josephine's eyes as the prejudiced onslaught rained down and she stepped back, her mouth gaping open in shock. She had been expecting some sort of look or comment from Sophia, but had not expected to be so viciously attacked.

'Yes, I know exactly what you are.' Sophia looked her up and down in contempt once more. 'And what you've done.' Her cold eyes shot up to meet Josephine's frightened gaze. 'And I can promise you this.' She stepped forward, pulling herself to full height in an attempt to reach Josephine's much taller level. 'I'm going to make you wish you had never even met my husband. I'm going to make you wish you'd stayed in whatever dirty fucking swamp you crawled out of.' Her lip curled up into an ugly grimace as she pressed her face closer to Josephine's. 'And I promise you that when you least expect it, I'm going to make you pay for what you've done. No one gets away with crossing me. *No one.*'

Without waiting for a response and not wanting to be walked in on, Sophia stepped back, turned around and swept out of the ladies as though nothing had happened.

CHAPTER TWENTY-SEVEN

Anna gratefully took the second cup of steaming coffee from Mollie and melted back into the kitchen chair, wishing the sun wouldn't shine so brightly through the window. Ethan walked round the table, filling everyone's glasses with fresh orange juice, a chirpy smile on his face.

'Me and Nan squeezed these oranges ourselves last night, didn't we, Nan?' he told Anna as he reached her glass.

'Nan and I,' she automatically corrected in a tired voice. 'I bet it's delicious, thank you.'

'Nan said you'd all have had too much lemonade and would need evening out. But…' A small furrow of confusion appeared in his brow. 'I've had loads of lemonade at parties before and it didn't do anything to me.'

'Well, sometimes it happens when you're old like us,' Paul said with a small chuckle. 'The curse of too many lemonades.'

'Oh, OK.' Ethan accepted this with a shrug. 'I just thought all the alcohol had given you hangovers.'

Paul glanced over at Freddie, who just shook his head with a crooked smile of defeat. The boy was too savvy for his own good sometimes.

'Right, here we are. Get this lot down ya,' Mollie said, bustling over with a serving dish full of juicy sausages, plump mushrooms, sunny eggs and bacon still sizzling from the pan. She placed it in the middle of the table and went back for the mountain of toast. 'Who else is coming? I'd have thought Tanya would have been with you.'

Mollie's family fry-ups were legendary among Freddie's inner circle. When she told them to invite the whole family, she really did mean the whole family. Bill and Sammy were almost always in attendance, as was Tanya these days. Mollie kept the food and coffee coming to the table until everyone had to practically be rolled out and they all loved her for it.

'Bill's not coming, he and Amy are off doing something out of the city today,' Freddie responded. 'But Sammy should be here any minute.'

'And I texted Tanya,' Anna added with a small frown. 'She wasn't in when we left.'

As Mollie opened her mouth to reply, there was a knock at the front door. 'Ah, well. That will be one of them now, no doubt,' she said cheerily. She scurried off to let whoever it was in, happiest as always with a full house.

A minute later a very dishevelled Tanya waltzed through to the kitchen and melted dramatically into one of the vacant chairs at the table, her wild red hair even wilder than usual and big black sunglasses covering her eyes.

Anna leaned forward and peered at her across the table. 'You look terrible,' she started. 'Have you still got last night's make-up on?' she asked in wonder. Tanya never left the house without full grooming, hangover or not, so this was unheard of.

'Yeah, alright.' Tanya's voice came out cracked and tired. 'Kick a bird whilst she's down, why don't you?'

Sammy waltzed into the lounge behind her with Mollie, casually taking the seat between Freddie and Paul. He looked as tired as the rest of them and leaned over to grab a corner of toast. 'This looks blinding, Mollie. Cheers,' he said.

Anna's sharp mind began to connect some of the dots. 'Did you two come together?' she asked, suspiciously.

'Yeah, I asked Sammy to pick me up. Don't think I should be driving my own car just yet,' Tanya answered.

'Pick you up from where? Where were you?' Anna continued, narrowing her eyes.

'What's this, the Spanish Inquisition?' Tanya said with a crooked smile of amusement. 'She ride *you* this hard after a night on the lash, Ethan?'

Ethan giggled but after a look at his stepmother's face decided wisely not to reply.

'Well, you weren't in, I checked,' Anna said accusingly. Tanya didn't reply, which just fuelled her curiosity further. There was something fishy going on here and Anna wanted to know what it was.

'So, other than the restaurant, what else is new, anyway?' Mollie asked brightly, changing the subject as she poured her two new guests a cup of coffee from the pot.

'Not much,' Paul said, leaning forward to help himself to some breakfast. He exchanged a look with Freddie. They told Mollie a certain amount, but not everything. Their new venture into gun-running was a good example of the kind of thing they kept to themselves. It would only keep her up nights, worrying about them.

'We've got a new member of the team,' Freddie piped up, reminded of the fact he had yet to talk to her about Jim. 'Says he knew Dad, actually.'

'Oh?' Mollie paused and looked over to her eldest son in surprise.

'Yeah, it was an odd one, I'll admit,' Freddie continued. 'He's been away on a long stretch, just got out. Says he used to work for Vince and Big Dom, back in the day. Came to me looking for a job, so I'm trialling him out at the moment. Jim Martin, do you remember the name at all?'

Mollie's skin paled to a deathly shade of white and the empty cup in her hand fell to the floor. At the sound of the porcelain smashing against the tile, she blinked and looked down.

'Shit,' she muttered, before grabbing a nearby tea towel and bending down to pile the pieces up in it.

Freddie and Paul looked at each other in surprise. Mollie never cursed.

'Mum? You alright?' Freddie asked.

'Yeah, yeah, I'm fine,' she said in a forced bright tone. 'Just annoyed I've dropped this,' she continued. 'Now I won't have a full set.' In reality, she couldn't care less about the damn mug. Clearing it up bought her some time to think.

Jim Martin. What the hell was he doing coming back here after all this time? And what was he doing, approaching Freddie?

Picking up the last of the shattered pieces of the mug, Mollie dropped them all into the bin and shook out the tea towel. As she turned back around to dump the towel in the wash basket, she caught the sea of confused looks being shot in her direction.

'Jim Martin,' she said slowly, as if racking her brain. 'Oh yes, I remember that name. If it's who I think it is, your dad wasn't that fond of him.' It wasn't a lie. Her Richard had hated Jim Martin with a passion – and with good reason. 'He's bad news, Freddie,' she said, shaking her head at him. 'Best to steer clear of people like him. Stick to those you can trust.'

Freddie frowned as he studied his mother. She had never looked so pale and flustered. And she could barely make eye contact with him. 'Why is he bad news?'

'Oh, I don't know.' Mollie swatted the air with her hand, as if batting the subject away. 'He just is, OK? Your dad would tell you the same thing, if he were alive.' Her voice became sharp as she turned away to the sink and Freddie closed his mouth into a hard line.

There was clearly something more to this than Mollie wanted to let on, but she wasn't going to tell him now. He'd have to come back on his own and try and prise it out of her then. Turning back to his breakfast, Freddie bit into his toast and moved his attention to his son.

'So, Ethan, good night last night?' he asked.

'Yeah, it was good. Not as good as yours though, by the looks of it,' he added with a cheeky grin. 'Was Auntie Tanya dancing on the tables again?'

'You cheeky beggar,' Freddie replied with a laugh.

''Course I was,' Tanya piped up. 'That's what they're there for on a night out – and don't let no one ever tell you otherwise, Ethan.'

'Tanya Smith,' Mollie scolded as a ripple of laughter made its way through the room. 'What a thing to say. He's a child, for Christ's sake.'

'Is he?' Tanya exclaimed in mock surprise. 'Well, knock me sideways and call me Barbara, I hadn't realised that. You sure?'

Mollie narrowed her eyes and put her hands on her hips, but Tanya was spared the scathing response as her phone began to ring.

'Oops, saved by the bell,' she said cheekily, winking at Mollie and taking the call. 'Hello? Oh…' Tanya's face dropped into a frown of deep concern and all previous conversation was forgotten. 'What! Is the fire out? Wait there, I'm coming now. Anna's with me. Just don't move.'

'Fire? Where?' Anna stood up, ignoring the protest inside her aching skull.

'The Sinners' Lounge.' Tanya shot her a meaningful look. 'We need to go.'

'Shit,' Anna cursed. She looked at Freddie. 'Can I take your car?'

''Course.' He stood up. 'I can come with you.'

'No!' both Anna and Tanya cried in unison. Tanya looked away and Anna stepped forward to continue more casually. 'There's no point. You stay with Ethan, finish your breakfast. I'm sure it's nothing major.'

'OK, if you're certain.' He threw the keys over to her and settled back in his seat.

'Thanks.' Anna leaned over and kissed him on her way out.

CHAPTER TWENTY-EIGHT

Rushing up the road towards The Sinners' Lounge as fast as they could from where they had left the car, Anna sighed heavily with stress as they reached the door. At first glance there was nothing hugely noticeable, but upon closer inspection Anna realised there were fingers of black soot clawing around the door from the inside.

'What the hell happened?' she demanded, as the door was opened by a miserable-looking Josephine. Her eyes were immediately drawn to the still smoking burns all around her and the charred remains of something on the floor.

Josephine stepped aside and waved them in, shooting a wary look up and down the road. There weren't many people around, but the street wasn't entirely empty. Anna and Tanya walked in and Josephine pushed the door back shut. Now they were inside they could see the true extent of the damage. Whatever it was had been small, something that burned out – or got put out – fairly quickly. The scorch marks didn't reach further than a couple of feet in, but even that was bad enough.

'Fuck's sake,' Tanya muttered. 'This whole hallway will have to be redone now. Carpet, walls, door, everything.' She stepped sideways and something crunched under her foot. Moving it to take a look, she found a scattered pile of broken glass.

'That was what set it off,' Josephine said, pointing down at the glass. I think it was a small bottle with some sort of flammable liquid and, you know…' Josephine flapped her hands as she tried to describe it. 'With a rag out of the top as a fuse.'

'A Molotov cocktail,' Anna said heavily. She sighed and shook her head.

'Well. Her calling card couldn't come any clearer than that,' Tanya said. She ran her hands through her hair in agitation, her expression sombre.

Anna frowned. 'But it makes no sense. She was all smiles last night, there was no indication that she knew anything about us...'

'She knows.' Josephine cut Anna off, her large brown eyes wide and watery with fear. 'She cornered me in the toilet before she left. I was going to tell you this morning, but then this happened...' She trailed off and looked around at the mess again, misery etched into her face.

Anna's gaze sharpened as she stared at Josephine. 'What did she say?' Her blood ran cold as all the possible future outcomes flooded through her head. None of them were good.

Tanya reached forward and squeezed Anna's arm. 'Let's go upstairs and have the hair of the dog, straighten ourselves out a bit so we can think straight. I don't know about you two, but I'm still absolutely hanging. This mess can wait until later. Go on, Josephine,' she urged, 'lead the way.'

They followed Josephine up to the bar and Tanya set about making three of her special-recipe Bloody Marys, her go-to hangover cure. Anna sat down at one of the tables and Josephine perched on the chair opposite.

'Well, go on,' Anna pushed.

Josephine sniffed and rubbed her tired eyes. She'd barely slept a wink, Sophia's cruel words running around in her head over and over and the worry of what was to come keeping sleep firmly at bay. 'She said she knew who I was, or rather, *what* I was. A disgusting creature, apparently.' Her bottom lip wobbled and she swallowed before continuing. 'That I would regret the day I met her husband and that no one crosses her. She said, *I know what you did.* She didn't elaborate but it doesn't take a genius.'

Tanya raised her eyebrows, her expression annoyed. 'She really called you that?'

'Among other things. All along the same lines.' Josephine looked down as she felt her cheeks redden and her eyes water. She didn't want to get upset about it in front of Anna and Tanya.

Tanya looked at Anna who shook her head, glancing down for a moment. She might still be angry at Josephine, but that didn't mean she didn't care for her deep down. And it certainly didn't mean she would accept one of her own being treated with such prejudice.

'Josephine, you mustn't listen to her,' she said quietly. 'Those are cruel and unnecessary words that mean nothing. You know who you are and you have every right to be yourself. Don't ever let someone make you feel otherwise.' She looked back at Tanya. 'We'll deal with that, eventually. But right now we need to focus on what sort of corner we're in exactly. Because at the moment we're still blind. We have no idea what she knows specifically or what she plans to do. She's certainly playing some sort of game, that's for sure, working with us yet making secret threats through you and doing what she's done downstairs.' Anna bit her lip as she tried to work out where Sophia could be going with this.

Josephine looked up at Anna, a feeling of hope shining through as her old friend gifted her the first kind words in weeks. As Anna met her gaze and hardened her expression once more, she looked down and tucked that hope away to mull over later. She wasn't out of the doghouse yet, but that had certainly been the first step towards it. The first chink of light in their broken friendship.

'Get the hallway cleaned up,' Anna ordered Josephine, her tone switching back to business. 'Get a new door, have the decorators do whatever they need and just put it through the books as renovation. I'll get Bill to put a camera on the front. We should have done that before now, anyway.'

'What do you want to do about Sophia?' Tanya asked, joining them at the table and handing out her freshly made Bloody Marys.

Anna took a sip and shot her a look of appreciation. She had no idea what secret ingredient Tanya put in these drinks – and she wasn't sure she wanted to ask – but they did always seem to soothe a lingering hangover. 'I'm not sure yet,' she answered. 'She needs to be pulled up for what she's done here. We can't be seen to let her get away with fire-bombing one of our businesses, even if it was just a small one to make a statement.'

'You think that's all it was?' Josephine asked. 'You don't think it was an attempt to burn the building down, with me inside?'

'No.' Anna shook her head. 'If she wanted to do that it would have been easy enough. That bottle was tiny, the liquid clearly chosen for instant impact and designed to fizzle out.' Anna twisted her mouth to the side as she thought. 'On the other hand,' she continued, turning back to Tanya, 'if she knows we covered things up, if she knows that Freddie *doesn't* know, we need to tread very carefully. We can't go in there all guns blazing and give her reason to strike back.' She rubbed her head and drank some more of Tanya's remedy drink. 'I need to give it some thought, figure things out. Josephine, you need to just stay out of her way for a while, keep your head down until we know where we stand.'

'Of course,' Josephine said dutifully. She pulled a wry smile. They had been telling her to keep her head down for a long while now, after everything with Aleksei. A little longer would make no difference.

'I wonder if it's worth pulling in Sarah Riley,' Tanya pondered, rubbing her chin.

'We can't tell her,' Anna replied with a frown. 'Her loyalty is with Freddie. She wouldn't keep this from him.'

'No, I don't mean tell her, not everything at least. Just tell her we don't trust Sophia. The facts rack up against her being trustworthy anyway. Make up some shifty look or conversation you half overheard.' She shrugged. 'It's enough to warrant setting a tail on her at least. And even Freddie can be in the know about that.'

Anna thought it over and nodded slowly. 'That would be a good start. Perhaps she'll trip herself up.' She paused. 'It could, of course, trip *us* up in front of Riley, depending on how much Sophia knows.' She and Tanya stared at each other for a long moment. 'But it's the best idea we've got.' She reached for her phone. 'Let's just hope and pray this works out in our favour. Because we sure as hell can't just sit here and wait for her to do her worst.'

CHAPTER TWENTY-NINE

Freddie marched down the busy street towards Heaven Sent, one of his more lucrative massage parlours. He had been so busy since getting out of prison, getting back up to speed with all the areas of the business, that he hadn't yet been able to find time to show his face. He knew it had been run well in his absence, he'd seen the books. It was a long-standing enterprise and Linda, the manager, was a competent woman who hardly ever contacted him for assistance. The odd do-good rookie policeman had needed to be dealt with, and a troublesome employee or two, but other than these occasional unavoidable issues, she ran a tight ship. It was still a Tyler business, though, and as such he needed to at least visit to make sure she had everything she needed and to let her know that they were around.

The bell above the door tinkled as he pushed it open and, as always, the scattering of men in the waiting area lowered their gazes even more. No one wanted to be recognised or make eye contact, for fear of people they knew finding out they frequented such an establishment.

A short, curvaceous woman bustled through from the back at the sound of someone entering. 'Welcome to Heaven Sent, how can I— Oh! Freddie!' Her homely face creased into a genuine smile which Freddie returned. 'I was wondering when I'd see you.' It wasn't a dig and Freddie didn't take it as one. They'd known each other long enough to speak frankly. 'How've you been?'

'I'm good thanks, Linda.' Freddie walked around the front desk and through to the back office, where he knew Linda would pour them a cup of tea and regale him with anything he needed to know about the business. She followed and they made their way down the long corridor dotted with doors to the booths where the girls carried out their work. 'You keeping well?' he asked politely.

'Oh, I'm grand,' she answered cheerily. 'Business is doing as well as ever. Well, I'll show you. Let me just get the tea on and we'll get into all that.'

The muffled moans and groans of pleasure seeped through the thin walls that separated the booths from the hallway as each client was given what they came for. As they reached the end of the hall, a door in front of them opened and one such client walked out, still tucking his shirt into his trousers. The young woman who had been servicing him lingered in the doorway behind in her lingerie, a fixed, fake smile on her face.

'Thanks, Janey, you do know how to make an old man young again, don't ya?' the man said with a small chuckle. 'I'll be back for that again in a couple of days.'

Freddie paused at the sound of the man's voice and looked into his face under the dim lighting.

'Jim? I thought you were on the rounds with Dean today?' Freddie said with a frown. That was what he had instructed anyway.

'Oh, Freddie, hello.' Jim was clearly taken aback, but he swiftly masked this with a smile. 'I was. Well, I am. We split off to get it done quicker and as I was passing I decided to take my lunch break in 'ere. Grab meself a little snack, if you know what I mean.' He winked at Janey and Freddie found it hard not to grimace at how leery the expression was.

'I actually wanted to talk to you about something,' Freddie said, changing the subject. 'Something that's puzzling me.' He smiled, but the action did not reach his eyes. 'Linda, would you mind if we use your office whilst you grab that tea?'

Linda caught on straight away. 'Not at all. I'll have a look for some biscuits too. I'm sure I have some, somewhere.' She disappeared round the corner and Freddie gestured for Jim to follow him into the office.

Jim rolled his eyes as Freddie turned away, feeling like he was being ordered into detention by the school master. He wondered if he was being pulled in for using the premises as if it was his own. But surely that was his right, as part of the firm? An employee bonus, so to speak. He'd been using this place for his sexual gratification every other day or so since he'd come across it on the collection rounds. The older bird running the show didn't like him much, he could tell, but she toed the line, knowing he was on the Tyler payroll. She still allowed him free access whenever he liked. And boy did he like it! He'd never had it so good, all these young girls, tight and ripe, professionals in the art of sucking him off and riding him like a horse. He didn't care whether they liked it or not, the point was they were good at pretending they did. And his balls were getting emptied more regularly than they ever had in his life. He wasn't giving that up without a fight. So, if Freddie was about to have a go at him for it, he'd just have to remind him of the long stretch he'd just done inside. Surely as someone who'd done time himself, he'd understand how raw his needs were right now.

Gearing up for this argument, Jim braced himself. The words that came out of Freddie's mouth, however, were not what he had expected, and for a second he found himself floundering, searching for a suitable response.

'You said you knew my dad, that you were mates. My mum, however, seems to be of a different opinion.' Freddie cut straight to the chase. He walked behind Linda's desk and sat down, leaning back in the chair with a frown. 'She seems to think you're bad news. Why is that?'

Jim blinked. 'Well, I er…' His mouth flapped a couple of times and then he laughed. 'Well, she might not have the fondest memories of me. I was your dad's mate, the one that used to drag him down the pub when she wanted him home and, admittedly, the one who always came up with the bad ideas.' He forced another laugh, studying Freddie's face for any clue that he knew more than he was letting on. He found none. He was clearly still in the dark. 'You know women. They always hate the Jack-the-lad of the group. Always nagging that they're the bad influence.' He rolled his eyes. 'Yeah, I'm sure she probably does remember me as that. But that was a long time ago. And certainly nothing to do with my ability in the workplace.'

Freddie nodded and bit his lip as he studied Jim. It sounded like a feasible excuse, only he knew his mum a lot better than Jim was giving him credit for. Mollie wouldn't have taken against him for something that simple. If anything she'd always loved the Jack-the-lads of his group, finding them entertaining and coming up with fantastic excuses for their cheeky behaviour, rather than taking a dislike. Plus, he'd never seen her pale so quickly upon hearing someone's name before. No, it was definitely more than that. But he wasn't going to find out what it was here.

In a swift action Freddie smiled and stood up. 'Thank you, Jim. That's all I wanted to know. You'd best be off.'

The door opened and Linda walked in with a tea tray.

'Yeah, 'course. Lots to do. Catch you later then.' Jim saluted Freddie with a smile and walked out as Linda put down the tray. She came to stand beside Freddie as they watched him walk off down the hallway.

'Can I be honest with you about something?' she asked.

''Course you can,' Freddie answered. 'Go on.'

'I don't like that one,' she answered quietly. 'There's something I just don't trust there.'

'Hmm.' Freddie nodded. He felt the same way too.

*

As Jim walked outside, he glanced behind him to check he was alone before pulling out his phone. Shoving his free hand in his pocket he marched off down the street and began searching his contacts for Sophia's number. He'd saved it as soon as he'd been able to do so after the party the night before and had been in two minds about whether to take her up on her offer, but that conversation with Freddie had made the decision for him. He was getting a little too close to Jim's ulterior motive, and this was not in his plan.

Jim had banked on Mollie being a lot more secretive with her son than this, about where they really knew each other from. But she had already made Freddie suspicious. Now, he would have to accelerate his plan and get to the crux of it sooner. And it certainly wouldn't hurt to make a bit of extra money on the side whilst he worked on that. Finding Sophia's number, he pressed the call button and waited for it to connect.

CHAPTER THIRTY

Tanya rolled off Sammy and onto her back as she tried to catch her breath and cool down after another steamy evening of sneaking around. Sammy put his muscular arm out and she shifted into it, pulling her hair up and over the pillow in an attempt to cool herself down.

She looked over at his chiselled face and smiled softly. The last week, since they had been running around together like teenagers, had felt like a complete whirlwind, yet oddly comfortable and familiar all at the same time. It was new and exciting, yet she knew Sammy better than she knew most people already. It was also a welcome relief to be with someone who knew her so well, all her faces and her colourful past, and who liked her anyway. She didn't have to worry that she'd let something slip one day and the façade they had fallen for would fade into a less attractive reality. She didn't have to worry about hiding anything either – or rather, not too much anyway. Sammy was one person who she could truly be herself around, and this was something she could definitely get used to.

'What you thinking?' he murmured, turning his head to face her.

Tanya half smiled as several quips immediately came to mind, but she decided not to tease him right now. 'Nothing much,' she answered. 'Just that this is nice. It's nice just being ourselves together, you know?'

'I do,' he replied. He leaned in and kissed her hungrily.

She pulled away with a laugh. 'I need a time out, not all of us were made at the Duracell factory.'

'It's called stamina. It's what I gain from that place you might vaguely remember called a gym,' he responded with a cheeky grin.

'Babe, you try running multiple businesses in London every day in six-inch heels and then tell me what you think a workout is,' Tanya said, raising her eyebrows at him.

Sammy laughed and pulled himself up on his side to face her. He ran his hands down her firm body and back up to her face. 'I'm well aware of the good working order you keep your body in, Tanya Smith. Though it would be fun to have you down the gym with me sometime so I can perv on you whilst you sweat.'

'Not for me, thanks,' Tanya replied, crinkling her nose. 'But it would be nice to do something other than just sneak around together like this.'

'We can, if you want. It's your call,' Sammy responded. Like Tanya, he was already appreciating the benefits that their long-standing friendship brought to the table in this new relationship. It didn't feel new, although that didn't take anything away from the fun of the honeymoon period. They had always got on well, but now things were just getting better and better. He had already decided that when she was ready to go official, he was fully on board. But, laidback as always, he was happy to leave it up to her as to when that would be.

'What do you think about getting away sometime? You know,' Tanya ran her fingers down his hard chest, 'like a holiday or something. A little getaway. Some fun in the sun.'

'You mean abroad?'

'Yeah, somewhere exotic,' she replied with a glint of excitement in her eyes.

'On your non-existent passport?' he promptly responded with a chuckle. She scowled. 'You could always just get one, you know. The application forms don't bite.'

Tanya's lack of passport, for someone with such desperation to get away, was a time hallowed joke within their circle. No one could understand why she hadn't sorted one out over the years.

'OK, fine,' she said with a defiant look. 'I'll get one. And I'll fill it out and then when that arrives, we should go somewhere straight away. A crazy, last-minute adventure. If you're up to that,' she challenged.

'Oh, I'm up to it,' Sammy replied. 'I'll take you on the biggest adventure you've ever had.'

'Yeah?' Tanya grinned and snuggled in closer. 'Where to then, Romeo?'

'Rome, Mexico, Thailand,' he reeled off. 'Hell, I'll take you to the dark side of the moon, if that's what you want.'

'Yeah?'

'Yeah. If you just get your damn passport,' he replied, sitting up and reaching over to get his boxers.

Tanya watched him for a minute, lying lazily back on the pillows. 'I think we might need more than passports to go to the moon,' she said eventually.

'How about dinner for now, then? Somewhere nice,' Sammy offered, running his fingers lightly up her arm. 'Anywhere you want. With zero sneaking.'

Tanya smiled. 'That sounds nice.' She leaned in and kissed him slowly and softly.

'OK, I'll book something.' Sammy moved back and eased himself up off the bed. 'Wait here, I'll grab us a drink.' He padded off and disappeared into the hallway of his flat. Tanya snuggled deeper into the bed and waited, feeling nicely at peace with the world. 'Oh, by the way,' Sammy called through, 'what was all that about, yesterday morning? Was everything OK? You said there was a fire.'

The peace Tanya felt suddenly shattered and was replaced with wary tension. 'Oh, that was nothing,' she lied. 'Josephine left her curlers on and there was a small fire. All sorted.'

'Oh, OK. Good stuff.'

Staring at the empty doorway, Tanya bit her lip as the shine of their situation began to cloud slightly. Things might be easier with Sammy than with anyone else in the world, but that still didn't mean she could be completely open. There would always be things in this life that they had to keep to their chest, even within the inner circle. She could not let her guard slip with Sammy now, or be fooled by the false sense of security that being with him made her feel. Not now. Not ever.

CHAPTER THIRTY-ONE

Jim looked up at the large comfortable family home and the neat front garden with its carefully tended flowers and foliage, his expression full of resentment. He checked the address one last time to make sure it was correct, though he already knew it would be.

'You jammy bitch, Mollie Tyler,' he muttered.

This house was a far cry from the one he had last known her to live in. Back when he'd last seen her, many years before, she'd been in a tiny house in the rows of the East End, renting off a landlord who didn't give a crap whether his houses were fit for people to live in so long as he got his few bob off them every week. She'd been a thorn in his side back then, a jumped-up bitch who paraded round like she was somehow better than him. Except she wasn't. She was no better than the shit on his shoe, in his opinion. But now here she was, living it up like Lady Muck in what was practically a mansion, all bought and paid for by her loving son.

His lip curled up in bitterness. She didn't deserve it. Not after what they had done to him. Not after all the years of his life they'd taken away from him because of her. *He* was the one who should be living it up now, not her. And that was exactly why he was here. To get his dues. And he would get them one way or another. Because if there was one thing he knew about Mollie it was that she'd do anything to hide the truth from people. Especially from Freddie. And this time she didn't have her precious husband, Richard, around to protect her.

Walking up the front path, Jim made a beeline for the front door and knocked on it loudly. The door swung open to reveal Mollie drying her hands on a tea towel, a half smile on her face as she began to greet whoever had come to see her. As her gaze settled on Jim, though, her expression froze and then turned into one of horror.

'Recognise me, do ya, Moll? Yeah, I thought you might,' Jim said, looking down on her with a sneer. 'We need to have a little talk, you and me.'

'I-I… Paul's home,' she said, her voice wobbling slightly. 'This isn't a good time.'

'No he ain't, Moll,' Jim replied, shaking his head. 'He's down the ring checking out some of the new fighters with Seamus. And Freddie's busy too. It's just you and me.' Moving forward, Jim pushed the door open wider and stepped inside, forcing Mollie out of the way. 'So, let's just get on with it, shall we?'

Mollie glanced outside quickly, checking that nobody had seen Jim enter, then shut the front door, closing her eyes for a second as she tried to overcome the surprise of him being here. Hearing his name had been shocking enough, but seeing him in the flesh like this, in her own home, was like a brick to the face.

She turned and looked him up and down. Of course she had recognised him. He hadn't changed so much. He was a lot older, that was a given. His hair was thinner and greying now and he had a lazy pouch across his belly where he had once been lean and fit in his younger years. He was softer and more filled out all round, but his face was still the same. And the piercing eyes that stared back at her still filled her with the same anger and hatred they had all those years before.

When all this had sunk in and she got a hold on her bearings, Mollie placed her hands on her hips and her eyes flashed dangerously. 'You need to get the hell out of my house, away from my boy and never come near either of us again. Do you hear me?

I ain't interested in anything you have to say, and if you think you were burned bad back then, you haven't got a clue how bad you'll have it if you start barking down this road again now,' she said fiercely. 'Get out. Go on.'

'I don't think so,' Jim said, his voice strangely calm, belying the bubbling anger written on his face. He took a slow turn around the hallway, pointedly looking around. 'Done well for yourself over the years, ain't ya? Suppose it's alright when you've got a gangster son looking after you, buying you big houses and filling 'em with expensive things.' He walked over to a painted vase that stood pride of place on the hallway sideboard. He picked it up, weighing it in his hand. 'This expensive, was it?' He looked back at her, then slowly dropped it onto the hardwood floor, watching her face as it smashed into pieces.

Mollie stared back at him. 'I'm warning you, Jim—' she started.

'No, I don't think you are actually,' he replied, cutting her off. 'Because Freddie has no clue who I really am, does he?' He tilted his head to one side and watched Mollie press her lips together, not willing to answer. 'No. He don't. And I'm betting you don't *ever* want him finding out who I am and what went down all those years ago. So, here's how it's going to go.' Jim looked around, as if calculating how much everything around him cost. 'You're going to get half a mill for me. Cash. And you've got a week to get it.'

'What?' Mollie exclaimed at the ridiculous request. Her eyebrows almost disappeared into her hairline and she barked out a humourless laugh. 'You are joking?'

'I'm not joking,' Jim answered. 'Five hundred thousand. I don't give a shit what you have to do to get it. Raid your piggy bank, steal from Freddie's hidden cash stash, sell your house for all I care. But you will get it for me. Because you owe me.' He stepped forward and stuck a finger in Mollie's face accusingly. She stepped back and tried to swat his hand away but he kept it there. 'You and Richard *both* owe me.'

'You're owed nothing,' Mollie spat, pushing him away from her with force.

Jim rocked back but kept his balance and narrowed his eyes at her. 'We both know that ain't true. So here's the deal. You get me that money and I'll leave you alone. I'll get out of London and set myself up somewhere with a nice house of my own and start again. I've had enough time to calm down now, that I'll accept that little amount as payment for the life you took from me. Well, that and a regular monthly payment to follow, too. But we'll get to that later. You get me that and I'll keep the truth to myself and we can all go on living our separate lives. But if you *don't*,' Jim continued with a slight pause, 'I'll tell your precious Freddie everything. And you can deal with the fall-out.'

Jim watched as Mollie's angry expression paled to one of dread and he stepped back. His job here was done. It was going exactly as he had thought it would. Taking a deep breath, he opened the front door and paused to look back at her one more time before stepping through it.

'One week, Moll. I'll be back here exactly one week today and I expect that money. Or I promise you, I won't hold back on the details. I'll ruin that *oh-so-special* relationship you have with your boy for the rest of your days.'

As the front door closed behind him, Mollie reached out to grip the banister and fell heavily onto the stairs. In all the years since she had last seen him, she had never thought that this could ever happen. She thought she was safe, that they were all in the clear. But that was the thing about living nightmares. One way or another they always came back to haunt you.

CHAPTER THIRTY-TWO

Anna sat curled up on the sofa, the wine in her hand and the book in her lap forgotten as she stared off into the distance. The room was dark, the lights all off except the reading lamp. Usually she liked it like this, dark and quiet whilst Ethan slept and she was left alone with her thoughts. Her life was always busy and chaotic, so she savoured the calm moments. But tonight the silence was not relaxing her. Tonight her mind would not be switched off as all her worries ran round and round in circles, chasing each other through her head.

What game was Sophia playing? What exactly did she know? She knew something, that much was certain. She had shown her hand the moment she revealed to Freddie that she knew where Aleksei was. If she knew that, Anna was certain that she must know of their involvement. The fire-bomb at The Sinners' Lounge only cemented this theory too, but why hide it? And why form a work alliance with Freddie of all people? It just didn't make sense. Did she somehow know that they had all lied to the brothers about it? How could she know that? And if she did, was stringing them all along as they struggled to work it out in the dark part of her plan?

Anna twisted the stem of the wine glass around in her fingers absent-mindedly and pulled her dark hair forward over one shoulder as she thought it all through for the hundredth time. *Had* the fire-bomb been about Aleksei's murder, or was it a dig at Josephine? After all, it was clear now that Sophia knew all about their affair. Aleksei had been merely a day away from ousting his beautiful Russian doll of a wife and moving Josephine into their home. Whether or not she'd loved him, the snub would be enough to send any woman crazy. Sophia had married him, borne two of his children, fled her own country and set up a new life in a foreign land when his actions had given them no choice but to flee – and then he wanted her to leave so he could move his mistress into her home? Anna snorted indignantly as she thought about it. As much as she neither liked nor trusted Sophia, she couldn't help but feel slightly sorry for her on this point.

As her mind rested once more on Josephine, Anna sighed and rubbed her forehead. No matter where Anna looked, Josephine was always there on the fringes lurking, watching, waiting to be forgiven. But she couldn't find it in her heart to be forgiving. All she felt when she thought of Josephine was resentment and rage. If she didn't care about the woman she probably would have been over it by now, but the fact that it had been a friend, someone she had taken into the family under her wing, still stung deeply. She knew deep down that Josephine had meant no real harm, but she had gone behind their backs. She had lied and snuck around with their enemy and it had almost cost them everything. It was disloyal, and although when it had come down to the line she had chosen them, this was what Anna just couldn't get her head around. Any type of disloyalty was betrayal. And in a family like theirs, there was just no room for it.

Once more her thoughts circled back round to her own guilt. Hadn't she shown disloyalty, too, by covering up Aleksei's death? She had killed the man in cold blood and buried him under several tonnes of rubble. And yet she had said nothing. She had sat back and watched as Freddie had sent his men out every day, scouring London for news of the man. He'd searched high and low, beaten down doors, tortured some of Aleksei's followers in the hope that they might give up his location, and the whole time she had just sat there in silence. She had sat on her throne of lies, watching the man she loved go almost out of his mind in his search for the Russian mobster. If Freddie found out now that she had lied to him – that she had covered up his death and the reasons for it, that she had protected a woman who had betrayed the firm – he would never forgive her. He would never trust her again.

She had done it to protect Josephine. If Freddie had found out what she'd done, he would never have allowed her to stay. He wouldn't have been so lenient. At the very least he would have slung her out and told her never to set foot in London again and at worst – well, that didn't bear thinking about. And she hadn't wanted that for Josephine. She'd made a mistake – a colossal one – but a mistake nonetheless. She wasn't a traitor at heart. But it was because of her that Anna now had to lie and show disloyalty herself.

The familiar feeling of resentment washed over her and she sighed in frustration. Was she ever going to find a way to move on from any of this? Not whilst Sophia's hand was still unplayed, that was for sure.

The front door opened in the hallway forcing Anna to rouse herself from her torturous thoughts. There was a jangle as Freddie dumped his keys in the key bowl before he walked through to the lounge, shrugging off his jacket. He smiled tiredly and dropped down on the sofa beside her.

'What's that you're reading?' he asked, pointing at the book in her lap.

'Oh…' Anna picked it up. 'It's called *No Escape*, by an author called Casey Kelleher.' *Apt*, she suddenly thought. A half smile crossed her lips. There had been no escape from her thoughts tonight either. 'It's really good.' She put it down on the side table and twisted to face Freddie, leaning her arm over the back of the sofa. 'How was your evening?'

'It was OK,' Freddie said, unconvincingly.

'Hm. Maybe you should tell that to your face,' Anna said jokingly. She reached forward and ran her hand through the side of his hair in an affectionate gesture.

'It's just my mum. She's acting really off at the moment. There's something about Jim Martin that's got her all worked up but she won't talk about it.'

Anna pulled a face. 'Maybe you're just imagining it?'

'No, I'm definitely not.'

'Maybe try talking to her again,' Anna suggested. 'Just the two of you, one on one. You're a convincing man, Freddie Tyler, when the whim takes you. You'll coax it out of her. And if not,' she added, 'you could always try Vince. You said he did a stretch for Big Dom, right? I know it's a long shot, getting information out of him these days, but you never know.' She shrugged. 'Might be worth a try.'

Freddie pulled a grim expression. Vince's dementia had cruelly taken so many memories from him, but he did have some good days when the light shone through the fog in his brain. It was a possibility, but he didn't fancy his chances. 'Yeah, well, I'll go round in the morning, see if I can get her to open up. There ain't many things I've ever seen rattle my mum. And the fact she's hiding it is worrying.' He frowned. 'I need to get to the bottom of it. Because secrets cause problems in this family. And the last thing we need is another problem right now.'

Anna felt her stomach turn over as her own secrets screamed at her from inside her head. She looked away and took a long sip from her wine glass.

'Anyway,' Freddie said, standing up. 'I'm going to go jump in the shower. Come join me if you like.' He flashed her a roguish grin and walked out unbuttoning his shirt as he went.

'I'll be there in a minute,' Anna called after him, her smile fading as Freddie's words echoed through her mind.

Secrets cause problems in this family. And the last thing we need is another problem.

She dropped her gaze and it rested once more on the book by her side. The words danced in front of her eyes taunting her, warning her.

No Escape.

CHAPTER THIRTY-THREE

Mollie stared unseeing out of the window of Thea's bedroom, as all the cars on their way to work passed by on the street below. She hadn't slept a wink after Jim's surprise visit to blackmail her the day before. After he had gone, she'd sat there on the stairs for a long time, all the long-forgotten memories of the past surging to the forefront of her mind. Her memories of the young woman she had once been and the world she had inhabited – a far cry from the comfortable one she resided in now – mixed with memories of her beloved late husband Richard and of all the drama that had unfolded.

Over and over it had all turned in her mind. Had the situation been dealt with in the best way? She would never be able to say for sure. There had been no perfect way. There had been no perfect people. But they had done what they needed to do to protect their family. Except now Richard was gone; he had been dead many years and she would have to face this consequence of their actions on her own. This realisation filled her with dread and made her feel more alone than she had felt for years.

She'd sat there in that hallway until her back ached and her legs cramped from the unusual position. It was only the incessant ringing of her phone that had finally forced her to move, rather awkwardly, back into the kitchen. The calls had been from Freddie, seven of them missed and the eighth just coming through as she reached it. He'd wanted to come over to see her, but she had made excuses. The last thing she had wanted yesterday was to see her eldest son. In the state she had been in he would have seen straight through whatever lies she told. She needed to figure out what she was going to do first, before she could face him.

As Mollie contemplated getting into the shower to try and force away some of the cobwebs still lingering from her sleepless night, a car pulled up in front of the house. She closed her eyes in distress. It was Freddie's. He obviously had no intention of giving up on his mission of talking to her face to face. She should have expected it, really. He was like a dog with a bone once he had his mind set on something. For a few seconds she wondered whether she should just jump in the shower anyway and hope something more pressing would call him away before she got out, but even as she considered it, she knew there was no point. Freddie would just wait her out or come straight back later. Tiredly she sighed and placed the one-eyed teddy of Thea's she'd been holding back in its place on the bed and walked downstairs to greet her son.

Freddie let himself in the front door at the same time she reached the bottom of the stairs. 'Alright Mum?' he asked, his hazel green eyes searching her face keenly.

'Alright, Freddie? What are you doing here so early?' she replied, tightening her dressing gown and shuffling through to the large kitchen at the back of the house.

Freddie followed her and sat down at the kitchen table, whilst Mollie began working the coffee machine on autopilot. 'Woke up early, had a bit of time on my hands. Thought I'd come and have breakfast with me old mum, that's all.'

'Less of the old, thank you,' she promptly retorted.

'Paul not up yet?'

'Just heard him stir a few minutes ago, so he should be down soon.' Mollie pulled three mugs out of the cupboard and placed them on the side as the coffee began to boil. She'd heard Paul come in during the early hours as usual, as she'd lain awake in her bed staring at the ceiling in the dark.

Freddie watched his mother as she moved around the kitchen putting bread in the toaster and pulling out all the breakfast things. She always liked to be on the move, never liking to be still, but her busy movements were more jerky today, more irritated. He could see the strain in her jaw and knew that this wasn't going to be a fun conversation. Whatever was bothering her since he had mentioned Jim, she clearly didn't want to talk about it. But he was going to try and make her, all the same. He decided to cut straight to the point.

'Mum, what's going on with you? You looked like you'd seen a ghost when I mentioned Jim to you a couple of days ago. What's all that about?' He sat back and waited, his gaze never leaving the side of her face as she rolled her eyes and turned away.

'Oh, leave it out, would you, Freddie?' she said, her tone irritable. 'I've told you already, I just remember him being bad news, that's all.'

'OK, give me an example of why,' Freddie said, holding his arms out beseechingly.

'I don't remember why, OK?' Mollie snapped. 'It was a bloody long time ago and my memory ain't exactly what it was. All I remember is he was bad news and that he weren't liked. That's all.'

Freddie tapped his finger on the table thoughtfully, as she turned her back with a huff and carried on with breakfast. 'You're lying to me, Mum,' he said eventually. 'I just can't figure out why.'

Mollie swung around to face him, frustrated anger flashing behind her eyes. 'Excuse me?' she exclaimed. 'Well, that's nice, ain't it? My eldest son dropping into my house, to my kitchen, just to accuse me of being a bleeding liar.' Her voice rose hotly with every word as her guilt and stress bubbled over. 'Lovely. Thank you *very* much.'

Paul appeared at the doorway, rubbing sleep from his eyes and shooting a look of confusion towards Freddie as he walked straight into their mother seemingly losing the plot.

'What a slap in the face. Well, I'll tell you what…' Mollie turned around and slammed the frying pan she had been about to add bacon to into the sink with a loud clang. 'You want breakfast somewhere you can insult the chef and get away with it, take yourself down the damn café.'

With one last glare at Freddie, she stomped past Paul, up the stairs and into her bedroom, slamming the door shut behind her.

'What the hell was that about?' Paul asked, his jaw dropping. He'd only been awake ten minutes and somehow in that short space of time World War Three had managed to break out in his kitchen.

'Jim Martin.'

'What is it about that guy?' Paul asked.

'I have no idea,' Freddie replied grimly. 'But whatever it is she's hell bent on hiding it.'

Paul turned to stare after his mother, completely stunned. He could count on one hand the times he had seen her lose her temper like that, and most of those had been when they had been outrageous teenagers asking for it. It just didn't happen like that these days. Something was getting to her about Jim Martin. Something very big indeed.

CHAPTER THIRTY-FOUR

Mollie sat on the bed upstairs and forced herself to breathe deeply and slowly until she calmed down. She felt terrible. Terrible for hiding things from Freddie, terrible for screaming at him to distract from the real issue and terrible because she knew she had to deal with Jim and get him away from her family once and for all. But how was she going to do that?

Angrily wiping away the tears of self-pity that had begun to fall, Mollie thought about Jim's demands once more. He wanted five hundred thousand pounds up front. Then a monthly payment, though he hadn't said how much he expected that to be. There was no other choice, she was going to have to pay it. It was the only way to protect her family from the fall-out. It was the only way to protect herself from it too, she finally admitted. She couldn't bear to think of how Freddie would look at her if he knew what had happened all those years ago. He would never see her the same way again. She just couldn't allow that to happen.

The problem was, Mollie didn't have access to that sort of money. She had savings for things like Christmases and birthdays, of course, from the allowance Freddie so generously paid into her account every month. He looked after her financially, had done for years. It was a family business, he always said. She had done her part bringing them up and working all her life, now it was time she benefitted from him doing his part, he insisted. But despite what he sent her being a very comfortable income, it was certainly not going to give her access to half a million pounds in a week.

Thinking over what assets she had, she shook her head help-lessly. There wasn't anything that would bring her even close to what she needed. Mollie wasn't a flashy person, she didn't own much jewellery. A few pieces her children had bought her as gifts were worth something, but not at that level. And besides, they held more sentimental value than anything else. She couldn't bear to part with them. The furniture in the house was decent quality, but again, this wouldn't raise much second-hand. She leaned forward and placed her face in her hands in despair. What was she going to do?

The memory of Jim looking around her house with a calculat-ing sneer popped back into her mind and she sat up.

The house.

Freddie had bought it for her outright. Their local bank manager had gone through all the paperwork with them, moving the house into her name. Freddie had said it was to protect her, should anything ever happen to him or if his assets ever got seized. She wasn't sure of the exact value, but it was a large house in a nice area in London. Surely that could be worth half a million at least?

She sniffed, a sudden ray of hope shining through the darkness that had been looming over her. If she could remortgage the house and get the money that way, Freddie need never be any the wiser. She wasn't that old, still of an age where a mortgage application should be accepted. And although she didn't work, she could prove she had a regular income from Freddie, a very comfortable one. She was sure she'd be able to cover the repayments. Standing up, Mollie pulled off her dressing gown and threw it on the bed before pulling open her drawers.

She was going to get dressed, wait for her sons to leave the house and then go down to talk to the bank manager about her options. It was a loss, but it was just money. Family would always be more important than that. Sniffing again, Mollie forced a brighter expression onto her face. It was all going to be OK.

CHAPTER THIRTY-FIVE

Jim stared through the gates that fronted the large family home and whistled in appreciation. The house itself was set back beyond a large drive, which housed three very uneconomical-looking cars. The double front door was set between two wide windows which stretched along the ample length of the property, and and cameras seemed to be dotted everywhere, covering every square inch. Clearly, Sophia's husband hadn't done too badly for himself.

He'd heard tales of Aleksei and of course had picked up that he was dead, after eavesdropping on Sophia and Freddie's conversation. But that and the fact he had been a Russian mobster was all he really knew for sure so far. He was curious to find out exactly what Sophia wanted from him.

A buzz sounded and the gates pulled back, allowing him entrance. He nipped through the gap as soon as it was wide enough and walked to the front door which was immediately opened by Ali, the man Sophia kept around as her personal bodyguard.

'Alright, me ol' mucker?' Jim greeted him cheerily.

He was met with a stony expression and a sullen response. 'Through there.' Ali pointed to a large, bright front room. It looked formal, probably not the one the family relaxed in.

'Oh. Cheers.' Jim wandered through and pushed his hands down into his jeans pockets as he awkwardly hovered. He considered sitting down but eyeing the pristine cream sofas he decided not to. He wasn't used to being somewhere this plush. It made him feel out of place.

The sharp taps of Sophia's heels rang through from the hall and he turned to greet her. She swept into the room, again looking as though she'd stepped straight out of the front page of a magazine, dressed in an elegant floating cream trouser suit.

'Jim,' she said with a tight smile. 'I was glad to receive your call.'

'Well, you know.' Jim shrugged. 'Only a fool turns his back when opportunity knocks.'

'Indeed.' Sophia beckoned him to follow her. 'Come with me. We will be more comfortable talking in here.' She disappeared and Jim quickly followed her out across the hall into a room on the opposite side.

The plush carpet was darker in here, to match with the dark wooden furniture that adorned the comfortable home office. Sophia took a seat behind the desk and Jim sat opposite, waiting to hear what she had to say.

'Would you like a drink?' she asked.

'Yeah, go on then. Couldn't say no to a tipple with a gorgeous girl like yourself,' he replied cheerily.

Sophia regarded him across the table. He was an imbecile, that much was clear. The goofy smile on his face – as though being here was some sort of treat – was already getting on her nerves. If one of her own men acted as he did, she would slap them hard around the face and remind them who they were working for. But he was not one of her men and he was potentially of great use, so she would tolerate him for now.

Opening the bottom desk drawer, Sophia rummaged around and pulled out two tumblers followed by a bottle of vodka. She eyed the label and forced an expression of grudging appreciation.

'He may not have had good taste in much else, but with vodka he knew what he was doing,' she said, pouring out two generous measures and handing one over to Jim.

Jim took it with a nod of thanks. 'I don't know,' he said. 'I'd say your husband had pretty good taste by the looks of this place. He definitely had good taste in women, at any rate.' He gave a wink to accompany his compliment, but Sophia's face remained unsmiling. She stared at him icily and Jim began to wonder if he should have just stayed quiet.

'This house was selected and furnished by me, without any input from my husband at all. And as for his taste in women, Aleksei was just one day away from moving me out of this home I created with my own two hands and sending me and my children away to Estonia, so that he could move his whore in to play queen of the castle. But then he died. So…' She pulled a cold half smile. 'Here we are.' Picking up her glass, she tipped it back and drank the clear liquid within.

'Oh.' For the first time since he could remember, Jim was lost for words. 'Jeez.' He blew out his cheeks on a long breath. 'So, no taste then, clearly.'

'Well,' Sophia topped her drink up, 'like I said, he knew his vodka.'

Jim frowned. 'So, his death was a good thing then, for you?' He found himself wondering if Sophia had been the cause of her husband's demise. She seemed more than capable, from what he had surmised so far.

Sophia seemed to consider it for a moment before she answered. 'I wouldn't say a good thing, no.' Her expression softened slightly and she looked down into her drink with a sad smile. 'I was unhappy with this new arrangement, of course. But I had known about Aleksei's preferences for a long time. There was no heartbreak, we had lived as friends for years.' Her eyes wandered to a small frame to the side of the desk. It was a picture of the four of them together, her, Aleksei and their two boys. 'We were close friends and I advised on business matters, behind closed doors. In many ways he was a very good husband.

He was also the father of my children and for that I will always love him. So, whilst yes, it saved me having to leave this home, no, it was not something I would have wanted. Not for Aleksei.' She stared at the picture for a few more moments before turning back to Jim, her expression hardening. 'What his death did mean for us, though, was a sudden lack of security. Without the income from his businesses we cannot live like this forever. Which means the people who killed my husband also put my family at risk of poverty.' Her brown eyes flashed darkly. 'And that is something I will not have. Not now, not ever. We have not come this far to see ourselves downtrodden.' She lifted her head defiantly.

'So, what are you thinking?' Jim asked, not really sure what any of this had to do with him.

'What I am thinking, Jim, is this.' Sophia reached into a small box on the desk and pulled out a slim cigarette. She offered one to Jim, who declined. 'I need the gun-running operation back up and working smoothly. You know of my plans to partner with the Tylers already.' Jim nodded. 'Well, I need that to go ahead. Most of Aleksei's men scattered when he disappeared, leaving me without the manpower I need to carry it out. I need Freddie's men to work with me, to become loyal to me, to believe my loyalties have switched towards them.'

'Right.' Jim shrugged.

'But privately my loyalties are still the same. I need to finish what Aleksei started and take Freddie and Paul out of the equation altogether.' She lit her cigarette.

'What?' Jim asked, surprised by the sudden turn of the conversation.

Sophia's level gaze bored into his. 'I realise that this may seem shocking to you. You might wonder why I would even say this to someone on their payroll. But you are not that loyal, I don't think.'

'Hey!' Jim sat up straight at the insult and his brow furrowed in annoyance.

'Don't take it the wrong way,' Sophia continued. She pushed his untouched glass of vodka towards him. 'I just had my man Ali do a little research on you. You are new to the firm. Not their usual type of recruit and not someone who has had dealings with them before.' She sat back and tilted her head to one side. 'You have no family, no proper home, no life to speak of after you recently left jail. I believe you are just looking for the right opportunity. I think that you are not so much loyal to the Tylers as loyal to the right employer, when you find them. And that is why I am telling you this. Because I have an offer for you. A *real* offer.' Putting her cigarette to her lips she took a deep drag and exhaled the smoke high into the air.

Jim picked up the glass and drank from it, feeling the smooth burn of the vodka slide down his throat. This conversation had become very serious very quickly and he wasn't sure whether he was going to like what Sophia was going to ask of him next. 'Go on then,' he said.

'The Tylers have you on the lower end of their payroll, running errands for them. They don't trust you. Or at least, they have not given you any responsibilities that would indicate that they do. They are just keeping you on a leash.' She watched as Jim's neck flushed pink and he cast his gaze away. 'That is not an employer who values you.' Leaning forward, Sophia filled Jim's glass back up. 'I am going to take the Tylers down one way or another. I'm in no rush, I can bide my time if needs be. But I'd rather not. I would rather have someone on my payroll working with me on the inside, who can help me get the job done quickly.'

'What would you want me to do?' Jim asked, in trepidation.

'I want you to get me information that will help me achieve this end goal. Assist me in the set-up.' She saw the worry fluttering across his face. 'You would not be expected to do it yourself,' she added. 'I do not expect that you are a killer.' The worry began to lessen. 'I just need a plan. And I think if you think hard enough, you can help me come up with that plan, with the knowledge you have of the Tylers, their businesses and personal lives. In return, I will put you on *my* payroll, starting on double what the Tylers currently pay you. You will work for me, ongoing, and if you manage to give me something valuable enough to pull this off well, I will reward you with a percentage of the gun-running profits.' She sat back and crossed her legs.

Jim swallowed, his mouth feeling dry. This was a huge step up for him and the small demon of greed inside him began to feel excited as he calculated how much money he'd be raking in if he took Sophia up on this. But then again, if he did join Sophia, this could all come crashing down around his ears once word got out. He'd been down that road once before and he wasn't sure whether he was more terrified of the idea of doing time again or of being on the wrong side of one of the most violent firms in London.

'What about the fall-out? How do you plan to deal with that?' he asked.

'The way I plan to do this, there will be no fall-out.' Sophia took another slow drag on her cigarette, her eyes not leaving Jim's face. 'I am making all the right noises and all the right moves to show that we are now allies. Technically, it would do me no favours to kill my business partners. So we are going to stage it to look like either an accident or a random attack from someone else. I will be shocked when I hear the news and worried for my own enterprise. I have children, after all.' She smiled sweetly and took one last drag on her cigarette before stubbing it out. 'They would obviously be my only priority. I will be no more a suspect in the Tylers' deaths than the next business partner. The men within the firm will keep to the agreement and will continue the gun-runs. Over time they will come to be working directly for me. That is the idea. I just need a suitable method.'

Jim picked up the refilled vodka glass and downed it once more. If what Sophia was saying was true, he really could have his cake and eat it. She was right about his loyalties. They weren't to the Tyler brothers. They were to the same person they always had been – himself. And if the brothers were out of the way, his blackmail of Mollie would never come back to haunt him. He could get that money off her and help Sophia get what she wanted, meaning he was then in the clear to live wherever and however he wanted with no threat of retribution.

But once more a feeling of wariness came over him. He was a coward at heart, an opportunist who preyed on the weak, not someone who took on the lions of society. He was already treading on dangerous ground, he wasn't sure his nerves could take any more. No, he was better off continuing the game he was already playing and seeing it out safely without the added risk. Half a million pounds hung in the balance.

'It sounds like a grand plan, it really does,' he said, sitting back in his chair, 'but it's not for me. Thanks for the offer and obviously I'll keep that knowledge to meself…' He licked his lips, suddenly realising he probably knew too much for someone who was trying to decline the offer. He began to feel hot under the collar and tugged at it nervously. 'I mean, I don't have any love for the Tylers,' he blustered. 'Like you said yourself, they ain't exactly given me a great position. But I've got my own stuff going on right now, and—'

'Let me make myself a little more clear, Mr Martin,' Sophia cut him off sharply in an icy tone. 'This was not really a request, more an instruction.' She sighed. 'I had hoped this could be agreed pleasantly.' She pinched the bridge of her nose and sighed before looking back at him coldly. 'You *will* be my eyes and ears and you *will* find me a way of getting to the Tylers or I will tell them why you're really here and who you really are.'

Jim blinked and looked taken aback by the sudden turn in the conversation and Sophia's threat. Surely she couldn't know that? No one knew except for him and Mollie.

'Oh please,' Sophia scoffed. 'It really wasn't that hard to find out.' She narrowed her eyes darkly. 'So, do we understand each other?'

She didn't actually know anything about Jim other than the fact he was an oddball hiding something. But she didn't need to know what it was, all she needed to know in order to threaten him into submission was that there was *something* he was hiding. Just watching his face pale as she had threatened to out him to Freddie told her that she had hit the nail on the head.

As the lump of dread settled into his stomach Jim started to nod slowly. He had no idea how she had found out, but he didn't doubt that she would use her knowledge to her advantage if he didn't do as she wanted. And that was something he couldn't afford to risk. 'I accept your offer then, Sophia.' It was the last thing he wanted to do, especially now, but it appeared he was left with no choice.

'Good,' she snapped. 'Now, think. What do you know that might benefit me, Mr Martin?'

He racked his brains trying to think of something to offer her, something to appease the beautiful but terrifying Russian woman who had claimed him as her pawn. As he thought over everything he had seen and heard since being around Freddie, his mind settled on something and he sat up straight.

'I have an idea that might be just what you're looking for…'

CHAPTER THIRTY-SIX

Anna stood with her hands on her hips and stared down at the puddle on the floor, then up at the gaping hole in the plaster of the ceiling of the new restaurant. She raised one neatly arched eyebrow at the maître d' who had called her in. He put his hands up in surrender.

'It wasn't me, I found it like this when I got here,' he blustered.

The arrival of Tanya was heralded by the sharp tapping of her stilettos across the marble floor. 'Gordon Bennett!' she cried, as she saw the damage. 'Well, that's all we need. We've only been open a bleedin' week.' She sighed and stared up into the gaping hole to the assortment of pipes in the abyss above. 'Pass me that table,' she ordered the maître d', pointing at the nearest one. 'Come on, chop chop, we ain't got all day,' she continued, when he looked confused.

He pulled the table over, placing it underneath the hole as Tanya indicated. Anna watched with interest. 'Surely you're not going up there?' she asked.

'I sure am,' Tanya replied chirpily, kicking off her Louboutins. She jumped up on the table and stuck her head up into the void. 'Yep,' she called down. 'Bust pipe. Looks like it's connected to the main but has its own stop valve. I should be able to isolate it and cap it off for now but we'll need it replaced.' She withdrew her head out and pulled a face at the devastated ceiling. 'We'll need to call that nosy plasterer back in too,' she added with a grumble.

'Since when did you become an expert in plumbing?' Anna asked with a smile. Tanya never ceased to surprise her.

'Oh, you'd be amazed at all the skills I've picked up over the years,' she replied. 'The benefits of a colourful dating history.'

Anna threw her head back and laughed as Tanya jumped back down and pushed the table back into place. 'Oh Tanya…' she shook her head and looked around at the mess. 'We'll have to close until it's fixed,' she said reluctantly.

They had sunk a lot of money into this place getting it up to scratch, and although the main purpose of the venture was as a front to launder money, it still wasn't ideal having to shut down so suddenly and so soon. From a marketing perspective it was an absolute nightmare. They were still dependent on the initial boost of attention. It was the latest hot new place to visit and they needed to ride the wave of excitement from food bloggers and local magazines to really cement their place in people's minds. If they shut down now the interest would deflate and the people they relied on to spread the word would move on to the next new opening.

Anna sighed and pursed her lips. She would have to think up something big to draw attention back to the restaurant when it reopened. Pushing her dark hair back off her face she shook it, then turned towards her best friend with a big grin. 'Come on, sod it. Let's call the plumber then crack open a bottle and forget our troubles for a while. We need a good laugh. Have you had any more terrible dates lately? You haven't shared any of your funny stories with me for ages.' She walked behind the bar and reached down into the wine fridge, running her finger along the rows until she found the one she was after.

Tanya slipped her shoes back on and followed Anna to the bar. 'Well…' she said reluctantly, glancing back towards the door. 'I actually have to go sort a few things out. But I could meet up later for that drink, if you're free?'

'Oh, come on,' Anna replied, holding the bottle up to tempt her. 'You know you want to.' She pulled a funny face and Tanya laughed.

'You're right, I do. But Candy has gone off the radar and Josephine's worried about her. I promised I'd go along with her to her flat, check up to see if things are OK. She's meeting me here any minute.'

'Oh.' Anna's eyebrows shot up in surprise. She put the wine back in the fridge. 'I hope she's OK. Candy, I mean. I heard from one of the girls that her boyfriend can be pretty volatile, so if she tries to palm you off just try to check her out for bruises if you can. We may have to sort him.' Her jaw tightened as she thought back to the scruffy, brooding guy who'd picked Candy up a couple of times. She had no time for men who knocked women around to feel better about themselves. Anna herself had been trapped in a violent relationship once, years before. Now, after all she had endured, she couldn't sit by and watch anyone being put through the same. If she ever found proof that the man was beating Candy, she'd make sure he was dealt with and that Candy was free to live her life without fear.

Tanya nodded. 'I'll let you know how it goes.'

The front door opened and Josephine walked into the restaurant, hesitantly. Anna's hands balled up into fists of stress underneath the counter upon seeing her. The resentment that Josephine's very presence ignited in her right now burned strong, and she tried to swallow it down.

Tanya bit her lip, noting the tension that immediately gathered in Anna's shoulders. She noted, too, the tension in Josephine as she approached Anna with caution, and sighed sadly. It was all such a mess. There was an awkward silence as Josephine walked up to them at the bar and Tanya shot her a bright smile. 'OK, are you ready to head over? I've got my car out back.'

'Yeah, 'course.' Josephine looked around at the posh new restaurant, noting all the changes they had made to the place. 'It's really nice in here,' she offered. 'You've made it so beautiful.' She shot Anna a tentative smile. 'Nothing like it was be— um…' She faltered, realising too late that her comment would only serve to remind Anna of her mistakes.

'Nothing like it was before,' Anna finished for her, looking up and meeting her gaze coolly. 'No, it isn't.' She turned pointedly towards Tanya. 'I'll catch up with you later, Tan. Good luck with Candy.'

Without bothering to wait for Tanya's reply, Anna turned and marched towards the back of the restaurant and into the office. When she'd closed the door behind her, she rubbed her face and stared at the reflection in the mirror. A cold face with hard red lips and smoky unforgiving eyes stared back at her and she wondered for a moment where the soft, naïve young woman she had once been had gone. Not that she wanted to be that person anymore, not really. Too much had happened and she had come too far to ever be able to go back now. And that came with hard decisions. Decisions that were not always the right ones.

Had she been right in letting Josephine stay after what she'd done? The feeling of betrayal and anger that came over her whenever Josephine was near was not fading. Perhaps she had been wrong covering her tracks and allowing her to stay. Perhaps it was time to start thinking over alternative futures for her whorehouse madam after all.

CHAPTER THIRTY-SEVEN

Freddie nodded to the receptionist as he walked through the entrance to the large retirement home and she offered him a friendly smile. 'Hello, Mr Tyler, it's been a while since we saw you here last,' she said.

'I know,' he replied in a regretful tone. 'I've been meaning to visit, but life has been hectic.'

In truth, Freddie found it hard to visit Vince these days. The guilt he felt at not being around whilst Vince's mental state had gone downhill ate him up inside. When he had initially got out, Freddie had made the effort to visit once a week, but as the weeks went on, watching Vince had become harder and harder to bear and Freddie's visits had slowed.

Sometimes when he came here, Vince would remember who he was and what they had done over the years. He would be almost feverish in his need to talk about the businesses and old times with Freddie, desperate to cling on to the small window of clarity. Other times Freddie would find him in a state of complete bewilderment, scared and confused, unsure who or where he was. This Vince was sometimes calm and guarded, or sometimes he would lash out violently and try to get away from everyone around him. Most of the time, though, he was stuck in a strange limbo, remembering some things but not others. The frustration this would cause him was painful to observe, as he struggled to place memories that were just out of reach.

'How is he today?' Freddie asked. The receptionist would already know without needing to ask one of the doctors. Vince had made a name for himself the second he arrived here and had cemented himself as a firm favourite with all the female staff.

She tilted her head and twisted her mouth to the side. 'He's OK. It's not a bad day, but it's not a clear one either. He's in and out, but seems pretty calm and happy enough.'

'OK.' Freddie nodded and reached for the pen to sign in. Squiggling his details quickly, he waited to be handed his visitor pass. 'Where will I find him?'

She glanced at the clock. 'He should be in his room around now. Do you want me to take you down?'

'Nah, I'm good. Thanks, Michelle.' Freddie waited for the door to be buzzed open, then strode through and straight down the corridor to Vince's room.

There had been a time when Vince had lived in the open part of this retirement home and could come and go as he pleased, but as his mental state had deteriorated he had been moved to a secure wing for his own safety. It was nice enough and the staff were as pleasant as they came, but it still reminded Freddie of the constraints of prison.

Reaching Vince's door, he knocked and then entered without waiting for a response. The room itself was spacious, one of the larger suites. The bed and the door to the bathroom were on one side and a comfortable lounge area was on the other, with a small breakfast bar with basic facilities. Vince was sitting in one of the armchairs, watching a documentary on a small flatscreen. He turned as Freddie walked in.

'Oh!' he said, his face creasing up into a genuine smile. 'It's you…' He blinked as he tried to pull Freddie's name from the fog in his mind.

'Freddie,' Freddie offered, smiling in return and taking a seat next to his old mentor.

'I know that,' Vince replied with a tut. 'Christ, I haven't quite lost all me marbles yet, son. Only a few of them.' He chuckled with a small shake of his head.

Freddie studied him. Vince was looking old these days. Something he had never really thought of him as, before now. Vince recognised him today though, so that was a good start. Even if he had momentarily struggled with his name.

'So, do ya fancy a drink? I ain't got much here, the bastards won't let me keep anything stronger than PG Tips,' he said, resentfully. 'But I still make a bloody good brew.'

'Nah, I'm alright, mate. I'm afraid this is just a quick business call, today. Need to pick your brains on something.'

'Well, good luck with that,' Vince replied with a crooked smile. 'I'm told there's slim pickings on that front these days.'

Freddie knew his condition bothered Vince much more than he let on. But as always he was fronting it out with jokes and style. That was just his way.

'Jim Martin.' Freddie cut straight to the point. 'Do you remember that name?'

'Jim Martin…' Vince mused for a few moments, his brow furrowing in concentration. 'Who is he? He causing you trouble?'

'He's fresh out the nick from a lifer. Handed himself in for a murder you and Big Dom were being investigated for, years back.'

Vince's brow furrowed more deeply as he tried to remember. Eventually he shook his head. 'I'm sorry, Freddie, it's not coming to me. Oh!' He shook his head as though he suddenly remembered something. 'The tea. I was getting us tea. Hang on.'

Vince stood up and moved to the small breakfast bar, pulling out two mugs and turning on the kettle. Freddie didn't remind him that he'd already turned down the tea. He didn't want to lead Vince into a spiral of confusion, as was so easy to do these days.

'So, how's the family?' Vince asked with his back still turned as he sorted out the tea bags and the milk.

'They're good, thanks,' Freddie replied. 'Mum's a bit off at the moment.'

'Mollie,' Vince butted in with a tone of satisfaction as he remembered her name straight off.

'Yeah. This Jim Martin has her spooked, but she won't say why. I was hoping you might have been able to tell me.'

'Jim Martin?' Vince asked again. 'Who's he then? He giving you trouble?'

Freddie swallowed his disappointment with difficulty. Vince definitely had known Jim, this much he was sure of from what he had already found out. But that no longer mattered. Jim could have been his conjoined twin for the majority of his life and it still wouldn't have made a difference. Those memories had been pulled into the fog of Vince's dementia today and they would not be released, no matter how much Freddie questioned. Jim Martin's effect on Mollie was a mystery that wasn't getting solved today.

'Nah,' he answered. 'It don't matter. Anna's well.' He continued answering Vince's question about family, putting all thoughts of Jim aside. 'She's been busy with a new venture we've got going. A restaurant. I'll have to take you to see it sometime.'

'Oh, yeah, I'd like that,' Vince said enthusiastically.

Freddie knew he'd never be allowed to take him out to the restaurant, but talking normally like this made Vince happy. 'Ethan's doing well at school,' he continued.

'Ethan…' Vince paused and squinted off into the distance.

'My son,' Freddie continued, not missing a beat. 'He's growing into a really smart young lad,' he added with pride. 'Seems every day he's learned something new. Something I'd never known before, anyway.'

'Ethan!' Vince suddenly shouted. Freddie paused and Vince swung around, his eyes wide and intense. He crossed the room and sat back down next to Freddie, leaning in and pulling him towards him. 'It's all dealt with, Freddie,' he said in a low, urgent tone, glancing back over his shoulder towards the closed door. 'It's done.'

'What's done?' Freddie asked with a frown.

'Her. Jules. She's gone. Dealt with.' Vince's hands clutched at Freddie's forearms and squeezed tighter and tighter. Freddie closed his eyes momentarily as Vince finally confirmed what he had suspected for some time. 'I couldn't have her do you over for all that money. She'd have been back for more too, and after how she treated the little mite… Nah.' He shook his head vehemently. 'She had to be dealt with.'

'You had her killed,' Freddie confirmed quietly.

'Did it myself. Some things you have to make sure they're done right,' Vince replied. 'The cheque went to the wind and the car, sad to say, to the bottom of a lake. That had to be done,' he added apologetically. 'But she can't come back to you now. And more importantly, she can't ever come back for your boy. He's yours. Yours and Anna's.'

Freddie nodded sombrely and gripped Vince's hands, gently removing his fingers from his arm. He bit his lip as he tried to find some words, but couldn't. Jules had been a waster, a terribly abusive and neglectful mother and someone who had played the game to fleece him for a lot of money. But much as he'd hated her for all of those things, he still hadn't wanted to see her dead. Because he knew one day he'd have to look into his son's eyes and answer some hard questions. He'd long suspected that she was dead, and that Vince may have had a hand in it. When her cheque was never cashed and he never heard anything from her again it seemed the most logical explanation. But until now he had been able to claim genuine ignorance. That was no longer a luxury he could be grateful for. Not now he knew for sure. He couldn't thank Vince for it, for killing the mother of his child, but he couldn't blame him for it either. Not after all she had done. In the end he decided it was best just to say nothing.

'You know, I could do with a drink,' he said, eventually.

Vince got to his feet. 'Where are my manners?' he asked, slapping his forehead and releasing Freddie's arm. 'Here you are come to see me and I haven't even offered you a drink. What can I get you? There ain't much on offer. Tight bastards don't allow me anything stronger than PG bloody Tips,' he repeated with a humourless chortle.

Freddie looked down at his watch, suddenly desperate to be out of this room with its dark secrets and cruel disease that had stripped his friend of his clarity. 'I'm sorry, Vince, I've just seen the time. I've got to get going.'

'Oh, of course, of course,' Vince replied. 'Business don't sleep. Go on, get off. You've got an empire to run, my son. Where you off to first?'

'Just to the gym. Seamus has a couple of guys…'

'Jim!' Vince interrupted, his face turning hard. 'Jim Martin.'

'Yes?' Freddie paused, his hopes rising.

Vince began to shake his head violently from side to side as he tried to hold on to the flash of clarity that had crossed his mind. 'No. You don't listen to him, boy,' he warned, pointing a finger at Freddie. 'You don't… You just don't… He's gone now.' His expression changed, his eyes turning glassy for a moment before his face cleared into a more resolute expression. 'He won't be talking to no one for a long fucking time, not now. He's taken the rap for Tom Long's death, full confession.'

'He did, Vince, but he's out now,' Freddie said gently. 'What happened between him and my parents?'

'Your parents?' Vince frowned, confused. 'He's gone. No one will ever hear him now, the fucking ponce. And he better hope I forget his name down the line too. Or I'll be sending him further into hell than prison next time, I tell ya.' Vince huffed and turned on his heel, pacing for a few moments before stopping to stare out the window.

Freddie waited for him to continue but he didn't, seemingly lost in thought. 'Vince?' he prompted.

Vince turned and stared at him. 'Sorry, what was I saying?'

'About Jim Martin,' Freddie replied, holding his breath in the hope Vince was still on the same page.

'Jim Martin?' He frowned in confusion and Freddie's heart dropped.

There would be nothing more to glean from Vince today. Perhaps next time, if he managed to catch him on a clearer day. Forcing a smile, Freddie reached into his inner jacket pocket and pulled out a small bottle of whisky. 'Hey, I snuck you in a bottle of your favourite.'

'Oh, you fucking diamond,' Vince said, his smile broadening from ear to ear. 'I can't wait to get some of that down me. Eh, hide it somewhere, will ya? The staff are a little bit cunty. They never let me keep any of the good stuff in here. There's a spot behind the bookcase look, over there.' He pointed.

Freddie walked over. 'Yeah I remember, this is where we put the last lot…' He trailed off as he pulled the bookcase forward and found the last bottle he'd snuck in, still full and with the seal intact. He slipped the new bottle back into his pocket and closed his eyes with sadness as once again the evil of the disease that had gripped his friend's mind hit him with full force.

Pushing the bookcase back, he stood up and gave Vince a swift hug. 'I'll catch you soon. Text me if you need anything, yeah?'

'Will do. Go on, get on with ya,' Vince replied, waving goodbye as Freddie went.

Walking back down the hallway, Freddie ripped off the visitor lanyard irritably. Now he knew that although Jim had taken the fall for Big Dom and Vince, he definitely hadn't been in their good books. He just didn't know why, and that made things even more frustrating. What was Jim hiding? What had he done all those years ago to make the faces he'd gone down for hate him so much? And what exactly about this guy was spooking his mother?

Pulling his phone out of his pocket, Freddie typed out a quick text to the man.

Meet me at the club tomorrow night after closing. Need to discuss some things.

As he hit send his jaw formed a hard line. It was time to solve the puzzle, one way or another.

CHAPTER THIRTY-EIGHT

Josephine ran her thumb across the butter knife to collect the excess jam still glistening and popped it in her mouth, savouring the fruity burst of flavour. Dumping the knife in the sink she picked up the plate of peanut butter and jam sandwiches and took them over to the couch, where she dropped into a comfy position in the corner. She smiled as she took her first bite. It had been ages since she had made one of these. It used to be her go-to food to cheer herself up when she was down, but somewhere along the way she'd forgotten to do simple things like that. As she'd lain in bed the night before, worrying yet again at the state of her world, she had made the decision to start looking after herself again, to start making herself smile. After all, no one else was going to.

The window was open, letting in a cool breeze, and she could just hear the low buzz of the lunchtime activities on the street below over the music playing through her radio. Taking another bite, she nodded, giving herself a mental pat on the back for choosing blueberry jam over strawberry.

It wasn't like she thought a good sandwich was going to take away the stress she was under or the grief and guilt that ran like a silent river underneath her skin on a constant basis. Josephine wasn't naïve enough to believe that. But it was a step in the right direction. If she could build up enough little moments in her life that brought genuine contentment or happiness, maybe eventually she could find a comfortable balance. Maybe she could even one day put everything behind her. She needed to believe that;

needed the positivity of that thought to help her carry on in a forward direction.

Sophia had upset her more than she had initially realised. Her degrading words, the way she had belittled the life Josephine had fought so hard to build for herself had been crushing. She had suffered cruel prejudice before, many times, in her old life. Ignorant biting words, taunts and even harsh beatings from people who couldn't understand why she couldn't just be the man whose body she had been born into. But that had been a long time ago. The memories never left, but they had become nothing more than a thing of the past. Here, in Soho, she was fully accepted for who she really was. She was liked for her unique personality and flamboyance, and as her self-confidence had grown it had been celebrated. To see such nastiness in Sophia's sneering face had been a sharp reminder that not everyone in this world was so forward-thinking and accepting. It was a reminder too that there would always be a Sophia, even when this nightmare was over. Or rather, *if* this nightmare was ever over. They still had no idea what Sophia's next move was going to be or what her overall plan was.

Josephine took another bite of her sandwich and stared out the window. The song on the radio came to an end and the sharp jangle that indicated the local news was starting took over. The dull, serious tone of the newsreader filled the small room and Josephine began to tune out. As she turned to pick up her phone to find something more interesting, her ears pricked up in interest. The name of a road – she was sure she had heard it before. She frowned and tilted her head to listen.

'... *which was set to become a block of flats later this year came down in what was described as a catastrophic accident. No one was hurt at the time with all contractors accounted for, and a few weeks on, the site was given the green light to be cleared. However, this morning, as workers reached some of the deeper levels within the rubble, parts of a crushed human skull was discovered, putting a stop to the clearance and reopening the initial investigation into exactly what happened the night the building came down. Our correspondent Hannah Jackson reports.'*

'Yes, hi, Claire. It's been a busy morning at the site. The police have arrived in force and have cordoned off the area. Forensics have been coming in and out in full suits as they search underneath the rubble. The workers on site are being interviewed and although there has been no comment from the police as yet, it would appear that the possibility of foul play has not been ruled out...'

Josephine felt the blood drain from her face and her jaw dropped in shock as she realised what they were talking about. They had found Aleksei. The events of that night jumped out of her mind and seemed to play out once more in front of her eyes.

She ran, Aleksei caught her and they fell to the floor. His hands tightened around her neck and she picked up the rock.

The rock. Would her DNA be on it?

Aleksei's blood trickling out as she smashed the rock over his head. His hands tightening harder when this didn't stop him. The loud, reverberating bang as Anna fired the gun, and the slump of Aleksei's dead body on top of her. Blood, so much blood going everywhere.

Josephine began to shake, the sandwich dropping from her hand and the plate to the floor with a clatter. They had found him. Or part of him.

Did they already know it was him? Could they tell he had been murdered? Were they on their way over now to arrest her?

Standing up suddenly as fright overwhelmed her, Josephine rushed into the bedroom to throw some clothes on, the mess on the floor completely forgotten. There was no time to lose, she had to go and find Anna and Tanya immediately. And now, more than ever, she couldn't afford to risk discussing it over the phone. They could already be listening. They could already be watching and waiting for an opportunity to trip them all up.

Josephine paused and shivered despite the warmth of the day, as she realised with certainty that if they were taken in for questioning, she would be the first to crack. It would be her who let them down, she knew it. Her emotions were fragile already, it would only take one savvy person to manipulate her and she'd end up a blubbering mess. She'd screw up, forget the story she was supposed to stick to, incriminate them all. And that was not acceptable in their world. When she tripped up – and it was *when*, rather than *if* now – not only would she be sending them all to jail, she'd be signing her own death warrant.

CHAPTER THIRTY-NINE

Anna sat staring at her phone, leaning forward on her elbows, one hand over her mouth, half covering the sombre expression on her face. Things were starting to fall apart. Now that they'd found a portion of Aleksei's skull, it wouldn't be long before they found the rest of him and most likely the bullet from the gun she had used to shoot him. The silver lining was that this alone couldn't be traced back to her. Even if they traced the bullet back to a type of gun, or even to the specific gun itself, it had been one of Aleksei's own illegal imports that Freddie had taken from him. At best, the police would end up going full circle, pointing the finger back at Aleksei's own firm for the shooting, if the bullet was all they had to go on. And the gun would never be found, no matter how hard they looked. It had been meticulously cleaned, weighted and dropped to the bottom of the Thames one cloudy night. No one would ever be able to uncover it from that deep, murky grave. It would lie there for eternity, holding its secrets close.

But of course it wasn't just the gun that could expose them. If their DNA was still floating around and was found, that would place them at the scene with no plausible reason. They had no connections to the site.

Anna rubbed her forehead and closed her eyes, trying to think the situation over from an emotional distance. There was a fairly good chance that their DNA could go undiscovered, even with forensics combing the place. What had been a half-erected building when they were there was now nothing more than rubble following the series of explosions that had brought it down. She had to give Aleksei his due, he had known what he was doing when he rigged the place to blow. And Anna knew from carefully hidden research that the chances of them finding their DNA in burnt rubble were fairly slim. If they had bled all over the place then maybe it would have been a different story, but they'd barely even touched anything in the short time they had been there.

She took a deep breath and sat up straight, trying to focus on this logic. If they were lucky, they might just get through this. *If* they were lucky.

There was a sharp tap on the door and it opened. Sarah Riley walked in with her eyebrows raised in question. It wasn't often she got a call from Anna, let alone one that sounded so urgent.

'Hey. What's up?' she asked, cutting straight to the point. Sarah had never been one for meaningless small talk.

Anna forced a smile and offered Sarah the seat opposite her. 'Drink?' she asked.

'No thanks, I can't stay long. What was it you needed to talk about?'

'No problem, I'll cut straight to it then,' Anna said, lacing her fingers together on the desk between them. 'The building site where they found that skull. It's in your area, if I'm not mistaken. Are you on that case?'

'I can be…' Sarah answered slowly. 'The team is still being worked out. Why?'

'The skull belongs to Aleksei Ivanov,' Anna replied.

Sarah's eyebrows shot up in surprise. Of all the things she had expected to hear today, this had definitely not been one of them. 'Right,' she said eventually. 'And how do you know that?' She frowned. 'No one knew where he went, you've had guys searching for him for months.'

Anna swallowed. 'Sophia told us,' she answered calmly. 'How she knows, I have no idea.' She shrugged dismissively. 'But it was one of the first things she told Freddie when she came looking to partner up on the gun-running.' It wasn't a lie.

Sarah watched Anna hawkishly. She hadn't spent so many years climbing the ranks in the police force for nothing. She picked up on things that no one else would notice. Things that gave people away. It was why she was so good at interrogations. Micro movements and changes in bearing revealed so much more than people ever realised. And although Anna had a good poker face, even she couldn't defy Sarah's years of experience and training. Anna's smile was confident and welcoming, casual too, as though she was in complete control of everything around her. But her body language said otherwise. She sat back in the chair and watching the other woman with curiosity.

'OK,' she said slowly. 'And why are you telling me this? What do you want me to do with that?'

Anna stared levelly at Sarah across the desk, her red lips forming a resolute line. 'I want you to bury it. I want you to make sure that he is never identified and that this gets put in the cold case files as soon as possible.'

Sarah's frown deepened. 'Why?'

'Because,' Anna glanced at a small picture of herself and Freddie which she kept on her desk, 'we need to protect Freddie and Paul. You know as well as I do that Hargreaves is looking for any way to lock them back up again.' She moved her gaze up to meet Sarah's again. 'This is too close to home. If they find out that it's Aleksei – the man who moved in on Soho the second the Tyler brothers were banged up – who's buried beneath the rubble, they will immediately start looking in their direction. Partner that with the fact that Tanya and I then secured Aleksei's club at a very reasonable rate the second he disappeared, and our links to Freddie and Paul, they're going to have the beginnings of a case.'

Anna paused to let it all sink in, realising herself that all she was saying was true. It may not be her real motive, but it was still valid.

Sarah nodded. 'That's true. But you know that burying a murder case isn't exactly that easy. This isn't slipping a stray parking ticket into the bin, this has made the news. People will want answers.'

'Who do we have on payroll at the morgue?' Anna asked.

'Melrose, but I'm not sure how that would help.'

Anna bit the inside of her cheek. 'Could he swap the skull out for one from a John Doe?' she asked.

'What?' Sarah sat upright. 'Jesus, Anna…'

'I'm just shooting round ideas,' she replied, holding her hands up in defence.

Sarah exhaled loudly and shook her head. 'I don't know about that, but…' She twisted her mouth to the side. 'If they haven't run the DNA through the system yet, I could maybe get Melrose to put a dummy sample through. The results would then state that whoever it is isn't on the general database. So long as nothing concrete is found at the scene that could lead us to Aleksei's identity, this would be the fastest route to a dead end.'

'Hmm.' Anna sat back and mulled it over.

'Though I have to say, I'm surprised that this wasn't already being looked into as a major incident or even terror attack,' Sarah continued. 'It's not every day that someone blows up a building.'

'It should have been,' Anna replied. 'But from what I gather from our contacts in the trade, the building company covered it up and reported it as a deliberate demolition. Apparently, their site insurance would be invalidated and they'd be shut down if it ever got out that there was an accident of this magnitude with explosives. The owner could even have faced jail time for negligence. They managed to get on site before the police did and sent them away, claiming they had it all under control.'

It hadn't been easy, casually dropping the site into a conversation with their business partner, Ralph. He owned one of the larger building companies in the area and she knew that if there was any gossip, he'd be in the know. But she'd had to steer the conversation very carefully indeed to get this out of him without her questions appearing odd.

'Well, you seem to know quite a lot actually, considering the news about this only broke this morning,' Sarah remarked, her tone tinged with suspicion.

Anna straightened up and her jaw hardened. 'I've found out all I can and quickly. Because that's what you have to do to stay ahead in this game. The normal rules don't apply to us and you know that. We have to stay one step ahead of the law at all times. If something can be linked to us, it can be the catalyst that brings us down. So I just need this dealt with. Can you help me with that?' She stared across the table at the other woman.

'What does Freddie have to say about all of this?' Sarah asked.

'I haven't discussed it with him,' Anna admitted. 'And I don't intend to. He has enough on his plate, he doesn't need to be bothered by every little thing. That's why I'm here. And the rest of the firm. To put fires out before they truly catch light.'

Sarah rubbed her chin thoughtfully for a few moments before she answered. 'Of course.' She stood up and gave Anna a tight smile. 'I'll find Melrose now and I'll put in a word with Ben that I want to run this case. It shouldn't be a problem.'

'Thank you.' Anna returned the smile and rose to see Sarah out. 'Let me know how things are going.'

'Will do.'

Sarah walked out of the small office and back through the club to the front door. As she exited into the early afternoon sun she turned the conversation over in her mind. Anna wasn't telling her the whole story. There was definitely something she wasn't sharing, something big. But what it could be, she had no idea.

If the firm had taken Aleksei out they would have no reason to keep it from her. Plus, if that were the case, they wouldn't have wasted so much time searching for him. So what could Anna possibly be hiding?

As she walked down the street she decided to file it away for now. Covering up Aleksei's identity would be enough to deal with. The mystery of whatever Anna was hiding could wait until another day.

CHAPTER FORTY

Jim paced the small office at Sophia's house, his shoulders hunched tensely as he gnawed at the skin around his thumb. He had made good on his promise to Sophia. He had handed her the information she needed and had given her the perfect time and place to take Freddie out. It had all just happened so fast that now the nerves were eating away at him. *What if something goes wrong?* But it was such a simple plan that surely it couldn't...

Sophia walked back in, having left him there whilst she went upstairs to change into suitable clothes for the occasion. Instead of one of her usual elegantly glamorous ensembles she was dressed in black jeans and a plain black polo neck. Her hair, usually so softly styled, was scraped back into a severe bun, not one strand out of place. No make-up adorned her face. Not – Jim noted – that she needed it.

'So,' she said, eying him up critically. 'You are sure that these codes have not been changed?'

'Nah,' Jim said, shaking his head. 'They won't have changed.'

'And Freddie should be alone?' she questioned.

'Most likely,' Jim replied. 'But I can't be completely certain.'

When Freddie had texted him the day before, Jim had initially fallen into a state of total panic. Why would the younger man want to speak to him after closing, when everyone had disappeared for the night? Perhaps he had underestimated Mollie, perhaps she had told him after all. Maybe he had gone in too high with his demands and she had considered the fall-out of telling Freddie the truth a lesser price to pay.

But after he thought about it some more, he decided this couldn't be the case. If Freddie knew what he was really up to right now, there was no way he'd just send a casual summons for a chat. He'd have rounded Jim up immediately and would be doling out some serious consequences. The seriousness of the situation had finally sunk in then, as he mulled this over. The game he had been playing was dangerous, and if he wasn't very careful indeed *he* would be the one pushing up the daisies.

Luckily for him Sophia had other plans and these now suited him just fine. Jim was no killer. For all his ducking and diving and dodgy dealings over the years, he drew the line at murder. In truth he didn't have the stomach for it. He was, as his mother would say, all mouth and no trousers. He hadn't ever even considered killing anyone, let alone someone as dangerous as Freddie Tyler. His plan all along had been to bully Mollie into giving him the money, then to disappear into the night. He hadn't wanted the hassle of getting embroiled in anything else. But as much as he hadn't wanted to be pulled into Sophia's game, the fact that she was planning to put an end to the Tylers was definitely a bonus for him. No repercussions to follow him as he made off with the money.

Now, more than ever, Jim needed Sophia to succeed. With this in mind, Jim had swiftly come up with a plan for Sophia to corner Freddie and take him out without being caught, using Freddie's own summons. It was simple, but hopefully effective. Freddie wanted to meet after hours which meant that there wouldn't be anyone around to see or hear what was going on. And Jim, ever watchful for an opportunity, had kept note of the codes he'd seen the men use on the security system for the club.

Sophia looked at the clock on the wall and nodded. 'It is time,' she said. 'Here, put these on.' She chucked a pair of leather gloves in Jim's direction and he caught them clumsily, looking confused. 'Ali and I will take care of things inside, you can drive the car.' She looked him up and down, her gaze resting on his pasty face. He wasn't up to this, she could tell. Usually she would have dropped a weak link like him way before this point, but Jim had been the one to give her the time, place and the details she needed to carry out her task, so she would keep him around. For now.

CHAPTER FORTY-ONE

An hour later, Jim pulled the car into a small side street just down the road from the club. It was the only club on this stretch of road, surrounded by pubs and smaller bars that closed a lot earlier, so once the club had shut for the night there were never many people hanging around. The last reveller had gone, the staff had all shuffled home to their beds and the place was deserted.

Sophia felt a glimmer of excitement as she thought through what she was about to do. Ever since Aleksei had died she had felt a burning need for retribution and tonight she was finally going to get it. Nobody had really understood the strange relationship she and her husband had shared. Those who didn't know his true nature were puzzled by his romantic indifference to his wife and the fact that she seemed at ease with this. Those who knew or suspected Aleksei's preferences were confused by the fact that Sophia was not enraged and hurt by it. The reality of the situation was that she and Aleksei had been best friends and two of a kind. The companionship they shared was special.

She had thought herself to be in love with him once. Indeed, Aleksei had tried his hardest to be a good husband at first. But once she realised that his love for her was not really the right kind and once she had got over the shock and analysed how this made her feel, she discovered that she wasn't devastated. They still had a close bond. They had a happy family and a good life together and neither of them had any intention of changing that. And that was what she really cared about. Not the romance or the sex – if truth was told, Sophia had never been much of a fan of that side of things anyway. She knew she wasn't normal, in that sense. But it was just the way she was built. She was as cold on the inside as the deep Russian snow. And unlike how most men would have felt, Aleksei loved her for it. He admired her cold, analytical mind and her strategic view on life.

The pair of them were as close as two people could be, and when he went off into the night to find his lovers Sophia didn't mind. She knew that when he was finished fulfilling his physical needs he would always come home to her. And they were happy. Or at least they had been until their lives were turned upside down.

Back in Russia Aleksei had been careful to hide who he really was. He'd had to. The other firms he worked alongside were not the tolerant kind. Anybody who was different to them was despised. Skin colour, religion, sexuality – if it didn't fit with their image of what was right, then it was classed as unacceptable. These were dangerous people to be around if you did not fit the bill and so when a competitor had come forward with photos and details and blackmailed Aleksei, they'd had no choice but to leave the country. It had been a choice between that and being burned alive for his secret choices.

They had fled to England with a skeleton of men to start afresh. But that had been when Aleksei had met *her*. Sophia's lip curled as her mind led her back to Josephine. Josephine had been different from the others. Sophia could tell from early on that it was not the same, Josephine wasn't just a booty call to scratch an itch. She wasn't just some toy he wanted to play with for a while before he got bored. Josephine had swiftly become someone he genuinely cared about. He'd begun spending more time with her, more energy on keeping her happy and less time and energy focusing on his family. Sophia had become jealous – not of their romantic connection, but because Josephine was suddenly a competitor for the deeper level of relationship that until this point had belonged only to her.

When Aleksei had come home one night, his face ashen and drawn, and asked to speak to her in his study, she hadn't expected the blow that was about to come. He had told her quietly that he was going to make some changes and that to do this he needed her to move with the boys out of their family home and into a new one he was setting up for them near her family in Estonia. As the words had registered, it had been like a hard slap across the face. She'd fought and they had argued, but in the end Aleksei had stood firm. This was happening and there was nothing more to say about it. Sophia would leave quietly and start a new life – a better one, he assured her – with the boys, and they would each begin living for themselves again. When he had told her Josephine would be moving in, her heart had almost stopped. White-hot ice pierced it and bloodlust like she had never felt before began to flow through her veins. And it had never dissipated.

Despite the fact the move had never happened, Josephine had very nearly ruined her life and taken everything from her. And for that, now that Aleksei was dead, Josephine would pay. *But first*, she reminded herself as her mind wandered, *Freddie Tyler*.

CHAPTER FORTY-TWO

Freddie rolled the empty glass that was on the desk in front of him around and around before checking his watch with a sigh of irritation. Jim was late. The club had been closed for over half an hour and his business was conducted for the evening. All he wanted to do now was go home to his warm bed and Anna. But he needed to talk to Jim first.

As he thought about going home to his girlfriend, Freddie's mind wandered to his son. He hadn't spent much quality time with Ethan over the last week. He made a mental note to organise a day out, just the three of them. If he could get into Anna's diary, of course. She was busier than ever at the moment.

A fresh wave of annoyance washed over him as he checked his watch again and he huffed. The other man was royally taking the piss now. Unlocking his phone, Freddie pinged across a message.

Where are you?

Pushing his phone away, Freddie's gaze swept over his desk as he searched for something to keep himself occupied until Jim decided to finally show up. His eyes rested on a set of blueprints for a new building Ralph Hines wanted to build. He had offered Freddie the chance to partner up on the project, but Freddie hadn't yet found the time to look over the documents properly. He sifted it out of the pile of paperwork that he'd shoved to one side, laid the documents out across the table and settled into the new task.

*

Sophia crept silently through the alleyway leading to the back of the club, hugging the wall where the shadows were at their darkest. She knew from Jim that there was a camera facing down this alley, but that the picture was low-contrast and grainy at night. It meant that when watching the video back later, the most anyone would be able to make out would be a few flickers in the darkness, not anything that would give their identity away. She imagined the Tylers had kept it this way to protect themselves, should they need to hide anything coming in. It was a clever move, but one that could be used against them – as they were about to find out.

She reached the back and allowed Ali to silently pass her to try the door. It was unlocked and Sophia gave him the nod to continue inside. As they slipped indoors out of the night, Sophia felt along the wall until she reached the box she knew to hold the keypad to the security system. Flipping the front open, a series of small blinking lights illuminated the keypad just enough for Sophia to see what she was doing. She punched in the code she had previously memorised and all the lights dimmed to black. The system was now completely offline. The alarm and all the cameras throughout the building were off.

Carefully walking down the hallway, the pair made their way into the main bar where some of the softer lights had been left on, and to the stairs that led up to the office. As they ascended, Sophia counted silently. The seventh step was creaky, Jim had warned her. They skipped this step and continued up without a sound.

As the door to the office came into her line of sight, Sophia's heart rate increased with excitement and her breath caught in her throat. She was so close now. Freddie was just inside that door, waiting for Jim, totally unaware of what was about to happen. With steady fingers she reached into the inside pocket of her black jacket and pulled out her gun. With her free hand she signalled for Ali to hang back. She wanted to be the one to do this. The need to pull the trigger herself was almost a physical pain now, as the rush of adrenalin began to fill her body.

Sophia pulled her black cap further forward over her forehead and took the last few steps to the door. It was slightly ajar, which was perfect. There would be no need to alert Freddie to her presence early by rattling the handle. Taking a deep breath, she exhaled slowly, savouring the moment, revelling in the feeling of power. Then without further ado, she gently pushed it until it silently began to swing open.

Without looking down Sophia pulled the silencer out of another of her pockets. With deft, experienced hands, she screwed it onto the end of the gun and lifted it ready to shoot. She licked her bottom lip, her eyes wide and alert like that of a predator. The bookcase came into view, then the filing cabinets and finally the end of the desk, bathed in the weak, warm glow of light from a desk lamp. Finally, as the door swung wider, he came into view.

Sophia studied him from across the room. She had been so quiet and he was clearly so engrossed in whatever he was doing that he hadn't yet turned around. He sat hunched over the desk, peering over a load of papers with his back to her and the door. There was no one else in the room, she noted. He was alone as she had hoped.

For a moment she considered getting his attention. It would be the icing on the cake to see his face as she ended his life. The great Freddie Tyler was about to be taken down so easily, so simply. Seeing the helplessness play out as he realised he was cornered would warm her for years to come. But the last warning Jim had given her held her back.

Freddie had a closed-circuit camera in this room which was not controlled by the main system. And she would not be able to disable it. In order to stay off it, she would need to shoot from the doorway. And if she let him know what was coming there was the chance that he would shout out her name before the bullet hit its mark. If she was going to continue in this world successfully and without being identified as his killer after he was gone, then this would do her no favours.

She swallowed her disappointment as sense won out and lifted her arm, aiming the gun at the back of his head. She calmed her breathing and let years of training take over. Sophia had always prided herself on the fact that she was a perfect marksman, able to tune the rest of the world out and focus on nothing more than her prey. And today her prey was Freddie Tyler. As she caught her breath Freddie froze, and as he began to turn, alerted too late to the presence behind him, she pulled the trigger.

The muted clap of the gun going off bounced through the room and faded away as the bullet found its mark. His body slumped forward and his shoulder knocked the small lamp off the desk and onto the floor, throwing eerie shadows around the room. The dim lighting made it hard to see at first, but a few moments later Sophia's face broke out into a wide, ecstatic smile and her eyes sparkled with glee as she saw the dark patch of blood begin to seep out of the wound in the back of his skull and down his neck. She didn't need to walk over to check. He was definitely dead. There was no way anyone would survive a direct hit to the head like that. It was over. Freddie Tyler was gone.

Ali held his hand out and Sophia stepped back and handed over the gun. Her body began to shake with elation. She had done it. She had avenged her husband's death – or rather, she was halfway to doing so. Paul was still to be dealt with. But she had overcome the biggest challenge tonight. And it felt amazing.

Freddie Tyler – the man who had run London for so long – was no more a force to be reckoned with. His businesses would crumble, his firm would fall into chaos and London would once more become fair game to those who wished to rise up from the positions they had been forced to stay in. A new day was about to dawn, and although for most life would still go on, it was about to change forever.

CHAPTER FORTY-THREE

Paul exhaled sharply in annoyance as Freddie's phone went to voicemail once more. It was early in the day, but that didn't usually stop his brother from picking up. Chucking his phone on the bed, he set about getting dressed. He'd heard his mother shuffle downstairs just a few minutes before, which meant that there would soon be some strong hot coffee brewing on the side. And he could certainly do with some of that today.

Shrugging on a fresh white shirt – one of the many identical ones he owned, being a creature of habit – Paul walked downstairs, doing up the last few buttons and tucking the tails into his trousers as he reached the kitchen.

'Very smart, as always,' Mollie said chirpily. 'What do you fancy? I've got some black pudding in today. I was at the butcher's yesterday getting me beef joint and he was just putting a fresh lot out. I thought to myself, *I know who'll like a bit of that.*' She grinned at him as he sat down at the large kitchen table.

'Not right now, Mum,' Paul answered tiredly.

'What do you mean, *not right now*? You can't start the day without a bit of breakfast,' she scolded. 'Growing boy like you needs to eat. Breakfast is the most im—'

'Most important meal of the day, I know,' Paul said, cutting her off. 'Not that I'd really class myself as a growing boy any more, Mum, I'm in my thirties.' He pushed a chair out and gestured towards it. 'Sit down. We need to have a chat.'

Mollie paused, her expression suddenly wary. 'A chat about what? This isn't your brother putting you up to this, is it?' she asked, her tone tinged with annoyance. 'Because I've told him—'

'The manager at the bank called me yesterday.' Paul cut straight to the point. 'They're under strict instruction there that if anyone in the family tries to make a big withdrawal, they're to check with us first, you see.'

Mollie paled and her expression turned to one of guilt. 'Wh-why have you set that up?' she stuttered, trying to brazen it out. 'I thought our family trusted each other.'

Paul shook his head sadly. 'It's not about trust. We're at the top of our game and have a lot to lose if someone smart enough decides to make us a target. So this arrangement is to make sure if one of us is ever in a corner being blackmailed and can't talk about it, we're alerted.'

He laced his fingers together and waited as Mollie slowly sat down in the chair he had offered her, her face as white as a sheet. 'So come on, Mum,' he said gently. 'What's going on? Why would you try and mortgage the house?'

Mollie sat there in silence for a moment, aghast. Of course they were watching the family assets, why wouldn't they be? Her sons hadn't risen to the position they were in today by taking their eye off the ball. She squeezed her eyes shut in stress and leaned forward on her hands. What had she done? More importantly, what was she going to do now?

'Does Freddie know?' she whispered eventually between her fingers.

'Not yet,' Paul replied, watching her carefully. 'But I can't keep it from him forever. So you need to tell me what's going on.'

Mollie sat up and leaned back, deep lines of worry etched into her forehead. Paul frowned. His mother looked as though she had aged ten years in the last two minutes. Whatever she was hiding had to be bad. Suddenly, to his horror, Mollie began to cry. Hot tears rolled down her cheeks and shallow sobs rocked her body as she tried and failed to gain control.

'Jesus, Mum!' Paul's eyes widened in shock and he moved forward to pull her into a hug. 'Christ, don't do that.' He squeezed her tight as she clung to him like she never had before. 'Come on.' He rubbed her back. 'It can't be that bad.'

'Oh, but it is, Paul.' Mollie pulled back and sniffed. She wiped the tears from her cheeks with her apron and swallowed hard, forcing herself to get a grip. 'It *is* that bad. And if I tell you, you'll never look at me the same again.' She squeezed away another tear, refusing to give into the fresh wave that threatened to fall. 'And if I tell Freddie…' She shook her head and stared out of the kitchen window, fear shining through her eyes. 'Well, I might just lose him for good.'

Paul felt the cold fingers of fear grip his heart. Mollie was truly beginning to scare him now and he didn't like that one bit. 'Mum,' he said strongly, 'you need to tell me what's going on right now.'

Mollie took a deep breath in and exhaled unhappily. 'OK,' she conceded, her whole demeanour suddenly quiet and defeated. 'About thirty-five years ago…' She paused as Paul's phone began to ring.

Paul pulled the phone out of his pocket and dismissed the call. 'Go on,' he urged.

Before Mollie could continue the phone began to ring again instantly. Paul tutted in annoyance and he warred with his priorities as he looked at the caller ID. It was Bill. For Bill to call this early in the day and so insistently there had to be something up.

'Answer it,' Mollie pushed.

'Alright, one second. Hello?' Paul listened as Bill spoke urgently down the line. 'What?' he uttered, his eyebrows shooting up towards his hairline. He stood up abruptly and his mouth gaped open. 'No…' he whispered. 'No,' he repeated, stronger this time. He shook his head and began to pace.

Mollie strained to listen, worried at her son's response to whatever news he was receiving. She could just make out Bill urging Paul to get to wherever he was as quickly as possible before Paul ended the call. There was a long silence as Paul stared down at the blank screen in his hand. Mollie bit her lip, waiting for him to lead the conversation. Eventually Paul blinked a few times as if seeing more clearly might undo what he had just heard. He turned to his mother.

'Um…' He tailed off and shook his head in disbelief. 'Er, look, um…' He stared off out of the window again, the shock beginning to settle in.

'Paul? What's happened?' Mollie asked, beginning to feel worried.

'I, um…' Paul ran his hands down his face. 'I need to go. I need to… I'll be back later, I'll explain then.' Turning on his heel, he walked out of the kitchen and Mollie stared after him as the front door was opened and then slammed behind him.

She blinked and twisted the bottom of her apron worriedly. *What on earth was going on?*

CHAPTER FORTY-FOUR

The tyres screeched on the tarmac as Paul pulled to a stop outside the back of Ruby Ten. He leaped out of the car, not bothering to lock it as he raced into the building and through to the main club. Terry, the general manager, was standing behind the bar, his face ashen. Paul glanced at him in question.

'Up there, in the office,' he said quietly, pointing towards the stairs.

Paul paused and nodded, trying to collect his thoughts. 'Um… lock the back door.' He cleared his throat gruffly. 'Don't let anyone else in now I'm here until I say otherwise. Did anyone…?'

'No, no.' Terry shook his head. 'I found him. I only came in to let the cleaner in and popped up to grab the staff rota. Lucky I did. I sent the cleaner home, she didn't see nothing.'

'Good.' Paul steeled himself for what he was about to see.

As he walked up the stairs, he felt the disbelief wash over him once more. He couldn't be dead, not really. The thought of that being a genuine reality just didn't seem possible. Not now that it had really happened, anyway. The possibility of any of their deaths was always there hanging over them, in their line of work. They lived and worked in a dangerous world. Not just that, but they were at the top of the food chain, a position coveted by many. A position many people would kill for.

Paul paused as he reached the door to the office and closed his eyes, briefly wishing he didn't have to walk in. Wishing that he didn't have to see what was inside. Because if he walked away now, then he could pretend that everything was OK for just a little while longer. But there was no point. Because it wasn't OK. Things would never be quite the same again. He took a deep breath, straightened up and walked in.

As he entered the room, his eyes were drawn straight to the body slumped over the desk and the lake of blood that had pooled and dried on the floor. He swallowed as his stomach clenched and threatened to eject whatever little was left in it from the night before. It wasn't that he was squeamish. He'd dealt with many a body in his time. But this was different. Because this was someone he cared about.

After a long moment, Paul turned to the two other men in the room and shook his head in defeated sadness. 'What happened?' he asked. 'Who did it?' He glanced back at the desk, misery etched on his face. 'What was Sammy even doing here anyway?'

Freddie exhaled heavily from across the room where he sat in one of the chairs, his shoulders slumped defeatedly as he stared at the body of his best friend. 'He was here running an errand for me,' he answered, his voice quiet and heavy with guilt. 'He was sorting through some files on a potential new job. You know what it's like, one set of documents, no copies, less risk… He was going to go over them then leave them here before he went off to do a recce for me. That's why he's dressed like that.' Freddie gestured towards Sammy. 'He was going to go to Sophia's place and scope her out a bit. She has cameras.'

Paul glanced back at Sammy's body. He was dressed all in black with gloves and a thin black hat covering his bright blond mop of hair. Not that it would have been particularly bright anymore without the hat, Paul realised, looking at the amount of blood that had come from the hole in his head.

Grief washed over him, as he stared down at his friend. Sammy had been like a brother to them since they were kids. He was their oldest friend – Freddie's best friend. He had been with them since the beginning, since before they were rich and infamous.

Sammy had been by their side since they were collecting rubbish off building sites as kids, to help make ends meet. He'd fought beside them in the alleys when bigger boys had fought them over which side of the street they lived on. From the moment they had all met, Sammy had been the most loyal friend and ally they had ever had. He was family. And now he was gone, it felt like someone had ripped off one of their arms.

Paul stepped to the nearest chair and sat down heavily. He wanted to cry. Looking over at Freddie, he could see his brother was barely keeping the tears at bay too.

Bill walked over and squeezed Paul's shoulder in a show of support. 'We don't know who did it or why yet. We still need to work that out. The strange thing is, no one knew he would be here. It was a last-minute arrangement.' Bill shook his head. 'It may have even been a chancer looking to rob the place.'

'Except nothing's been taken,' Freddie interjected.

Paul frowned, trying to make sense of it all and failing. He cast his eyes over again towards Sammy's body before looking away, unable to look for very long and keep a hold on his emotions. 'What do we do now? I mean…' he glanced at Bill and then Freddie, 'we can't exactly call it in. A murder in one of our clubs with a known associate – we can kiss our parole goodbye. They'd have us linked to this in seconds.'

Freddie nodded. 'I know.'

'But we can't just get rid of him either. It's Sammy…' Paul's voice cracked and he paused to clear his throat before continuing. 'If he disappeared he wouldn't be buried, and that – that, er…' He looked down and swallowed hard, shaking his head.

'That don't bear thinking about, you're right,' Bill finished for him, gently.

'That's why we ain't doing either,' Freddie replied. He sat up in his chair and sniffed, before leaning forward and putting his face against his clasped hands. 'We're going to move him.'

The desk phone rang out shrilly, making them all jump in the quiet room. Bill stepped forward and answered it. 'Yeah? Good. Send her up.'

'What do you mean?' Paul asked, looking over at his brother.

'I mean we're going to move him somewhere he'll be found. It will be investigated, of course, but we'll make sure we leave no link to us or here, then the case will just go unsolved. But it means we get his body back and can give him a proper burial like he deserves,' Freddie answered. 'It's risky, but it's better than the alternative.'

Paul blew out his cheeks. 'OK. But how exactly are we going to make sure we properly cover our tracks?'

There was a brief knock at the door before it flew open and Sarah walked in, hands casually pushing down her jacket pockets and a slightly distracted expression that swiftly disappeared as she clocked Sammy. Jumping back, her hands flew out of her pockets and up to her cheeks as her eyes widened in shock.

'*Motherfucker!*' she exclaimed loudly. 'Is that... is that *Sammy*? What the hell happened?' Her eyes darted between the three of them as she waited for answers. 'And you have to be kidding me right now. Tell me I am *not* looking at a dead body in your office, Freddie.'

'Believe me, I wish I could,' he replied.

Sarah leaned forward on her knees and grimaced. When Freddie had called her in citing an emergency she'd expected a number of things, but this had certainly not been one of them. Her gaze roamed the room critically. It was a bad situation. There was blood everywhere.

'Well,' she said eventually. 'You need to tell me that you've got one hell of a plan here, Tyler. Because it's going to take something big for me to keep your head off the block on this one...'

CHAPTER FORTY-FIVE

Anna stared across the lounge at Freddie in shock. Ethan was in his room playing on his Game Boy, much to her relief. Breaking the news that Freddie had just imparted to her was going to be hard. Ethan had grown very close to Sammy, especially whilst Freddie had been in prison. Sammy had made a special effort to take him to places like football practice and out for one-on-one time at least once a week in Freddie's absence. It had shown how true a friend Sammy had been to Freddie, that he had taken such special care of his son during that time. As this thought rested in her mind, her heart broke. He had been such a special friend to them all.

She crossed the room and knelt at Freddie's feet, picking up his hands in hers. 'Freddie, I'm so sorry,' she breathed.

Freddie leaned forward and put his forehead to hers, letting the tears that had been threatening all morning silently fall. 'He was family, you know?' he said, his voice full of pain. 'I just didn't see it coming.'

'No one could have,' Anna replied, putting her hand to his cheek in comfort. 'There was no reason to think anyone would do this. I mean, who would have had beef with Sammy? I think there may be something in what Bill said, that this may have been a break-in gone wrong.'

'But nothing was taken, Anna.' Freddie sat up and wiped the tears from his cheeks, clearing his throat and regathering himself. 'That's what doesn't make sense.' He sighed, tiredly.

'Maybe they got spooked,' she replied. 'Maybe they spooked themselves – guns can be louder than people expect. Perhaps they decided to forget their plan and run, thinking someone would have heard.'

'Maybe…' Freddie didn't sound convinced.

The doorbell sounded and Anna stood up, brushing off her skirt. She leaned down and kissed the top of Freddie's head. Freddie breathed in the sweet floral smell of her hair as it brushed over his face, grateful that she had been at home when he got in. It wasn't often he felt so taken aback, but right now he did and he was glad of the comfort her presence brought him. He rubbed his face as she walked away and grabbed a tighter hold on his emotions. Standing up, Freddie moved into the kitchen and set about making a pot of coffee. Whoever it was at the door he was not about to show them this moment of vulnerability. That was reserved for Anna's eyes only.

Mollie gave Anna a watery smile as the door was opened and bit her lip, her resolve wavering now that she was here.

'Oh, hi, Mollie,' Anna greeted her with a smile and a look of surprise. She hadn't expected to see her today. 'Come in.'

'Hi, Anna.' Mollie stepped inside and took off her jacket, placing it carefully on the same hook she always did. 'Paul said Freddie was heading home for a bit – is he here? I really need to speak to him about something.'

Paul had only flown into the house for a few moments to change his clothes before running back out the door again. He'd seemed distracted and Mollie still hadn't found out what had been said on the phone call that had spooked him so much, but she had at least managed to find out where Freddie was. After Paul had left that morning, Mollie had sat down and thought over things long and hard. She was up against a wall now, and there was no getting out of it. Paul knew that something big was going on and he wouldn't keep it from Freddie for long.

And once Freddie knew, there would be no stopping him. She knew that for certain. He wouldn't give up until he had found out every last detail.

Mollie's worst nightmare was finally coming true. She wanted nothing more than to bury it all back where it had lain all of these years, but whether she liked it or not this was no longer possible. Freddie would soon know one way or another and although the thought of telling him terrified her, she knew that it was the best way for him to find out. So, after hours of attempting to find the right words – and a very large glass of wine – Mollie had worked up the courage to come over. The day she had dreaded for the last few decades was finally here. It was time.

'Yes, he's home,' Anna said, walking back through to the lounge. 'We're just in here. Do you want a drink?' Anna paused and properly looked at Mollie. The older woman looked pale and anxious, unusual for the typically unshakable Mollie Tyler. 'Mollie, are you alright?' Anna frowned. Was it the news about Sammy that had her in such a state? Freddie had said they were keeping things under wraps until they'd had a chance to move him, but perhaps Paul had told her already.

'I'm OK, thank you,' Mollie replied with a slight wobble.

'Mum,' Freddie greeted her with a curt nod. He had gained a grip now and was busy pulling cups out of the cupboard. 'Coffee?'

'No, I um…' Mollie glanced at Anna. 'I need to talk to you about something. It's… well, it's… can we speak alone?'

'Oh, sure.' Anna stepped back and shot them both a quick smile. 'I've got to get ready anyway, I'll leave you to it.'

Freddie frowned as Anna left the room. What could his mother have to say that Anna couldn't be privy to? They shared everything. There were no secrets between them. He watched his mother with curiosity. He was still annoyed with her for clamming up about whatever her issues were with Jim, but then perhaps that's what she'd finally come to talk about.

'Here.' He gestured towards one of the bar stools that stood by the breakfast bar he was currently the other side of. 'Sit down, Mum, take a load off. I've just brewed a fresh pot.' He waited until she had sat down and poured her out a steaming mug. 'So, come on. What's up? You look like you've just walked into the ghost of Hitler or something,' he joked, trying to lighten the mood.

'No, that would have been more pleasant,' Mollie muttered.

'Eh?'

'Nothing. Look…' Mollie leaned her forearms on the breakfast bar and swallowed the dry lump of fear that had formed in her throat. 'There's something you need to know. I had hoped that it was something I would never have to tell you. And, to be clear,' she added, 'I'm not sorry for keeping it from you.'

Freddie's eyebrows furrowed together in a deep frown. 'OK,' he said warily.

Mollie looked up into the face of her eldest son. The son she was the most proud of, if she was honest. Not that she would ever admit her favouritism out loud. He was so handsome, with his dark hair, strong jaw and bright greeny-hazel eyes. Like all of her children, he had the look of her side of the family, the Irish blood in him too strong to be weakened. She loved him so much that sometimes when she looked at him her heart ached. It was both a mother's blessing and curse, the depth of the love felt for one's children. She sent a silent prayer up to the heavens that he didn't turn away from her.

'You wanted to know what my issue is with Jim,' Mollie began, taking a deep breath. 'Well, it all started a very long time ago.'

'When Jim went to prison?' Freddie asked.

'No.' Mollie shook her head. 'A long time before that.' She turned to look out of the window, her eyes glazing over as the memories all came flooding back. 'I was very young. Barely just turned eighteen. Back in those days we grew up a lot later than you young people do today. So I was very naïve.' Mollie's eyes welled up and she blinked the tears away before they could fall. 'I'd just started a job as a secretary in this big office near our estate and felt very grown up and flash. I still lived at home back then and my mum was quite strict when I was at school, but then suddenly I was out of school and earning my own money and finding my feet in the world. I started going out with my mate Linda to the local pub on a weekend. And that was where I met your dad.'

'Yeah?' Freddie smiled. 'You've never really talked about how you guys got together.'

'Well, we didn't get together straight away,' Mollie said, casting her eyes down. She picked up her coffee and took a few sips. 'We became friends at first and started hanging out in a group, a few of us. We had a grand old time together, we did. Then, one Saturday night, someone introduced us all to Jim.' She paused, trying to quell the quiver of resentment in her stomach. 'Looking back now he was always a bit of a wideboy. But to a young girl like me who hadn't seen much of the world, he just seemed… I don't know… Confident, I guess. Sure of himself. Exciting.' She glanced at Freddie. 'He took a shine to me and asked me out for a drink. I was flattered. He was a good-looking bloke back then and no one had ever asked me out before.' She began to twist the coffee cup around on the worktop. 'I started seeing him and at first I felt like I'd won the jackpot. There I was with my posh job and my nights out and this handsome boyfriend… I just thought Linda was jealous when she started trying to warn me off him. But then everyone else started trying to warn me off too. Even Richard.' She smiled sadly. 'I should have listened to him. To all of them. But I didn't.' She closed her eyes and forced herself to continue. 'One day, I realised that something had changed. In me, that is. I was pregnant.'

Freddie blinked and opened his mouth in shock. A cold wave flushed through his body. Where was this story going? He watched his mother's face grow crimson with shame and her body began to slightly shake. He swallowed. 'Go on,' he urged.

'I was scared. I told Jim, assuming that this was something we would both deal with together. I thought he would do the right thing, stand by me, tell me everything was going to be OK. But when I told him he got angry. He told me we were over, that I was no longer of any use to him and that he didn't want to see my face again.' Tears began to fall down Mollie's cheeks as she was forced to relive one of the hardest times of her life. 'I got angry too then. I told him I wasn't going anywhere and that he needed to step up. That it had taken two to get into this position. When I did that, he slapped me round the face, hard.' Her fingers reached up, in a subconscious gesture, to where he had hit her all those years ago. 'I had never been so shocked in my life. No one had ever hit me before. He told me if I ever went to him again or told anyone that the baby was his, he'd punch me in the stomach and make sure it never saw the light of day.'

Freddie swore under his breath, the anger building up inside him like a ball of fire. So many questions swirled round in his head but he forced them down. He needed her to continue. He needed to hear the rest of the story before he could respond. He gripped the edge of the counter top so hard his fingers turned white and waited.

'He also told me that if I told a soul he'd tell my mother I was a whore who slept around and had got knocked up by who-the-hell knew. He knew that she'd throw me out if she found out I was in the family way out of wedlock and that I'd have had nowhere to go. She was a very devout Catholic, your grandmother. After that he walked away and already had the next young girl on his arm by the very next day as if I had never existed. I didn't know what to do. I called into work sick and stopped going out. I couldn't tell anyone, I was too ashamed and scared. Eventually one night I went out for a walk. I needed some fresh air. I ended up walking down to your dad's old gym. He was just coming out as I walked past and came after me. He'd been worried when he hadn't seen me out.' Mollie gave a sad smile. 'I ended up telling him everything. I couldn't help it, I'd bottled it up for far too long. He just sat with me for hours while I cried, that night. He was so angry. He wanted to go straight over and batter Jim for what he'd done, but I couldn't let him. I knew if I let him, Jim would follow through with telling my mum out of spite. And then I'd have been totally screwed.'

For a few long moments Mollie turned silent as she thought back to that awful time. Freddie took a deep breath and exhaled slowly, trying to stay patient with her despite the turmoil this was creating inside his head. *What had happened to the baby?* He needed to know.

'Mum?' he prompted eventually.

'Right, yes.' Mollie cleared her throat. 'I spent the next few months trying to prepare, still hiding the pregnancy. With baggy clothes it wasn't too hard. I went back to work and saved every penny I could, thinking about renting a room somewhere and started buying a few bits here and there. Nothing too big, just things I could hide under my bed. Your dad was by my side the whole time, helping me. The best and most loyal friend I could have ever hoped for. I realised then that he had feelings for me, had done for a long time. I realised, too, that I felt the same. But it was terrible timing, so I said nothing. I mean, how could I declare feelings for him when I was such damaged goods?' Mollie looked down to her hands in her lap and her face flushed an even deeper shade of red. 'But Jim saw me and Richard going about together and saw how happy he made me, even considering my situation. And even though he'd cast me aside, Jim couldn't bear to see me happy. He was a spiteful bastard, even then.' She shook her head and pursed her lips. 'He went to my mum and told her that I was sleeping about and had got pregnant. Didn't mention himself in all this, of course.' Mollie's grey-blue eyes dulled. 'She threw me out that night. Had my bags packed for me when I came home. Never spoke to me again.'

Straightening her back, Mollie sighed. She couldn't bring herself to look up into Freddie's face. 'I found a cheap B & B and holed up there for a while. But one night your dad turned up late, all agitated, asking to speak to me. He told me then that he'd loved me for a long time and that he wanted us to be together. I tried to refuse at first, not wanting to drag him down, but he wasn't having it.' A small half smile lifted the corner of her mouth. 'He said he wanted both me and the baby. That it didn't matter how the baby had come about, what mattered was who was there for it in the long run. Because that's what a real parent is, Freddie, the person who raises it. And that was who he wanted to be, the father of my children. At that point no one knew I was pregnant and we knew even when it did come out that Jim wouldn't ever admit to it being his. So, your dad and I got together and pretended as though Jim had never existed.' Mollie's hands began to shake. 'We found a little house and your dad came home soon after with a ring. We got married quickly, one of the best days of our lives. And…' She swallowed again. 'And when the baby was born, we just told people he had come early. No one ever questioned it. We were so in love by that point. Love's young dream. It was just one of those things as far as people were concerned. Accidental baby, quick marriage…' Mollie trailed off, waiting in dread for the question she knew was coming.

'And the baby's name?' Freddie asked, his voice husky and full of fear.

Mollie forced herself to look up into the horrified eyes of her eldest son. 'Freddie,' she whispered. 'We named him Freddie.'

CHAPTER FORTY-SIX

Tanya strutted down the busy high street and lifted her face to the sun, breathing in the warm summer air. The sickly sweet smell of sun lotion and various perfumes mixed with the smoky essence of the city that always clung to everything it touched. Tanya smiled as it once more reminded her how much she loved where she lived. The busy chatter of stallholders on the market buzzed over the constant hum of traffic and she nodded to one or two of them who recognised and greeted her. She held her new Furla bag close as she quickly nipped across the road between two cars. She had only been to the bank and the post office, not a trip she would usually break out a new Furla for. But she had picked up something very important today too, and for that she'd decided it was worth it.

Sammy was going to be shocked when she dramatically pulled it out to show him later, but then he was going to be very happy with her indeed. She couldn't wait to show him. Pulling out her phone she couldn't help but grin as she wrote out a quick text.

Hey sexy. I have something to show you. Come by my flat when you're done for the night. I'll leave the key under the mat. Get naked…;-p X

Slipping the phone back into her bag she laughed and shook her head. If someone had told her even a few weeks ago that she and Sammy would soon be an item she wouldn't have believed them. But yet here they were. And now she suddenly couldn't work out how they had spent so long getting here. They were perfect for each other. So long as it all worked out, of course. As the thought resettled in her mind the smile faded slightly, but she pushed the worry away. They'd done it now. And there was no point approaching it with such negativity if they wanted it to stand a chance. Holding her head high she shook her long red hair back over her shoulder and marched onwards towards the front door of her building.

The lift doors opened and for a moment her finger hovered over the number for her floor. She and Sammy hadn't officially agreed to tell anyone yet, but keeping it a secret was eating her up inside. She needed an outlet for her happiness or else she was going to explode. She pressed the number for Anna's floor instead and grinned in excitement as the lift doors closed.

Reaching the front door, Tanya breezed through into the flat without bothering to knock. 'Hello?' she called out. 'Anna, you home?'

'In here,' Anna called from the kitchen.

Tanya walked through and shot her friend a dazzling smile, full of the promise of gossip. She laid her bag on the floor by the sofa and joined Anna on one of the stools by the breakfast bar where her friend sat nursing a cup of coffee.

'Do you want one?' Anna asked, gesturing to the half full pot.

'Nah, I'm good.' Tanya straightened up with a little wiggle. 'I've got something to tell you.'

'I've actually got something to tell you, too,' Anna said. She rubbed her forehead tiredly and Tanya suddenly realised how down and drawn she looked.

Her smile dropped into a look of concern. 'Hey, what's up? Are you OK?' Her news could wait if there was something wrong with Anna.

'Yeah, I'm OK…' Anna pulled a sad face. 'But I have some bad news. Terry, the manager at Ruby Ten, he found Sammy this morning, up in the office. He'd been shot at some point in the night.'

'What?' Tanya felt her body grow cold and a wave of ice seemed to wash through her stomach. 'He, um…' She heard her voice shake as she spoke. 'He… where is he? Where was he shot, was it just a flesh wound?' She felt the hope inside her die as she saw the look on Anna's face.

'Tan, he didn't make it,' Anna said softly. 'Sammy's gone.'

'No.' Tanya shook her head. She couldn't believe that this was true. She *wouldn't*. 'No, he's not.' Tears prickled at her eyes and she pulled back away from Anna.

'I'm so sorry, Tan,' Anna said, her own tears forming. 'I know you've known him a long time.'

'No.' Tanya stood up and shook her head once more with a frown. She sniffed and wiped away the stray tear that fell. 'No, he's not gone. Not Sammy. Not him.' He couldn't be gone. They had a future together. She was about to tell Anna all about it, that's why she was here. She shook her head again in disbelief. This couldn't be happening.

Anna looked away. She'd known it would be difficult for Tanya, but she was surprised at the resistance her friend was showing to the news. It was devastating for all of them, but it had happened and they all had to get used to it.

'I'm sorry, Tanya,' she said again. 'The bullet was to the back of the head. He wouldn't have felt it and he didn't see it coming. It doesn't make it any easier, but… at least he didn't suffer. We're all going to miss him.'

Tanya backed up into the lounge and took a couple of deep breaths, placing her hands on her hips as she tried to get her head around what Anna was saying. How could Sammy be dead? He was with her just a couple of days ago, laughing, joking, holding her, kissing her… She closed her eyes as the pain pierced her heart like an arrow.

'Why?' she asked, barely keeping the tears out of her voice. 'Who was it?'

'We don't know yet.' Anna sighed and looked out of the window. 'Listen, just so you know, Freddie has to move him,' she said quietly. 'He couldn't have him found at the club and he couldn't make him disappear otherwise he wouldn't have had a funeral. He's doing it tonight. No one outside the inner circle is to know anything until it's done, so that's between us for now. Mollie, Amy, everyone else is still in the dark. And obviously if you're questioned for any reason, you knew nothing about it…'

Anna's voice blurred away into white noise as Tanya's head spun in horror. They were going to be happy together, her and Sammy. They were going to make a go of it, finally find the peace and happiness in a relationship that neither of them had been able to find before. But now they couldn't do that. Someone had taken all of that from them. Someone had taken away Sammy's future from him entirely. Steady, strong, charismatic Sammy. He was larger than life, always filled the room with his presence even when he was silent. How could he just suddenly be gone?

'…Tanya? Tanya, are you listening to me?'

Tanya focused on Anna and realised her friend was looking at her in confusion. Anna didn't know. Suddenly Tanya knew she couldn't tell her. She couldn't bear the look of sympathy she knew would come next. She needed to be alone, to try and understand why this had happened.

'I need to go,' she muttered, backing away from Anna.

'What?'

'I just… I need to go,' she repeated. Picking up her handbag she turned and fled, hurrying out through the door and down the stairs to her own flat.

With shaking hands, she pulled the keys out of her bag and after dropping them twice managed to open the front door. She quickly closed it behind her and walked through to her kitchen, placing her bag carefully on the side. As she leant forward over the kitchen counter she took a deep breath, then another and another. She could feel it coming, the grief. It was going to overwhelm her at any moment and she wasn't ready for it. She wasn't ready for any of this.

Sammy had been found this morning, which meant he had been killed last night. All day she had been waltzing around with her head in the clouds, dreaming of what their union would bring, making plans, sending him messages, whilst he'd been sat cold and lifeless, with a bullet in his brain. She squeezed her eyes closed and shook her head, feeling so stupid.

As she opened her eyes her gaze landed on the Furla bag standing proud on the side in front of her, and the tears began to fall. She reached into the bag and pulled out the pile of papers she had been so excited about just half an hour before. She stared at them for a moment, thinking back over all the things they said they were going to do together. Things that would never happen now. As the sobs she had been holding at bay finally broke through, she dropped the passport application into the bin, closed the lid and walked away.

CHAPTER FORTY-SEVEN

Jim walked out of the small corner shop on the estate where he currently rented a room and breathed in the air with a broad smile. The stench of bins and weed was as prevalent as ever in the rundown area, but today it didn't bother him. This would not be his home for much longer. Soon he would be able to afford a nice big house somewhere with a view. And hopefully nice and close to a good local pub, he thought cheerily.

Clutching the brown paper bag that held the bottle of whisky he'd just purchased, he began to whistle as he crossed the street. Today was a day for celebration. The information he had passed to Sophia had paid off, which meant not only was she indebted to him, but his biggest potential problem had been exterminated. All he needed to do now was drive home the pressure on Mollie. She would be in a complete state, having just lost her eldest son, but it would make her easier to manipulate if he played his cards right.

The thought of what he had been part of caused a small stab of guilt to pierce his happiness for a moment, but he swiftly shrugged it off. She had always planned to take Freddie out, anyway. His participation made no difference to the outcome, but at least by being involved he benefited from it.

He passed a group of youths and ignored them as they stared him out. One ran off, pushing past him in his haste to get down the alley before him.

'Oi, watch yourself,' Jim yelled, annoyed. He had nearly dropped his whisky, and he hadn't just bought the cheap stuff. No, this time he had splashed out on the top-shelf stuff. He couldn't wait to get home and toast his bright new future.

He wrinkled his nose at the strong smell of urine as he made his way through the narrow alleyway between the buildings and sidestepped a bag of rubbish that had been dumped there and foraged through by a cat or fox at some point. As he reached the end of the alley the youth that had run through appeared up ahead and smiled at him. He frowned as he stepped out onto the pavement beyond.

'What's your game then, ya little—'

But he didn't get time to finish his sentence before the wooden baseball bat that was swung from around the corner caught his head with full force and knocked him unconscious.

The icy water hit his face like a sharp slap, waking him up and making him jump in fright. Crying out in fear and confusion he tried to move his hands but found he couldn't. They were bound behind his back, lashed to whatever it was he was seated on. Jim squeezed his eyes shut and blinked them open a couple of times, trying to clear his vision. It was blurry, partly from the water and partly due to the double vision he was experiencing.

That's right, he remembered as he began to collect his thoughts. *I was knocked out…*

'Oi, what – what's the meaning of this?' he spluttered, trying to keep his eyes open despite the throbbing pain coming from his head.

Was it those kids?

He blinked once or twice more and then squinted as he looked around. He was in some sort of old barn. His heart skipped a beat as he registered this. The Tylers favoured barns, it was well known they had several dotted about for when they didn't want people to hear what was going on. But would Paul really have already found out about his part in Freddie's demise?

Sure enough, as he twisted his head, he clocked Paul. He groaned in dismay, but then his groan turned to a gargling choke as he saw who was with him. It was Freddie. His jaw dropped. How could Freddie be there? Sophia had killed him the night before. She had gone up there, aimed at his head and pulled the trigger. She'd confirmed that he was dead. This didn't make any sense.

Jim's head reeled as he tried to make sense of it all. *What had happened? How had Freddie survived?*

The expression on Freddie's face was murderous and Jim felt a flood of dread wash through him. Putting two and two together he came up with a sharp four as he realised that he wasn't getting out of this barn alive. He started whimpering and tears filled his eyes.

'Oh, don't you dare,' Freddie said with disgust. 'You were ballsy enough to try and blackmail my mum, knowing the possible consequences, so be fucking man enough to take them.'

Jim squeezed his eyes, trying to dispel the tears. So that's why he was here. He tensed his body and tried to think of anything he could possibly say to get out of this, but no matter how hard he wracked his brains he couldn't think of anything. Mollie had told them. Which meant he'd crossed the ultimate line as far as the Tylers would be concerned. He'd gone after their mum. A civilian. An innocent loved one under their protection. There was no coming back from that. He swore under his breath, kicking himself. He hated Mollie in that moment, more than he ever had before. This was all her fault.

Freddie walked towards the man tied in the chair and looked him up and down in disgust. He felt sick to his stomach that this pathetic creature was the man who had fathered him. When the penny had dropped during his conversation with Mollie he'd felt as though his whole world was collapsing. Everything he thought he'd known about himself had been a lie. His dad – his beloved dad – who had raised him in the early years and who he'd idolised, was just a stand-in. It wasn't Richard Tyler's blood running through Freddie's veins, it was this guy's.

He had sat down and listened as Mollie had quickly continued and told him all about the blackmail and how she had tried to mortgage the house in order to keep this from him. At first he had been angry, livid even, that she had kept this a secret for his whole life. He was angry too that she'd been stupid enough to fall for a slimeball like Jim and get herself pregnant. But then as he tried to find the words to throw at her, he thought about everything she had done for him ever since, and although his head was reeling he realised he couldn't blame her. She had just been a young girl in a bad situation and had done the best she could.

Freddie had watched her cry from across the room as he processed everything that this meant, understanding her predicament but unable to go to her and hold her just yet. Then, when she was finished, he told her to go home and that he was going to sort it all out. Family was family, however it had come about. And she was his mum. He'd always have her back.

Clearing his throat, Freddie tried to get his head firmly in the game. However sick he felt, however many questions were swirling around in his brain, he needed to focus on dealing with Jim right now. He stared at the other man, hatred burning through his eyes.

'So, you're the piece of shit that put my mum in the family way and then cast her off,' he stated. Bile rose to the back of his throat and he swallowed it down.

Despite his fear, Jim barked out a small laugh and tried to brazen it out. 'If I'm a piece of shit what does that make you then, *son*? Half piece of shit and half what… slag?'

Freddie jerked forward and smashed his fist into the other man's face with force, knocking both him and the chair over. His nostrils flared as the insult to his mother sent him over the edge.

Paul grabbed his arm. 'Don't let him push you into making this easy for him,' he murmured.

Freddie shrugged Paul off roughly and sniffed, straightening his jacket and pacing up and down to walk it off. As he calmed back down to a simmer he nodded at his brother and Paul tactfully stepped back. This was Freddie's fight.

Jim spat out a mouthful of blood and half a chipped tooth and tried to move from the awkward position he'd landed in. His hands were still tied tightly behind the chair and he was on his side, face pressed uncomfortably down on the ground. He quietly seethed as he heard Paul's words. He was many things but stupid wasn't one of them. After assessing the likelihood of getting out of this alive was zero, he quickly realised his best hope was to rile Freddie into ending him quickly. But it seemed that Paul had sussed out this tactic too.

Holding out hope that Freddie was hot-headed enough to be riled up anyway, he continued. 'Ahh come on, *son*,' he mocked. 'Is this any way to treat your old dad? Not that I ever wanted kids. Nothing but thankless parasites really, aren't they? I wasn't going to be tied down just because your mum was too stupid not to get sprogged up. Nah, I let that oaf Richard take that bullet. Stupid twat that he was.'

Freddie clenched his jaw and, with difficulty, resisted the urge to smash his foot into Jim's face. 'Richard Tyler was ten times the man you could ever hope to be,' he growled. 'You're not fit to wipe the shit off his shoe.'

'Not that he has any need for shoes these days, though, eh?' Jim shot back with a mocking laugh.

Freddie's lip curled and he turned and smashed his foot into Jim's stomach viciously. 'Got a lot to say for a dead man, haven't you?' This time Jim turned quiet and Freddie narrowed his eyes into a hateful glare as he stared down at him. 'Not that you're going to hell just yet. You've got some debts to repay first.' He shook his head. 'You said you were friends with my dad. That was a fucking lie. Why?'

'Ha!' Jim spat. 'Your dad was the bane of my fucking life,' he snarled, finally discarding the mask of lies he'd worn all this time. 'I lost twenty-five years of my life because of him.'

'What do you mean?' Freddie's attention sharpened. Something had always been off about the way Jim had taken that life sentence. He just hadn't been able to put his finger on what it was.

'What I mean,' Jim said, trying to shift into a less uncomfortable position, 'is that *he* was the one who sent me down. I didn't work for Big Dom and Vince. Nah, I was never *good enough* for them,' he said bitterly. 'I was desperate for an in back then, desperate to show them what I could do and earn some real wedge for once. I made out alright on me own, but I could have doubled it overnight working for a firm like theirs. But Richard Tyler was their golden boy. He could do no wrong. When I went asking, he told them not to hire me and they listened. For years I tried, but it was always the same answer. Honestly, you make one fucking mistake with a bird and it never fucking leaves you.' He grunted, finding it difficult to continue talking in the position he was in.

Paul reached down and yanked the wooden chair upright. Jim rocked to one side and then the other before he righted himself in the middle. Blood trickled from his mouth and broken nose, down and off his chin. He looked up at Freddie with eyes bloodshot from age and alcohol and once more Freddie wondered how he could possibly have ever been fathered by this man.

'So one day I decided if I couldn't make money *with* them, I'd make it *off* them.' His bloodstained lips curled into a nasty half smile. 'Richard was set to go up against another boxer who was top of his game. It was rigged, he was set to win it, but the odds at the bookies had swayed people to bet the other way.' He spat out a mouthful of blood to the side. 'I put on several big bets against him, like the rest of the crowd. Then I drugged him with a bunch of muscle relaxants half an hour before the fight. It weren't hard, sneaking into the changing room and lacing his drink. He was busy out the back with you and your mum. She'd brought you kids to watch the great Richard Tyler, *your dad*,' he mocked. 'The drugs kicked in, in the second round. His punches were pathetic and he started swaying all over the place.'

Jim paused to chuckle. 'It was funny as hell. The other guy couldn't exactly just stand back and not take his chance, not with so many people watching. They'd have known it was rigged. He had no choice but to knock him out. I made a lot of money that night, as did a lot of other people. But somehow...' his smile faded and his expression darkened, 'your mum found out. She told Richard and Vince and they took me out to an old warehouse – not much different to this, actually,' he said, looking around at the dark barn. 'They gave me a choice. Not that it was much of a choice,' he growled. 'And that was how I ended up taking the lifer. They stitched me up and took the best years of my fucking life,' he said, his voice rising to a bitter shout. 'So, you want to know why I've got such a grudge against your mum, *that's* why. She stole my life from me. And she damn well owes me. They all do.'

Freddie looked at him, not really seeing the bloodied, angry man in front of him, but seeing Mollie in a whole new light. He remembered that night. He had been excitedly watching in the audience, eating the popcorn he was always allowed as a treat on fight nights and helping to keep an eye on his younger siblings. Richard had suddenly begun to act strangely. Freddie had been worried for his dad, scared he had fallen ill. There had been no celebrating after this fight or even the good-natured commiseration drinks that were the norm after a loss. After this fight Mollie had ushered them home quickly to their beds and hushed conversations had wafted up the stairs through the night as different people came in and out of the house. Now, after all these years, he knew why. Now he also knew why everyone hated

Jim so much and the lack of recognition he'd received for the life sentence finally made sense.

He cocked his head to one side and looked at Jim. 'I really couldn't care less what you think you're owed. Sounds like you were *owed* what you got, to be honest. And you were lucky at that – if I found you pulling that with one of my set-ups you wouldn't have got away with a holiday at Her Majesty's pleasure,' he said, pointing a finger at Jim. He shook his head and began to pace. 'You know, funny enough, your first mistake wasn't abandoning my mum when you found out she was pregnant,' Freddie continued. 'Nah. Not that I condone that, but I guess, like her, you were young and naïve. I don't respect you for that, but I won't take a pound of flesh for it either.'

A pound of flesh? Jim's ears pricked up and he widened his eyes with dread.

'No, your first mistake was slapping her round the face and threatening to punch her in the stomach if she told anyone I was yours.' Freddie walked over to the side of the barn where a multitude of items lay on an old trestle table. He picked up a large, sharp knife. '*That* you're going to pay for with a finger.'

'What?' Jim paled. 'Come on. You want me dead just do it, Freddie.' His eyes darted back and forth between the brothers. Paul stared back at him levelly, no emotion in his face. Freddie seemed more interested in the knife than anything Jim had to say. 'Come on,' he said again, panic beginning to colour his tone. 'Just do it, come on.' His voice rose in panic. He couldn't deal with torture. He didn't have the stomach. 'I've been through enough,' he whined. When Freddie continued to ignore him, he tried to wind him up again. 'Your mum was a slag, would open her legs for anyone, that one. I couldn't wait to be rid of her.' He began throwing all the insults he could think of. 'And – and Richard, he was like a potato on legs for all the brain power that geezer had. Fucking tosser. Come on, Freddie, *do it*!' he roared.

'Nah, I don't think so, Jim,' Freddie replied calmly. He had a tight grip on his emotions now and although rage was fuelling him it was running cold and calculated rather than hot and rash. 'I want you to hurt first,' he said with feeling. 'Really hurt.'

Paul reached down and untied one of Jim's hands from its bindings, then pulled his arm forward and held it at the wrist, tightly. Jim struggled and bucked against Paul, but Paul's grip didn't waver.

'Get off me! Get the fuck off me!' Jim yanked as hard as he could, but the chair just moved closer to Paul rather than his hand coming free. 'No!' he yelled, as Freddie walked over. 'No!'

Freddie prised open Jim's fist and got a good hold on his little finger. 'This,' he spat, 'this is for threatening my mum the first time, when she was at her most vulnerable.' Pressing the sharpened blade down into his finger he gritted his teeth and forced it through the joint connecting it to the hand.

The bloodcurdling scream that escaped Jim's mouth was almost feral as the pain set in. After a few seconds he went quiet and swayed dangerously to one side. The severed finger dropped to the floor and blood began gushing from the open wound. Reaching into his back pocket where he had placed it earlier, Freddie pulled out a cloth. He bunched it up and pressed it tight to Jim's hand.

'Can't have you bleeding out before we finish now, can we?' he asked. 'Now, where were we? Paul, can you recall?'

'That was his first finger for his first crime, Fred,' Paul answered in a matter-of-fact tone.

'Ah, yes.' Freddie turned his stare on Jim once more, his eyes flashing dangerously. 'Your second mistake was turning my nan against my mum. Did you know she went the rest of her life never talking to my mum again? Mum wasn't even invited to her funeral,' Freddie said. 'Eats her up inside, that does. All because of you.' Freddie pointed the bloody knife in Jim's face and the other man flinched away.

'Fr-Freddie,' Jim wailed, trying not to be sick from the pain. 'You've made your point. Please…'

'Please?' Freddie questioned. 'Please what?'

'Please stop. Come on.' Jim groaned. 'I'm your dad, I'm blood. Whatever I've done you can't deny that. How can you do this to blood?' He knew it was a weak argument even as he said it, but it was worth a try.

'*Dad?* You ain't my dad.' Freddie paced a few feet away from him and then turned and came back. 'Richard Tyler was my dad. He was the one who was there for me, who picked me up when I fell over and cheered whenever I won. The one who kept me clean and fed and taught me how to ride a bike. Who taught me how to be a man.' Freddie bit his lip as the grief for the man who raised him rose up from where it always lay, just beneath the surface. He pushed it back down. 'You know I used to think blood meant family. I used to believe blood was thicker than water and all that bollocks. But then over the last few years our family has grown, and I would take a bullet for each and every member of that family. And do you know, barely half of them are actually blood-related.' He nodded to himself. 'Family…' He leaned into Jim's face as he emphasised the word. '*Family* is what you make it.'

Without another word, Freddie grabbed Jim's bloodied hand again, throwing the cloth stemming the blood to one side and grasping the next finger.

Jim began to fight against his captors once more, but again it was no use. Freddie pressed the blade down hard and the sickening crunch of bone being broken was drowned out by Jim's screams. As the second finger dropped, Freddie picked the blood-soaked cloth back up off the floor and pressed it back down, his expression never changing. Jim's screams dulled to heaving sobs as he could no longer contain them.

'Your third, and honestly your most stupid, mistake,' Freddie continued in a deadly tone, 'was coming back here and trying to blackmail my mum.' He shook his head and tutted. 'That was a *big* mistake. I mean, did you really think that we wouldn't find out? What do you take us for? You know who we are. You know also that stealing from her would be stealing directly from us. And that in itself is something we would never allow. Bigger men than you have tried to steal from us and failed. I don't know what made you think you could get away with it. Do you, Paul?'

Paul shook his head. 'It's beyond me, Fred.'

'I'm sorry,' Jim sobbed, spittle and snot mixing with the tears now running freely down his face. 'Please, I'm sorry…'

'You're sorry? I don't think you are, Jim. Not really. I think you're just a fucking coward saying anything he thinks might help him now that he's been caught out. I think that's what you've done your whole life. But it's far too late for that,' Freddie said.

Walking away, Freddie began stripping off his clothes, dropping them one by one into a plastic bag next to the trestle table. Paul yanked Jim's arm back behind him and with deft fingers tied it back up with the other one. Jim cried out as he was moved, half from the pain and half in surprise. *What was happening? Were they stopping?*

Freddie undid a bottle of water as he stood stripped down to his underwear and poured it over his hands to wash away the blood. He stared at Jim, his expression unreadable, as he reached into a gym bag and pulled on some sweats.

Making sure Jim's hands were once again secure, Paul joined Freddie and mirrored the same process. Freddie held the bag open for the last piece of Paul's clothing then dropped it into an old metal drum before lighting a match and letting that drop in after it. After a few seconds the flames began to grow and took hold, licking the sides of the drum as they devoured the contents.

A few beads of sweat formed on Jim's forehead, as the throbbing pain of his lost fingers began to get worse. He closed his eyes, praying to whatever god might listen to put a stop to whatever the

Tylers had in store for him next. But even as he thought this, he knew it was no use. Nobody knew he was here. The only person who might question where he was eventually was Sophia, and as far as she was aware Freddie was dead. Even if she did somehow put two and two together, she'd never find the barn and by then it would be far too late anyway. Jim knew when his cards were up. There would be no escaping from this one.

For a moment he wished that he'd just left London when he'd got out after his murder stretch. He wished that he'd just forgiven Mollie and Richard for what had happened all those years ago. He shook his head in self-pity. He should have just left the past in the past and moved on. Revenge never worked out how it was supposed to.

'We have some business to attend to,' Freddie said, rousing Jim from his thoughts. 'You're going to stay here for a few hours. It's getting dark out, so the rats should be out to play soon. And they love the smell of blood.' He smirked coldly. 'So, bleed away. And when I come back, you're going to find out what the punishment is for your third and biggest mistake. I'll leave you guessing for now.'

Freddie hadn't wanted to put a pause on things this way, but then he hadn't planned on having two such pressing issues to deal with in one night. Sammy's body still lay in the office and it needed to be moved. Sarah had come up with a plan, but it involved waiting until dark to get him out. At the time, torturing and disposing of Jim hadn't been on Freddie's to-do list. But perhaps this had ended up working to their advantage, he reasoned eventually. Leaving him to suffer these initial wounds and to worry about what was coming next would cause him much more pain than if Freddie killed him quickly. And after all the other man had done, Freddie wanted to cause him pain. A lot of pain.

Rubbing his head, Freddie felt the weight of what he was about to do push down on him. He was about to go and move his best friend's body. Sammy's body. Sammy was gone. It still didn't feel real. It still didn't make sense.

'Let's go,' he said to Paul. 'There's a lot to do.'

Jim watched them walk out together, the feeling of dread intensifying as the barn fell into heavy silence. Leaning to one side he rolled his arm slightly, trying to ease the agonising pain in his hand. It was the worst pain he had ever felt, shooting all the way up to his elbow. He cried out as the small movements he was making made it worse. Tears filled his eyes and spilled over in fear and self-pity and he began to shake. Hours, they said they were going to leave him here. Hours of this pain lay ahead of him before they came back and finished him off. And he was under no illusion that this wasn't the plan. If he was lucky, all he could hope for was that they finished him off quickly and spared him any further torture.

But as his eyes slid across the barn to the selection of tools they had left on the trestle table, his hope swiftly faded.

CHAPTER FORTY-EIGHT

The club was in darkness, a sign on the door stating that there had been a water leak and that the club would be closed until this had been resolved. As a precaution, Freddie knew, Sarah had broken a small pipe in the ladies' bathroom and allowed it to flood over half of the flooring before turning off the mains. It was no issue, it was only the flooring which would be damaged and this was easily replaceable. Paul had found it a tad extreme, but Freddie understood that it was a necessary precaution. If ever anyone did come snooping around trying to find a connection between Sammy's death and them, they needed to make sure their stories were watertight.

In stark contrast to the eerily silent club, the office was a hive of activity. Freddie and Paul walked in with heavy hearts and grim expressions. Sammy had been moved and now lay on the ground wrapped neatly in several layers of plastic sheeting. Freddie closed his eyes and looked away, unable to stop the stab of guilt and pain that pierced his heart. If he hadn't asked Sammy to look at those plans – if he had just waited to show him the next day – he'd still be here. Who had done this? *Why* had they done this? The questions swam around and around in his mind until he could barely take it any longer. He rubbed his forehead.

The desk had been removed and burned earlier in the day by Dean and Simon, who now sat to one side of the room waiting for everyone to leave before they took up the bloodstained carpet and laid the new one that Simon had waiting outside in his van. They looked drawn and pale and were silent for once, as the weight of what had happened sat as heavily on them as everyone else in the room.

Bill shone a hand-held UV light on the bookcase nearest the desk. He paused as he found what he was looking for, then reached into the bucket full of industrial-strength cleaning products next to him and selected one. He didn't look round as he began to scrub, his jaw set tightly as he continued his methodical in-depth clean-down. Freddie didn't take this as a slight. He knew Bill, like the rest of them, was finding it hard to contain his feelings. It was easier sometimes, just not to interact with people whilst processing something like this.

Sarah was dressed in dark sweats and a hoody like the brothers, ready to go with them to move Sammy. She had organised everything and overseen everyone whilst Freddie and Paul had been busy dealing with Jim. Freddie's first instinct had been to leave Bill in charge, but it was Sarah's plan they were carrying out, so it had made sense to do things this way.

'Are you ready?' Sarah asked, her tone quiet and slightly less abrasive than usual. She knew how much Sammy had meant to Freddie. To all of them.

'Yeah,' Freddie said, clearing his throat. He wasn't ready, not at all. He would never be ready to do this. But there was little choice.

'Freddie?' Simon piped up from the corner of the room.

'Yeah?'

'We don't know who did this yet or how they got in here or even how they knew he was here… Do we need to assume we're all targets?'

It was a good question, one Freddie had been pondering all day. 'I wish I knew. Yeah.' He nodded. 'I think we all need to assume that for now, until we know more. Keep yourselves safe, keep one eye over your shoulders. And stay tooled up,' he added.

Simon and Dean exchanged a look. Freddie had always urged them not to carry weapons unless for a specific reason and to hide them somewhere outside their homes. There had been many a clever criminal who'd got away with murder, only to be sent down for possession of an illegal weapon. It was a rookie error to be caught out that way. If Freddie was warning them to stay armed, that meant he was worried. And that was something no one was used to.

'Look, whoever the fucker is who did this, we're going to find them,' Freddie said, his voice hard. 'And we're going to bury them. Sarah's going to work this on the quiet. So don't worry. Just be careful.'

Simon nodded. Bill paused what he was doing and gave the plastic sheeting that was wrapped around Sammy one long last stare. As he pulled his eyes away, his gaze met Freddie's. The raw misery he saw in Bill's eyes was echoed in his heart and as they broke eye contact again Freddie had to swallow hard to dislodge the lump of grief in his throat.

'Come on,' he muttered to Paul.

Gently, the brothers picked Sammy up, taking one end each awkwardly. The plastic was bound securely by thick tape but Sammy's body had turned rigid with rigor mortis whilst he was still seated at the desk, sprawled forward, and so he was curled over, almost in a foetal position. Without a word, they carefully walked down through the club with Sammy's body and out to the car which was right by the back door. Sarah darted ahead and opened the boot for them, checking the alleyway was still deserted. They slipped Sammy in and Paul winced as the body shifted forward with a dull thud, then they got in and drove off, Sarah following behind in another car.

Driving through the back streets away from the club, Freddie glanced in his rear-view mirror. Sarah was following at a distance. At the next set of traffic lights she would overtake them and lead them to the place she had discussed with them earlier in the day. Freddie gripped the steering wheel tightly in an attempt to stop his hands from shaking, but it didn't work. Having a body in the boot wasn't what was causing him to shake. He wasn't nervous, he'd done this kind of thing more often than he cared to remember. But this was Sammy. It just didn't feel right.

Freddie's gaze flickered sideways at Paul. His brother's expression was a mixture of sadness and anger. This was something he understood. He felt the same. As if feeling his brother's gaze on him, Paul shook his head and began to talk.

'Who the fuck was it, Freddie?'

'I really don't know, mate.' Freddie let Sarah's car pass them and then hung back so that they were not too close in convoy.

'I mean, it's Sammy, for fuck's sake,' Paul continued. 'Sammy had no beef with anyone.'

'That we know of,' Freddie interjected. As sure as he was too that Sammy had no real enemies, he couldn't rule out the possibility.

Paul tutted and brushed this off. 'We knew everything, Fred. Aside from the odd pissed-off customer at the bookies, Sammy didn't have anyone who would want to cause him harm.'

Freddie's thoughts moved back to Bill's suggestion that it could have been a robbery gone wrong. 'We don't know what's happened yet. When we're done tonight Sarah's going to go over the footage again.'

'I still can't believe he turned off the cameras,' Paul said, shaking his head.

'Well, that is what it is,' Freddie answered. They had found the main security system turned off when they arrived, but this made sense. Sammy had been dressed like a cat burglar to go and spy on Sophia for Freddie later that night. Whenever they were dressed for an illicit occasion or were ferrying goods they'd rather not be caught on camera with going through the club, they often turned them off on the way in.

Freddie still had a closed-circuit CCTV camera in the office, though this had not proved to be much assistance. He'd played the footage back earlier that day, hoping to find out who it was, but their faces never came into view. Whoever it was, they'd stopped at the door, aimed and shot. All he could see was the hand holding the gun and a partial section of their black-clad arm for a second before it disappeared again. There wasn't much information to gain from that. The only thing they had ascertained was that Sammy had never seen it coming. Freddie was thankful for this small mercy. At least their friend had not suffered in any way.

Paul sat brooding as Freddie drove, the anger building up inside him like steam inside a pressure cooker. The pain of losing Sammy was eating away at him. How could he not be on this Earth, walking, breathing, just *being*, any more? He couldn't remember a time in their lives when Sammy had not been by their side. Every single week, day in, day out, he was there. But now he suddenly wasn't. As it all overwhelmed him Paul growled and lashed out, punching the glove compartment of the car with force. He pulled his fist back and punched, over and over, roaring in anger at the unfairness of the world.

The plastic underneath the clean-cut leather cracked and the clasp broke under the onslaught. As it dropped, Paul smashed his fist down onto the open door of the compartment and it snapped off, falling to the floor.

Freddie drove on in silence as Paul let it all out. The glove compartment didn't matter. It was just a car. That could be fixed. What couldn't be fixed was their family. Suddenly, all the members of their family who had died for the sake of the firm flashed through his mind and Freddie felt old.

And suddenly, he wasn't sure what really even mattered any more.

CHAPTER FORTY-NINE

Sarah pulled over on the side of the short dead-end road backing onto the edge of Hampstead Heath and got out of the car. She looked up at the clear sky and nodded to herself. There was enough moonlight to see what they were doing, but not so much that it would illuminate them to anyone looking down from the main road. She knew of this secluded little road from a case she had worked on years before. The body of a young girl had been found just a few feet in from the walkway into the heath. The killer had obviously known the area well, as he'd managed to keep off any cameras nearby and he obviously knew that this small bit of road was not overlooked. Large houses stood on either side but the road was flanked by tall trees, blocking the view from the windows, and whilst both sides had CCTV, they were trained to view only inside the treeline, not beyond. She had never found the culprit and the case had turned cold. Something that still didn't sit right with her to this day.

Freddie pulled up behind her and she walked over as the brothers got out of the car with grim expressions. 'I'll scope it out and be back in two secs – wait here,' she ordered.

Shoving her hands down into the large front pocket of her hoody where all the things she'd brought to set the scene jangled around together, she marched into the thick treeline. Just beyond, there was a wide clearing. She peered up and down and squinted, double-checking no one was hiding in the distance. When she was satisfied that they were alone, she jogged back.

'Quickly, come on,' she urged.

As Freddie and Paul pulled Sammy out of the boot, Sarah's heart leaped into her mouth and her pulse began to race. She looked around once more at the trees either side of them. Earlier today she had double-checked that nothing had changed since the last time she'd been down here, but what if she had missed something? What if someone suddenly appeared? Sweat began to form on the back of her neck and she wiped it away, trying not to panic. Freddie and Paul were moving as fast as they could towards the trees with Sammy between them. She glanced back towards the main road. What if someone drove up the road and saw them? What if a *police patrol car* drove up here? Catching her breath, she turned and ran after the brothers, trying to get a hold of herself. She had been working with the Tylers for a long time now, had committed numerous illegal acts to help protect them and cover their tracks. But this was the first time she had ever had to do something like this and the risk factor of what they were doing was high at best.

They broke through the trees into the clearing and Sarah pushed ahead, leading them down the shadowy edge of the treeline towards a larger copse of trees. They covered the ground quickly, none of them wanting to be here any longer than was necessary. Under the cover of the trees, away from the beaten track, Sarah felt slightly better. She breathed out slowly into the night air and turned to Freddie, but as she did so she noticed a pinprick of light bobbing up and down in the distance.

'Get down!' she hissed, her heart jumping up into her mouth. Someone was coming this way. She crouched behind a large fern, ignoring the sharp stone that stabbed at her leg.

Freddie and Paul melted back further into the darkness and quickly knelt down behind two large trees, Sammy still between them. They exchanged a worried glance and then turned to stare at the newcomer as he approached. Whoever it was, he appeared to be running, as the light grew slowly clearer. Freddie squinted, trying to make out who it was in the dark. Calming his racing heart the way he'd taught himself over all the years he'd spent in dangerous situations, he focused on getting through the next few minutes. Next to him, he saw Paul slowly pull a knife from his inner pocket with a grim expression. Freddie's jaw tightened. As much as he didn't like the thought of threatening an innocent bystander, if they were seen they would have no choice. He just hoped it didn't have to come to more than that.

The moon shone down, highlighting the man as he ran down the beaten path. He was dressed in jogging bottoms and a sports top, a sweat band around his head and a wire running from the phone in his hand up to his earphones. The sound of his music carried through the still night air.

Freddie licked his dry lips, not taking his eyes off the man for a second as he drew nearer. The tension in the air was palpable. He was almost at the edge of the treeline when, to everyone's horror, a loud vibrating sound came from where Sarah was crouching. Freddie's heart almost stopped and he turned to her with a furious glare. As quickly as she could and with shaking hands, Sarah reached into her pocket and turned off the phone. She stared back at Freddie with wide, terrified eyes before tearing her gaze back to the runner.

The runner slowed down to a stop right in front of them and for a few moments Freddie was certain that he had heard. But the man never turned to look in their direction, instead scrolling down his phone for another song. He selected his favoured tune and picked up the pace again, turning with the path and eventually disappearing from sight.

'Jesus fucking Christ,' Paul growled at Sarah as they all stood back up.

Freddie exhaled heavily through his nose and shot her a dark look, but decided to drop it. There was no time for pointing fingers and arguing now. The guy had gone, and they needed to hurry up and leave too if they were going to pull this off.

'Why here?' Freddie asked in a whisper, straightening his back before attempting to pick Sammy back up. Sammy had been a muscular hulk of a man. Carrying him was not the easiest task.

'The rocks.' She pointed at a mound of rocks pushing up out of the ground. 'His positioning is too precise to leave him on a flat surface. It will be too obvious he's been moved and they'll start looking for the original murder site. Here...' She pointed at the largest rock, glancing back over her shoulder to make sure the runner hadn't reappeared. 'This is where you need to lay him, face down over it. It should naturally look like they shot him and he landed there. I'm hoping anyway.' She pulled a large pair of scissors out of her front hoody pocket and gave them to Paul. 'Here, get the plastic off.'

As Paul set about doing as she'd asked, Sarah pulled a bottle of dark liquid from the same pocket and Freddie squinted, trying to make out what it was. 'Is that...'

'Blood, yes,' she answered, unscrewing the lid.

'Sammy's?' Freddie asked, frowning. Sarah nodded. 'How did you get that?'

'The rug under your desk was thick, as was the carpet beneath it. There was so much blood that even though a lot of it dried, they were both still wet. I cut through and wrung it out.' She glanced at the bottle and suppressed the grimace the memory brought forth. 'There isn't a lot at all, not enough really. But I'm hoping if I place it to look like most of it was soaked into the mud, this will go unnoticed.'

'Isn't that a bit of a reach?' Freddie asked, his frown deepening. They were pinning a lot on this and he was now worried they'd made a terrible mistake. Perhaps they should have buried Sammy somewhere he would never be found after all. But even as he thought this, he felt a pang of guilt. Sammy would never let him disappear without the funeral and burial site he deserved. And he couldn't do that to Sammy either. No matter what the consequences could be.

Sarah shook her head. 'This is my area. I'll be assigned the case and I'll make sure it's classed as a low priority. He was a known criminal. Officers tend to have less sympathy for those anyway. Plus…' She thought back to the conversation she'd had with Ben, her boss, only the day before, about taking on the Aleksei case. 'My team will be stretched across a couple of large cases, so I can make sure they don't give this one too much time.'

'You'd better be sure about this, Riley,' Freddie warned, his eyes glinting hard under the moonlight.

'I am sure,' she barked back, bristling. It wasn't going to be easy, but she had committed herself to it now. And if things went wrong, she would be going down alongside them. So she would make damn sure they didn't. 'Even if someone does smell something fishy, we've made sure they can't put anything on you. That office is cleaner than a nun's browser history. A damn bloodhound wouldn't be able to find evidence in there now. So, let's just get this done, shall we?'

Shrugging the tension off, Sarah eyed up the rock before pouring the blood where she estimated Sammy's wound would drip, making sure to show it leaking into the ground. As the bottle almost emptied, she turned and splattered the last few drops in another direction. Small blood spatters would be expected, even with a wound as clean as this one. And the wound was very clean. Whoever had shot him had excellent marksmanship.

'Come and lay him here, face down over the rock.'

Freddie and Paul hoisted Sammy up between them and tried not to look at what was left of their once so charismatic friend.

'How long before he's found here, do you think?' Paul asked, trying to focus on anything other than Sammy as they placed him down carefully.

'He'll be found just after dawn,' Sarah replied with a tone of certainty.

'How do you know that?' Freddie asked. 'Have you set someone up to find him?'

'No,' she replied, checking they had laid him just right. 'I just know people run through here in the morning. Had a case nearby once. Hadn't expected anyone to be running through here so late at night though,' she added.

She nodded as the brothers stepped back. She'd been right about the rock – Sammy looked as though he had slumped forward over it naturally. There would be no initial reason to believe he hadn't died here. So long as the blood she had laid was accepted, this would be classed as the murder scene.

People commonly thought that cases like these were uncovered by the most minute detail, found by some geeky-looking forensic when no one else had thought to question things. In truth, if there was no reason to question something like place of death, it wouldn't be questioned. Not deeply anyway. Even DNA wasn't as hard as people thought to keep away from a scene like this. Sammy had been carefully preserved in plastic in the office. No one had touched or breathed too near the body. And the three of them in the woods were covered up from head to toe. Despite the minute or two that Sammy's body had been exposed to these surroundings and moved by the Tylers, they were too well covered for DNA to find its way onto the body. The public watched far too much *CSI*, in her opinion.

'This is all we can do for now,' she said, stepping back and casting a critical eye over Sammy once more. 'We need to go. Your clothes, gloves, shoes, everything needs to be burned tonight. And you need to firm up your alibis,' she added.

As they walked out of the trees, Sarah used a broken branch to brush over where they had walked in case of any noticeable footprints, then looked up to see what had made Freddie pause.

He was staring back at the dark cluster of trees and for a moment under the moonlight she could have sworn she saw a tear form and fall from his eye as he said his silent goodbyes. But as he turned back towards her, she cast her gaze down, knowing better than to ever let him know she had seen.

CHAPTER FIFTY

Freddie rubbed his tired eyes and gulped down the takeaway coffee in the passenger seat as Paul drove them back out of London. It had been the longest and most shit-filled day known to man, so far as Freddie was concerned, and all he wanted now was for it to end. But they were a long way from that happening yet.

After leaving Sammy and parting ways with Sarah, they'd driven to the warehouse where Simon and Dean were burning the office carpet. They had already finished with the desk earlier in the day so all that remained were the metal handles from the drawers. Here the brothers washed down and changed and burned their clothes once more before heading back out.

Paul glanced sideways at Freddie, noting how drawn his brother looked. It was a hard day for them all but especially for Freddie, considering the news Mollie had imparted.

'Fred?'

'Mm?'

'You sure you want to finish him?' Paul asked.

'He tried to blackmail Mum for half a mil, Paul,' Freddie responded. 'No one tries that and gets away with it, not in our family. You know that.'

'Yeah but…'

'But what?' Freddie frowned, irritated.

Paul exhaled slowly through his nose. 'I just mean he's… Well, I don't know.' He shifted uncomfortably in his seat. 'Don't you have questions for him or anything?'

Freddie turned towards Paul, his expression resolute. 'I have nothing to say to or ask of that scumbag. I don't give a shit what part he played in things back then, he never has been and never will be any part of our family.' He turned back to stare out of the window into the darkness. 'You know Dad told Mum that it didn't matter how I came about, what mattered was who raised me. And you know what, he was right. I won't pretend it don't stick me in the gut to know that I don't have his blood in my veins…' Freddie felt the familiar twist in his stomach as he thought about it. 'But he was the one who moulded me into the person I am today. He taught me all the things I needed to become who I am. Mum's still Mum, we're still brothers and our family is still the same family it was yesterday.' He reached into his pocket and pulled out his cigarettes, lighting one up and cracking open the window. 'And that's all there is to it,' he concluded, blowing out a long plume of smoke. 'So that piece of shit in there,' he continued darkly, 'the one who tried to steal from us, who hurt Mum and apparently drugged Dad to make a quick buck – he's going to regret the day he was born.' Freddie's expression clouded over. 'He's going to beg me for death until I finally see ending his life as a fucking kindness.'

Ten minutes later Paul drew the car to a stop outside the dark barn and switched off the engine. He pulled on his gloves, ready for the task ahead. It was clear that Freddie was not in the mood to make this quick, so it was set to be a very long night indeed. He checked his watch. It would only be a few hours before the sun came up. He made a mental note to remind Freddie of this in a little while. They would still need to dispose of Jim's remains. It wouldn't be the most pleasant task, but at least it would be easier than what they had just been through. Placing a body somewhere it would never be found again was oddly a lot easier than placing it somewhere it *would* be found.

Freddie took one last drag on the cigarette in his hand. He'd been chain smoking all evening, another indicator of exactly how stressed he was right now. Exhaling, he flicked the butt to one side and clamped his jaw. He knew that he was letting his emotions get the better of him, drawing out Jim's demise this way. But the thought of being in any way related to a snake like him was eating him up, and after all he had done to Mollie Freddie was ready to make him pay the ultimate price.

It was rare for Freddie to find any pleasure in this side of things. Violence and murder came with the territory, but he wasn't a savage. He did what needed to be done to remain on top and for his family to thrive. It was never done for pleasure. Tonight, though, Freddie wanted to hear every ounce of pain and suffering that he could draw from the creature his mother had once trusted.

Freddie walked over to the barn and pulled the door open, walking a couple of feet in and pausing to allow his eyes to adjust. It was dark outside, but they'd had the moon to guide them. In here, barely any of the moonlight reached the centre of the room where they had set themselves up.

'Did you miss us, Jim?' he taunted, in a low deadly growl.

Reaching into his pocket, he pulled out his phone and switched on the torch. They had a portable camping lamp on the table with their tools, but he needed to be able to find it first before he could switch it on. Shining it over towards the table, he went to locate it, eager to get on.

'What the fuck?' Paul suddenly cried.

'What?' Freddie turned with a frown which quickly deepened as he saw what had caused Paul to curse.

Where Jim should have been sat, still tied to the chair, possibly unconscious from loss of blood, there was no one. The chair was on its side, the ropes that were holding him in a messy pile on the floor and a trail of blood led across the floor and out of the barn the way they had just entered.

'Fuck!' Freddie roared. He bolted to the door and ran outside, frantically searching the immediate area as if Jim might reappear. When this didn't happen he ran his hands through his hair in frustration and turned back to find Paul. 'How the *hell* did he get out of that? I thought you had him held tight?'

'I did!' Paul replied, stressed. 'He shouldn't have been able to get out.' He turned in a circle, looking into the corners desperately as though he might still find Jim hiding in one.

'Fuck.' Freddie slammed his fist into the barn door. '*Fuck!*' he yelled again, his anger echoing into the night.

CHAPTER FIFTY-ONE

Jim leaned back against the cool leather of the back seat of the car and tried to control the shaking. He held his hand upright, the rag too bloodstained to soak up any more. He had lost so much blood at this point, he was amazed he'd made it this far without passing out.

After the brothers had gone, he'd tried to come to terms with what was happening – then he realised there was a bit of give in the rope that held the hand Paul had hastily retied before they'd left. The pain had nearly killed him, but he had wriggled that hand around until eventually, and with great difficulty, he'd managed to pull it free. With the two fingers and thumb remaining on that hand he had worked the knots tying his other hand, then untied his ankles. He'd barely dared to believe it, but he was actually about to escape. Through every second that passed as he worked on the ropes, he expected to hear the brothers return. When they didn't, Jim turned his face to the heavens and thanked God for the first time in his entire life. He'd grabbed his phone and keys from where Paul had slung them and jogged out as fast as his weakened body would allow. It had taken until halfway down the road before he'd found a phone signal and as the little bars on the screen flashed up, he'd placed his call for help.

Sophia turned back to him from the passenger seat and stared critically at the rag covering his hand. 'Did you pick up the fingers?' she asked.

'No, I didn't think,' Jim replied. 'Shit, I should have…' He kicked himself for not thinking of that before he ran away.

'No, it doesn't matter.' Sophia shook her head. 'It is likely too late to reattach them now anyway. We'll go back to mine and then Ali will stitch you up.'

'What?' Jim blinked. 'No, I need a hospital. And painkillers. Morphine, something,' Jim replied in a panic.

'No.' Sophia's tone was harsh. 'You have Ali and vodka. That will do. Now, tell me everything about what happened. What did they say to you?' she urged. 'And who the hell did I shoot, if it wasn't Freddie? Why was he not there himself?'

She still couldn't believe that Freddie was alive. It had been dark, but she had been so sure it was him. He was supposed to have been there.

'It was Sammy, their right-hand man. I think I got the wrong club.' Despite his wounds, Jim's cheeks coloured in embarrassment. 'I think Freddie was waiting for me at his other club.'

'You fool,' she hissed. 'How the hell could you get this so wrong?' Sophia felt rage begin to boil inside her at the man's stupidity.

'I know, I know.' Jim hung his head.

Sophia swallowed her anger and tried to compose herself. Now was not the time to lose her head, there was too much at stake. 'How did they know it was me? How did they realise you had helped me?' she asked. They had picked Jim up so quickly, she must have missed something.

Jim's head shot back up and his gaze met hers. 'Oh, they don't know any of that,' he said, his face brightening slightly. 'This was for something else, something personal. I'll explain all that later, but the good news is that they're still in the dark.' He leaned forward. 'They have no idea we had anything to do with Sammy. Absolutely none at all.'

CHAPTER FIFTY-TWO

Sarah arrived on the scene bright and early, coffee in hand, dressed in her smartest trouser suit and made up to the nines. Today she had taken extra special care to ensure her make-up covered the bags under her eyes. The last thing she needed was someone questioning why she looked so tired.

Dan, the newly promoted DI she had requested as her second-in-command, rushed over to greet her. 'Ma'am,' he said respectfully. 'The forensics are all set up ready to go. The body's over here.'

Sarah felt her insides freeze at the mention of forensics. She calmed herself, remembering the lengths she had gone to to ensure nothing of significance would be found. She forced herself forward, following Dan through to where she could see two people in full white suits cordoning off the area.

'We have an IC1 male, I'd guess somewhere in his early to mid thirties. Gunshot wound to the back of the head,' Dan continued.

'Well, no need to guess at cause of death then,' Sarah replied, taking a sip of her coffee.

'James is on his way in with the camera to take photos to run through the system,' he said, holding the police tape up for his boss to duck under.

Sarah greeted the forensics with a nod. She was familiar with them both – in turn, they were used to working with her and trusted her instincts. *Good*, she thought. The situation was nicely manipulatable.

As she reached the body, she was careful to react in an exaggerated manner, raising her eyebrows and making a sound of surprise. She squinted at Sammy's face again, as if double-checking something.

'Ma'am?' Dan asked, his keen brown eyes darting back and forth between Sarah's face and Sammy's.

Sarah sighed wearily, as if this was the last thing she needed today. 'There's no need to run photos through the system, Dan. This is Samuel Winters. Bookkeeper by day, known associate of several criminal firms by night.' She was cautious to make his criminal association vague rather than tie him directly to the Tylers.

'Oh.' Dan glanced at Sammy again. 'Convictions?' he asked.

'None that stuck,' Sarah replied in what she hoped was a resentful tone. 'But he's been on our radar many times.' She turned and rolled her eyes at one of the forensics. 'Just another mob fall-out, it would seem. And they chose their location well.' She gazed up into the trees. 'All this foliage would no doubt have muffled the sound, especially if they used a silencer.' She knelt down next to Sammy's body and inspected the scene she had laid just hours before. 'Bullet still inside by the looks of it.' She straightened back up. 'I want him moved to autopsy as quickly as possible.'

'OK, I can get some more feet on the ground here to make this quicker…' Dan reached for his phone by Sarah stopped him.

'No. These guys know what they're doing.' She smiled at the forensics. 'See if you can find anything, but I doubt you will. If it's a professional killing, which I'm almost certain it is, they'd have taken precautions. You've seen it before, Mac. If we're going to find anything, it will be on the body.'

The older of the two forensics nodded in agreement and she saw the veil of resignation fall over his eyes. Mac had been on several of her cases where nothing had been found at the scene, so it was a fair assumption. He wouldn't bother looking too hard now, she was sure of it.

'Hey,' she said, as if just realising something. 'Mac, you're on the team over at that building site, right?'

He nodded. 'Yeah, right mess that one is. Going to take weeks to get all the remains together. I heard you were put on it.'

'How much more have you found?' she asked.

'Some bone fragments, clothes. There are tools nearby too. By the looks of what was there the guy could have been the one rigging the place. Might be that he pressed the detonator by mistake before he got out. I never did believe the story the building company told. Who blows a half-built building in the middle of the night?'

Sarah nodded and made a sound of agreement. She'd looked into it, after her conversation with Anna. The owner of the building company had gone to great lengths to cover it up, even spinning an elaborate tale to the client whose building it was, about water pipes and damaged foundations which had forced them to pull it down and start again. He might have even got away with it, had Aleksei not been found by one of the workers clearing the rubble. Now, the owner was in more trouble than he would have been if he'd just been honest in the first place. He'd been arrested the day before and she was due to question him in an hour.

She felt sorry for the guy, if she was honest with herself; he was just an ordinary businessman whose site had been caught up in something that was nothing to do with him. But she knew she had to push these feelings aside. If the worst came to the worst and Aleksei was identified despite her best efforts, she might need to use him as a scapegoat.

'Thanks, Mac. I'll see you over there later this afternoon, yeah?'

'Sure thing,' he replied.

'Come on then, let's go back to the station, get the team together,' Sarah said to Dan, walking back down the beaten path to where she'd left her car. As they reached the mouth of the road, she pointed to the large houses set back behind the trees. 'Go knock and ask about their security cameras before you get in your car,' she instructed. She eyed the treeline in the light of day, checking once more that she hadn't missed anything. 'I doubt they will show anything over here, they appear to be trained on the house and drive, but you never know.'

'Yes, ma'am. Oh, and ma'am?' Dan asked as she unlocked her car.

'Hm?' she turned back towards him with an eyebrow raised in question.

Dan cleared his throat and pulled himself up to his full, rather short, height. 'I just want to say thanks. For the opportunity, I mean.'

Sarah smiled, the first genuine smile she'd given in days. 'This is your first murder case, right?'

'Yeah.' He grinned back, a slight flush colouring his young cheeks. 'I didn't expect to get something so big so quickly, being a new DI. So just wanted to say thanks. And that I won't let you down.'

Sarah forced herself not to laugh. The very fact that he was as wet behind the ears as a new puppy was exactly why she'd requested him on this case. He was the least senior second-in-command she could get away with. It had been just one week since his promotion to DI. He'd follow her lead without question and that was exactly what she needed.

'Oh, I know you won't, Dan,' Sarah said slipping into her car and starting the engine. 'I know you won't.'

CHAPTER FIFTY-THREE

Freddie kicked at the pile of dirty washing on the floor of the small room Jim had been renting. The whole flat was dingy, but this room was the worst. The wallpaper peeled off the tobacco-stained walls and patches of damp were visible in the corners. The smell of the damp permeated the room and the sound of music and people arguing boomed through from the flat next door. 'I wouldn't stay here if someone paid me,' Paul muttered, looking around with disgust.

The bedsheets were rumpled and grubby and half pulled off the mattress, and a rotting apple core had been left on the pillow. Freddie turned away, sickened that anyone could live like this. It didn't cost a thing to keep things clean and tidy.

'It doesn't look like he's been back here,' he said eventually. He rifled through an disorganised pile of papers and magazines on the desk. At the bottom of the pile there was a slim wallet with a zipped top. Freddie looked inside. There was around a hundred pounds in notes and change. It was probably all Jim had left of his weekly wedge. It was highly unlikely he would have forgotten that if he had made a trip back.

Freddie turned back around and put his leather-gloved hands on his hips, perplexed. 'Where the fuck is he?' he wondered aloud.

Paul shook his head. 'Not a clue. He hasn't got any friends or family around here and he hasn't gone to hospital.'

'Unless he checked in under a fake name.'

'Possible,' Paul conceded. 'But the bird on the front desk at the nearest A & E didn't have any recollection of a man missing fingers.' He'd claimed concern for a friend who'd lost fingers in a machinery accident in an attempt to find out if Jim had checked in, but the receptionist had no details of anyone with missing extremities.

'She took quite a shine to you, that one,' Freddie recalled with a chuckle.

Paul grinned. 'Yeah. Shame she ain't my type.' They both laughed.

The smile faded from Paul's face as this reference to the dating world reminded him of his ex, James. He still missed him a lot.

'Come on,' Freddie said. 'There's nothing to be found here.' Jim had very little to his name, as was to be expected of someone who'd just been inside for as long as he had.

As they walked back out of the door, someone quickly pulled back and shot around the corner. Freddie was quick off the mark and chased the eavesdropper down the hall. He swiftly caught up with the skinny young man and grasped the back of his hoody, twisting him round and slamming him up against the wall. He grabbed his neck in a vice-like grip and began to squeeze. The young man struggled helplessly under Freddie's grasp and his eyes widened in panic.

'Who the fuck are you and why were you listening at that door?' Freddie demanded.

'I – I wasn't,' he squeaked.

Freddie pulled him off the wall and slammed him back against it once more, harder this time. 'Try again,' he growled.

'OK, OK!' The man held his hands up in surrender. 'Please, I can't breathe.'

Freddie loosened his grip but still held him firm. 'Start talking.'

'I was just trying to work out if he was coming back soon, that's all.' His thin voice shook in fear. 'This is my flat, he owes me rent.'

With a sigh Freddie dropped him. The man stumbled forward, rubbing his neck. Freddie looked at Paul. 'Another dead end then,' he said resentfully.

'We could try The Black Bear again, see if anyone's heard rumours,' Paul suggested.

'Might as well,' Freddie responded. He doubted there would be anything of value there either, but they didn't have any better ideas. He turned back to the terrified man he had just held against the wall and stared at him menacingly. 'You tell that fucker – if he does come back here – that we're looking for him. And that his days are numbered.'

'Wh-who should I say left the message?' the man stammered.

Freddie's expression darkened as he began to walk away. 'Oh, he'll know,' he called over his shoulder. 'He'll know.'

CHAPTER FIFTY-FOUR

Freddie sat opposite Bill in his usual booth at The Black Bear pub and stared into his pint glass. He still couldn't wrap his head around the fact that Sammy was gone. It still felt as though his best friend was about to walk through the door any minute to join them.

'I um…' Bill sighed unhappily. 'I can go and sort things out at the bookies. I know the system, since I put it in. I can keep things ticking over there until you decide what's to be done long term.'

'Thanks, Bill,' Freddie replied. 'I appreciate it.' He knew he was going to have to sort out a replacement for Sammy there, some sort of manager at least, but he just couldn't think about that yet. Perhaps after the funeral, whenever they were able to get Sammy's body back to do that.

Where usually there would be music playing in the pub, there was just silence, as a mark of respect. Everyone in their world already knew about Sammy, either the truth or the news version of it. His death had been reported a few hours earlier. Apparently, a morning jogger called Jane had been the first to come across him and had decided to extend the fifteen minutes of drama by calling the local news station. It had spread through London's journalist community like wildfire.

Freddie heard the front door of the pub open but didn't bother to turn around. Bill looked up and annoyance flashed across his face. Freddie shot him a questioning look, but Bill turned his gaze away as whoever it was approached their back-corner booth. Freddie turned with a frown.

'Mr Tyler, Mr Hanlon.' Sophia greeted them with relaxed smile. 'How are you both?'

'We've had better days, Ms Ivanov,' Freddie answered. 'What are you doing here? This doesn't strike me as your kind of scene.' He was curious. He couldn't imagine what business she could have in The Black Bear at this time of day, and he hadn't told anyone where he was so she couldn't be here for him.

'I was driving past and noticed your car outside. I thought I would come in and see if you were available to discuss how things are going,' she replied.

Freddie nodded slowly. 'I'm sorry but I won't be conducting any business today. You're welcome to stay for a drink, though.' He knew they still needed to iron out a few small points with regard to the gun-runs, but he couldn't think straight right now. He had enough on his plate with Sammy gone, his killer at large and Jim still out there somewhere. They had wracked their brains for ideas of where to look next, but the truth was the trail had gone oddly cold.

'Is something wrong?' Sophia asked. She cocked her head to one side and her perfectly arched eyebrows furrowed into a frown of concern.

Freddie looked down to the beer mat he was twisting around in his fingers, his tone matter-of-fact, masking his pain. 'One of our men was found dead, up at Hampstead Heath. We need to sort a few things out, but we'll be back to business as usual tomorrow.'

'Oh dear, I'm so sorry to hear that.' Sophia took care to widen her eyes in surprise and to add a note of concern to her tone. 'What happened?'

Freddie looked up and met her gaze, searching her eyes for any sign of possible knowledge. In a situation like this where there was no obvious culprit, he had to consider everyone around them. 'We're not sure yet. He was shot in the back of the head.' He waited to see if there was a reaction. Sophia didn't flinch but she did shake her head in pity. Perhaps being married to Aleksei for so long had numbed her reaction to things like this. It was a reasonable assumption.

'Well, I hope you find out what happened soon. It's not good for enemies to be running around unchecked,' she replied. She twisted her mouth to one side as if thinking about something. 'I'll get Ali to ask around the Russian community, though I doubt it would have had anything to do with them.'

'And why do you doubt that?' Bill chimed in.

'Because, Mr Hanlon, if it were anything to do with us Russians, I would have heard about it.' She smiled sweetly at him, a slight challenge in her eyes. 'Anyway…' She turned her attention back to Freddie. 'I shall leave you in peace.'

'Let's get together over the next few days and we can go over things then,' Freddie offered. The gun-running was a lucrative business for them both. He didn't want to let things slip too much.

'I'll be in touch.' With a smile and a nod, Sophia turned and walked out, Ali following dutifully behind. As she walked, her smile grew. Jim was right. They had absolutely no clue that she had been the one to kill Sammy, nor that she had every intention of making sure Freddie and Paul met the same fate.

Freddie studied Bill's face as the other man watched the pair leave. 'You don't trust her,' he stated.

'Do you?' Bill asked. He waited but Freddie didn't answer. He shook his head with a sigh. 'I don't think getting into bed with the Russians is a good idea at any point, but especially not her.'

'Because of Aleksei?'

'Well, yes, there's that. But there's also just something off about her. She has this way, that…' Bill grimaced, trying to work out how to explain it. 'It's like her reactions are always a second too late. Like she has to work out what emotion to show before she acts it out. It ain't natural.'

Freddie nodded. He knew what Bill meant. He'd seen it before, in his youngest brother, Michael. The brother who had turned out to be a cold-blooded psychopath. But that wasn't necessarily a reason not to work with Sophia. When you lived and worked in the dark, illicit underground world of London, you had to work with all sorts of dangerous or unsavoury people. A certain level of coldness was a good thing in a new business partner, in Freddie's opinion. They had stronger stomachs when times got rough. So this wasn't a deterrent.

'And Sammy,' Bill continued. 'He was shot.'

'And?'

'*And*, who has ample access to a large range of guns?' he asked, leaning in towards Freddie. 'Don't you think it's a little bit suspicious?'

'Anyone can get hold of a gun on the black market, you know that,' Freddie responded.

'Yes, but that don't mean they do. I've been thinking about it. If this was a bodged robbery, they're more likely to have taken knives, right? Statistically speaking, here in London.' Bill leaned back and took a sip of his pint. 'And if it was another firm looking to pay him back for something they wouldn't have done him in your office. They'd have taken him somewhere and we'd have never seen him again.'

Freddie took a sip of his own pint as he thought it over. Bill had a point. It didn't mean it was likely to be Sophia, but there was an element of logic to his argument.

'I don't think it's Sophia. What would she have to gain by taking Sammy out? It makes no sense.' Freddie chewed his bottom lip as he mulled it over. 'Who else would favour a gun, who might have had an issue with Sammy? Or, if your original robbery theory is correct, who would tool up with guns for a late-night break-in?'

'That's just it though, Freddie, I can't think of anyone. And no one has heard anything either.' They fell into silence for a few minutes until Bill changed the subject. 'You got any further with Jim?'

'No,' Freddie said, his expression darkening. 'We've searched everywhere we can think of, but there's nothing. And at the site itself there was a trail of blood that went halfway down the road but then it just stopped. He must have been picked up, but by who we can't work out. He doesn't exactly have a lot of friends.'

'And you're sure there are no cameras anywhere close? Nothing I can look into?' Bill asked, although he already knew the answer.

'No. It's why we bought the damn place,' Freddie responded, pulling a face. 'No one can trail you within two miles of it. And even then, it's patchy.'

'Well, he's got to be somewhere. He can't have just vanished. Especially in his condition, he'll be in agony.'

'Good,' Freddie growled as the hatred he felt for Jim flowed through his veins. 'I wish that cunt the worst pain imaginable whilst he's on the run. And I can assure you, what he's going through now will seem like a happy memory compared to what he's going to suffer when I finally catch up with him.'

CHAPTER FIFTY-FIVE

Sarah peered closer at her laptop screen and squinted. She rewound the footage and watched the brief few seconds that the shooter's arm came into view again. Her finger paused as it played out, then she clicked the back button again several more times. As the arm holding the gun pulled up into view, she hit pause and sat back.

The quality of the footage wasn't the problem, the equipment inside Freddie's office was top-of-the-range. But the room was fairly dark and the only visible part of the shooter was half a forearm and the gun. It could have been a slender man or a woman, the only thing Sarah could safely rule out was someone who was on the heavier side. Whoever it was had dressed in black and the only other thing that Sarah could pick up on was a gold chain bracelet. This didn't give much away, not even the sex of the person wearing it as the style could have been worn by either a man or a woman. There was something about it that was niggling at her though, and had been since she'd spotted it. She was sure she had seen it before somewhere. If only she could remember where.

Frustrated, she stood up, shutting her laptop. Perhaps if she had another coffee she might remember. She opened the door to her office and walked through the main floor towards the kitchen, half listening to the hum of conversations around her as she went. As she passed one of the members of her team it suddenly hit her where she had seen the bracelet before and she stopped dead in the middle of the walkway.

'Ma'am?' Anita asked, tentatively.

'That's it,' Sarah breathed, ignoring Anita entirely. She had figured it out.

Turning on her heel she marched back towards her office, a determined gleam in her eye. She knew who it was, she was almost certain. She just needed to double-check to be sure, before she told Freddie. But as she reached her office she found someone about to knock on the door.

'Ah, there you are,' Mac said with a small smile. 'I need to talk to you about the Samuel Winters case. Have you got a minute?'

Sarah paused, her breath catching in her throat for a second before she composed herself and smiled back. ''Course. Come on in. What's up?'

She opened the door ahead of him and walked around the desk to sit down, waiting patiently until he had closed the door behind him and taken a seat opposite her.

'I've just been going over the samples from the soil that was collected from under the body.' He frowned and scratched his head. 'Something isn't right. There's barely any blood.'

Sarah shifted her weight as her mind raced through her options. 'The shot was pretty clean, right? Bullet still inside? Maybe he wasn't much of a bleeder.'

Mac shook his head. 'The scene still wouldn't be that clean. I think it's been set up. It was cleverly done, I'll give them that,' he admitted. 'But I think we need to begin working on the assumption that this body has been moved.'

Sarah felt her blood run cold and she shifted her weight again as she tried to control her panic. Lacing her fingers together on the desk in front of her, she forced a smile. 'I see,' she said. She swallowed hard and nodded, as if on board with the idea. 'I see,' she repeated.

Mac frowned and his gaze sharpened as he looked at her. Sarah sniffed and sat up straight again, suddenly aware that she must be acting oddly. She sifted through all the options she had that might bury this issue right here and now and realised that there were none.

'Who else knows about this?' she asked. She had an idea and turned it over quickly in her mind. It was a bit close to the mark, but it should buy her some time at least.

'Just us at the moment, I've come straight from the lab. Why?'

Sarah nodded and leaned towards him, lowering her voice. 'Listen,' she said, looking past him out through the glass wall of her office into the main room beyond. 'I need you to keep this between us, just for today.'

'Why?' Mac's frown deepened.

She took a deep breath and exhaled it slowly. 'Samuel Winters was linked to some very high-profile people and I've had suspicions for a while that those particular people have eyes and ears in this very station.'

'What?' Mac responded, his jaw dropping.

'You know the kind of people I'm talking about, don't you?' She eyed him meaningfully. Mac had worked on several cases that involved the larger underground firms in the city. He should be able to connect the dots without her giving up too many details.

'I gather you're talking about one of the ones you and I have worked on trying to bring down over the years. Is this why we've failed so often?' he asked, joining the dots. If any of the mob firms had moles in the force, that would explain why so many of them slipped through their fingers on technicalities and missing evidence.

Sarah nodded sagely. 'If what I suspect is true then we need to tread very carefully with this information. I'll need to talk to Ben personally about how we approach this particular case before this becomes general knowledge. He isn't available today,' she lied, 'but I can get into his office in the morning. Can you keep this between us until then?'

Mac shook his head in disbelief. 'Sure. Tomorrow it is.' He glanced around into the main office, clearly wondering who Sarah suspected as a rat. 'I'll be off then, for now.' He stood up and nodded goodbye, then left the small office and closed the door behind him.

Sarah watched him go, dread settling into the pit of her stomach. As he walked out of sight she reached into her bag and pulled out her second phone. She switched it on and placed a call, waiting impatiently for it to connect.

'We have a problem…'

CHAPTER FIFTY-SIX

Finally finished for the day, Mac cleaned down his workstation in the lab and tidied everything away. He was meticulous in his methods and liked to keep everything in its rightful place, so he never had to lose concentration in order to look for something.

Brian, his lab partner, laughed as he inspected the glass inserts for his microscope. 'If an atom farted, you'd find it,' he joked.

Mac grinned. 'It's always better to be overprepared than underprepared, Brian.' He glanced at his workmate's messy station, papers with scribbled notes strewn across used tools and sample pots. 'I'm surprised you find anything in there,' he added with a laugh.

'Ah, there's method in the madness, Mac. Method in the madness. Anyway, I'll see you tomorrow.'

'Yeah, OK. Have a good night.'

Brian left and Mac took one more look around before walking away with a satisfied nod. He grabbed his brown jacket, hanging by the door, then locked up and walked to his car.

It was takeaway night tonight and it had been his week to choose, so they were having Chinese. He couldn't wait. His wife had put an order in with their favourite restaurant and he would pick it up on the way home, like always. Amber, their daughter, would be waiting excitedly at the table with her hands full of knives and forks – it was her job to set the table, being at the important age of six now. Mac started the car with a smile, imagining the look on her little face when he walked in and handed her the prawn crackers. Amber loved prawn crackers.

He drove home with the radio on, singing tunelessly to Abba as it kicked off the golden classics hour on the local radio show, stopping only to grab the Chinese. Home was just a few minutes away from his lab, so he pulled up on the drive in no time. The Chinese bag rustled as he grabbed it from the passenger seat and closed the car door. As he began walking up the pathway between the drive and the front door there was a small sound in the alley running down the side of the garage. Mac paused and peered into the darkness. The sound came again, closer this time.

'Hello?' he called out. There was silence. A ripple of unease ran up his back and suddenly Mac felt cold, despite the warmth of the evening.

Mac had never been someone who was easily spooked. It was why he was able to do the job he did and still sleep at night. But the conversation he'd had today with Sarah Riley had left him on edge. If there really was a mole within the force reporting back to one of the London mobs, then this undermined everything they stood for. It could jeopardise whole cases and put innocent people at risk. He had always felt safe doing what he did for a living. He wasn't front and centre battling the bad guys like the Sarah Rileys of the force. He was in the background searching through the details, keeping his head down. He had helped bring many a murderer and thief to justice over the years from behind the scenes, then had come home safe in the knowledge that no one knew who he was. But what if now they did? What if whoever was spying on the force for those involved in the Samuel Winters murder had told them who he was and that he was the lead forensic on the case?

Sarah had seemed more than a little on edge when he'd spoken to her about it. And he had never seen that woman's feathers ruffled in all the years he'd served on the force. If she was scared, things must be pretty bad.

Mac stood there, frozen to the spot by the worrying thoughts running through his mind, his gaze trained on the dark mouth of the alley between him and the front door. He had walked past that alley a million times without so much as glancing down it. So why was he so spooked by it now?

Tutting to himself, Mac forced himself forward. The Chinese was getting cold in its bag. If he didn't get it on the table soon, he'd have a very unhappy family on his hands and that wouldn't do. As he reached the mouth of the alley, he forced himself to look forward but as he passed there was a loud clatter and he gasped and jumped back as something hurtled out of the darkness towards him.

The cat hissed as it ran off into the night, irritated that he had spoiled its foray into the bins. Mac grasped his chest with his free hand and laughed.

Light flooded the front garden as the door opened and his wife, Fiona, appeared. 'Mac?' she asked. 'What are you doing? Did you pick up the food?'

'Yes, yes, I've got it,' Mac replied with a wry smile. He walked up to the front door and kissed her on the forehead. 'Sorry, I was just thinking over some work stuff.' He took his jacket off and handed her the bag, as she closed the front door. 'You wouldn't believe what happened today.'

'Oh?' Fiona asked, her smile open and interested.

'Yes,' he replied heavily. 'I should probably wait until Amber is in bed before I tell you though. It's a bit worrying.'

'OK. You have a guest by the way, he's been here about half an hour. I told him you wouldn't be long.' Fiona led the way through to the dining room at the back of the house.

'Oh? Who?' Mac asked, following her through and racking his brain with a frown. He didn't think he was expecting anyone.

'He says he's an old friend from uni,' Fiona replied, opening the door and stepping through ahead of him.

'Uni…?' Mac walked through into the dining room. His next words died on his tongue as he registered the sight that met him. The sight of Freddie Tyler sitting at his dining room table, listening to his six-year-old daughter tell him the names of all her favourite Barbie dolls.

CHAPTER FIFTY-SEVEN

'Mac! So good to see you,' Freddie said enthusiastically, putting on a charming smile. 'I was just telling your lovely wife here that I can't remember the last time I saw you in person.' He cocked his head to one side and stared Mac out with a challenge in his eyes.

Mac closed his gaping mouth and swallowed. 'Yes,' he said. 'It's certainly been a while.' In truth, he could remember exactly when he had last seen Freddie Tyler, and it was not at university. It had been several years before, when he'd been investigating another murder. The Tylers had been in the frame at the time, but they had never been able to pin enough evidence on them to get an arrest. Mac knew enough about the man to know that he was ruthless and ruled the majority of the London underworld with an iron fist. The rumours and tales about him were endless – he was a dark, dangerous legend. But unlike most legends, Freddie Tyler was very much real. And here he was, lying in wait for him in his home. This was not good.

'I'll just pop this in the kitchen,' Fiona said cheerily. 'You'll stay for dinner, won't you, Freddie?' she called over her shoulder as she disappeared.

'Perhaps,' he answered, not taking his eyes off Mac. 'I just need to check something first, Fiona.'

Mac swallowed and edged around the table towards Amber. He caught a glint of amusement in Freddie's eye and his heart began beating hard against his chest, as he gently pulled his precious daughter away from the cold-blooded killer. 'Why don't you go and play upstairs, Amber?' he suggested, trying to keep his tone neutral. For a moment he thought she was going to argue, but as she looked into his face she closed her mouth and nodded as if she somehow understood the severity of the situation. She couldn't have done, of course. But Mac was just thankful that she had agreed. He forced a smile as she gathered her dolls and took them upstairs. She was out of immediate danger now at least, but he was under no illusion that this meant she was safe.

They were now alone and Mac felt like throwing up. Freddie being here could only mean one thing. The eyes and ears Sarah had been talking about had given his personal details up to the Tylers. Which meant, in turn, that they must have been the ones who murdered Samuel Winters and were worried they were about to be uncovered. Freddie was here to make sure that never happened. He suddenly felt hot beneath the collar as the quandary this put him in hit home.

'You know who I am,' Freddie said, his voice low and deadly. It was a statement rather than a question, but Mac nodded just the same. 'Good. Then you'll know what I'm capable of.'

Mac licked his lips. They suddenly felt very dry. 'I do,' he confirmed.

Freddie nodded. He waited a few moments before continuing, allowing the other man's discomfort to grow. He knew that his mere presence here was enough to scare the life out of a man like Mac. He was a good citizen, a hard worker and most of all a family man. Whilst he took pride in his work, he would never compromise his family's safety for it. Which was exactly the reason Freddie was here.

The Tylers had a strong code, one that involved never harming an enemy's family. Enemies were fair game, but as far as their partners and children went, that was a no-go area. They may be killers but they were not savages. However, Mac didn't know that. And so this was something Freddie could use to his advantage.

He tilted his head to one side. 'Your Amber's a bright little thing, isn't she?' he mused, with a calculating smile. 'Such a sweet girl.'

'Don't you talk about her,' Mac hissed, his face turning red with worry. 'She's just a baby.' As soon as the words escaped his mouth he cast his gaze down. He did not want to anger the dangerous man in front of him, yet he needed to try and protect his family.

'Yes, she *is* just a baby…' Freddie leaned forward when Mac didn't answer, his face a mask of terrified misery. 'Now listen here,' he growled in as hard a tone as he could manage at low volume. 'I know you've figured out something is off about where Sammy was found. How I know that isn't your concern. Just know that I have access to everything you so much as set your eyes on and always will do. I know you found barely any blood in the ground, I know you thought something was off about his positioning and I know you shared that first bit with your DCI, who just so happens to be rummaging around her office looking for my moles. Not that she'll find them. They're always just that one step ahead.'

Freddie made sure to keep up with Sarah's story. It would do none of them any good for Mac to start questioning her loyalty to the force. 'Now I'll tell you this – we had nothing to do with Sammy's death. And that's the truth,' he continued. 'He was my best friend in the world.' He looked away for a moment and gathered himself before continuing. 'But for reasons that you don't need to know, I need the situation dropped as soon as possible. So here's what's going to happen.' He glanced towards the closed door that led to the kitchen. Fiona was still pottering around with plates and cutlery. 'You're going to forget your suspicions about the murder site. That's where he was killed. There is no evidence you can find that will lead you anywhere worth going, and you need to publicly come to that conclusion quick-smart. The case needs to be closed and his body released as soon as humanly possible. I will be keeping tabs to check that you've made this happen.'

Freddie stood up. 'You'll start by going to that bloodhound you call a DCI and telling her that you were wrong. And you'd better be convincing.'

'And what if I don't?' Mac asked, growing angrier by the second. His fighting spirit kicked in. Who the hell did this guy think he was, turning up at his home, talking to his family and threatening him in his own dining room? Finding the evidence to put away guys like this was Mac's job. He wasn't about to help a criminal get away with the crimes he was paid to uncover. He'd sworn an oath.

Freddie lunged in closer and Mac flinched, reminded that this was not someone to mess with. 'There is no *if you don't*, Mac,' he whispered menacingly in his ear. 'Because we both know you don't want to find out what the consequences are if my wishes are not carried out. I have a lot of people under my command and a very, *very* long reach. There is nowhere you could go to escape me, no matter how hard you try.' Stepping back, Freddie sniffed and looked around pointedly at the photos filled with happy memories on the walls. 'Lovely family you've got here, Mac.' He smiled coldly. 'Truly lovely.'

They stood opposite each other in the small dining room with locked gazes for a few long seconds, until Mac finally dropped his to the floor with a defeated slump of the shoulders. Freddie smiled. 'I can't stay for dinner, Fiona,' he called out. 'Something's come up. But thank you so much for the offer.'

'Ah, what a shame,' she called back. 'Another time, then.'

'Another time, then,' Freddie repeated to Mac quietly. He stepped around the other man and made his way to the door. 'I'll expect to hear back from my contacts that this has all gone away first thing tomorrow morning, Mac. Make it happen and you need never see my face again.' Satisfied with the small nod Mac gave in response, Freddie walked out of the house and down the path towards his car, buttoning up his jacket as he walked.

It had been quick thinking on Sarah's part, to set the scene the way she had. It had left the other man wary and cast the light of suspicion away from herself. All Freddie had needed to do was add on a bit of pressure and scare the man into submission. He hadn't enjoyed implying that Mac's family were in danger. No matter what the situation was, Freddie would never touch his wife or child. That was a line he'd never cross. But fear was a great motivator and if Freddie could get away with keeping order through fear rather than violence, he would always choose to do so.

Mac would lie awake at night now, terrified that the Tylers were going to come and hurt his family. It was a terrible thing to leave him thinking, but it would definitely ensure that the Sammy issue was dropped. And that, as far as Freddie was concerned, was all that really mattered.

CHAPTER FIFTY-EIGHT

Freddie pulled up to his mother's house and cut the engine, sitting in silence for a few moments before he opened the door. He didn't really want to go inside. He wanted to avoid his mother for a while, just until he had begun to come to terms with everything he had learned. But he knew that this would cause Mollie pain and worry, and that was something he couldn't do.

A large part of him was still angry with her for lying to him all these years and for being so stupid to have fallen for a scumbag like Jim in the first place. But the more reasonable side of his brain reminded him that he wouldn't be here if she hadn't and that she had just done the best she could with a bad situation. She had also been the best mum anyone could have possibly been, ever since he could remember. Even when Richard had died and she'd been left all alone with four children, she hadn't crumbled, she'd stood up despite her pain and had fought every day to give them everything she could.

There had been days when the money Mollie had made from the cleaning jobs and the ironing she took in just hadn't been enough to stretch to everything they'd needed, but still this never deterred her. No matter what, there was always food on the table, even if it was just bread and dripping with a fried egg. Their clothes were always clean and darned, even if they weren't always new. The rent man always got his due, even if that meant they went to bed with extra layers on so that they didn't have to turn on the heating. Looking back, Freddie couldn't imagine how hard it must have been for his mother back then, with such a large burden on her shoulders. But not once had she complained or let her children see her tears.

He forced himself out of the car and up the path. The front door was unlocked and he let himself in, walking through to the back of the house where he knew he'd find Paul, Ethan and his mother in the kitchen.

Mollie was sniffing, barely managing to keep back the sobs that were trying to make their way out into the open. She was busying herself with the washing up, totally ignoring the top-of-the-range dishwasher Freddie had had fitted for her a few years before. She always did the washing up by hand when she was upset, it was a sign the brothers knew well.

Freddie glanced at Paul questioningly. He gave Freddie a sad look in response. 'I just broke the news about Sammy,' he said, his gruff voice sounding awkward in the quiet room.

Mollie turned around and looked at Freddie warily. He had listened to everything she'd told him the other day, had sat in silence as she'd poured her heart out and voiced the secrets she'd held so close for so long. She had watched his face twist in pain as she crushed the deepest connection he had to the man he'd called dad. Afterwards he had sat still and silent for so long she hadn't known what to do. She'd babbled, begging his forgiveness, but he had cut her off and quietly told her that she wasn't to worry any more. He was going to sort it all out. Then he'd left.

Paul had told her that everything was alright, but she knew deep down that it wasn't. It couldn't be. She hadn't been able to sleep from worry. But he was here now and that was the main thing. If he was meeting Paul at the family home like normal, that was a good thing, surely? She just wished it was under less terrible circumstances.

'I'm so sorry, Freddie,' she said tentatively. 'About Sammy, I mean.' She didn't want him to think she was still harping on about the other thing, when he so clearly didn't want to discuss it.

Freddie looked down at his mother and saw the lines of worry around her eyes and the grey streaks in her hair as if for the first time. Her life had been hard for the most part and as she aged it had begun to show. The truth about his parentage might have been hard to swallow, but he knew in that moment that he would forgive Mollie that. He would forgive her anything. She had earned that right. He laid a hand on her shoulder gently. 'We all are, Mum,' he replied.

She reached up and grasped his hand tightly as relief washed over her. Feeling his hand on her shoulder, so gentle yet firm, felt like a life raft being thrown out to her. She had been drifting away from the safety and security that Freddie brought to the family into the darkness of her own past, and he was pulling her back in. The tears began to swell in her eyes and she looked down, not wanting to let them fall in front of him.

'Sammy was a part of this family. He meant a lot to all of us.' Freddie looked round and locked gazes with Ethan, who sat at the kitchen table looking miserable. In hazel-green eyes that mirrored his father's, Freddie saw the hurt and the pain that the young boy felt at losing yet another important person from his life. 'I'm so sorry, mate,' Freddie said. 'I know you were close.'

'Why would someone want to kill Uncle Sammy?' Ethan asked, his voice quivering. His gaze moved between Freddie and Paul as he searched for answers. 'He was nice to everyone. One – one time…' He sniffed and wiped his eyes with the back of his hand as he struggled to speak calmly. 'One time we went to dinner and there was a man outside who lived on the street and when we left it started raining and Uncle Sammy went to the shop and bought him an umbrella so he didn't have to get wet. 'Cause he's just nice. Wh-why would anyone want to kill him?' Ethan's voice rose an octave and he squeezed his eyes shut as the pain of losing his 'uncle' overwhelmed him.

Freddie moved across the room and quickly gathered his son up in his arms, holding him tight as he began to truly sob. He put his face to the top of Ethan's soft head and closed his eyes. The boy had seen and been through so much in his short life that he had developed a mature wisdom that was seldom seen in men twice his age. Sometimes he forgot that he was still just a child underneath it all. And right now that child had lost one of the only people who had been a constant in his life over the last few years. It had been Sammy who had been there to take him to football and for dinner and to talk to him about guy stuff whilst Freddie had been in prison. It had been Sammy who'd helped him adapt to his new life after his mum had sold him down the river. And now Ethan would have to say goodbye yet again to someone he loved. It wasn't fair and in that moment the hatred Freddie already felt for Sammy's killer burned hotter than the fires of hell.

'I can't answer that, son. Because I don't know either,' he murmured, rocking Ethan gently back and forth as he held him. 'But what I can tell you, is that when I find out who did it, we'll make sure they pay.' He raised his eyes to Paul's and they exchanged a hard look.

'We certainly will,' Paul agreed.

Glancing back at Mollie, Freddie saw her look away as if worried to lock gazes with him. His mouth formed a grim line. He didn't want to talk about what had been said but it lay between them like a heavy weight. He needed to clear the air and let her know where he stood if they were going to be able to properly move past this.

'Paul, do me a favour, go ahead with Ethan to football, will you? I'll meet you there in a few,' he said.

'Sure. Come on, mate, let's go.'

Still sniffling but trying to put a brave face on, Ethan followed his uncle out, saying a brief goodbye to his grandmother on the way.

As the front door shut and the two of them were left alone, there was an awkward silence. Freddie rubbed his hand over his face, not sure where to start. Mollie twisted the tea towel in her hands, the anxiety she felt building to a crescendo.

'Listen,' Freddie said, backing away from Mollie and sitting on one of the chairs around the kitchen table. 'I can't pretend finding all that out was easy. I can't imagine it would have been easy finding that out at any point. So I get why you didn't want to tell me.'

'Richard was still your dad, Freddie,' Mollie said quietly, her bottom lip wobbling. 'He was your *real* dad.'

'I know.' Freddie nodded. 'It stings, knowing his blood doesn't run through my veins,' he admitted. 'But he will always be the man who taught me the most important life lessons. He'll always be the man who made me into the person I am today. And that's enough. That's what's important.'

There was a short silence as mother and son stared at each other across the room. Mollie sniffed and wiped the tear that was threatening to fall from her eye. 'What now?' she asked. 'Can you forgive me?' The question turned to barely more than a whisper as she dreaded his answer.

Freddie cast his gaze to the floor, rubbing his forehead tiredly. 'There's nothing to forgive,' he said eventually. 'You're my mum. You're a *good* mum. You always have been.' He smiled sadly. 'You're also only human. And that's a curse that leads us all to have to make difficult choices sometimes.' He looked up at her. 'I need a bit of time to process things. But I love you very much. That never has and never will change.'

The tears in Mollie's eyes spilled over and she wished more than anything that she could run forward and envelop her eldest son in a huge protective hug, but she knew Freddie was not ready for that right now. He needed space and then when he was done, he'd be back and everything would be OK again. So instead, she nodded and wiped away the tears with a watery smile. 'I love you too,' she said. 'So much more than you'll ever know.'

'I know, Mum.' Freddie stood up and straightened his jacket. 'Listen, Jim managed to get away from us before we could solve the matter properly.' He didn't elaborate and he knew Mollie wouldn't ask. The darker side of his job was something they didn't talk about, for his mother's peace of mind. 'But I promise you…' Determination darkened in his eyes. 'We *will* catch up with him. And when we do, you won't have to worry about him bothering you ever again.'

CHAPTER FIFTY-NINE

Sarah knocked on the door and pushed it open, walking into the bright, clinical room. She wrinkled her nose slightly at the smell, but said nothing. Careful not to drop either of the two coffees in her hand she walked across the room to where Melrose was busy looking down into a microscope.

'You know you're not supposed to be in here without an express invite,' he said without looking up.

'I figured you'd fill out the paperwork later,' she replied, putting one of the coffees down in front of him. 'Double shot, soya, decaf, caramel latte. Just how you like it.'

Sarah was used to difficult people in her line of work. She herself was a difficult person, a trait she was both well aware and proud of. But in all her years of working with difficult people she had never met anyone quite as awkward as Melrose. He seemed to enjoy making people squirm at a level she wasn't sure could be classed as normal, when the mood took him. So, abandoning her usual bull-in-a-china shop approach, she handled him with care whenever she needed something.

Melrose glanced at the coffee with interest, then at her with slightly less interest. 'What are you here for?'

'I take it you got my message about the DNA sample for the John Doe at the building site?' she asked.

Melrose smirked. 'You mean Aleksei Ivanov?' He laughed as her face froze. 'Oh, don't worry. I ran him through off the record.

I've kept the files clear like you asked me to do until we spoke. What's happening?'

Sarah glanced over her shoulder, checking the room was still clear of anyone but them. 'I need you to run an unidentified sample through for his file. No one can know it's him. There is nothing else at the site that can identify him, so ID would then be dropped.'

Melrose frowned. 'Why don't you want him ID'd?' he asked.

'This is for the Tylers,' she said with a meaningful look.

'Ah.' Melrose paused and moved his attention back to the microscope. 'I see.'

Sarah waited for him to say something more but he didn't, seemingly engrossed with whatever he was looking at. 'So you'll do that?' she prompted.

'Well, if I don't, I imagine I'll be given a talking-to about earning my keep, seeing as I take regular payments from the Tylers to be on call for situations such as this. So I don't really have much choice,' he said in a casual tone.

Sarah exhaled and relaxed the muscles she just realised she'd been tensing for the last few days. 'Great.' She nodded. 'I'll leave that with you then. Thanks, Melrose.'

'No worries. Thanks for the coffee. Nothing I like more than the sweet taste of caramel with my dead bodies in the mornings.' He picked up the paper cup and took a deep appreciative swig.

Sarah raised her eyebrows and walked out of the room without response. He really was an oddball, Melrose. As she left the building and stepped into the sunshine she shrugged the thin suit jacket off and folded it over her arm. It was a hot day, far too hot to be working, but as usual she was on a double shift. Once she'd finished her official investigations, she still had her unofficial ones to get stuck into. Her livelihood – and potentially her freedom, these days – depended on it.

Her next stop was only around the corner, so she decided to leave the car and walk the short distance instead. Her court shoes clipped out a sharp rhythm on the pavement as she walked and she fluffed her short dark hair back.

The ugly one-storey building that the forensic team were housed in came into view and she picked up the pace. Reaching the door, she pushed the buzzer and waited to be let in. There was a short click and she pressed forward into the building, waving briefly to the familiar security guard in the office as she passed.

Mac was at his station, sitting on his stool and staring worriedly into space. He was so lost in his own thoughts that he didn't notice her until she waved a hand in front of his face.

'Hello? Earth to Mac?' she said with a slight laugh. 'Are you with us?'

'Oh, Sarah!' he exclaimed. Relief flooded through his face and he glanced around the room before lowering his voice. 'I've been trying to call you. I need to talk to you.'

'Yes, I saw your calls but I was in a meeting round the corner. I need to talk to you too,' she said seriously. 'Is there somewhere more private?' The room was a hive of activity.

'Yes, let's go to the break room. That's probably best.' He led the way down a long corridor towards a small room at the end. Sarah followed him in and waited until he had shut the door.

'Listen,' she said, sounding as urgent as she could. 'I've got a meeting set up with Ben in an hour. If you're free to come with me, we can take this all to him then. I've got—'

'No, stop.' Mac cut her off and put his hands up in protest. 'Listen…' He licked his lips and shifted to one side. 'I got it wrong. I mixed the samples up.'

'What?' Sarah asked with a deep frown.

'I mean, I made a mistake.'

'But you never make mistakes,' Sarah pressed, making sure to put on a good act.

'Well, I did.' He wiped his forehead, sweat beginning to form. He wasn't used to lying like this, the stress was getting to him. 'I used the wrong soil sample. I ran the right soil samples and they contained the correct amount of blood for what I would expect to see at the site.'

'You're certain?' She made sure to sound like she was not entirely convinced.

'I'm positive,' Mac confirmed with a nod. 'I double-checked everything. I was too quick off the mark to bring it to you. I should have checked it again first. Sorry, I'm not sure how this happened, but it won't happen again.'

Sarah tilted her head to one side as if she was mulling over the information. 'OK,' she said eventually. 'I guess I was wrong about the whole thing then. Huh. I was sure there was something off about it…'

'Nope. Well, other than the fact a guy's been murdered, of course,' Mac replied.

'OK. I'll cancel Ben then, don't worry about it. And your little slip-up can stay between the two of us.' She smiled and opened the door, stepping back out into the hallway and heading for the exit. 'No harm, no foul.'

'Thanks, Sarah,' Mac said with a small smile of relief. He didn't like having to lie the way he just had, but the safety of his family meant more to him than anything else in the world. Even the law.

'No problem. Keep me updated, yeah? There must be something.'

But there wouldn't be something, she thought with a smile, as she left the building and headed into the office to start her official working day. Because Freddie had made sure that Mac was so scared that the Sammy case would be over and pushed to the side in no time. There would be nothing found that linked the body to Freddie's office where he actually was murdered, and then maybe they could all stop holding their breaths and start living their lives once more.

As she reached her car, Sarah's smile melted away. Now that these issues had been dealt with, there was one more thing she needed to do. She needed to see if her suspicions about the owner of the gold bracelet were right. Because if they were, everything around Freddie was about to blow up, big time.

CHAPTER SIXTY

Josephine draped the royal blue feather boa over her shoulders and flicked one end back around with a flourish, before turning slowly in the mirror to check that it was sitting just where she wanted it. Really it was too hot for such adornments, but it matched perfectly with the long floaty dress she wore and she had never been one to let something as trivial as the weather get in the way of a good outfit.

She picked up the box of macarons she had purchased earlier in the day from her favourite French patisserie, Ladurée, and made her way down the stairs and out onto the busy Soho street. Raising her face to the sun, she enjoyed its warmth for a moment before marching forward with determination. She was only going around the corner, to Club Anya, but each step towards it felt like an uphill struggle.

She clutched the box and hoped that her peace offering might do the trick. Anna hadn't exactly warmed to her, but she had been around her a lot more lately, due to all the unforeseen issues that had arisen. Josephine was hoping that perhaps she was beginning to thaw a little. After all, their shattered friendship aside, Josephine did work for Anna. She ran the whorehouse and lived there too. Surely Anna couldn't keep up the iciness forever. She knew that they weren't about to bounce back to being close pals again, it was too soon, and Anna had made her feelings perfectly clear on that front. But she hoped that perhaps if she kept persevering, they could at least get to a more civil and comfortable level with each other again. Because the tension between them was almost unbearable.

Reaching the side door to the club, Josephine used her keys to get in. It was still too early for the doors to be open to the general public. She walked through to the bar and greeted Carl with a nervous smile.

'Hello, Josephine,' he said in a warm tone. 'I haven't seen you in here for ages, how you keeping?'

'Hi, Carl, I'm OK, thanks. You?'

'Oh, I'm dandy. Love the scarf, very nice shade on you,' he replied.

'Why thank you.' Josephine preened and gave him a wink before continuing on to the office.

She paused at the office door and exhaled slowly, trying to muster up the courage to enter. 'Oh, come on, you silly fool,' she muttered to herself. She lifted her hand and knocked, then pushed forward into the room before she could change her mind.

Anna sat at her desk. She was frowning at a piece of paper, running her finger down rows of data and holding up a bunch of other papers in her other hand. They hung, suspended in the air, as if they were awaiting their turn on the gallows of Anna's disapproval. Josephine knew how they felt.

Anna looked up and briefly raised her eyebrows in surprise before focusing back on the task at hand. 'What do you need, Josephine?' she asked in a clipped tone. Her red lips pursed together firmly, a clear sign that she was not a fan of her visitor.

'I, er…' Josephine stepped towards the desk. Anna was dressed in black. Not an uncommon colour for her, but Josephine knew that today it was on purpose. She doubted there would be much brightness to Anna's wardrobe for a while. At least until after the funeral. 'I wanted to offer you my condolences. I heard about Sammy,' she said, tentatively. 'That he… that he died.'

Anna's finger paused on the page, her dark red nail pressing down into the paper for a moment. 'Yes. Well.' She swallowed. 'You heard correctly.'

She tried to refocus on the list in front of her but found suddenly that she couldn't. She had been trying to stay strong for everyone around her – Freddie, Paul, Ethan. But she had felt Sammy's death too. They all had. They were a family and each of them had had a special bond with Sammy in their own way. Having him gone so suddenly felt as if someone had removed a limb. Nothing worked quite so smoothly. Nothing felt quite right anymore. It was going to take a long time to get used to and they would never fully heal from it, the way they had never fully healed from losing Thea, Freddie's sister. But that was something Josephine couldn't possibly understand.

Anna felt her heart harden once more against her once so-called friend. She had taken Josephine in at a point in her life where the other woman had wanted to end it all. She had given her purpose, a home, a family to be part of and who accepted her for who she was. But Josephine had betrayed them. She had carried on behind all of their backs with the one person who had been out to destroy them, destroy everything they had worked for. So how could she stand there now and feign sorrow for the death of a member of that family? Anna felt the anger swell up inside and she tried to swallow it down.

'Was there something else?' she snapped.

Josephine blinked, taken aback by the sudden aggression. 'Um…' She looked down at the box in her hand, the pale green ribbon around it tied neatly into a bow. She placed it down on the edge of the desk. 'I bought you these. I thought that perhaps a sweet treat might make you feel a little better.' She tried giving Anna a hesitant smile.

Anna stared at the box in disbelief. 'Someone we all loved dearly just died,' she said slowly, 'and you think some cupcakes will make it all feel better?' she asked.

'Macarons,' Josephine corrected, her cheeks colouring. 'And no, 'course not. I just thought—'

'You just thought,' Anna butted in, 'that you could walk in here with some macarons and a smile and all would be OK with the world, right?' She stood up, her agitation reaching boiling point. 'What world do you live in, Josephine?' she demanded, anger flashing across her face. 'What fantasy world do you think this is – that macarons could take away the sting of someone *dying*? I mean,' she barked a humourless laugh, 'that just brings a whole new meaning to the term "sugar-coating", doesn't it?'

'I didn't mean to upset you,' Josephine mumbled, dismayed that her attempt at peace had gone so terribly wrong.

'Well, you have, Josephine,' Anna responded, her tone harsh. 'You upset me with these stupid macarons, you upset me by turning up here at a time when I *really* don't need the added stress, and you upset me with your total betrayal of this family after all I've done for you.' She glared at Josephine for a few long moments and then closed her eyes and rubbed her forehead, her shoulders slumping defeatedly. 'I just need you to go, Josephine. I can't do this right now.'

Josephine's eyes filled with tears and she bit her lip in an attempt to stop it wobbling. 'I'm sorry, Anna,' she whispered. 'I'm sorry.' She turned and fled, before Anna could say anything more.

Anna sighed heavily, immediately feeling guilty. She shouldn't have taken it out on Josephine. The woman was trying really hard to make things right and get back onto a normal footing and Anna knew that she should be trying too, however burned she felt by it all. Whether she liked it or not, it had happened. But the past was the past and she knew that, like Josephine, she should be focusing on trying to rebuild the present so that the future had a fighting chance.

With a groan she moved around the desk and opened the door, dashing into the bar area. 'Josephine?' she called.

'She's gone. Ran out crying,' Carl said from his position behind the bar. He placed the cocktail jug he'd just polished down and picked up the next one. 'What did you do to her?' he chastised jokingly. 'Poor girl…'

Anna bit back the retort that Josephine was anything but a *poor girl* and instead took a seat at the bar. 'Nothing,' she replied, brushing it off. 'She just caught the back end of my bad mood.'

'Drink?'

'Sure. I'll have a glass of wine.'

Carl poured one out and handed it to her in silence. He waited until she had taken a few sips. 'When will the funeral be? Do you know yet?'

'Not yet,' Anna replied with a glum sigh. 'But I'll let you know as soon as I hear. We'll obviously shut the club for the night, whatever day it is.'

Carl nodded and continued his methodical polishing of the glassware. Anna pulled her phone out of her dress pocket and checked the screen with a frown. It was still blank. She checked the signal but there were four bars, so it wasn't that messages weren't coming through. She had been texting and calling Tanya all day and hadn't heard anything back from her. She typed out another text.

Tan, can you PLEASE get back to me? I'm swamped, could really do with you here!

'Hey, did Tanya come in at all yesterday?' she asked Carl.

He shook his head. 'No, I haven't seen her for a couple of days.'

Anna tutted in irritation. 'Me neither and I really need to talk to her. This is *not* the time to disappear off the radar.'

'Well, I think she's just, you know…' Carl pulled a face. 'Grieving.'

Anna's frown deepened. 'We're all grieving, Carl,' she replied. 'We all miss Sammy. But that doesn't mean everything else stops. We have businesses to run, things to do.' She shook her head.

'Yeah, but, it's *Sammy*,' he reiterated with a meaningful look.

Anna stared back at him with a blank expression. 'I'm aware of that,' she said. 'And like I said, we all miss him. But we still need to carry on with life. The world doesn't stop, much as we would like it to at times like this. And I don't think that's why she's disappeared. She's so resilient. Even when Thea died, that hit us just as hard, but she held her head up and got on with things.' She took a sip of her wine. 'And I mean, I know that she's known Sammy a long time, but they barely hung out. She wasn't as close to him as she was to Thea. They were friends, sure, but it's not like he was her boyfriend or anything.'

Carl stopped what he was doing and his usually neutral expression fell into a frown as he stared at her.

Anna caught the stare and blinked. 'What?' she asked, self-consciously.

'You don't know?' he asked slowly.

'Don't know what?'

Carl's eyebrows shot up and he exhaled slowly, blowing out his cheeks. 'Wow. OK. I thought you knew.'

'Knew what?' Anna urged, worried now. She stood up, her wine forgotten. 'Carl, you need to tell me what's going on, right now.'

Half an hour later Anna rushed out of the lift on Tanya's floor of their building and pulled out her keys from her purse. Without bothering to knock, she unlocked the door and let herself in. The flat was in darkness, all the curtains closed and a slightly stale smell in the air, indicating that fresh air had not been invited inside for a while.

Princess, Tanya's fluffy white cat, pranced over and wound itself around Anna's ankles. She bent down and stroked the feline, who began to purr warmly. 'Hey, where's your mum, Princess?' Anna asked quietly. 'Where's she hiding?'

Standing up straight she leaned into the lounge and glanced up towards the open-plan kitchen. Tanya wasn't in there, but the usually tidy side was covered in glasses and a nearly empty bottle of cherry vodka stood beside the sink. Anna pursed her lips and moved through the hallway towards the bedroom. She walked in and squinted in the darkness, allowing her eyes to adjust. As they did, she saw Tanya – or rather, the shape of Tanya – buried underneath her thick quilt in the middle of the bed. Another half-empty bottle of vodka sat beside her and one hand poked out from beneath the covers, holding on to the glass she was drinking from.

Without a word Anna kicked off her shoes and climbed into the bed beside her, gently taking the glass and placing it on the side before pulling Tanya into her arms for a hug. She looked down at her friend and her eyes immediately filled with tears of sorrow. Tanya's wild red curls that usually bounced and shone were flat, knotted and unkempt. Her face was pale and drawn and her eyes were puffy and red, a dullness where there had once been life and sparkle.

'I'm so sorry, Tanya,' she said. 'I'm so sorry that he's gone and that I told you the way I did.' She closed her eyes, cringing at how callous she must have seemed. 'I didn't know.' She lowered her head to Tanya's and stroked her friend's hair.

When Carl had told her she could have kicked herself for not seeing it sooner. She had been so wrapped up in all their troubles that she hadn't taken the time to notice all the things that were going on right in front of her. She was Tanya's best friend. Even though Tanya hadn't told her, she should have picked up on it. Looking back, Tanya had had an extra glow to her recently, despite their worries. She'd sneaked off at times and had often been vague about the things she'd been up to when Anna had enquired about her evenings. There had been all the signs of a budding romance, but they had all gone over Anna's head. She felt terrible. What sort of best friend was the last to notice something like that?

Silent tears poured down Tanya's face. 'We were going to be happy together,' she said in a pained voice, barely more than a whisper. 'We'd finally figured it out.' She squeezed her eyes shut as the pain once more broke through the fuzzy layer the alcohol had wrapped her in.

'I know,' Anna said, holding her tighter. 'I'm so sorry, Tanya. I'm so, so sorry.' She shuffled deeper into the bed, trying to find a comfortable position. Because she wasn't going anywhere. She may have been a neglectful friend of late, but she was here now. No matter what life threw at them – and life had certainly thrown them some bad times – they had always pulled each other through. And this was no exception. Anna was going to get her through this. Because whether they wanted it to or not, life went on – and this was just what she and Tanya did. They weathered the worst times together, no matter what.

CHAPTER SIXTY-ONE

Sarah stared up at the tall, imposing gates that led to Sophia's property, her hands jammed down in the pockets of her thin leather jacket. The security was impressive, she had to give them that. Probably installed by Aleksei when he bought the place. When you were a Russian mobster taking over enemy territory you couldn't be too careful, she supposed.

Before she had reached forward to press the buzzer, a whirring noise started up and the gates opened, allowing her entry. She pulled a face and walked forward down the wide gravel drive and up to the front door. It opened as she reached it and Ali gestured for her to come inside.

As the door closed behind her, Sarah took in her surroundings with appreciation. Whatever else she was, Sophia was certainly a talented decorator. With soft hues and elegant furniture running throughout, it was a stark reminder of Sarah's lack of talent in this department. Her small flat was filled with a mismatch of whatever had taken her fancy over the years. All sorts of colours and styles haphazardly thrown together. She had often thought that the chaos of it all lent it a homely charm, but as she compared it in her mind to the home she was in now, she realised that this was no more than wishful thinking.

They entered a lounge area which could have been plucked straight from the pages of a magazine and Sarah spotted Sophia lounging on a sofa, her attention on the pages of the book she was reading.

'So, Miss Riley, are you here as an officer of the law, or as the Tylers' paid pet?'

Sarah ground her teeth and held her neutral expression with difficulty, as the caustic comment hit its mark.

When Sarah didn't answer, Sophia put down her book and looked her up and down. She took in Sarah's casual jeans and jacket and the lack of any type of sidekick and made a sound somewhere between a huff and a snigger.

'Paid pet is it then, today. And what brings you to my home, Miss Riley?'

Sarah forced a smile, although it did not reach her eyes. 'This is a courtesy call. I just thought I should let you know that Aleksei's body won't be officially identified.'

'Oh?' Sophia raised one perfect eyebrow in interest.

'I've had it buried to protect your new business partners from any unnecessary scrutiny.'

'How good of you to let me know.' Sophia's words dripped with sarcasm.

Sarah gave her a small frown of confusion. 'Surely you're pleased that they are protected? I mean, they are helping you prop up your only source of income now.'

There was a short silence and Sophia gave her a tight smile. 'Of course. But don't forget, Aleksei was still my husband, so I can't really celebrate the news that he will just forever disappear without being shown any of the usual honours that death brings someone of his standing.'

'Of course,' Sarah replied gravely.

'It is my sons that I'm thinking of,' Sophia continued. 'It is they who have missed out.'

'Indeed. And may I just say,' Sarah stepped closer towards her, 'that I commend you for doing such a great job with them in the face of this all. It must be incredibly hard for you, raising them alone.'

Sophia narrowed her eyes. What was Sarah playing at? They were not on terms to share compliments and sympathy – they were not on civil terms at all.

'Honestly,' Sarah continued, extending her hand. 'I have a lot of respect for people who have no choice but to go it alone and you're doing a better job than most. I'd like to shake your hand.'

Sophia raised her eyebrows. The praise was unexpected and very odd, but then perhaps it was an English thing. She found English people often shared far too much with each other and always seemed to offer opinions and advice in business that wasn't theirs to mind. She held out her hand, deciding to meet Sarah's halfway. Perhaps she should lay off the insults for a while. She despised the scruffy Amazonian woman, but perhaps she would come in useful down the line as an ally, once she had succeeded in doing away with the Tyler brothers.

Sarah grasped Sophia's hand and shook it vigorously, deliber-ately causing the other woman's sleeve to rise up her arm. There it sat, on her slender wrist. The gold chain bracelet from the video footage. She had been right. Sophia was the shooter.

'What a beautiful bracelet,' she commented. 'Though it doesn't seem your style, somehow.' She tilted her head to one side in question, looking from the bracelet up to Sophia's face.

Sophia retracted her hand and pulled her sleeve back down. 'It was Aleksei's,' she said, her dark eyes suddenly wary. 'I bought him it as a wedding present.'

'Ah, I see.' Sarah nodded her understanding and looked away, her mind racing.

Sophia seethed inside, realising that the whole conversation about her children had been nothing but a trick to get close enough to see the bracelet. 'Was that everything, Miss Riley?'

'Yes, that was all I came for.' Sarah smiled, a genuine smile this time, and noted that Sophia did not return it. 'I'll leave you in peace then. Catch you another time.' Without waiting for Ali to guide her, Sarah walked back out the way she came.

Sophia rose from her position on the sofa and glided to the window. Her lips pursed and her eyes turned hard as she watched Sarah leave. The door that led out from the lounge towards the back of the house opened and Jim walked through from where he had hidden away from the unexpected visitor.

'What did she want?' He sidled up to her as the gate closed once more behind Sarah.

'To compliment me on how I'm raising my children,' she replied, drily.

'Really?' Jim asked in surprise.

'No. Not really,' she answered, her look darkening. 'We need to pull up the new plan to tonight. We have, as you Londoners say, been made.'

CHAPTER SIXTY-TWO

Freddie hurled his glass across the newly decorated office with a growl and it shattered into pieces as it hit the wall. So it was her. It was Sophia who had killed Sammy. He turned in a slow circle, holding his head in horror. He had been the one to allow her into their lives, into their business. He thought he'd read the situation well. She was just a mother trying to provide for her children, a woman of the underworld making use of the skills and knowledge that she had. Aleksei hadn't even been a proper husband. The story had been so easy to buy, with her cold indifference to the issues of the past. But he had been wrong. And it had cost Sammy everything. The sickening realisation that this was all his fault hit him like a ton of bricks and he pulled his hands forward over his face with a groan.

Paul caught on to his thought process almost immediately. 'No.' He shook his head. 'Fred, I know what you're thinking but this ain't your fault.'

'Yes, it is,' Freddie groaned through his hands. 'It *is* my fault. I fucking fell for it, thinking I knew better, thinking I could trust my gut over pure fucking fact. And the fact is, she's the enemy. She always has been.'

'You thought she was after the money, which was the logical explanation,' Paul reasoned. 'You couldn't have known she was playing this game.'

'Bill did,' Freddie replied, looking up at his brother. 'Bill knew. He didn't like this from the beginning. He told me not to trust the Russians at any point, but especially not her. I should have fucking listened.' He closed his eyes in torment, kicking himself for not paying more attention to the warning signs.

Sarah shifted uncomfortably from one foot to the other. She had been elated that she had finally figured out who the killer was, but she had not been looking forward to telling Freddie. She had known it wasn't going to go down well. She eyed the door, wishing she had positioned herself a little closer to it. She could have slipped out unnoticed and carried on with her day. There was still a lot to do and she didn't want to be missed at the station.

Paul exhaled slowly. He wanted to make Freddie feel better, to take off the mantle of guilt his brother had decided to adopt, but he couldn't find much of an argument. Freddie had fucked up. 'Look,' he said eventually. 'Even if you had told her to sling her hook, she still would have been out for blood. Chances are it still would have all panned out the same way.'

Freddie stared off into space, not really hearing Paul's words. He frowned. 'How did she get in? How did she get the information she needed?' He turned to Paul.

Paul shrugged. 'I don't know, maybe she just chanced it.'

'No.' Freddie shook his head. 'Sophia isn't a chancer. She's methodical, careful.' He'd seen as much with the gun-running and in the elaborate set-up to get close to Freddie. It was doubtful that she would then go running in all guns blazing to kill Sammy without a well-thought-out plan.

'It did seem rather convenient that all the cameras were off,' Sarah remarked. 'But how would she know where to look? And the fact she never stepped into this room…' Sarah glanced towards where she knew the closed-circuit cameras were hidden. 'It was like she knew the cameras in here were on their own loop.' She frowned and looked at Freddie. 'Who had access to the security system?'

'No one who would tell her anything about it,' he replied with certainty. Before he could continue, a message pinged through on his phone. He looked at the screen and his expression darkened. It was Sophia.

Paul glanced at the screen and his eyebrows shot up. 'Well, go on, open it,' he urged.

Freddie read it out loud. '"Mr Tyler, I need to meet with you tonight to discuss some of the details of the next run. Let me know where is best to find you after the clubs close. Sophia."'

'I suppose asking her to report directly to the shallow grave we'll be digging for her is out,' Paul said.

'She'll be in it soon enough, brother,' Freddie replied, his expression darkening. 'But not before I get some answers.'

CHAPTER SIXTY-THREE

Anna sat at one of the empty tables in the bar of The Sinners' Lounge, her legs crossed and her hands folded in her lap as she waited, hiding the tension she felt running through every inch of her body. Freddie paced up and down the long room nearby, not able to hide his agitation as successfully.

'What time is it?' he asked.

Anna looked at the watch on her wrist. 'Ten to.'

They heard the door open downstairs and froze. They exchanged grim glances and braced themselves for what was coming. 'They're here,' Anna breathed. She reached under the table and her fingers curled around the handle of the revolver she'd strapped there earlier. Freddie was unarmed, to keep up appearances until things took a turn for the worse.

Anna strained her ears as they heard footsteps on the stairs. Only one pair, it seemed. She frowned. That was odd. The door opened inwards and as Tanya walked into view she exhaled the tense breath she had been holding.

'Tan, what are you doing here?' she asked, standing up and walking towards her.

'I had to come,' she said with a sniff.

She didn't look at all like her normal self, dressed casually in a pair of skinny jeans and a khaki hoody Anna had never seen before. Her face was devoid of the usual expertly applied make-up, which made her look younger and more vulnerable somehow, and her arms were wrapped around her torso as if she was protecting herself from the outside world.

At least, Anna noted, she had showered and run a brush through her hair. And she had left the flat to come here. Which meant that there was still some fight in her, no matter how much she was hurting.

'You shouldn't be here,' she said, rubbing Tanya's arm. 'This is just going to upset you more.'

'This is just going to *anger* me more,' she replied, a hardness breaking through the pain in her eyes. 'Which is exactly why I *should* be here.'

'I'm just—'

'No, she's right.' Freddie cut her off, his tone full of the fury that was seeping out of his every pore. He began pacing once more, unable to stand still, so strong was the rage running through him. 'She should be here. She has every right to look that murdering bitch in the eye before she disappears off the face of the fucking planet. Sammy's been taken from all of us, her included.'

He glanced over at Tanya and she nodded her gratitude. He looked away and shook his head sorrowfully. He'd suspected something had started up between them anyway, but Anna had confirmed the details. The two of them could have been very happy together, had Sammy not been killed. He knew it was the lost future, as much as Sammy himself, that Tanya was mourning, and he felt her pain. They had been friends for a long time, he and Tanya.

Freddie searched for the right words, for anything to say that could be of some comfort but there were none. Instead he kicked out at a chair and sent it flying. Anna picked it up and placed it back in its rightful place.

'Sorry,' he said, taking a deep breath. He ran his hands through his dark hair and straightened his jacket. He needed to get a handle on himself before they got here. Mixing emotions with business was the fastest way to make a mistake, and none of them could afford to make a mistake tonight.

After they'd got over their initial shock, they'd started to work through all the possible reasons why Sophia had killed Sammy and a sneaking suspicion had entered his mind. Perhaps Aleksei wasn't dead. Perhaps this had been the long game and Sammy was just the first to fall. They had never actually found Aleksei, after all. Sophia had told them a neat little story about him being buried in a building site, but what if that had just been to throw them off? Maybe all this time Aleksei had been lying in wait, using his wife to get close to them so that he could pick them off one by one. It seemed like a lot of effort to go to, but it was the most likely explanation Freddie could come up with. Either way, it had stopped him in his tracks. He needed to find out what was behind the killing before he dealt with her.

When Sophia had messaged, Freddie had agreed to meet, inviting her to The Sinners' Lounge as if nothing was out of the ordinary. Then they had worked out the best strategy to get answers out of her before dealing with her for good. Now here they were, ready and waiting for her and whoever else she brought along for the ride.

So many questions buzzed around Freddie's head. Would Sophia still act as though they were allies for a while longer or was she only coming here to take him out? Was he the next on the hit list or would she still be playing the long game? Would Aleksei come with her, if Freddie's theory was correct? Why did she take out Sammy first, of all people? What did she have to gain by that? He rubbed his forehead. None of it made sense.

The door below them opened again and the atmosphere changed immediately. It was time. They all exchanged glances as two pairs of footsteps made their way up. Sophia marched into the bar area, Ali close behind. She stopped dead, just a few steps inside the room, and raised one eyebrow at Freddie.

'I thought we agreed we were to meet alone?' she asked, nodding towards Anna and Tanya who still stood together by the bar.

'I thought that applied to both parties,' Freddie responded coldly, nodding towards Ali.

As he stared at her across the room, he found he could not mask his anger and contempt. Sophia just smirked humourlessly as she read his face. Clearly Sarah had already told him about the bracelet. She could have kicked herself when the penny had dropped earlier. The second Sarah had commented on it, she'd realised her mistake.

'You don't look very happy this evening, Mr Tyler,' she said. 'Is something the matter?' She walked a few paces forward and then stopped, leaving a few feet between them.

Her tone was carefully innocent but the mocking challenge in her eyes fuelled Freddie's rage and he clenched his fist to stop himself lunging for her throat. This was the woman who had shot Sammy and ended his life – who had shot him in the back of the head like a coward. He'd never even stood a chance.

Freddie deliberated for a few moments over which way to take things. He decided to cut to the chase. There was no point playing around, they both knew what was going on now. What he didn't know was why – and what or who was behind it.

'Let's cut the crap, Sophia,' he said in a low deadly tone. 'Why did you do it?'

'Why did I do what?' Sophia asked, cocking her head to one side as if curious.

'Sammy. Why did you kill him?' Freddie felt the familiar stab of pain as he mentioned his best friend's name. He saw Tanya twist uncomfortably out of the corner of his eye as if she too was trying to keep her emotions in check.

Sophia smiled coldly. 'So we're not here to talk about the gun-run?'

Anna studied Sophia as the other woman's gaze remained locked on Freddie. She reminded her of a snake. Cold, calculated movements and a slyness which held a promise of imminent attack. As the stand-off between the two continued, Anna's eyes were drawn to the bulge underneath Ali's jacket. He had a gun.

Suddenly she remembered the gun underneath the table and she silently cursed. She had planned to sit there with one hand on it, ready to pull it out at a second's notice. When Tanya had arrived she'd abandoned her post and now it was several feet away. Training her gaze back on Sophia, she began slowly making her way back to the table.

'I don't think so, Miss Davis,' Sophia immediately remarked. She reached behind her back and as quick as lightning pulled out her own handgun, pointing it directly at Anna's head.

Freddie immediately reacted with an enraged cry, but as he began to lurch towards Sophia, Ali pulled out his gun and turned it on Freddie. He pulled himself up short and swore loudly.

Her heart racing at the sudden turn of events, Anna raised her hands and backed up against the bar once more. 'Jesus Christ, Sophia,' she exclaimed. 'I was just going to sit down. There's no need for this.' She tried to sound reasonable, buying them some time and keeping the pair distracted. 'We just wanted to talk things out. Surely we can do that like civilised people?'

Tanya gripped Anna's arm, murder in her eyes as she stared at Sophia. She wanted to shout and scream at the woman, but she'd caught on to what Anna was doing, so she kept silent for the time being.

'You really expect me to believe that you just want to talk things out?' Sophia scoffed. 'Oh please… I just killed someone you all love. Apparently, I was not quite as discreet as I'd hoped,' she added, 'but there we go.' She chuckled and shook her head. 'Oh no, Miss Davis, you did not bring me here to talk. You brought me here to pay my debt. A life for a life. Let's be honest, shall we? But you did not plan this out very well, considering we have two guns and you have none.'

'You really expected me not to have arranged back-up?' Freddie piped up, a glint of triumph in his eyes.

The tip of Paul's gun touched the back of Sophia's head and Ali turned his gun away from Freddie towards Paul in alarm. Freddie saw his chance and started towards the table, but before he could get more than a step Ali realised his mistake and swung back around, stopping him in his tracks. His gaze jumped from Freddie to Sophia and back to Freddie again as he panicked, but Sophia didn't even flinch.

'Hello, Paul,' she said calmly, not taking her eye off Anna. He cocked the gun and she smiled. 'You really expected me not to anticipate this?' she mocked.

The sound of the front door being locked and bolted came up through the hallway and into the bar. Paul and Freddie exchanged looks. If the door was bolted, Bill had no chance of getting into the building after whoever had entered made their way up the stairs. That really did put a spanner in the works. Paul gave Freddie a meaningful look and Freddie tensed, ready to leap towards the gun Anna had left under the table. Paul then gave him a curt nod and without removing the gun from Sophia's head, kicked out at the back of Ali's knees, hard.

Ali gave a small cry of surprise as his legs gave way and he crumpled to the floor. He dropped his gun and as he grappled to find it again Paul dove forward, hoping to get to it first. Catching on quickly, Ali grabbed him and the pair ended up fighting with their fists as each tried to get ahead of the other. Freddie jumped towards the table once more.

'Don't you dare,' snarled Sophia, swinging her gun towards him and away from Anna.

Freddie stopped in his tracks, frustration boiling over at how close he'd been to getting the gun.

Without pausing to think, knowing that she couldn't afford to lose even a second, Anna dived towards the table. Sophia swiftly turned the gun back in her direction and let off a shot, missing Anna by millimetres. Anna recoiled and put her hands back up, aware of how close Sophia had got to hitting her, and Freddie started forward with a cry of outrage.

'*Yebat*,' Sophia cursed angrily in Russian as she swung the gun back round onto Freddie once more. 'Back up,' she shouted.

Freddie did as he was told, anger burning dangerously in his eyes. He had no doubt that Sophia would shoot again without a second thought and this time they might not be so lucky.

Sophia exhaled as she tried to collect herself. She was losing control of the situation, which was unacceptable. But she hadn't anticipated so many people and whilst she did not know exactly why the pair of them kept trying to get to that table, she had a pretty good idea.

Tanya used the chaos to sidle around the bar and silently picked up a large bottle of vodka. She was just behind the grappling pair and her mind worked quickly as she thought through the ways she could use this to her advantage.

Ali managed to land a blow that sent Paul reeling and quickly grabbed his pistol. Realising his chance to take Ali out of the equation had passed, Paul jumped up and pointed his gun at Sophia once more. Freddie was still right in her line of fire.

Ali righted himself a little further away from Paul and aimed at the other man's head with a growl. His boss seemed to have both Freddie and Anna under control without need for his assistance. Right now, Paul was a more immediate threat.

Sophia rolled her shoulders, satisfied that she had regained enough control to ensure the situation went her way.

Anna watched as Tanya crept forward towards Ali, Paul and Sophia. With their focus trained in the other direction, they hadn't noticed her approach. 'Sophia, put your gun down now or I promise you that you will seriously regret it,' she said, trying to keep their attention away from her friend.

'I highly doubt that, Anna,' Sophia replied, her tone calm and confident. 'And you're hardly in a position right now to be making demands, are you?' She sighed as if the whole situation was tiring. 'Now, I came here to finish the job I started, and you all came here for answers and to send me along to the next world. Only one of us is going to end up satisfied and I intend for that to be me. So…' She recocked her gun and her gaze darkened as she focused on Freddie.

Anna urgently gestured towards Sophia with her eyes, as Tanya looked to her for direction. Tanya mashed her lips into a hard line and hatred burned in her eyes as she lifted the vodka bottle, ready to run forward and smash across Sophia's arms. If she could just disarm her, they stood a chance of overpowering the two of them. All she had to do was make sure she got there before Ali realised what she was doing.

'Well,' Anna said, trying to keep Sophia talking. 'I guess we're going to have to disagree on that one, aren't we?'

'Why did you do it, Sophia?' Freddie repeated, his gaze locking with hers. 'I still don't get what you're doing here. It doesn't make sense.'

Tanya took a step forward. She was still a few feet away from Sophia but there were two creaky floorboards between them and she needed to stay silent if she had a chance of getting close enough.

'Put the fucking gun down, Sophia. Seriously,' Paul growled, weighing in, 'or I'll take you out even *with* your guy pointing his gun at me.'

Tanya glanced at Ali. Maybe she would be better going for him. But the grief and anger gnawing through her heart drew her back towards Sophia. She wanted to cause that woman pain like she had never wanted to cause another person pain before.

Before she could take another step, though, whoever had locked the front door mounted the stairs and entered the room. Tanya swivelled round and blinked in surprise. It was the new guy who worked for Freddie. A smile of relief spread across her face, but then quickly faded as he pointed his own gun straight at her.

Keeping the gun trained on Tanya and gesturing for her to back away from his new boss, Jim looked across the room into the furious gaze of his biological son. 'Hello, Freddie,' he said, as his mouth turned up into a dark, crooked smile. 'I guess you're now wishing you'd killed me when you had the chance.'

CHAPTER SIXTY-FOUR

Josephine heard the shot upstairs in her flat and froze in horror. Anna had been up just an hour before and told her under no circumstances was she to come downstairs tonight, that there was to be a showdown with none other than Sophia Ivanov. Apparently, it was Sophia who had killed Sammy. Josephine hadn't been able to think about anything else since. She had huddled up on the sofa for a while, then paced the room for what seemed like an age but what was in fact no more than just a few minutes. Eventually she had poured herself a strong drink and sat staring at the wall, too tense to even put on the TV.

She'd heard people coming in and out and her heart had raced each time. Was it Sophia? Would she stop downstairs or would she come up here to take her revenge? Josephine had never been a violent person. She doubted she even had anything in the flat that could be used as a weapon to defend herself. Even the kitchen knives barely cut through food any more, so dull had they become with age and neglect.

The knowledge that Sophia was just downstairs had set off a train of thought that once more led her back to Aleksei. They had been so happy together, for a while. Sometimes she could forget how sour things had turned and just remember the good times for what they were. He had been a flawed man through and through, but he had loved her in his own way. Love was not always enough though, in this cruel world. It was dog eat dog. Survival of the fittest.

The shot had made her jump and cry out in alarm. Her vodka tonic had spilled all over her lap and she'd cast the empty glass aside as she'd leaped to her feet. Now she just stood there rooted to the spot, a rabbit caught in headlights. Except the headlights had passed and now there was nothing but an agonising silence roaring through the air.

What was happening? Who had been shot? These were questions that Josephine needed answers to and no matter how insistent Anna had been, she could not obey her orders any longer. If it *was* Sophia who had fired the shot she could not stay up here like some sitting duck for her to pick off if she decided to mount the next flight of stairs. And no matter who had fired the shot, her friends were down there. They might need her help. It didn't matter what else was going on between them at the moment, she wanted to be there for them. They meant the world to her. She'd never let them down – intentionally at least – before, and she wasn't going to start now.

Mustering up what little courage she could find, Josephine wrapped the long pale grey cardigan she wore around her then walked out into the hall and tiptoed down the stairs as quietly as she could. As she approached the landing she could hear voices in the bar area. She crept along the hallway and stopped just outside the door, her hands flat against the wall as she strained to listen.

CHAPTER SIXTY-FIVE

Sophia stared down the barrel of the gun at Freddie with pure hatred. This was not the situation she had envisaged now that a gun was aimed at her own head, but it was not going to stop her achieving her goal.

'How can you not know what's going on here?' she asked, her own anger beginning to rise as she stared at his furious expression. 'I made it clear the first time I met you that I knew what had happened to my husband,' she said. 'Oh, I know I seemed as though I didn't much care, and I suppose with all you know about him it was easy for you to accept that. But despite our marriage not being what is expected of a normal marriage, Aleksei and I had a very strong bond indeed.'

For the first time since he had met her, Freddie saw some emotion break through her cold, hard shell and, despite the precarious position he was in, he watched with interest.

'We were two of a kind, Aleksei and I,' she continued. 'We saw the world in the same way. In a way other people didn't always understand. That was why we worked, despite the lack of romantic attachment. Or perhaps because of the lack of that. Romance is nothing but a distraction from the things that matter, like business and children,' she spat.

The memory of Aleksei asking her and the boys to leave and start afresh somewhere new so that he could move Josephine in came rushing back and her anger intensified. That whore had turned his head. It was her fault he was distracted that night.

'I'm sure that's all true,' Freddie replied. 'But I still don't see what that's got to do with us or why you killed Sammy.'

'Oh please,' she scoffed bitterly. 'Do you really still think you can pull the wool over my eyes? I *know*. I knew the whole plan; I helped Aleksei cook it up.'

'What plan?' Freddie asked, exasperated. If he had any clue what Sophia was talking about he could have figured out how to deal with it, but he didn't. He eyed the gun. Despite her sudden outburst of emotion she still held it steady and firm. He needed to try and distract her for just a second. If she dropped it even slightly, he could lunge for it. Paul already had his eye on him, ready and waiting for his move.

'The plan to kill you, Mr Tyler,' Sophia answered. 'I know why he was there that night, because it was me who had sourced and planned out the arrangement for the explosives within the building. That was always *my* forte, you see, not his.' She lifted her chin, a glint of dark pride in her eyes as she shared this. 'He had his little whore message you from your girlfriend's phone, to lure you there. It was so simple. All he had to do was get you up to a higher floor and detonate from a safe distance. But something happened.' She frowned. 'I still don't know how you did it, how you figured it out and turned the trap on him, but I know you were there. I know you were responsible. I know that *you* ended up being the one who walked away and it was *me* who was left without a husband.'

Freddie's mind whirled as he took this all in. This was the first he had heard about any of this and none of it made any sense. 'Sophia, I don't know what you think you know, but until right now I had no idea that any of this had taken place. And I definitely wasn't there.'

If he had been, he certainly wouldn't have started working with the woman afterwards, that was for sure, he thought to himself. And who was Aleksei's whore? Who could have been close enough to Anna to send out a message from her phone without her knowledge? He turned to look at her in question, but she was staring intently at Sophia and did not turn back towards him.

'Your lies won't help you now, Freddie,' Sophia snarled. 'I'm done playing nicely. The only reason you're still here is because your *father* here led me to the wrong club the other night. I thought it was *your* brain I'd lodged that bullet in.'

Freddie let out a low growl of anger at the use of the word 'father'. Jim deserved many titles but that was not one of them. And as the reason for Sammy's death became clear a deep feeling of regret washed over him. It had been a case of mistaken identity. Sammy hadn't needed to die. What a terrible waste of a life.

He shot Jim a look of contempt. 'And how did *you* end up working for her then, eh?' he asked. When Jim didn't answer he shook his head in disgust. The man was a snake through and through. And he was right. Freddie did wish he'd killed him when he'd had the chance.

'Sophia, I really don't know what happened that night, but I can tell you now that whatever it was, clearly your plan failed. I never got any text, I never met him that night. I've been searching for your husband ever since he disappeared, assuming he was just in hiding. And yeah,' Freddie said, raising his voice as his temper started to get the better of him, 'I was planning on taking him out as quickly as possible, and anyone else around him. He waltzed in here and took over land that wasn't his whilst I was in prison. And when we came out he tried to kill me and my brother here. So damn straight, he was number one on my fucking hit list. But whoever did kill him that night, it wasn't me. And that's the truth.'

'Lies,' Sophia spat. 'And I've had enough of them. So say goodbye to your girlfriend, Mr Tyler.'

'Don't you fucking dare,' Paul yelled, getting ready to shoot her.

As all tensions swiftly rose Ali stepped towards Paul and shouted something in Russian, and Anna and Tanya both cried out as they realised the worst was about to happen.

'Stop!' Josephine fell into the room with her hands in the air and panic in her eyes. 'Stop, Sophia.' She hurried forward and placed herself between Sophia and Freddie. 'Please. It wasn't him.' Her voice wobbled as she stared into the eyes of the person who hated her the most in this world. 'Sophia, it wasn't him.' Her terrified voice was barely more than a whisper. 'It was me.'

CHAPTER SIXTY-SIX

'You?' Sophia was taken aback. This was the last thing she expected to hear.

'I couldn't do it,' Josephine breathed. 'I couldn't hurt my own people the way Aleksei wanted me to.' She was terrified now that she was in the room and the truth was spilling out. She'd rushed in without thinking it through, but she didn't regret it. She couldn't allow other people to die for something she had done. The guilt had eaten away at her like a cancer ever since it had happened and it haunted her every waking moment. That was already hard enough, she couldn't cope with the blood of more people she cared about on her hands. And she couldn't watch Anna lose the man she loved, the way that she had.

Anna's eyes widened in horror as she realised what Josephine was doing. This was what she had been protecting her from, all this time. Retribution for what she'd had no choice but to do. 'Josephine, no,' she cried.

'It's OK, Anna, you didn't know,' Josephine said quickly. She eyed Anna meaningfully. 'You didn't know,' she repeated.

Anna had saved her that night. Josephine had tried to stop Aleksei, had planned to kill him herself but when it had come to it she hadn't had it in her to finish the job. He had overpowered her and strangled her and she had given up fighting, had accepted that it was the end of the road. But Anna had followed her and had shot Aleksei, saving her and unbeknown to her at the time, Freddie too. Anna and Tanya had then covered it all up, protecting her all this time from anyone finding out. They had lied to everyone, even Freddie, knowing that he would not understand or forgive her the way that they had decided to.

But this had put them in a precarious position too. They'd lied in a family where there could be no lies. If Freddie knew the whole story, the trust between them would be broken and the family would fracture even more than it had already. Josephine couldn't let this happen, not after all they had done. It was her fault, all of this. None of it would have happened if she had not started up a relationship with the enemy in the first place and it was time to put it right as best she could.

'You would not harm Aleksei,' Sophia said, doubt creeping into her tone. 'You loved him. He was about to give you the world. *My* world,' she added with a hiss.

'I did love him,' Josephine admitted. 'But I loved this family too and he tried to make me choose. Someone who loves you back doesn't make you choose.' She shook her head and a tear rolled down her cheek. 'He didn't love me the way I loved him. And in the end I couldn't let him do it.'

'So you did it to him?' Sophia asked, her tone incredulous.

'I did.' Josephine's gaze flickered around at all the stunned faces staring back at her. 'I never sent the text from Anna's phone. I went to the site instead that night. I stole the detonator and I was going to bring it down on him, but he followed me. He knew something was up.' She sniffed. 'So I shot him. And then I pulled the building down. It was the hardest thing I've ever done and it has haunted me ever since.' Several more tears fell as she finally let it out. 'But it had to be done. I had to protect the people who had taken me into their family, who *truly* cared for me.' Her gaze moved back to Anna. 'I may have made some bad decisions, but I remembered where my loyalties lay when it came down to it. And I will always protect these people,' she added with feeling. 'For as long as I live.'

'You were seeing Aleksei?' Freddie asked, a shocked anger colouring his tone. 'And you were going to help him lure me there?' He glanced over at Anna. Her face was as white as a sheet, her expression unreadable. He realised this must be hard for her to hear. Josephine was one of hers. She had taken the woman under her wing when no one else had been there for her.

'You stupid creature,' Sophia breathed. 'You were not content enough to manipulate my husband into moving me away and moving you in, you had to take his life?'

'I didn't manipulate him, Sophia,' Josephine replied, a sad smile shining through the tears. 'He did that all on his own. I don't know what you think you had between you, but whatever it was was all in your head.' Her passion began to shine through as she thought back to what they had shared, to how unhappy Aleksei had told her he was with Sophia. She stepped forward and held her head high, her fear momentarily forgotten. 'He didn't want you any more, Sophia. And he told you that. He didn't want someone so cold and rigid and calculating, he wanted warmth and love, and—'

The sound of the shot reverberated through the large room as Sophia swung her arm round and shot Josephine in the centre of her chest. Josephine fell backwards to the floor, choking noises coming out of her mouth, and her eyes widened in shock.

'Josephine!' Anna ran to her and managed to catch her head just before it hit the floor. 'No... No, what have you done!' she shouted.

Almost frozen in shock but roused by seeing her chance as Jim dropped his gun, Tanya smashed the bottle of vodka down on Sophia's shoulders, hard. Paul barged sideways into Ali, knocking him to the ground, and began grappling with him again as Ali fought fiercely to get back up.

As Sophia stumbled and all hell broke loose, Jim turned and fled out through the door. He had felt confident with a gun in his hand whilst Sophia had everything under control, cocky even. But things had suddenly turned and he was reminded that he was not cut out for this sort of thing. He'd hoped to get his revenge on the brothers for what they'd done to his hand, but he was not up for a fair fight. He only liked to play the game when the other side was already in a weaker position.

Taken by surprise as she'd fallen, Sophia had dropped her gun and Tanya kicked it away out of her reach. Leaving Josephine momentarily, Anna quickly crawled over to the table where her own gun was stashed and retrieved it with a small sigh of relief as she wrapped her fingers around the cold metal. Freddie waited to make sure Anna was OK, then turned and ran out of the room after Jim.

Rising to her feet, Anna marched across the room and aimed the gun down at Sophia's head. Sophia tried to move but Anna just jammed it closer and cocked it.

'Don't even think about it,' she growled. 'Tanya, how's she doing?' Her tone became more urgent as fear gripped her heart.

Tanya had rushed to Josephine's side and was frantically moving her hands across their friend's chest in an attempt to stop the bleeding but it was no good. Josephine's breathing was laboured and raspy as blood began to fill her lungs. 'It's not good, Anna,' Tanya said, her tone panicked. Tears began to fill her eyes and her hands shook as she realised that there was nothing more she could do.

'You bitch,' Anna hissed, shaking her head as her own eyes began to fill. 'You fucking bitch.'

Sophia looked up at Anna with a mocking defiance in her dark eyes. A spiteful smile began to curl up at the corners of her mouth. 'She got what she deserved—' she started.

'No, she didn't,' Anna cut her off vehemently. 'But you sure as hell will.' With vengeance in her heart and not the slightest trace of regret, Anna squeezed the trigger and let off a shot. The bullet sank into Sophia's forehead and Anna held her gaze as the life dimmed out of her eyes and her body slumped back to the floor. She stared at her for no more than a second. She felt no remorse. She felt nothing for the woman who had taken so much from them.

Ali stopped struggling for a moment, horrified to see his boss was now dead, and Paul took the opportunity to smash the butt of the gun around his head, knocking him unconscious. Anna turned back to Josephine and knelt beside her, opposite Tanya who was now openly weeping over her as she struggled to take her last few breaths.

'Josephine…' Anna's lip wobbled and the tears began to flow as she realised that there was nothing more they could do. The shot was fatal and the lifeblood was draining from Josephine's body at a terrifying speed. Suddenly everything that had been going on shot into horrifyingly clear perspective and Anna felt sick to her stomach. 'I'm so sorry, I'm so, so sorry,' she said, her voice quietening to a heartbroken whisper. There was so much to say, so much to apologise for. She had been awful to her. She'd been so angry with her for so long, but it was only because she loved her so much. She needed to tell her, to make things right. 'I… Josephine, oh God, Josephine…' She needed to tell her how she felt, explain why she had been the way she was, but she couldn't find the words.

Josephine's hand reached up and grasped hers, slipping slightly as it was slick with blood. *It's OK,* she mouthed, no longer able to properly speak. *It's OK.*

'No, it's not,' Anna replied, her voice breaking. She stroked the hair back off her face with her free hand. 'Oh, Josephine.'

Josephine's own eyes filled with tears at the gesture of affection and she gripped Anna's hand tighter as she gazed up at her. As Anna opened her mouth to speak once more, Josephine's body suddenly convulsed and then stopped moving as the last bit of life left her. Her eyes glazed over and the room fell into total silence.

EPILOGUE

Anna walked out of the small church with her head held high and her eyes cast low in respect. Freddie walked beside her, his suit black to match her dress and the outfits of all the other attendees of Sammy's funeral. They all stood together in silent unity by the graveside as his coffin was lowered into the ground. Anna gripped Tanya's hand tightly with one hand and squeezed Ethan's shoulder gently with the other, while the vicar read the text they had carefully chosen for the occasion. Freddie kept one hand on the small of her back, quietly standing as her rock while she stood strong for everyone else.

It had taken a while to get Sammy's body released, but Sarah had made it happen as quickly as she could. Getting Josephine's body had been slightly easier. After Freddie and Paul had rear-ranged the guns a little, it had been an open-and-shut case. A shoot-off between two women over the same love interest. Both had died and it had been assumed no one else had been involved. Josephine had been cremated the week before and now lay in a corner of the graveyard with an array of colourful flowers planted to mark her grave. It suited her, somehow, leaving her as colourful in death as she had been in life.

Anna and Tanya had taken the night after her funeral to celebrate Josephine's life and talk about the good times, just the two of them. No one else would ever know what Josephine had done for them in the end. They would never know that she took the blame for Aleksei's murder and lied about the events of that fateful night to protect them both from the fall-out that would come from the truth. In the end she had been the most loyal and loving friend of all, and for as long as she lived Anna knew that she would never forgive herself for treating Josephine so coldly in the last few weeks of her life.

After some deliberation the brothers had allowed Ali to go free on the condition he take Sophia's children over to their family in Estonia and never return. Freddie had kept tabs to make sure he did as he was instructed and, to his relief, Ali did so quickly and quietly. The man seemed heartbroken over the loss of his employer, leaving Freddie to wonder whether there had been something more between them behind closed doors. But that was none of his business. The children were looked after and Ali had retired from London gracefully. All loose ends were tied up as far as he was concerned.

All loose ends except for Jim, that was. Freddie had run out of The Sinners' Lounge after him but somehow Jim had disappeared. He had jogged down the road in each direction, looking down the side alleys and any likely hiding places, but the man was gone. He had disappeared into thin air like smoke in the wind. That was something they were going to have to deal with at some point, but it could wait for the time being. Freddie's reach was long and he had all the time in the world. Jim wouldn't be able to stay off their radar forever.

As the vicar's sermon came to a close Freddie stepped forward and picked up the first handful of earth. He dropped it onto Sammy's coffin below and stepped back as Paul and Bill followed suit. Next came Anna, followed after a pause by Tanya. Ethan bravely took his turn and Freddie nodded in approval.

This was Sammy's family. Some families were bonded by blood, theirs was bonded by something deeper. These were the people Sammy had lived and died by, the way all of them eventually would. There were days when Freddie wondered if he should try and steer them towards a straighter path, a path less wrought with heartache and danger. But deep down he knew that he never would. This life was in his blood. It was in all of their blood – Paul, Bill, Tanya, even Anna. It had always been there, deep down. It was what had drawn them together, the underlying darkness in each of their souls.

Freddie held Anna's waist a little tighter. Today the family suffered a loss. They'd had to say the final goodbye to one of their own. It wouldn't be the last time and Freddie had no idea when the next blow would come, or from which direction. But, as always, he would fight with everything he had to keep this family safe and on top. And no matter what life threw at them next, the one thing he was certain of was that they would face it together.

A LETTER FROM EMMA

Dear readers,

Well! What a rollercoaster ride this has been. *Ruthless Girl* is the seventh and final book in the Tyler series. For now, at least. And looking back it all feels a little surreal. *Runaway Girl* was the first book I ever wrote and to see it turn into a series and to watch my characters develop through seven whole books has just been incredible. A huge part of me is so sad to bring this series to an end. The characters, Freddie, Anna, Tanya – they feel like family to me. I've probably spent more time with them than I have all the real people in my life these past three years.

If you like my books, please do sign up to hear about new releases. Your email address will not be shared and you can unsubscribe at any time.

www.bookouture.com/emma-tallon

Writing this last book, *Ruthless Girl*, has been a journey in itself for me. I wrote the first half of it heavily pregnant and the second half with a newborn baby sleeping next to me. I pushed on through sleep deprivation, heavy post-C-section painkillers and mid pandemic lockdown to get this written. I laughed and cried, cursed and celebrated, but I got there in the end. And I'm really pleased with the result. I just hope you've enjoyed it too.

Now it is time to move on to something new. The next book I release will be the beginning of a new series, involving a new crime family called the Drews. I've had Lily Drew, the matriarch of the family, in my head for a while now. She's been dying to come out and meet you all, so I'm finally putting her on the page. You may have noticed a sneaky mention of her in this book, so keep your eyes peeled for a little cross over with the Tylers down the line!

And so, it is time to say farewell. Thank you for coming on this journey with me. It's been a blast. See you all on the next book.

All my love,
Emma X

emmatallonofficial

EmmaEsj

@my.author.life

www.emmatallon.com

ACKNOWLEDGMENTS

To my readers. I say it in every book and I mean it more and more every time – thank you for all your incredible support. Seeing so many of you enjoy my books, reading your reviews and hearing from you through various different pathways means the world. I love what I do, but I wouldn't be able to do it without you. So I am eternally grateful for that.

To my editor, Helen, you were the person who gave me and my books our chance in the publishing world, the first person to really see the potential and where we could go with these characters. You'll never know just how much that changed my life. And now here we are, seven books in and counting. Words barely touch the surface, but thank you. For everything.

To all of my friends in the writing community, through thick and thin you keep me laughing and you keep me sane. (Or perhaps you keep me insane?) You bring the sunshine into my working day and I am so glad to have all of you amazing, crazy people in my life. Please never change.

And lastly, to my husband – you may have not read even one of my books… but you are the most supportive person of all. When life has been crazy but the deadlines keep coming, you're the one who takes the load off my shoulders so I can get things done. When I'm sat worrying, full of self-doubt, you're the one who believes in me whole heartedly. You've had my back through thick and thin and I love you for it. You'll always be my ride or die.

Printed in Great Britain
by Amazon